# Out Of Control

# Out Of Control

## G. Gordon Liddy

ST. MARTIN'S PRESS, NEW YORK

80-   71201

**Library of Congress Cataloging in Publication Data**

Liddy, G. Gordon
  Out of Control.

  I. Title.
PZ4.L7130u [PS3562.I34] 813'.5'4 79–16366
ISBN 0–312–59065–2

For Francie P.

# Out Of Control

# I

If patience is a virtue, Edward Zlin thought to himself, I am not a virtuous man. The fact that he had been practicing patience for more than five hours did not enter into his self-evaluation; he did not *feel* patient. Quite the contrary, he felt decidedly *im*patient and therefore guilty of the failure to develop a character trait acclaimed universally.

Almost furtively, Zlin checked his watch. He did so with a penlight, stabbing the operating button quickly so that the flash of light on the dial would be as brief as possible. If he could not read the time in an instant, then his just punishment for using the light again so soon would be denial of the solace of knowing exactly how much longer he had to wait.

Zlin's intelligence told him that his attitude toward the penlight was illogical. There was no danger its use would betray his presence. While the interior of the utility closet he occupied was dark, relieved only by a strip of light marking the bottom of the door, the hall outside was lighted. The fact of the matter, he acknowledged reluctantly, was that his desire to know the time arose from the fact that knowing the time helped him endure its slow passage. That help was a crutch and using it, a display of weakness. So Edward Zlin felt guilty and resolved not to look at his watch again until it was operationally necessary to do so. That would be close to the time he was scheduled to leave the closet and proceed upon his mission.

He had, of course, read the time and even the date: 0106 hours, 4th April. Twenty-four minutes to go. It was reasonable to get ready, and the first thing to do was stand. His legs were numb, "asleep" his children termed it, from sitting motionless for so long on the bottom of an overturned bucket, the rim of which cut into the backs of his thighs shutting off the circulation of blood.

Zlin tried to rise and was unsuccessful; his legs would not hold him. He congratulated himself on his foresight in recognizing the problem while there was still time to deal with it, without either missing his scheduled departure time or leaving in less than total physical readiness. He lifted each leg with his hands, stretching it outward and shifting his position on the bucket. He began to rub his legs and they responded first with a tingling sensation, then with excruciating pain. He grimaced in the dark, caught himself at it, chastised himself mentally and forced his features to return to normal. Finally the pain was succeeded by a rush of warmth and he was able to stand.

As he stood, Zlin became aware of an urgent need to relieve himself. That, too, was reasonable and he proceeded to do so into the low-set utility sink to his right. The gurgle of his urine going down the drain was louder than he had anticipated and made him feel anxious until he was through and the sound stopped. He would have run a little water in the sink to flush it but for the noise he now knew it would cause; noise that could not be justified by any operational imperative. Nevertheless, he felt a twinge of guilt about not flushing. It would leave an odor, and well-raised people not only did not urinate into sinks, they *never* neglected to flush.

Zlin comforted himself with the thought that any odor he left would be masked by the stench of the disinfectant-laced water that half-filled a wheeled mop bucket with wringer attachment standing in a corner of the closet. His expensive, conservatively cut clothes, an operational requirement, were now probably permeated by the same acrid disinfectant odor. The thought annoyed him.

By feeling for it, Zlin recovered his topcoat from the mop-hook on the wall to his left and donned it. Then he retrieved his hat from an overhead shelf it shared with a supply of scouring powder and settled it on his head at what he hoped was an appropriate angle. He put the penlight into his topcoat pocket and withdrew two golfer's gloves. Sold individually (the left-handed one was difficult to find), they fit tightly, allowed his hands to breathe as rubber gloves would not, yet transmitted the sense of touch nearly as well.

A time check was now clearly justified: 0128. Close enough. He picked up a morocco attaché case and leaned toward the closet door, listening. Hearing nothing, he opened the door a crack and inspected the hallway. Clear. Edward Zlin stepped out into the hall and, feet silent on the thick carpeting, strode confidently toward the elevator lobby of the ninety-sixth floor of the forty-year-old Manhattan skyscraper now owned by, and housing the headquarters of, the multi-national conglomorate, Comco.

Paradoxically, Zlin's confident appearance was a reflection of his anxiety. He reassured himself of success against the danger he knew to be present by a deliberate review of facts which would induce confidence in any logical man: he had been trained in the techniques and mechanics of surreptitious entry and the defeat of alarm devices and locking systems by the Federal Bureau of Investigation. He had perfected and proven his skills on dozens of assignments against sensitive targets defended by the finest technology. Had not his wits and fine physical condition gotten him out of some hairy situations in the last sixteen years?

Not every black bag man could have detected the high explosive set to blow when the alarm on the safe in the communications room of the Netherlands embassy was disconnected. And the time those pricks on the heavy squad just beat it and left him there when they realized the East German they were snatching was the wrong man. Jesus! He'd had to slug the Kraut himself and then do the Good Samaritan bit until he could disappear into the crowd. Pricks! It still angered him to think about that one.

Zlin had thought it was all over after the post-Watergate attacks by all three branches of government upon the intelligence community, the show trials of top officials, and men such as himself disciplined and forced into retirement. But an interesting thing happened. A new job fell into his lap so easily it must have been pushed and, in his own case at least, a cryptic admonition to "stay loose, you never know." If he had any problems, he was to call someone he had never heard of and, somewhere in the conversation, mention his aunt Agatha, the one with TB, in Longmont, Colorado. Zlin had no aunt Agatha, tubercular or otherwise.

That's how they had gotten back to him. The man who had approached him and set up this piece of work had said he was aunt Agatha's attorney. She wasn't well and needed her nephew's help. That was all Zlin knew or cared to know. The pay was top dollar, the back-up of first quality—back-stopped alias identification and pocket litter. But most important of all, the operation was familiar and sensible. Duplicate the technique of a professional New York safe-cracker of the first rank. Penetrate the private office of Gregory Ballinger, board chairman of Comco. Hit his safe, steal the cash and anything else in it of easily fenced value, photograph any documents and leave. The camera with its exposed film went to drop number one, a pay locker in Grand Central Terminal. The valuables went to drop number two, a similar locker in the Port Authority Bus Terminal. Neat, clean and professional. And the best part was that they had chosen him, Edward Zlin, when they needed help. You bet your sweet ass he was good!

Zlin had himself psyched up by the time he gained the elevator lobby with its exhibition of modern sculpture. The exhibits had been changed since he was there two weeks before on the feasibility and vulnerability study, when he had discovered that all the locks but two were "mastered"—operable by a master key, one of which he created for himself after removing the lock temporarily from an out of the way door. Only the entrance to the office suite and Ballinger's private office would require picking.

The master key worked easily on the glass double doors into the vast reception area, and the light through the doors was sufficient for him to thread his way quickly through the furniture to the door to the Ballinger office suite; offices that housed Ballinger's private secretary, three stenographers and two male assistants—one of them a middle-aged Oriental of unknown function.

Zlin would be visible from the lobby, so the quicker he got through the lock the better. From his inside jacket pocket he took a wallet-like container. It held neatly in place a selection of slender metal rods that he himself had tortured into their odd shapes years ago in an FBI workshop that was secret even from other special agents. The tools were as familiar to him as his fingers and he used them as dexterously.

Selecting a rod having an end bent into a right angle and flattened, he slipped the flattened end into the keyway. This was his tension bar, a "wrench" in criminal parlance. Next he chose a miniature button-hook, a pick or "rake." Zlin twisted the tension bar to apply torque to the cylinder, inserted the pick and began expertly to move the pins upward. As he worked, he applied just enough torque to retain the pins in their upward position, but not enough to make it impossible to raise them with his pick. Within moments the pressure on the tension bar released suddenly as the cylinder turned and the lock opened.

There was some risk to his next move. Overhead on the inside of the door, Zlin remembered, was a television security camera pointed ahead and down so as to cover the door at the end of the short corridor—the door to Ballinger's private office. Because the camera pointed downward, should Zlin open the door too far, the top of it would register on the screen. It was a chance he had to take and he took it, opening the door just far enough to slip through quickly and stand with his back to it upon closing.

Zlin was not so much concerned with the personal consequences of discovery and apprehension as he was with mission failure. Failure would plague him, give him no rest. The personal consequences were provided for in the event of capture. His tools and *modus operandi* would mark him as a longtime professional safe-burglar who had finally run afoul of the law of averages. In keeping with that role he had no handgun or other armament. Upon apprehension he would resist interrogation and take under advisement the inevitable offer of the police to see to it that reasonable bail was set and that he would receive a short sentence as a first offender, in exchange for a plea of guilty to this burglary and a confession, without being charged, to all other similar burglaries in the precinct still on the books as unsolved.

Pending his agreement, high bail would be set. Someone would make it for him and, released, he would disappear. Zlin's fingerprint record, both at the New York Police Department and the Identification Division of the FBI would be expunged of the alias booking and that would be the end of it. No, it was just failure that was intolerable.

Fishing in his topcoat pocket, Zlin brought out a device approximately the size of a small matchbox, wrapped in friction tape. In it was a miniature signal generator powered by a number of wafer-type camera batteries wired in series. One side was coated by an adhesive. Zlin moved a contact which activated the device then, reaching above him, pressed the adhesive-coated side to the surface of the camera housing. The picture transmitted by the camera promptly dissolved into a meaningless jumble which would be blamed on anything but the camera. That accomplished, he walked past the doors of the auxiliary offices to that of Ballinger's at the end of the hall.

Again the tension bar and pick were employed. Zlin worked by sense of touch alone, looking vacantly to the side as he concentrated.

Ballinger's office ran the entire length of the north wall of the building. As that consisted entirely of a series of floor to ceiling windows, more than enough light seeped up the near quarter-mile from Manhattan's brightly lighted midtown streets to reveal the office to Zlin as his pupils enlarged to compensate for the reduced light. All was as it had been two weeks before, but the office seemed even more huge. The old tower had very high ceilings designed for summer coolness before the age of air conditioning; fourteen feet, he estimated.

Zlin took it all in. The windows across from him could still be opened and through them he could make out the dim shape of the heavy granite balustrade which was all that protected anyone daring enough to venture out upon a shallow balcony into the ever swirling winds ninety-six storeys above West Thirty-eighth Street. He could hear the wind moaning and it lent an aura of menace to the darkened room. The windows on the east side had been covered over and the wall hung with a priceless medieval tapestry rivaling those of the Cloisters.

Six feet out from the east wall and its tapestry, placed so that it ran north and south, was a long, ornately carved wooden table of unusual height and massive construction. It was bare but for two items: a fifteenth century monk's writing desk which, its height added to that of the table, was at the correct level for writing while standing, and a plain walnut chest which, Zlin knew, contained a telephone. A *Forbes* article provided him as homework for this mission had explained the paucity of furniture. Ballinger believed he thought best on his feet; so that was the way he worked. He was also obsessed with the value of time; no subordinate ever sat down in Ballinger's office, there was no place to do so. Standing uncomfortably, one disposed of one's business with Ballinger in the quickest way possible and departed. Chairs were available to be brought in for the occasional visitor from whom Ballinger wanted something.

The high ceiling held an incongruous maze of metal tracks which served a multitude of small spot lamps able to be arranged into infinite combinations to illuminate a frequently changed display of paintings which took up the whole south wall. The spot lamps were probably used only at night, Zlin surmised, the north light from the opposite windows serving very nicely during the day.

The west wall was given over completely to shelves filled with first editions and rare examples of the bookbinder's craft. A really smart thief, Zlin thought, would say to hell with the safe and try to figure a way to get the books down ninety-six storeys to the ground and out of the building.

The window draperies were velvet, a blue which picked up the dominant color of a chinese rug so magnificent in quality and size it might have been created for the palace of an emperor.

Zlin directed his attention to the southeast corner of the office. There stood a large, dark, carved teak cabinet. Its double doors were opened by golden handles fashioned in an orientally stylized likeness of a pair of flying fish. Most took it for a liquor cabinet, but Zlin knew that it housed a large, modern Mosler safe into which, he had been told, Ballinger cleared his desk whenever he left his office, even if he intended to return but minutes later.

Zlin approached the cabinet. He put down his attaché case and removed his hat, topcoat and suitcoat, placing them on Ballinger's table-desk. He took off his wristwatch and put it into his pocket, then opened the cabinet doors and looked at the door of the Mosler. He frowned and grunted aloud as he focused on the combination dial and spindle. In the two weeks since he had "cased" Ballinger's office, they had been replaced.

Slipping the penlight out of the pocket of his overcoat where it lay on Ballinger's desk, Zlin squatted down in front of the safe, shielded the light with a cupped palm and played it on the new dial and spindle. They were black, and the combination numbers were visible only through a cutout "window" in the top, not enscribed around the circumference in the usual manner. In the center of the spindle appeared the logo *S/G* and, around it, the legend, *Sargent & Greenleaf, Inc., Nicholasville, Kentucky.*

Zlin recognized the newly installed locking equipment immediately: a Sargent & Greenleaf 8550 series "manipulation proof" locking mechanism with a "spy proof" combination system. The restriction of the visibility of the numbers to the cutout was intended to prevent the combination from being gained by telephoto lens as the safe is opened. Inside the locking box, the tumblers were of nonconductive plastic rather than metal so as to defeat attack by a sonic device seeking to line up the gates by wavelength variances. The safe was now also protected against "punching" because of a collar around the spindle, and defeat of the relocking bar by "pulling" was prevented by a strong metal pin.

None of the new equipment on the safe presented a problem to Zlin, nor would they cause him to change his plan of attack. What concerned him was the fact of the change. Had he somehow alerted someone when he was in the building two weeks ago? Was his attempt this evening anticipated? Had he walked into a trap? Ought he to abort?

Zlin forced himself to analyze his situation professionally. First, were he in a trap, it would probably have been sprung before now. Secondly, the S&G equipment was the latest and the best; it would be logical for Ballinger's security people to upgrade the resistance of his safe to penetration by using it, especially as they were probably relying on the Mosler's "drill proof" steel to eliminate an attack by drilling, and the new S&G locking equipment was to cover the long lens, manipulation, sonic, punching and pulling methods. Burning would require heavy oxygen and acetylene gas tanks to be hauled up to the ninety-sixth floor, most probably by a multi-man crew, and would therefore be eliminated as unlikely or, if attempted, easy to detect and prevent.

Edward Zlin knew, because it was his business to know, that the door to the particular model of Mosler safe before him consisted of an eighth of an inch exterior steel plate behind which was two and a half inches of a plaster-like asbestos insulation, backed by a half-inch plate of "drill proof" steel protecting the locking box which was his target. Ironically, it was the "drill proof" steel which was to prove the vulnerable point of this safe. No technical advantage is able to hold out very long against counter-technology, and Zlin carried with him in his attaché case the very latest fruits of counter-technology—Borazon drill bits. A diamond is rated at 10 on the Mohs scale of hardness, but the bits he would use against the Mosler were of boron-hydride and rated from 11 to 14 on the Mohs. He calculated that it would take him but fifteen minutes to open the safe.

Getting to work quickly and methodically, Zlin opened his attaché case and removed a ruler and marking pen. Using them, he measured from dead center of the spindle and made a small guide mark between the dial and the handle of the safe. As he was attacking the locking box via the bolt protruding from its side, he had a bit of leeway and was not concerned that the measurement he was using was based upon a Mosler, not Sargent & Greenleaf box. Next he selected one of two Black & Decker electric drills of the kind marketed nationwide to "do it yourself" types, attached an extension cord to it and plugged the cord into a continuous receptacle running along the baseboard and concealed by millwork. Returning, he took from the attaché case a length of heavy chain with a slip-link on one end and a snap attachment on the other that was designed for use on a heavy dog leash to snap quickly onto a collar. Zlin smiled as he remembered the remark of the salesman when he had bought it: "This one here'll keep a Great Dane from a bitch in heat!"

The chain was followed by a steel bar as thick in diameter as his thumb and sixteen inches long. One end had been bent over several inches at an angle that made the bar look like an enlongated numeral 7.

Zlin moved with an economy of motion that was unhurried but nevertheless swift. He slip-linked one end of the chain to the handle of the safe, then picked up the drill and chucked into it a three-inch long, one quarter-inch diameter Borazon bit. He adjusted the length of the chain with the dog leash attachment, then hooked the angle of the 7 bar into it. Placing the point of the bit precisely on the mark he had made, he laid the bar across the drill handle and applied leverage against the drill by leaning on the free end of the bar, using the drill as a fulcrum, as if he were trying to pull off the handle with the chain. The end of the bar in his right hand, Zlin operated the trigger switch on the drill with his left, securing it with the catch provided on the drill housing for that purpose.

Zlin bore down hard as the boron-hydride bit cut into the Mosler. The Black & Decker whined and groaned at the abuse to which he subjected it, sometimes slowing down to a full stop from the pressure he exerted. Within three minutes he had drilled through the eighth-inch outer plate and the bit sank immediately up to the chuck as it encountered the insulation. Zlin switched to an eight-inch long bit, adjusted the chain length and applied himself once more to his task. In a moment he was through the insulation and against the "drill proof" steel backplate protecting the locking box. He stopped and put a mark on the drill to indicate another half-inch of penetration as a warning. There was a third of an inch gap between the rear of the protective steel plate and the bolt and Zlin didn't want the bit suddenly to go through into the gap. If it were to do so at full pressure and spinning at the high speed permitted by the sudden absence of resistance, the bit, whose hardness made it brittle, might break off in the hole and thwart him.

The first Black & Decker burned out shortly after Zlin began his attack on the back-plate. He was perspiring heavily now. Zlin switched to the second drill, readjusted the chain and went back to work. He had to readjust the chain twice more before he came to the warning mark on the drill bit. He stopped immediately, then continued, using maximum concentration and all his sense of touch and experience. Suddenly he sensed that the pointed leading edge of the drill had penetrated the rear surface of the steel plate. Again Zlin stopped. This was the critical point. Carefully he withdrew the Borazon bit from the hole. So far so good. He removed it from the drill gingerly because of its great heat and replaced it with an "end mill"; a different kind of bit designed to finish the hole, reaming out the remaining metal with an industrial-diamond cutting edge. Guiding the end mill into the hole, Zlin worked the drill with the trigger switch, using exactly the right touch until he had accomplished his purpose. Then he withdrew the drill once more, laid it aside carefully and detached the chain from the handle.

From his attaché case, Zlin produced a hammer and a drift pin of quarter-inch diameter. He slid the drift pin into the hole he had just drilled, seating it firmly against the bolt protruding from the locking-box. The hammer in his right hand, Zlin struck the drift pin precisely while he applied turning pressure to the safe door handle with his left hand. After several blows, the locking-box had been knocked back sufficiently so that the handle rotated suddenly and the door to the Mosler swung open at his pull. The task had required something more than fourteen minutes.

Zlin looked into the safe interior and reacted with a small smile of satisfaction. The information given him by his contact had proven correct. The interior of the safe contained no locked chest which would have required further and more difficult penetration. Such a chest is an option on a Mosler and a covert check of the records of purchase had disclosed no extra charge for one in Ballinger's office safe.

There were eighteen thousand dollars in currency in the safe, along with several thousand each in sterling, deutchmarks and

Swiss franks. He knew the amount of dollars because they were in eighteen packages, each bound by a paper wrapper imprinted with the figure *$1,000* and the logo and name, *Bankers Trust*. The foreign currency was contained in separate plain manila envelopes for each variety and Zlin did not bother to count it as he stuffed it all into his suitcoat and topcoat pockets.

As he took Ballinger's money, Zlin did not consider his act theft, nor himself a thief. He was acting on behalf of his government and would retain none of the money, nor derive any gain from it. Indeed, it was a bother to have to carry it away and he did so only because it was necessary to the cover of his operation. Zlin had used the technique before and, though he had long since stopped concerning himself with such things, there was once a time when his strict Czech-Catholic background had led him to think about it and he had been grateful for the handy Jesuit ethical loophole called the "principle of double effect."

Zlin did recall an article he had once read in *The Wall Street Journal* commenting on the fact that, although Comco held as a subsidiary a major credit card company, Ballinger never carried a credit card. The seeming inconsistency was attributed to Ballinger's aversion to the "electronic tracks" left by credit card usage. No Hughes type recluse, Ballinger nevertheless attempted to keep his movements unobtrusive so as not to give out clues business rivals might use to fathom his financial maneuvers. Zlin found that reasonable.

There were fewer documents in the safe than Zlin had expected. He attributed that fact to Ballinger's absence from the country which, his principal had assured him, would be for all of the week. It was an important factor in timing the operation, as Ballinger was known to work in his office at all hours, seemingly oblivious to time.

Zlin removed the documents and placed them in a neat pile on the floor a few feet from the safe where the light from the windows seemed a little stronger. He removed an Olympus motor-driven camera from his attaché case. It was the smallest 35mm single lens reflex available with an air-dampened mechanism which was very quiet. The camera was loaded with an ultra-high ASA speed film furnished by his contact. He needed nothing more than the dim available light in the office to photograph the documents, which he proceeded to do with the same economy of motion with which he had opened the safe.

Zlin's equipment made the photography easy. There was no need to advance the film and cock the shutter between exposures as that was done rapidly by the motor drive unit. All he had to do was to move the target document from the unphotographed pile, photograph it, then move it to an adjacent pile of completed work. He photographed thirty-four documents in all, having read none of them. He had not been asked to do so and Zlin was professionally incurious about that which he had no need to know.

Completing his photography, Zlin replaced the documents in approximately the same place in the safe they had occupied when he had found them, then swept them to the floor with the hurried motion of a burglar whose only interest in them was as objects which could be concealing further cash. Satisfied with the look of things, Zlin repacked his attaché case.

There are two schools of thought, Zlin knew, among professional safe-crackers. Some leave every tool at the scene of their crime on the theory that, if apprehended, they cannot be charged successfully with the separate crime of possession of burglar's tools. Further, the police must first link them to the tools before being able to use them as evidence. Such men walk out with nothing but their loot.

The second school, adopted by Zlin in his pose as a criminal, takes the position that if the police have probable cause to detain and search one en route from a job, they will find the loot. The tools are then mere icing on the cake. Either the search is legal or it is not. If not, the evidence will be suppressed by the court and the case will fail. If legal, one has lost his calculated risk and accepts imprisonment for a time as an occupational hazard.

As would an adherent of the latter school, Zlin would discard any striking or cutting tools, such as the drift pin and the drill bits, because the marks they made on the safe, like fingerprints, could link them directly to the crime. He would discard his expensive clothing too, as the insulation used in safes is also telltale, each manufacturer using his own formula and furnishing a sample to the FBI laboratory and those of major police departments throughout the country.

It is impossible to clean one's clothing well enough to be sure that microscopic particles of the insulation, reduced to a powder-like consistency by the drill, do not remain. Such a particle, he knew, could be identified not only as safe insulation, but as that from a safe of particular manufacture. But Zlin would discard the potentially incriminating items later. He could, after all, hardly leave the building without his trousers. Then there were his lock-picking tools; he couldn't bring himself to throw them away. He had made them and they were a part of him now. He donned his suitcoat, topcoat and hat, put his watch back on his wrist and, picking up the attaché case, left the office to retrace his route.

The locks on the doors he had picked were spring-loaded latch types which opened by hand from the inside. It was not necessary to repick them as he made his way quickly back to the elevator lobby, pausing only long enough to remove the television signal scrambling device.

Hours before, when many others were in the building, he had ascended via a series of elevators. But it would not do to set one in motion at this hour from the ninety-sixth floor where Ballinger had his office. Zlin was resigned to the arduous task of descending on foot and, as he entered the stairwell, resisted the temptation to divert himself by counting the steps all the way down. He realized he was quite tense when he felt the pain from gripping the handle of the attaché case so tightly that his fingernails cut into his palm. Zlin was acutely aware that an operation is never over until one is away safely, the fruits delivered and debriefing completed. With ninety-six floors to negotiate on foot, Zlin was in no mood yet for self-congratulation.

By the time he reached the eighty-fifth floor, Zlin's tension had eased and he was almost lulled by the rhythm of his hoplike descending steps. So much so that it was a moment before he reacted as he passed the door on the eighty-fifth floor landing and then felt a sudden breeze blowing on the back of his neck. He ducked, saving his skull, but something took his hat off from the rear with a great deal of force.

Zlin whirled, holding the attaché case up before him as a shield. It took the full force of the second blow from a linked-stick flail wielded by a thin oriental in a dark business suit. Zlin lifted his right leg from the hip and snapped it forward from the knee. His shod toe caught his opponent in the hollow below the lower end of the breastbone, smashing into the network of nerves behind the stomach. The oriental went down, paralyzed, and lay in the light of the exit sign above the door, one leg preventing the door from closing.

Now Zlin could hear footsteps approaching rapidly from above and below him on the stairs. Jerking the oriental's leg out of the doorway, he left him on the landing and entered the eighty-fifth floor.

Adrenalin poured through Zlin's body and he perspired profusely. He was in trouble. He had to get rid of the camera. It did not fit his pose as a burglar after loot, and he might not be able to elude capture.

Zlin tried the door to a women's rest room. It was locked against the possibility of an ambushing rapist. He ran to his right down the hall and, as he expected, came upon a men's room. It was unlocked and he darted inside. Before the door to the hall closed, Zlin saw that the room was small, windowless and was provided with three booths, two urinals and a sink. Over the sink was an eighteen-by-twelve-inch metal dispenser for paper towels.

To steady himself, Zlin stood still and took a deep breath, letting it out slowly. It was pitch black save for a line of light seeping under the door from the hall. He put down his attaché case, took off his topcoat and laid it along the bottom of the door. Now there was no light at all. Quickly, he opened the attaché case and felt for the Olympus. Finding it, he removed it and fired off the two remaining frames to get all the film out of the unexposed cassette. Now he opened the camera and took out the reel of exposed film. He put the camera down and pulled the exposed film off the reel, winding it into a tube which he placed in his suitcoat pocket.

With an effort, Zlin resisted an urge to listen for his pursurers. He took his lock-picking tool kit from his pocket and, by touch, selected the torsion bar. He felt before him for the sink, located it, then felt for the paper towel dispenser. Finding that, he continued feeling until he found the keyway of the rudimentary lock securing the cover. A second with the tension bar and the lock gave way. Zlin snapped the empty reel back into the camera, closed it, then placed the camera on top of the paper towel supply inside the dispenser. He was careful as he lowered the cover and relocked it. It made no sound.

Turning, Zlin retrieved his topcoat from the floor, felt for a booth, entered it and hung up his top and suitcoats, all by touch. Then he dropped his trousers and shorts and, feeling for the toilet seat with the backs of his legs, sat down on the stool.

# II

"Fucking birds!"

Carmine Burgio stared through the windshield of his junker Chevrolet at the latest of a continuing series of outrages: a large white and yellow liquid splatter directly in his line of vision. It dribbled down toward the windshield wiper.

Burgio hated seagulls. They were big, dirty birds with cruel beaks; eaters of carrion and garbage who fouled themselves and everything around them. They stank. Their shit covered his car. He could use it for nothing but commuting to his job here at the garbage dump below the Sheepshead Bay bridge in Brooklyn. At the other end of his commute he had to park it blocks away from his home. The car shamed his wife.

The City of New York called the place where Burgio earned his living a "sanitary landfill." Burgio, who saw life with the clarity of a hard-working Italian-American, called it a garbage dump. He worked on it five days a week, six when he could get the overtime, operating a giant, diesel powered D-8 Caterpiller bulldozer, burying garbage by the ton.

Burgio backed his Chevy up against a chain-link fence. The fence was papered by trash blown from the dump it surrounded and held against it by the prevailing winds from the Atlantic. Slamming the door, he walked slowly out over the track-rutted, earth-covered portion of the dump toward the edge of hundreds of acres of garbage. Two hundred yards away, his machine waited silently. Scores of the hated birds waddled over it, their droppings covering its yellow paint with a thick layer of off-white excretion.

Bald, stocky and thirty-seven years old, Burgio saw no beauty in the spectacle of hundreds of gulls rising, wheeling, swirling and descending in continuous mass movement over the dump as they fed. What appeared to be white wings against the morning sky were, he knew, dirty yellow at the trailing edges, matching the belly and the underside of the tail feathers. The big, semi-hooked beaks dipped deeply into rotten flesh. Lice flourished among the body feathers. The air was filled with high-pitched screeching.

Burgio couldn't wait to fire up the big Cat's engine. The roar of the mighty diesel would drown out the din of the birds. He'd never been able to do it, but maybe today, Burgio thought, he would succeed in trapping a gull behind his blade and crushing it.

About halfway to his machine, Burgio saw what appeared to be a pile of gulls swarming over each other. He picked up a piece of splintered board from a broken produce crate and scaled it at the center of the cluster. One the birds rose some three feet in the air, then settled right down again on the dark object of their attention. Curious, Burgio moved closer. He cocked his hand behind his right ear like a quarterback and passed an empty beer can expertly. Once again the birds rose, swirled slightly, descended. Closer now, Burgio made out the object as a dark green plastic garbage bag. The birds seemed to be tearing it apart with their beaks. That meant it was fresh.

Something registered as wrong in Burgio's mind. This was a filled portion of the dump. The trucks hadn't started to arrive yet and the bag, sitting out there alone, was obviously not part of a misdirected load. As much out of gratitude for a reason to harass the birds as from curiosity, he walked directly to the bag.

If it was possible, what Burgio found increased his unreasoning hatred of the gulls. Through the torn bag he saw the head of a corpse.

Burgio looked around, spotted a piece of rusted coathanger lying partially buried in the dirt and picked it up. He used the wire to pull apart more of the bag, and the corpse, which had been in a knee-chest position inside it, fell over on its side toward Burgio's feet. He jumped back, then glanced around, sheepishly. When he turned back to the bag, he froze.

The corpse had no face. It's eye sockets were empty. The nose, lips and both ears were missing. The gulls had eaten them. Deep gouges in the flesh of the remainder of what had been the face and in the tops of both shoulders attested to the sharpness of the tearing beaks. He looked at the chest. It had been a man.

Burgio wasn't sure what to do next. He had to report finding the body to the police, but he hated to leave it, even for a moment, to the waiting gulls. He thought of covering it up with loose dirt, but the cops wouldn't like that; they'd want it the way he had found it. Well, he wouldn't leave it to them for long.

Burgio turned and ran to his bulldozer, mounted it and flipped on the master switch. He picked up the microphone of the transceiver used for communication with his supervisor, other bulldozer operators and dump truck drivers. No one responded to his call. Cursing silently, he switched to a citizen's band channel used by truckers on the road. He had installed the crystal himself.

"Break, break, break. Caterpiller to any rig inbound Sheepshead Bay."

"Go ahead, Breaker, you got Billy the Kid here."

"Billy, I'm workin' the dump off to yer left. I got a stiff here in a plastic bag. How 'bout flaggin down a cop for me?"

"Ah, tell ya what, Cat. I got a toll booth comin' up in a few minutes. I'll give it to them, okay?"

"Thanks, Billy. Take care."

The squelch on Burgio's transceiver broke twice as the truck driver acknowledged him by hitting his mike button in quick succession.

Burgio went through the start sequence on the D-8. The big diesel buzzed, barked, then roared into life. Braking the right track caused the steel behemoth to pull to the right, and crawl rapidly, blade raised, toward the plastic bag. It was covered again by a heaving mass of gulls.

The gulls were not in the least intimidated by the huge, snorting machine. Long familiarity had bred contempt. Burgio hadn't expected the gulls to move, but their nonchalance infuriated him just the same. He stopped the bulldozer six feet away from the bag and its grisly contents, jumped to the ground and ran toward the feeding gulls waving his arms and shouting to be heard over the idling diesel:

"Cocksuckin' scum-bag hard-ons!"

Reluctantly, the gulls fluttered a short distance away, then settled back to earth and eyed him warily. Waiting.

Paul Farington picked up the phone on his desk, punched three digits and waited.

"Ginny? Paul. He wanted me waiting for him when he came out. What's it look like?"

"Breaking now. Come ahead."

"How's he look?"

"Unhappy. Hurry up."

"Gotcha. Thanks."

Farington, six feet one and lean, hung up the phone and left his desk in one motion. His office was small and he was out of it in a moment, hurrying down the hall to the stairwell door. He yanked it open, took the steps two at a time to the seventh floor and headed for the entrance to the office of the director of the Central Intelligence Agency. Before he could get there, the door popped open. A short man of extraordinary thickness through the chest and shoulders came through it with a twisting motion, as if not to brush his shoulders on the door jambs. He resembled a bison. Even his hair was shaggy.

The bison's name was Constantine Kazalakis and he came down the hall charging. Head down, torso bent forward, he moved at a pace Farington knew from experience was exhausting.

Approaching Farington, Kazalakis did not break stride. He just stuck out his left arm and swept him along with him, speaking as if Farington had been with him for hours. There was no greeting. Farington almost fell down trying to reverse his field so fast.

"What time is it?"

Kazalakis was wearing a watch, but he had an assistant with him, so it did not occur to him to look at it. That was what assistants were for; instant service, even in matters of trivia, so that Kazalakis could continue concentrating on whatever problem occupied him at the time. And there was always a problem. Kazalakis was Deputy Director for Operations; the euphemistic title of the chief of what was left of the clandestine service of the CIA.

"Twelve-twenty," said Farington.

"Who've you got doing it?"

"Dr. Seidman."

"Good. I want to talk to him myself. How soon?"

Farington consulted his watch again. "Let's see. Figure fourty minutes to La Guardia, an hour and a half to Andrews—should be at TSD in ten, fifteen minutes. Any special plans for lunch?"

"Fuck lunch," snapped Kazalakis as he opened the door to his office and leaned in.

"Connie, I'll be at TSD downtown. So will Paul. Any calls?"

"Just Mr. Keneally again. I'll call a car."

"No. I don't want every clerk at State wondering who's going into TSD and why. What's that?"

Kazalakis stared at the top of his secretary's desk. On it was a sandwich wrapped in cellophane, a half-pint container of milk and a partially eaten dill pickle lying wetly on an opened plastic wrapper.

"Ham and swiss on white. Mustard. No butter."

"Thanks," said Kazalakis as he tucked the container of milk under his left upper arm, put the sandwich in his left hand and waved the rest of the pickle at her before putting it into his mouth with his right.

Farington held the door open as Kazalakis exited. He rolled his eyes heavenward behind his superior's back and drew a resigned smile from Connie before he was swept out in Kazalakis' wake.

Farington followed Kazalakis into the stairwell. Waiting for an elevator was a form of suffering too painful for Kazalakis. Bounding down the stairs, he handed Farington half the stolen ham and swiss. Farington accepted it, assuaging his feeling of guilt with the rationalization that Connie was a bit overweight anyway. But he waved aside the proffered swallow from the container of milk as they sped across the great seal of the agency set in the floor of the lobby and through the glass doors.

Kazalakis led the way left and down the path toward the private bus stop at the side of the sweeping, semicircular approach to the main entrance to CIA headquarters in Langley, Virginia. The small buses made regular runs to the State Department, the Pentagon and other CIA installations in the Rosslyn and Arlington areas of Virginia, just across the District of Columbia line.

The two men boarded a State Department-bound bus and sat all the way in the rear. They waited silently as a handful of others boarded soon after and sat in the front. One woman isolated herself by sitting in the middle. The bus was small, but there was sufficient separation for the two men to carry on a low conversation without being overheard after the bus got underway.

"Okay, give me what you've got," said Kazalakis. He didn't look at his subordinate, just stared at the back of the seat in front of him.

Kazalakis did not have to tell Farington that his own career was on the line along with Kazalakis'. That Kazalakis was going with him to TSD was itself extraordinary. It was no secret that the new director, the latest in the series brought in after Watergate and from the academic community, did not interpret his role as serving to change only the image of the agency. He believed he had a mandate to change the Agency's fundamental approach in the areas of activity most under fire in recent years. Kazalakis was an old school advocate and practicioner of the aggressive, pragmatic deployment of clandestine assets to advance the national interests. He was effective; even his worst enemies gave him that. He was also ruthless, abrasive and an assertive "ethnic" in a WASP preserve; appreciated by his peers only if they made a special effort to achieve a detached view. If Kazalakis had a friend anywhere in the world, Farington had yet to learn of it.

"He went in on schedule just before 1800 so he wouldn't have to sign in. When he didn't come out of the steam tunnel by 0300, we used our P.D. asset. We checked the drops first, just in case the tunnel was blocked or something and he used an alternate route out. He never made it to the drops. We got the call at 0746. They found him in a plastic garbage bag on a landfill in Sheepshead Bay, near the bridge."

"Who made the I.D.?"

"We did. We were ready to check out every corpse that turned up this morning. You know how many bodies they find every morning in New York City?"

"Never mind that. Keep going."

"Not much more. We alerted TSD and arranged to get him there. They'll go over everything; the body, the bag, everything. Whatever's there, we'll get."

"Any trace of the film?"

"No sir. Nothing."

Farington lapsed into silence and Kazalakis said no more until the bus arrived at the west entrance to State. Kazalakis left the bus with uncharacteristic slowness, ambled over to a *Washington Star* vending machine on the sidewalk, bought a paper, tucked it under his arm and strolled north to the next corner. Farington in tow, he crossed west, then turned south again.

To Kazalakis right, just across the street from the squat, boxlike State Department headquarters which took up a square block, was a wrought iron fence guarding a steep, lawn-covered hill. At the summit, approached by a winding driveway, was what appeared to be a late nineteenth century mansion; the home, perhaps, of an Alexander or McClean. The building housed an installation of the Technical Services Division of the Central Intelligence Agency. At one time that fact had been secret. People who thought about it, and few did, speculated that the building was a residence maintained by State for the convenience of visiting foreign dignitaries. The curious were informed by a small sign that the property belonged to the Department of the Navy. No Trespassing.

It was different now; the United States Senate had seen to that. Tourists viewing the State Department had the added attraction of a peek at "where they kept all that poison!" For that reason the installation would be abandoned shortly. The same reason explained Kazalakis' discreet approach.

The guard at the desk just inside the door checked the two men into the building. Kazalakis resumed speed to the stairway and down to a basement room which he entered without knocking.

The room was small and windowless. Opposite the door, behind a waist-high table, a man in a surgical gown and mask was adjusting a weight and balance scale. Even through the mask, Farington could see that he was annoyed by the abrupt intrusion. Farington sought by a solicitous tone of voice to smooth it over:

"Mr. Kazalakis, Dr. Seidman."

What could be seen of Seidman's smile was forced. "I wasn't expecting such distinguished company."

Kazalakis was oblivious to Seidman's reaction. "That him?" he asked, nodding toward a naked corpse without a face, lying on its back on the table between them.

Kazalakis stared at the mutilated body. The only sound was the quiet whirring of an exhaust fan.

"How was he identified?"

Seidman lifted up one of the dead arms by the wrist and rotated it against the rigor so that the inside of the hand faced Kazalakis. The fingertips were black.

"Fingerprints," said Seidman.

Edward Zlin's head was propped up on a wooden block, much in the manner of a Japanese pillow. The table that bore his body was of a laboratory utility type. It had a raised edge all around it and a gutter running just inside the edge to a drain at the end of the table opposite Zlin's head.

The room was illuminated by a single, multi-tube fluorescent light fixture centered over the table. It gave the raw flesh of what had been Zlin's face a purplish tinge. From the ceiling there hung a microphone directly over the corpse's waist. It was at Seidman's mouth level.

Kazalakis had noticed something when Seidman displayed Zlin's right palm to him. He picked up Zlin's left hand and examined the palm. The flesh was cold and unresilient. The left palm bore the same marks he had noticed on the right; four shallow, half-moon cuts, in a line across the palm.

"What's this?"

Seidman examined the right palm again, then the fingertips.

"Judging from what appears to be dried blood and bits of tissue under the fingernails, I'd say those wounds were caused by the nails biting into the palms under great pressure. But I really don't know. The proper way to go about this is to recover a sample of the substance under the nails, determine first whether it is human blood and tissue, then whether it's the same blood group of the deceased, etc. Really, it's going to be some time before I can tell you anything with any degree of certainty. There are certain standard procedures we follow—"

"I understand, Doctor," Kazalakis cut him off. "I just want to get what I can, as soon as I can. What do you make of that?" he said, nodding toward the head of the corpse.

"Consistent with partial devouring by scavenger birds; in this case seagulls, I understand."

"Cause of death?"

Seidman looked as if he was about to give another lecture on proper postmortem procedure, but before he could draw a full breath Kazalakis cut him off again.

"I mean anything obvious, like a bullet hole in the skull."

Seidman sighed. He lifted Zlin's right arm again and pointed to a small discoloration centered over an even smaller scar on the inside of the forearm.

"This man had a subcutaneous capsule. Installed years ago, I understand. Looks like he may have used it."

"A capsule? A Roman Catholic with an FBI background?" Kazalakis looked at Farington questioningly.

"A few, a very few of the top entry people in Hoover's heyday, had them installed unofficially by their lab. It wasn't a defense against hostile interrogation or anything like that. It was a last ditch defense against exposure of the embassy penetration program for NSA and what that would do to the Bureau and Hoover. A sort of die for the emperor thing, with Hoover the emperor. It also guaranteed their family would be taken care of. There was no official or unofficial sanction and it wasn't encouraged. But it wasn't *dis*couraged, either."

"Could it have been broken accidentally? Any evidence of torture?"

"Nothing apparent at first glance," said Seidman. "No burns from electrodes on the genitals and so on. I doubt it was accidental. Its placed so that direct pressure wouldn't break the capsule, it would just sink in deeper. It was meant to be ruptured by crushing within the flesh. By a strong pinching action, for instance."

"And that's how it was done?"

"I don't *know*, sir," said Seidman with a hint of exasperation. "I haven't done any more than measure the body. I haven't even dictated the measurements yet—"

"Right, right, go ahead," said Kazalakis.

Seidman reached up and flipped a switch on the suspended microphone.

"Washington D.C., 5th April, 1313 hours. Edward Zlin. The body is that of an adult male caucasian, age forty-two. Good muscular development. Well nourished. No obesity."

Seidman's voice slipped into a monotone. "Body weight, seventy-five kilograms, fourty point five four grams. Height, one hundred eighty-one point nine seven centimeters. The eyes and eyelids, nose and both ears are absent and there is extensive postmortem tissue damage and loss at the anterior of the skull, consistent with consumption by scavenger birds. Similar but less extensive damage appears at both deltoids. Multiple slight cuts appear across the palms consistent with infliction by the fingernails while the hands were in the closed fist position. A hematoma with a diameter of twelve millimeters appears on the inside of the right forearm, four centimeters below the joint of the elbow. A six millimeter scar appears at the center of the hematoma. Genital development is normal adult male. The appearance of the remainder of the body is unremarkable except for a substance consistent with dried blood appearing under the fingernails, a sample of which is being taken."

Seidman scraped under the fingernails of the corpse and

deposited the specimen collected in a pillbox, labeled it and put it aside. Then he picked up a scalpel.

"The body," said Seidman into the microphone, "is opened with the usual $Y$ incision."

Seidman pressed the cutting edge of the scalpel under Zlin's left breast and pulled it along a descending diagonal to the center of the body, just below the breastbone. The blade sliced through the skin, a thin layer of yellow fat, then a layer of muscle tissue. Under the fluorescent light, ribs gleamed dully white through the incision. Seidman repeated the maneuver from under the right breast. The two incisions formed a $V$. Placing the scalpel at the base of the $V$, Seidman sliced carefully, straight down the center of Zlin's body from the breastbone to the base of the penis. The distinct layers of skin, fat and muscle tissue lay bare to the view of the three men. A membrane, no longer held in by an overlayer of muscle, bulged with the contents of Zlin's body cavity.

Something was bothering Farington, annoying him. He couldn't place just what it was. As Seidman bent over the corpse once more and carefully slit the bulging membrane, it hit him: Seidman was *humming*.

As the slit membrane parted, Zlin's stomach and intestines glistened. Farington smelled a gas generated by decomposition and released when the membrane parted under Seidman's knife. He started breathing through his mouth.

Next, Seidman picked up a small electric saw. Its motor whined into life and Seidman laid it into the cut under Zlin's left breast, against the exposed ribs. The saw cut through them quickly and neatly. He repeated the procedure under the right breast, the other arm of the $Y$, then snapped off the saw. As the blade stopped whirling, Farington noticed that the teeth of the saw blade were clogged with bits of bone dust and damp tissue. He wondered who had to clean it up.

Seidman slipped his gloved hands up under the arms of the "Y" and lifted back Zlin's chest, freed by his severing of the ribs. Zlin's heart and lungs were now exposed. Seidman addressed the microphone again, describing them. He noted the marbling of fat on the heart and then, with a few deft strokes of his scalpel, removed it. He weighed it on the scale he had been adjusting when Kazalakis and Farington entered, and duly reported his findings to the microphone. Then Seidman placed the heart on a wooden block and dissected it. He reported on the presence of a buildup of plaque, much like the mineral deposit in an old water pipe, appearing in the blood vessels of the heart, then turned his attention to Zlin's lungs.

These, too, were removed, one at a time, inspected and weighed. After weighing, Seidman placed the lungs on the small wooden block and sliced across them, sectioning them. Frowning, he noted to the microphone discoloration and tissue damage. Working on the second lung, he spoke to Kazalakis and Farington, ignoring the microphone:

"Wish I had a healthy lung here to show you. You really can't appreciate the lesson without it. This man smoked. Look at it. In a normal lung, this tissue would be fresh and pink!"

There was a touch of outrage in Seidman's voice. Self-destructive behavior, especially *knowingly* self-destructive behavior such as smoking, angered him. Kazalakis and Farington, the former an inhaler of cigars and the latter a smoker of whatever filter cigarette promised lowest tar and nicotine at the moment, said nothing.

Seidman continued working easily and efficiently. He removed liver, spleen and kidneys. Each was described in detail to the microphone, weighed, dissected and described again. Each was then preserved for later pathological examination. Seidman would be working far into the night before he was through.

Still, there was no certainty of the cause of death. If the poison of the subcutaneous capsule, whatever it was, had been the agent of death, that information waited the completion of the chemical tests necessary to identify it. All Seidman could say at this point was that Zlin's heart had stopped beating. He was not sure yet why, or even when.

Seidman reached in to remove Zlin's intestines. They gleamed in the fluorescent light like a nest of wet snakes. He reached down for the end of the colon to sever it from the inside and separate it from the anus and sphincter muscle.

"Hold on," said Seidman quietly to himself.

"What is it?" demanded Kazalakis. The time being consumed was exasperating him even though he knew it was absolutely necessary. He couldn't remember when he'd last spent so much time as a passive, though interested, observer.

"There is a possible foreign object in the rectum," said Seidman, "although it may just be an abnormal piece of feces."

Farington forced himself to look closely at Zlin's intestines. His complexion was healthy no longer. His face was as white as Zlin's skin where the blood had been drained away by gravity to a purple pool, around his buttocks.

"Wait a minute!" Kazalakis commanded. Seidman looked up at him, inquiringly.

"Could you remove whatever that is in darkness, Doctor? I mean absolute darkness?"

"Yes, I suppose so, but—"

"Paul, kill the lights. Go to the photo lab and get a light-proof container. No. Get the head of the lab down here right away and let *him* pick the light-proof container."

"Yes, sir." Farington answered, opening the door and snapping off the light switch. He closed the door behind him. The room became pitch dark.

Seidman did not ask Kazalakis why he wanted him to extract the object from Zlin's colon in the dark. He didn't have to. The dispatch of Farington to the photo lab had told him why. Nor would he have asked if he hadn't guessed, though he felt he should have been told as he was conducting the autopsy. He waited.

"There's light leaking under the door," said Kazalakis, whose eyes were becoming accustomed to the darkness.

Seidman did not answer. There was nothing he could do about it.

Within moments, the door opened. The light in the hallway had been extinguished. *Somebody's* thinking anyway, Kazalakis thought. When the door closed there was no light leakage. There was no light at all; it was absolutely black in the room.

"Steve is with me." It was Farington's voice. Steve would be the chief technician from the photo lab. There being no need for the others to know his real name, the standard practice of using a ficticious name, and only a first name at that, was being followed. Kazalakis approved mentally.

"Steve," he said, "have you been filled in?"

"Yes, sir," came the reply out of the darkness. "I understand there's a chance of recovering an exposed roll of ultra-fast thirty-five millimeter. I've got a light-tight container here to hold whatever's recovered and take it to the lab. Can you give me anything about any unusual conditions its been exposed to?"

"Body temperature heat for at least some time," answered

Seidman. "Moisture and possibly some light may have filtered through partially translucent body tissue just now."

"Um," said Steve. "There's probably damage but we'll salvage all we can."

There was another moment of silence. "Here," said Seidman.

"Where?" replied Steve.

"Over here. Hold the container out in front of you. Do I just drop it in?"

"Right."

"What does it feel like?" asked Kazalakis.

"Can't tell for sure through these gloves but it seems the right size for your film."

There was another pause.

"Is that your arm I've got, Steve?"

"Right."

Farington heard a hollow clunk, like an ice cube dropping into a plastic bowl.

"Okay. You've got it."

"Let me know when I can put the lights on," said Farington.

"Wait a minute—okay."

The fluorescent fixture glowed dully for a moment, then made them all wince at its brightness.

"Paul, why don't you stay with Steve and bring whatever he comes up with back with you. Dr. Seidman, when you've completed all your tests, send them to me immediately by courier. I don't care what time it is."

Kazalakis did not wait for an acknowledgement of his instructions. He turned, strode out of the room and up the stairs to catch a cab back to Langley.

Farington followed Steve up the stairs toward the photo lab. He tried to suppress a thought that kept making him want to smile, though it wasn't funny. The more he tried to suppress it, the worse it got. He couldn't help it. Farington kept wondering what Steve's reaction would be if what he found in the light-tight container turned out to be feces.

In reaction to the autopsy experience, Farington's mind continued to pursue silly imaginings. What an opportunity, he thought, for a classic one line report: "TSD can't develop shit."

# III

"This, of course," said Alexander McKenzie, "is precisely what I was trying to avoid."

The CIA director put a forkful of liver into his mouth and chewed it, waiting for a reply from his Deputy Director for Operations. He received none. Constantine Kazalakis' response was to put a forkful of steak into his own mouth and begin to chew. Kazalakis wielded his fork in the European manner, upside down, in the view of McKenzie who, seeing that he would receive no reply, continued:

"I inherited this pool business. I have never agreed that the agency should continue to involve itself in domestic clandestine operations. But my predecessor sold the president the notion that we should preserve the capability, and that the pool arrangement would provide protection from any political consequences. Now I employ it for the first time, on your strong recommendation, and find that the net result is one man dead and nothing to show for it."

Kazalakis' hand stopped its slicing of another piece of steak. McKenzie knew very well that Kazalakis had been the father of the pool concept, the literal pooling of clandestine operational specialists from among the several agencies that comprised the intelligence community, and the assigning of them to tasks laid on by any but the agency which had employed them formerly. All had been retired or resigned and now held jobs with cooperative corporations and labor unions. Each operation was to be done on an *ad hoc* and cash basis with no records kept. McKenzie was out to kill the baby before it was baptized.

"If I gave you that impression," Kazalakis said, staring directly into McKenzie's eyes, "I misled you. We *have* something to show for it. Most of the film was recovered intact. It's just that it appears, and I stress the word *appears,* to be of no significance."

"To whom?"

"To us. We've had our best people go over it. It is their considered opinion that it's nothing more than what you'd expect to find in such a place."

"And you disagree?"

"I don't know. Our analysts looked at the stuff from the point of view of legitimate, even though very sophisticated, businessmen."

"What do you want to do?"

"Bring in an expert."

"An expert?" McKenzie put down his knife and fork. He looked intently at Kazalakis, sitting across the table from him in his private dining room. McKenzie's expression indicated that he was fast running out of patience. Whatever Kazalakis had in mind had better be good.

"A rogue," said Kazalakis.

"As in 'worthless, dishonest person'?"

"As in 'elephant'; one that's gone bad and left the herd. On his own, shrewd and dangerous. Follow me through on this: A few years ago, the *Nachrichtendienst* passed on to the legal attaché in Bonn a rumble they picked up in the east that Ballinger was a Soviet 'sleeper'. The Bureau checked it out and couldn't prove it—but they couldn't *dis*prove it, either. They try to keep an eye on him but he's out of the country as much as he's here and they're afraid to make any real moves or the Justice Department will indict them for mopery. Now, in quick succession, we get word from MOSSAD—so strong it's clear they think for this information alone we should give Israel another squadron of F-15s—that the Soviets are cooking up an economic move against us that'll make the wheat deal into a kid's lemonade stand; and the *Gaimusho* rings in to State with much the same thing."

"There is nothing to assure us, however," said McKenzie, "that all that smoke is coming from the same fire."

"True," acknowledged Kazalakis, "but we can't ignore that smoke. Maybe Ballinger's wrong and maybe he isn't. But if he is, he's got so much going for him he can do a lot of damage on his own, and if he's hooked up with the Soviets—Jesus! I hate to think of it! Either way you figure it, though, he's a rare bird and to play against him we need someone who can think like him."

McKenzie's smile was mirthless. "Well, he's got you mixing your metaphors if he's done nothing else. Whom do you propose as a peer of Gregory Ballinger—Robert Vesco?"

McKenzie's sarcasm wasn't lost on Kazalakis. His voice took on a note of defiance: "Someone I would not propose if I didn't think him capable."

"Of course, of course," McKenzie backed off. "Who is it?" He began to eat again.

"Richard von Randenburg."

McKenzie's pause was only momentary. "I don't believe I've ever heard of the gentleman."

"He's no gentleman. And you wouldn't, not by that name. Try Ricky Rand."

"If you mean the man I think you mean—"

"I do."

"A playboy and associate of gangsters—"

"Hear me out."

"Wouldn't miss it for the world," said McKenzie in the tone he once employed when dealing with bright students with whom he disagreed. "I'm fascinated."

Kazalakis forgot his food. He was making his pitch and it absorbed all his attention.

"Rand is a strange duck. He doesn't even begin to be in the same class as Ballinger as far as wealth is concerned, but he's got a lot of money. He earned it all, though probably a good half of it illegally. He inherited nothing. His father died in World War II. He was on the losing side and left nothing but a few medals.

"Rand's mother left his father before the war over the question of allegiance. She was American. Came back to the States and changed her name and the boy's to Rand; von Randenburg was not a popular kind of name to have around here in World War II. She never divorced her husband, though. He became something of a hero flying with the *Luftwaffe*. Two hundred and two kills until he ran out of fuel over the Ukraine in '44 and was killed."

Kazalakis took out a cigar and gestured with it toward McKenzie.

"Do you mind?"

McKenzie gave his head a slight shake and Kazalakis fired a battered Zippo under the cigar. McKenzie caught a glimpse of a Marine Corps emblem on the Zippo as Kazalakis snapped the cover shut and returned the lighter to his jacket pocket.

"The boy had tremendous admiration for his father, but there was never any question of his loyalty to this country."

"How do we know something as subjective as that?"

"For one thing, he's a native born citizen. The mother saw to that. For another, I flew with him as a Marine aviator in Korea. In fact I broke him in, or tried to. He was good. Kept arguing that the tactics his old man had used were better than the ones we were using. When he was assigned to liason with the Air Force, he decided to prove it. He got hold of one of their P-51s and actually shot down two Mig 15s with it, then got pissed off when they wouldn't let him put his father's old squadron markings on the 51."

"Where's the alleged financial expertise come in?"

"He went to the Wharton School. Graduated at the beginning of the Korean War as an ROTC Distinguished Military Graduate. With that he could pick his service. He took Marine Corps aviation. The old thing about his father, I guess. When Korea was over and there was no more flying action, he used his fluency in German to wangle assignment to ONI. The von Randenburg's come from what's now East Germany and his accent is perfect. When they set up DIA he was assigned there. In the meantime I came here. Never did like jets. Sneeze and you're in the next county."

"How did your man do?"

"Well, and not so well. He didn't last long."

"What happened."

"He was lent out a few times for some executive actions in East Germany. He was very good. But he made a bad marriage, at least from the government's point of view, then got himself personally involved as a result of it and ended up in jail. From then on it was all down hill in every way but financially."

McKenzie took a sip of a good claret, touched his lips with his napkin and asked:

"What constituted a bad marriage from the government's point of view?"

Kazalakis studied the ash on the end of his cigar. It was half an inch long.

"He married the niece of a Mafia Don. And he knew damn well who she was. Said she wasn't involved in anything and he was probably right. They tend to keep their women out of it and she was only twenty-two. At any rate, while he was abroad on a trip she was staying with the uncle. Her father had died years before of natural causes and the uncle took in his widowed sister and her child. Brought her up. Strict convent schools and so forth. The uncle had a golf cart he used to get around his estate with. The girl borrowed it one day and was blown up. Now, remember I told you this guy's a strange duck?"

That, McKenzie thought to himself, makes an elephant, a bird and a duck. A veritable zoo. But he repressed the urge to comment upon it.

"I assume," said McKenzie, "his response to the stress was unusual."

"You assume correctly. He was in West Berlin when he got word of what had happened. He went directly to the embassy at Bonn and resigned his commission. Didn't even wait for the resignation to be accepted; just tore out of there, technically AWOL, and hopped a plane for New York."

"All right," said McKenzie, "he's immature and impetuous. Not desireable qualities in an officer, especially not an intelligence officer; but hardly extraordinary in the circumstances."

"Agreed, but—"

The phone on the table to McKenzie's right had a row of lucite buttons below the numbered push-buttons. One marked "intercom" was flashing on and off. Somewhere in the room a muted gong kept time with the flashing light. McKenzie said "excuse me," lifted the handset to his ear, listened a moment, said "Thank you, Mrs. Lacey," and hung up.

"You left instructions to be advised when Paul Farington arrived?"

"Yes. Thank you, sir." Kazalakis did not explain further. He was eager to continue his biography of Rand.

"I'll agree the man's reaction was not startling. Up to a point. That point arrived when he got home. He went directly to the uncle's place. Now, the next part is in dispute, but what we have is from the FBI; information they've put together from ELINT and informants. I'd say it was at least ninety percent accurate."

McKenzie glanced at his watch. "All this is interesting, but so far all I have that is to the point—this man's knowledge of finance —is that he graduated—some time ago I might add—from the Wharton School. You're sponsoring him, in effect, to second-guess mature and experienced economists and financial analysts who have been with us for years and, one supposes, doing a good job or they wouldn't still be here."

Kazalakis frowned. "Yes, sir, I *am* sponsoring him. And for that very reason I'm trying to give you all the negative information I have about him first, so that we go into this with our eyes open."

"If we do so at all."

"Of course."

"All right, but do get to something positive and to the point as soon as you can."

"Yes, sir." Kazalakis took a breath and plunged ahead. "According to our information, Rand and the uncle had a helluva row. Rand insisted the uncle knew who did it and demanded his identity. He invoked his right under some obscure Mafia or Sicilian custom to take vengence himself as the girl's husband. The uncle, whose own honor was gravely offended, didn't want to give it up to someone who, as far as he knew, was just a young Marine officer who wouldn't know how to handle it. What's more, Rand demanded that the funeral be postponed until he could avenge the girl."

"I wonder," mused McKenzie, "how much was for the sake of the girl and how much was for the sake of your man's own ego?"

"That's a good point. I don't know. At any rate, they compromised. Rand was to settle with the underling who set the device and the uncle would take care of the rival Don who had tried to kill him. In nine hours an obscure thug was found in his own garage screaming his life away with a broad-bladed hunting arrow all the way through his gut and out the back. They got him to the hospital alive but he died in the emergency room from shock. But it wouldn't have done him any good anyway. The arrowhead was found to have been coated with a flourescent powder poison. It takes days to kill, but there's no antidote."

"What do you make of the bizarre choice of weapon?"

"A message—a signature. That's not the way the Mafia kills. He wanted everybody to know he'd done his duty as a husband."

McKenzie reacted with a grunt. "What happened to the other man; the rival Don?"

"Shotgun. Eight months later. No repercussions. It was cleared in advance with the other family heads."

"And your man?"

"Subpoenaed before a grand jury and refused to testify, even with immunity. Went to jail for contempt for ten months. That was it."

"I assume we are now going to get to the part about his financial acumen."

"Right." Kazalakis stopped talking while a waiter brought in coffee, served it expertly and left.

"When he got out, Rand had earned the respect of the Mafia people. That plus the fact that he was still an in-law, so to speak, got him a stake. It was supposedly a lot of money and with no strings. You can get all kinds of guesses on the amount, up to a million dollars. I doubt it was that much and I doubt there were no strings attached. They just don't operate that way. At any rate, to make a long story short, within two years Rand had run it into a small fortune."

"Wait a minute. That long story you just made short is the point of this whole exercise. If he won it on a horse race he's of no more value to us than—"

"I understand," Kazalakis interrupted, holding his hands up, palm out, as if to ward McKenzie off, "I understand. I'll give you what we've got, but you've got to appreciate that a lot of people are still trying to figure out the details of how he did it. Basically, he followed the classic pattern of recognizing an opportunity arising from a fundamental change in society. In Rand's case it was the revolution in air travel time brought about by the introduction of the commercial jet."

Kazalakis warmed to his task. He had not only a professional appreciation but a personal admiration for a clever scheme. "Rand," he said, "recognized that while the new jets could get him to, say, Switzerland in a matter of hours, international monetary transactions were still in the steamship era. It *still* takes 10 days for a check drawn on a Swiss bank and deposited in the United States to arrive in Switzerland. So Rand just took advantage of the time differential. He started out with sheer manipulation of deposits, checks, letters of credit and so forth. If you've got enough money to work with, you can keep quite a float going and pick up a helluva lot of interest on other people's money. Just takes an intimate knowledge of the way banks work internally, a damn good memory so you know what you've got going and where, and a good set of balls. Jet travel was brand new then, remember, and nobody was looking for it. He ran wild."

"What you've described," said McKenzie, "is no more than common check kiting."

"Kiting, yes," retorted Kazalakis, "common, no. And that's not all of it. When he got a big enough stake he went in for highly innovative manipulation and started taking over whole businesses. Some he'd keep and some he'd use to trade, sell or whatever suited the needs of his latest scheme. As I said, he's not in the Ballinger or Ludwig league yet by any stretch of the imagination; but if he can keep out of jail, he's on his way."

McKenzie raised both his eyebrows. "That's it?"

"No. The word is that Rand's success led his Mafia friends to start coming to him for financial advice. Lansky's illness and age have made him cut way down in his activities. Rand is believed to be his replacement."

McKenzie's face grew bleak. "It's all been for nothing, hasn't it? All we went through over the liason with Giancana for executive action against Castro. I can see we've learned nothing. Well, I can assure you that *I* have no intention of ever having to go up on the hill to try to explain another such incident to an oversight committee!"

Kazalakis had been expecting a negative reaction to that information, but it's vociferousness surprised him. McKenzie was by nature dour and reserved. He pressed on:

"There's more. Depending on how you look at it, it could be either positive or negative."

McKenzie's outburst had apparently spent his quota of passion for the day. Resignation filled the void. "Well," he sighed, "we've gone this far. I might as well listen to it all. If, that is, you think you can wind it up before they start serving supper in here."

"I'll do my best," said Kazalakis. He took a long drag on his cigar. It was dead. Fishing out the Marine Corps Zippo again, he continued, his first few words interspersed with pauses as he puffed the cigar back to life:

"For the last few years, despite the fact that he's seen all over the place with a succession of young, rather vacant little knockouts, Rand's real love and mistress has been a mature Oriental woman named Li; T'sa Li in the Westernized version, Li T'sa Xiao correctly. Like most Chinese who settle here, after a few losing battles with license bureau clerks who refuse to accept that in China the family name comes first, she and her family gave up and made the switch."

McKenzie, who required no explanation of Chinese naming customs, sighed impatiently and looked pointedly at his watch. Kazalakis got the message and rushed ahead:

37

"At any rate, she's a pure Mongolian, in her late thirties, who beat him in a gold deal in Macao. Instead of getting mad, he fell in love with her, so he says, and had her, her widowed mother and her brother admitted permanently through a private bill he bought from a Congressional chairman. Less charitable people say she's the only person ever to beat Rand and what he's really in love with is her brain."

"That's very romantic," said McKenzie, "but—"

"There's more," Kazalakis interrupted. "The brother, T'ang Li, turns out to be a red belt master of Fu Dong, a particularly deadly Mongolian martial art. Fu Dong means 'strong lock'. He fights in the style of the tiger—high T'ai Chi. According to DI-6, whose source is in Hong Kong and rated most reliable, T'ang Li runs the enforcement apparatus for the consolidated Tongs—a sort of Chinese Mafia reputed to exist wherever there is an overseas Chinese community of any size. Which takes in a lot of territory in the free world these days."

"How," said McKenzie, "can that bit of information be viewed as positive?"

"Because the liason has reportedly led to Rand's also becoming involved with the Tongs as a financial advisor; perhaps as a joint venturer, if one credits some rumors."

McKenzie opened his mouth to speak, but Kazalakis didn't give him a chance.

"What we have here is a financial genius completely without scruple. Even better, a genius at manipulation on a grand and creative scale with extraordinary contacts, entré, and human assets in the international underworld."

McKenzie smiled. "All I have to hear now," he said, "is that his sister is married to a Corsican bandit chief."

"I wouldn't be surprised," said Kazalakis, smiling at the relief of tension between them.

"But," said McKenzie, "I'm afraid any association with your man is quite impossible. Just too risky in today's climate."

Kazalakis' disappointment did not register in his face. It settled in his stomach. "Not," he continued doggedly, "if we handle it correctly. Look. Lets try it a step at a time. We bring Rand in here and sit down with him and a couple of our top financial people. Test him first. Let them ask him questions about anything in the field. If everybody's not satisfied, we're out no more than a free lunch."

McKenzie didn't like the reference to 'everybody' being satisfied. He still felt very much the outsider—a new boy transfering into prep school in his senior year and being appointed president of the student council. "And if *I* am satisfied that he's as able as you say he is?"

"Then we give him the problem," said Kazalakis. "Let him analyze the film. See if he can give us any idea what Ballinger's up to."

"If anything."

"If anything," Kazalakis agreed.

McKenzie was silent. He stared at a wrinkle in the table linen while necessity struggled with caution for control of his will. "All right," McKenzie said finally, his voice tired. "Get him down here."

Kazalakis fought back a smile of triumph but his voice was full of suppressed energy as he said "Yes, sir. May I use your phone for a moment?"

McKenzie nodded his assent, rising.

Kazalakis hit the intercom button and picked up the receiver. "Mrs. Lacey? Would you ask Mr. Farington to step in here for a moment, please?"

Kazalakis had barely hung up when the door with the one-way lock on it leading into McKenzie's office from the dining room opened and Farington entered.

"Doctor," said Kazalakis, trying to please and sooth McKenzie by using his academic title, "I had hoped that you would decide as you did and took the liberty of trying to save us some time. If you had decided against it," he reassured hastily, "I'd only have had lunch with an old Marine buddy. I had Paul contact Rand and tell him I'd like to see him."

Turning to Farington Kazalakis said, "How soon can Rand get down here, Paul?"

Farington looked decidedly uncomfortable. "I'm afraid there's a problem, sir. Mr. Rand won't be able to come down."

"Why?" asked Kazalakis. "What problem?"

"He didn't say, sir."

"Well what the hell *did* he say?" Kazalakis barked.

Farington was the picture of misery. He hesitated, then seemed to make up his mind. "Well, he said—his exact words were, 'go fuck yourself', sir."

Farington looked as if he wanted to disappear. Which is exactly what he wished he could do. Kazalakis appeared to be strangling, quietly. For the first time in the memory of either of the other two men, McKenzie burst into unrestrained laughter.

A moment later, under control but still grinning with a mouth that was never meant to do so, McKenzie spoke:

"You get him down here any way you have to. I want to meet that man!"

# IV

T'sa Li wakened to the morning light streaming through the baroque window of the Plaza Hotel. Below it, the oasis of Central Park swept north to the asphalt badlands of Manhattan. She came awake instantly, like a bird at first light, then, realizing where she was, smiled and abandoned herself to a warm and sensual langour. Morning was good, life better and being a woman best of all.

T'sa Li listened to the slow, regular breathing that told her that Richard Rand was fast asleep. She nestled closer to his naked body, feeling it's long, lean hardness against her own softness and stared at the nape of his neck. The hair just faintly curling there was very blond; such a contrast, she thought, to the iridescent jet of her own.

Shifting her body slightly to relieve a protesting muscle, T'sa Li felt a warm wetness lubricate her thighs where they touched when she moved. Pursing her lips against her lover's neck, she tasted more than kissed it. Salty, T'sa Li thought. The flavor complemented his masculine aroma and, blending subtly with the scent of her own womanhood seeping up under the covers from her loins, rekindled still glowing embers of last night. T'sa Li felt her nipples harden. Perhaps this would be the morning she would win; it was worth a try, anyway.

Slowly and carefully, so as not to waken him, T'sa Li sat halfway up, resting on one arm, and regarded Rand. In sleep his face was almost boyish, closed lids covering his terrible eyes. She pictured those eyes as they were when he looked at her—looked *through* her would put it better. Never had she seen any like them; so pale a blue that there was almost no pupil, nothing to focus upon when trying to return his steady gaze; like looking through cloud-less sky into infinity. It was impossible to tell what Rand was thinking until he spoke or acted. For some, that had proved too late. For T'sa Li it was always disconcerting. But, she acknowledged, it was one of the things that attracted her to him. He was so unusual, so *interesting;* a perpetual challenge.

Leaning over Rand, T'sa Li began kissing him gently on the flank, just below the blond hair curling from the deep recess under his arm. Like a golden serpent, her left hand slid under the covers.

Richard Rand rolled over on his back, smiling. The sea was warm. So warm he must be floating over some undersea well-spring of warm water; a volcano, perhaps, thousands of fathoms below. The current centered under his buttocks. Rand permitted his legs to drift apart, letting the warm flow bubble up between them. Small fish were trying to bite him with smooth, toothless little mouths. A buoy had somehow floated between his legs. As he rocked in the gentle swell, the buoy became part of him; he could feel the waves wash over it. The pleasure was exquisite. He was drawn up, up . . .

"Stop that, you devil!"

Startled, T'sa Li froze, her lips still enclosing Rand's glans, the hard shaft held lightly between her thumb and fingertips. She dared a glance at him. The awful eyes were upon her, but he was smiling. She gave his glans a little bite, then lifted her head.

"Sure you mean that?" T'sa Li said, smiling teasingly. She started to move her fingertips up and down slowly.

"You know damn well I mean it," said Rand. Then the stern tone of his voice melted into complaint, almost a plea: "How'm I going to run out there," he said, gesturing out the window toward Central Park, "if I leave my legs up here?"

T'sa Li, sitting now, hands in her lap with fingers laced together, gazed at Rand's erection and sighed. "Such a waste!" she exclaimed. Then, like a striking cobra, her hand shot out and snapped a finger hard against the base of Rand's penis.

"Ow! Damn it!" Rand yelped as his erection toppled like a felled tree, "Where the hell did you learn that trick!"

"Kung Fu!" T'sa Li crowed in mocking triumph, shaking a fist above her head and grinning from ear to ear. Then, giggling like a schoolgirl, she bounced out of bed just in time to duck the pillow Rand sailed after her and disappeared into the bathroom.

Rand was getting out of bed, still grumbling, when the telephone rang. He snatched it up.

"Good morning, Mr. Rand," said the voice of Constantine Kazalakis. "In exactly five seconds your ass will self-destruct if you don't get it down here!"

"Greek?" Rand barked, "Listen you bushy-haired bureaucrat, I gave my answer to that errand boy you had call me after a short pause of only fifteen years. Who the fuck do you think you are? Better yet, who the fuck do you think *I* am—"

"Rick, Rick," Kazalakis interrupted, "You're right, you're right, okay? I should have called myself. Sorry if I woke you, but I couldn't reach you all yesterday afternoon and evening and figured you were duckin' me. Look, Rick. I won't bullshit you. I need help."

"You need help, all right. Professional help. Or do you think I'm the guy who needs it? You bastards don't even bury your dead anymore, much less bring out your wounded. Forget it, pal!"

"Rick, look. I'll level with you. I made a mistake and said I could produce you without checking first. I never thought you'd turn down an old wingman. It's no big deal. Some people just want to talk to you; get your slant on something, that's all. You blow a day, pick up a free lunch and get my ass off the hook. How about it?"

"No way, sweetheart. You're not talking to some cherry, you know. I've been waltzed into the garden by experts."

"Rick," said Kazalakis, "did your old man ever let down a wingman?" For a moment, all that could be heard on the line was the hollow electrical distance between them. Finally, Rand spoke:

"You're a real low-life son of a bitch, Greek. You know that, don't you?"

"Aw Rick, c'mon. How soon can you get here?"

"How's one o'clock?"

"Great. And Rick, do me one more favor, will you? Come commercial. I haven't told anyone here yet about that plane of yours."

Rand might have yielded, but it didn't do to let Kazalakis have his way completely. It could be habit forming—a bad habit. The anger in his voice was an act when Rand said, "Negative! I choose my own transportation." Then he softened his tone: "Hell,

Greek, you of all people should know I've got to put in the hours to keep up proficiency on that ship. Thinking any other way can get you dead."

"Yeah, I suppose," said Kazalakis, grudgingly, "where you coming in? I'll meet you and fill you in on the way out."

"National. General Aviation North Terminal."

"National! Jesus Christ, Ricky! Why don't you just hire a brass band?"

"That ship's gotta be hangered, Greek. It'd be stripped to the frame in five minutes if I ever left it out. Now do you want me there or not?"

"My God!" said Kazalakis. "When are you ever gonna grow up? One o'clock!"

Rand pulled the receiver away from his ear sharply as Kazalakis slammed it down at the other end. Grinning, Rand hung up the phone, crossed to the bathroom and knocked on the door. T'sa Li gave a wary "Yes?"

"Sally, do you have to get home right away?"

"Not necessarily," T'sa Li pouted, "why? Trying to get rid of me?"

"On the contrary. I thought if you weren't in a hurry I'd go run and then we could have breakfast together."

"I'm taking a bath. Feels good. Why don't you join me? I guarantee you more exercise than your silly jogging."

Rand laughed. "I run, I don't jog! Anyway, I've gotta do *my* exercise just to stay in shape for yours."

T'sa Li was needling him, Rand knew, because he had called her "Sally." It was bad enough having to turn her name around without his slurring it into an anglicization. Calling him a "jogger" evened the score.

"Whatever," T'sa Li replied airily, "you'll probably get yourself mugged either way."

"Thirty minutes." said Rand. "Keep the water hot with your little water heater."

Crossing the room to a large, polished walnut *armoire*, Rand donned an athletic supporter, shorts with the seams ripped halfway up the sides, a T-shirt and a sweatshirt. He folded a towel twice, lengthwise, and wrapped it around his neck like a scarf, tucking the ends down inside the front of his sweatshirt. He put on a pair of thick, white wool athletic socks and then laced on a pair of ultra-light running shoes, triple soled and with flared heels.

Rand bent over, letting his upper body hang down for a moment. Then he placed both palms flat against the oriental rug on the floor. Satisfied, he donned a trenchcoat to appease the Plaza management and left his suite.

Riding down in one of the slow, beautifully ornate elevators that are a trademark of the Plaza, Richard Rand stared at the floor and tried to imagine what had prompted Constantine Kazalakis to make contact again after so many years. Once as close as only combat pilots in the same unit can be, Kazalakis had sided with the government on the advisability of his marriage to Carla. Rand had resented it bitterly at the time. He could understand it now, but, although he respected the man, his feelings for Kazalakis were reserved at best.

Crossing the lobby quickly in deference to the sensibilities of the day manager, Rand emerged on Central Park South to a magnificent April day. Spring, he decided, had come to New York. Jaywalking quickly across the street, he remarked on that fact to Alfredo Matarazza, a short, thickset man in his early fifties. His dense black hair framed a face as rutted and sunblasted as the Sicilian hills from which he had immigrated at the age of four.

Alfredo Matarazza had no thought for spring. He was standing next to a hansom cab, uncomfortable in an ancient formal jacket.

"Boss," he asked, "do I gotta wear the fuckin' hat?"

Rand grinned. The hat in question was a battered topper of the kind affected by the hansom cab drivers who plied their trade in Central Park from hackstands along Central Park South. Matarazza, however, was no cab driver. He just acted the part every morning in good weather when Rand was at home in the Plaza.

Alfredo Matarazza was third cousin to Rand's deceased wife, Carla, and a member of the Scarbacci family in more ways than one. His assignment in life was to look after Rand. Matarazza's real boss, as they both well knew, was Luigi Scarbacci, Rand's one time quasi father-in-law. Scarbacci had a lot beside a family tie invested in Rand and, considering him a bit rash, had assigned Matarazza to take care of him. Rand, having little real choice in the matter, and liking Matarazza anyway, went along with it to the extent he could do so reasonably.

"Nah, 'Fredo," Rand smiled, "who needs a hat on a day like this?"

Gratefully, Matarazza tossed the offending hat into the cab and mounted to the driver's seat. The cab was rented at three times the going rate just so Matarazza could drive. The costume he was wearing was thrown in as part of the deal. So was the right to keep concealed under the seat a sawn-off over-under Browning shotgun, its top barrel loaded with double-O buckshot and the lower one with a 12-gauge rifled slug.

Rand peeled off his coat, tossed it into the cab with the topper and started running east, just off the street. When he came to the road going north into the park he turned into it, Matarazza following. They had tried it with a car, but after being accused a number of times of blocking traffic, switched to the hansom. Matarazza had insisted upon the arrangement. Rand ran there so often that it was a natural occasion for an enemy to move against him as he would be alone, unarmed and vulnerable in a relatively quiet area.

Rand was running now. As did his other passions, flying and hunting, it brought him alive, heightening his senses and honing his discipline and will. Rand settled down into a powerful lope, running against the sweep of the OM-1 Omega on his wrist. The idea was to exhaust himself at the end, and that meant constant time pressure and a maximum-effort final sprint.

Good weather made this a five mile day and he reveled in the feeling of limitless reserves of strength as the ground flowed beneath him. Rand monitored his body mentally. Six strides to one breath cycle. He was not yet in "cruising gear," as he thought of it. After about a mile and a half, his body would shift automatically to four strides per breath cycle. In that gear he could run on indefinately, needing only water to sustain him.

The familiar landmarks slipped by. His arms became a bit tired and Rand realized that he had been carrying them too high. He let them hang loosely and shook them. The fatigue vanished. A buildup of sweat formed in his eyebrows, then broke through and trickled down his face. He brushed it away. Only an occasional whiff of auto exhaust spoiled his pleasure.

A mile and a half from his finishing point, Rand threw a mental switch. It would override all pain. With a command of his will he downshifted, lifting his legs, stretching them out. Rand's body seemed to lift inches off the earth. He expelled his breath with a powerful contraction of his diaphram; to passersby old enough to remember, it sounded like a steam locomotive under forced

draught. The last mile was a concentration so intense Rand became almost totally unaware of his surroundings. Anoxia made
his legs gain weight increasingly. Despite his resolve, pain infil-
trated his mind and fought with Rand's will for control of his
body. He reacted by lashing himself into even greater effort:
more, more, MORE!

Rand passed the five mile mark with his vision blurring, his
body out of fuel. He coasted to a walk. With remarkable swift-
ness, his breathing rate slowed and his pulse dropped. In the
short time it took him to walk back to Matarazza, Rand's breathing rate was back to normal and his pulse elevated only slightly.
Greeting the burly guard he removed the towel from around his
neck and dried his face and wrists. Then Rand donned his trenchcoat and hurried back up to his suite at the Plaza. A tub containing hot water and a hot woman awaited him. Right now, it was
the hot water he craved.

The exhaust pipe leading from the turbo-charged three litre
overhead cam racing engine gave out a high rpm *whoop* as
Richard Rand stabbed the throttle of the BMW 630 CSi in a
double-clutched downshift. The tachometer needle swung up
sharply as he accelerated the black coupé into the traffic stream
crossing the George Washington Bridge. Past the toll booth on
the New Jersey side, he headed for route 46 west.

Rand sat upright, relaxed, his arms nearly straight out as he
gripped the steering wheel and put the BMW's superb Alpina-
modified suspension to good use in snaking through the heavy
traffic. Rand was happy. He had dropped an equally content T'sa
Li downtown before heading north, rejecting the more logical
route through the Lincoln Tunnel in favor of one that just
seemed more appropriate to a beautiful Spring day. The traffic
thinned and Rand opened the sunroof of the BMW.

The thought of T'sa Li stirred Rand even now. She received
and expressed pleasure so well, and Rand's own pleasure was
directly proportionate to that he was able to give. The two of
them together, he thought, were like compound turbines increasing each other's rpm reciprocally until they went through
the red line and fused from the heat of a passion that exceeded
human design limits.

"Christ!"

Rand braked hard and cut back over to the right lane to cool down. He had been doing 86 mph and accelerating when he realized what his sexual reverie had done to his usually precise driving. Moments later he was surprised to see Little Falls exit go by. He had really made time. Rand decided to stay in the right lane. The Passaic Avenue exit would be coming up in about one minute.

Rand's estimate was precise. He cut right, paused for the stop sign, turned hard left and negotiated the highway intersection overpass. A few hundred yards more and Caldwell-Wright airport was on his right. Rand downshifted again to use engine braking as he turned in the driveway.

Caldwell-Wright had a good runway. It had served the old Curtis-Wright Propellor division during World War II and was designed to accomodate the four-engined B-17 Flying Fortress. There were still some big, strong wartime hangars there, and the people operating the place now were dedicated aviation professionals.

The line boy driving the red avgas truck braked to a halt when he recognized Rand's BMW, then ran to catch up with him as Rand entered the fixed-base operator's operations shack.

"You gonna take her up, Mr. Rand?" the boy asked excitedly.

"If the weather's as good where I'm going as it is here, I am."

The grizzled FBO grinned at the boy's enthusiasm as Rand phoned the FAA Flight Service Station for a weather briefing for New York—Washington. The whole northeastern seaboard was in the middle of a high pressure system extending from Cape Hatteras to Cape Cod. Ceiling and visibility unlimited. Light clear air turbulence reported north of Baltimore.

"CAVU, kid," said Rand to the delighted youth as he hung up, "we got severe clear all the way. Let's go."

The youth darted out to a small tractor and drove it to the door of a big hangar east of the runway. Rand caught up with him and used his key to unlock the hangar door, entered through a small door cut into the larger one and threw a switch. Light flooded the interior of the hangar as the main door lifted like a theatre curtain, rumbling into the overhead to the accompanying whine of an electric motor.

The two of them stared into the interior of the hangar. The look on their faces was that of an art student viewing Michaelangelo's *Pieta*. Before them was a masterpiece in the history of aviation and of war. Mottled green-gray color, blunt prop spinner and deeply underslung oil-cooler intake making it look for all the world like a great white shark with wings, there stood a completely restored and airworthy Bf 109E-3; the sleek and deadly Messerschmitt with which the *Luftwaffe* dueled the R.A.F. over the English Channel during the Battle of Britain.

Breaking their reverie, the two went about the task of towing the plane, tail first, out of the hangar and onto the hard stand, swinging it around so that the nose of the ship was headed in the direction of the taxiway. That accomplished, Rand began his preflight inspection with a walk around, examining the exterior of the ship minutely, even rocking the wing from the tip to test the strength of its bond to the fuselage. He peered at hinges, put his fingers into openings such as the air and oil cooler intakes and drained gasoline into a glass to check for moisture.

The boy brought a step ladder and the two of them checked the oil. Rand checked the fuel level with his fingers. He finished by inspecting the undercarriage and landing gear wells. Satisfied at last, he mounted the ship and lifted the cockpit greenhouse canopy up and swung it on its side hinges to the starboard of the ship.

Reaching inside the cockpit, Rand picked up a parachute lying on the bare metal seat and donned it, then hoisted himself over the side and settled into the metal bucket. There was little room. He handed a metal crank to the waiting youth. The boy fitted it into the right side of the fuselage ahead of the cockpit and began to crank. The crank started a flywheel spinning. Rand's left hand fell readily to the cylindrical handle of the throttle projecting from the port cockpit wall. He cracked it a little, set the mixture full rich, slipped his feet into the roller-skatelike rudder pedals complete with straps and waited for the sound to tell him that the flywheel was up to speed. Detecting the proper note, he motioned to the line boy who promptly disengaged the crank, handed it back to Rand, then ran off to the side of the ship.

"CLEAR!" Rand shouted, then hit the master switch and let the clutch in to link the crankshaft of the engine to the spinning flywheel. There was a loud, descending whine as the clutch engaged and the three propellor blades started to pass across his line of vision at the end of the long, steeply angled cowl.

Suddenly there appeared a puff of blue-black smoke from the exhaust stacks under the cowling. It was accompanied by a cough, then a rapid, machine gun series of reports which melded into a roar as the great inverted V-12 fuel-injected engine came powerfully to life.

The rush of prop-wash buffeted Rand, prompting him to don the *Luftwaffe* flying helmet stored in the cockpit; then he began carefully to taxi out to the holding area adjacent to the runway. It didn't do to spend too much time on the ground in the Messerschmitt; it's cooling system was designed for flying, not taxiing, and it would overheat quickly if allowed to idle very long on the ground.

Rand's view forward was terrible. The ship was a "tail-dragger" with the resultant raising of its long snout up in the air at an angle that blocked his view while on the ground. Added to that was the gunsight placed squarely before him and which could not, as it could in later model craft, be swung to the side when not in use to improve forward vision. As a consequence, Rand craned his head out the side of the cockpit, first left and then right, and used differential braking to snake the ship *S*-fashion down the taxiway. En route he checked the wind sock to decide in which direction to take off. A small cluster of people had materialized outside the operations shack to watch and listen with a touch of residual dread as the alien eagle hurled itself into their native sky.

Arriving at the holding area to the side of the end of the runway, Rand worked his rudder, elevator and aileron controls to be sure they were free, checked his fuel gauges, saw to it that his coolant and oil were within the correct temperature limits and then turned his attention to additional equipment necessary for modern flight on the eastern seaboard of the United States: dual miniature Collins Nav/Com radios and a transponder. Chosen for their small size, it was still a tight fit. He switched on his Nav/Coms and set in one of them the Caldwell-Wright Unicom frequency. Then he set the Visual Flight Rules code into the transponder, but left it in the "off" position.

Standing on the brakes, Rand advanced the throttle, bringing up the engine rpm. He switched from both magnetos to one only, observed the rpm drop to be within limits, repeated the procedure with the second mag and then returned the ignition to dual magneto and eased off the throttle. Next he cycled the constant-speed propellor from fine to coarse pitch and back again, then set his altimeter to the altitude of the field as announced by a small sign stuck in the grass low and to the side of the runway.

Rand keyed his microphone: "All aircraft vicinity Caldwell-Wright be aware imminent take-off high speed traffic."

There was no response. Rand pulled over the cockpit canopy and shut it down on top of him, latching it. Then he divided the surrounding sky into quadrants and searched it meticulously. Satisfied that there were no aircraft approaching to land, he applied hard braking to one wheel and opened the throttle to ease the ship out onto the runway and line it up with the center-line. Rand paused long enough to set his gyro-compass to the runway number painted in huge white numerals on the asphalt before him, then smoothly fire-walled the throttle.

Blue flame stabbed from a dozen stubby exhaust stacks as the mighty Daimler-Benz DB 601Aa responded with a roar that set nearby building walls atremble. The Messerschmitt rolled forward, gathering speed. Its tail came up and the straining *Emil* hurtled down the runway under 1,175 horsepower.

Rand held the stick hard forward. There was a slight rocking motion as the craft accelerated and Rand held it on the ground deliberately for a few moments after his senses told him it would fly. A heartbeat later he pulled back on the stick and the legend-ary fighter leaped into the air, climbing at more than 3000 feet per minute. Adrenalin rushed through Richard Rand. He didn't realize it but, as he brought up the gear and switched on the transponder, he started to think in German. His name was once again von Randenburg, and he and the machine were one.

As the earth dropped away rapidly beneath him, Rand made a coordinated forty-five degree turn out of the pattern, then banked around sharply to pick up Victor Airway 3 heading south-west. He throttled back to hold his airspeed below 200 knots and leveled off to stay beneath the New York Terminal Control Area; then tuned to the Pottstown VOR signal on the Collins Nav radio, twisted the OBS knob and took up a heading that brought the needle in toward the center.

Once out of the New York TCA, Rand climbed to 3,500 feet. His maximum range cruise speed at that altitude was 202 mph, ideal for holding airspeed below 200 knots to avoid controls on high-speed traffic. From time to time he glanced at the OM-1 on his wrist and consulted a low-level sectional chart to tick off check points, confirm his navigation and calculate ground speed. He'd make it to D.C. with a good margin of time in case Washington Approach Control gave him the runaround.

Rand relaxed a little, but kept his head turning slowly in a constant scan of his instruments and of the sky, looking for traffic. He saw some from time to time; Cessnas, Pipers and Beechcraft at the lower altitudes, the general aviation craft that make up half the nation's air transport capacity. Overhead, commercial jets were silver winks as the big oil burners climbed or descended on their way to or from the great airport complex of Newark, La-Guardia and Kennedy that make up the New York TCA. For all that though, the sky was uncrowded, still open, free and, today at least, crisply beautiful.

A sense of power came over Richard Rand as he felt the twelve super-charged cylinders of the Daimler-Benz throb through every part of his body in contact with the aircraft; he felt mastery as the ship responded instantly to the controls. The curious phenomenon he had noticed before made itself manifest again. He began to hear music, the stirring martial music of his boyhood, as if played by a symphony orchestra. The hair rose at the nape of his neck. As if in a trance, Rand began to advance the throttle of the Messerschmitt. In moments he was streaking forward at three hundred knots, the Daimler-Benz in full-throated song.

An irresistible impulse came over Rand. He had obtained and installed in his E-3 model 109 a GM-1 unit from a later model, the F-4/Z. At a weight penalty of 400 lbs, it gave him the ability to inject nitrous oxide directly into the engine with an extraordinary effect upon speed, especially at altitude.

Rand engaged the GM-1. The effect was instantaneous. Rand was mashed back in his seat as the Messerschmitt screamed through its exhaust stacks and shot forward as if, at 300 knots, it had been standing still.

The reaction brought Rand back to his senses. He had no business travelling at such tremendous speed at that altitude. Furthermore, he knew only too well that bearings for the Daimler-Benz were rarer than moon rocks, and GM-1 use, especially at low altitude, put an enormous overload on the entire engine. He cut off the GM-1 and throttled back immediately, annoyed at himself. Still, for just a moment, he had experienced rapture.

The jolt of clear air turbulence snapped Rand out of it. Now he was all business, cold and precise. Below 200 knots the effect of the turbulence was far less severe; like slowing a car down on a bumpy road. He checked the ground and his charts. Baltimore International coming up to starboard. He dialed radials from two different VORs into the two Nav radios, then kept an eye on their presentation heads while continuing to scan for traffic around Baltimore International. He was also staying alert for two 1,200 foot transmission towers his chart indicated were nearby.

Rand dialed in a frequency on his number one Com radio, then a second frequency on the other. He listened intently to the first, copying such ATIS information as weather, active runways, altimeter setting, wind speed and direction. Then, switching from the number one to the number two Com radio, he stared at the Nav presentation heads on the panel before him. As the needles centered he keyed his microphone:

"Washington Approach, Messerschmitt four-oh-one-niner Bravo with you at fourteen hundred over Salt Point intersection at one-niner-five knots with information Juliet squawking twelve hundred VFR."

"One-niner Bravo, Washington Approach. Say again make and type aircraft."

"One-niner Bravo is a Messerschmitt, single engine, land."

"One-niner Bravo, you by any chance an Me 109?"

*"Bf* 109," corrected Rand, "E-3."

There was dead air for a moment, then:

"One-niner Bravo, squawk two-oh-three-oh and ident."

Rand set 2030 into his transponder and pressed the "ident" button. It glowed, then went out only to blink on and off as it indicated the plane was being swept and interrogated by radar.

"One-niner Bravo radar contact. Say intentions."

"One-niner Bravo requests instructions land Washington National, destination General Aviation North Terminal."

"One-niner Bravo take heading two-oh-five degrees climb to two thousand take river route report over bridges." The controller ran it all together on a stream of instructions; a compliment indicating he believed he was communicating with an experienced pilot. Rand replied in kind: "Niner Bravo out of fourteen for two heading two-oh-five for river route." He banked right and took up a heading of 205 degrees to pick up the Potomac river beyond McLean, Virginia. He was there in minutes and banked left to follow the river as instructed.

"Washington Approach Messerschmitt one-niner Bravo have you in sight over Chain Bridge."

"One-niner Bravo three-sixty to the right follow United seventwo-seven cleared to land runway one-eight contact Ground Control frequency one-two-one point seven good day sir."

"One-niner Bravo, Roger."

Rand banked around to his right applying power. Multi-wheeled gear down and looking ungainly with both leading and trailing edge flaps out to increase the lift of its swept wings, the big aluminum United jet sank past him with a roar. Rand swung in behind it. He could see the Pentagon to starboard, the White House and the Washington monument to port. Somewhere, someone couldn't resist a remark:

"United seven-two-seven, Messerschmitt six o'clock high!"

The old pro in the left seat of the United flight wasn't phased: "Just like the old days," he drawled.

At 100 knots, Rand dumped his flaps and gear. When the flaps went down, his ship's nose dropped ten degrees and he eased it back to correct attitude with the large trim wheel on his left; then he brought his air speed down to 90 mph for final and set 121.7 Kz on the other Collins. The Arlington Towers slipped by to starboard.

The E-3 Messerschmitt had a tendency to drop its left wing if a wheel landing was attempted, so Rand flared a little high and held it off the runway as long as he could. The ship settled slowly and smoothly to a three point landing, nose very high. Once more Rand had to *S* his way along the taxiway in response to instructions from ground control.

Word of the rare ship's imminent landing had gotten round and there was quite a crowd of the curious gathered as he taxied up to the General Aviation North Terminal, leaned the engine all the way to kill it and cut the switches. Swinging back the canopy, Rand reached behind the seat for a small suitcase, then climbed down to the ticking of cooling exhaust stacks under the gaze of the crowd awed by the full wartime *Luftwaffe* markings on the aircraft. He spotted Kazalakis' bulllike figure in the back row. Kazalakis wasn't awed.

Rand gave precise instructions on the care and feeding of his treasure to the representative of Page, the FBO, then walked over to Kazalakis. He thrust his hand forward in greeting, smiling, and said, "Greek, how do you do it? You look great!"

Kazalakis took his hand but, instead of shaking it, used it to spin Rand around and hustle him toward the street. With a glower he said:

"You crazy son of a bitch, let's get out of here before we're both on *Eyewitness News!*"

Rand and Kazalakis walked quickly through the Page waiting room and exited through the glass doors. Outside, Kazalakis headed for a nondescript sedan parked at a twenty minute limit meter, went round to the trunk, opened it and grabbed Rand's suitcase without asking.

"Christ!" said Kazalakis, "What've you got in here, bricks?"

"Bolts," said Rand, grinning.

"Bolts?"

"Yeah. You wouldn't want me to break the law, would you?"

"What the hell are you talkin' about?"

Rand sighed, then said, with a touch of exasperation, "That's no Hollywood mock-up I flew in here, you know. What'd you think that armament was, painted broomsticks? That's the real thing, friend: two 20mm Oerlikon cannon with 60 rounds per gun in the wings, two 7.9mm MG-17 machine guns on the fuselage with 1,000 rounds each and one of the big Oerlikon 20mm tank-busters mounted on the engine firing through the prop hub. That one's got 200 rounds. Cost me twelve hundred and fifty bucks just for the Federal tax stamps to make 'em legal, but I still can't go into most states with loaded automatic weapons. So I carry the bolts locked up in the bag there in case some do-gooder wants to make an issue of it."

"But why go to all that trouble, for Christ's sake," Kazalakis protested. "Why not just pull out the armament and forget it?"

"C'mon, Greek. You know better'n that. Did you forget about trim already? That stuff's *heavy,* pal. That ship's in the *Zerstörer* configuration. Pull it all out and you completely fuck up the trim.

No way the trim tabs could keep her ass up. You want to get me killed?"

"I suppose it never occurred to you," said Kazalakis, "that there's a much simpler way to keep yourself from getting killed?"

Rand's eyes went wide in mock innocence. "What might that be?"

"Fly commercial like I asked you!" roared Kazalakis, banging down the trunk lid in angry emphasis, "Like everyone else who's not a fugitive from a nut house!" He stomped off to the driver's door and got in, slamming it. Rand laughed and got in the other side as Kazalakis started the car. His door was barely closed when Kazalakis backed out too fast, braked hard, abused the transmission as he put it into forward, sped out of the parking area without pausing at the stop sign and turned onto the George Washington Parkway in the direction of Washington.

"Langley," said Rand, gesturing over his shoulder with his thumb, "used to be that way."

"Still is," snapped Kazalakis, "but, in spite of your grand-standing, we still hope to keep this meeting quiet."

Rand shrugged his shoulders and remained silent as Kazalakis turned east onto Maine Avenue and followed the Potomac waterfront down past the Arena Theatre to the Tiber Island townhouse complex in Washington's "new southwest." Pulling into the entrance of an underground garage, Kazalakis gained entry through the electric gate with a magnetic card, drove down to the far side and parked. They left by a different gate, emerging on the block opposite the one they drove in.

The street was lined on both sides with three-to five-bedroom townhouses, all in an identical modern style. Rand memorized the number of the one Kazalakis led him to more out of habit than anything else. He knew that safehouses are changed regularly, and always after a visit by an outsider.

Kazalakis let them in with a key. The lights were on inside even though it was the middle of the day as the blinds were drawn over the large amounts of floor to ceiling glass. In the artificial light, Rand could see that the place was sparsely furnished. There was a throw rug in front of the front door, but no runner up the stairs.

To the right, through an arch, was a living room in which four men were seated. Three were grouped together uncomfortably on a small, cheaply made sofa. Across a plain, glass-topped cocktail table there was one man seated opposite the three. He lounged in an easy chair covered in an atrocious, liver-colored plastic. Two chairs had been brought in from the dining room and sat, empty, across from each other so that the glass-topped table formed the center of a rough circle. The blue rug on the floor was the kind sold by Montgomery Ward from its stores located in poor neighborhoods.

When Rand and Kazalakis entered, the three men on the sofa rose. Alexander McKenzie, seated in the liver-colored horror, remained there.

"Good evening, sir," said Kazalakis to McKenzie. Then, though McKenzie had, of course, been identified publicly at his confirmation hearing in the Senate, and Rand's photograph appeared frequently in gossip columns as a certified "jet-set" playboy, Kazalakis introduced them to each other in the traditional manner:

"John," he said to McKenzie, "this is David. David, John." The two men nodded to each other, then Rand turned as Kazalakis completed the introductions: "David," he said, gesturing to one after another of the standing trio, "Edward, Vincent and Phil."

Rand was well aware that these false names were as much a part of each man now as their true ones, having been assigned to them years ago; still, he couldn't resist saying, albeit with a smile that belied malice, "Let's be consistent and make it Matthew, Mark and Luke, shall we; it'd be easier for me." Then, turning to Kazalakis, he said, "I'm sorry, I don't believe I got *your* name . . ."

Kazalakis flushed. "William," he said, "call me Bill." He sat down, followed by Rand and the three newly christened saints of the New Testament.

Kazalakis recovered quickly. "David," he said to Rand, "our friends here would like your opinion on something." He nodded to the three men on the sofa.

"Some of us," said the man introduced as Edward, "are concerned by reports we see increasingly in business journals and the press in general, to the effect that the OPEC nations may use their huge dollar surpluses, especially in view of their devaluation against the mark, Swiss franc and yen, to buy up U.S. industry and take it, for all practical purposes, out of American control. Could we have your thoughts on that possibility?"

It was a test question, Rand knew, to probe the breadth of his understanding of economic reality. He didn't think much of the question. "Forget about it," he said, "it won't happen."

"That's comforting," said McKenzie dryly, "why not?"

"All right," said Rand, with a hint of the patronizing in his tone as he remarked what he considered to be the obvious. "First, you can eliminate Iran, Venezuela and Algeria. They've got about twenty-five years worth of oil reserves and a combined population of some seventy million with a lot of economic development in mid-stream. For at least another ten years, they're going to have to concentrate on completing that internal development. They've already done a lot, but it will take that long at least to do what they've committed themselves to do."

"They could change their minds tomorrow," interjected Vincent, "then what?"

"Uh uh," said Rand. "Not with those seventy millions breathing down their necks. The taste of the good life in the future is already in their mouths. Shah or Ayatollah, they've got to finish what they've started now, which won't leave them with enough surplus to even consider intervention in the U.S. market."

"That leaves," said Phil, "the Saudis, Kuwait, Libya and Quatar."

"And Abu Dhabi," Rand added. "Together they've got about two thirds of the worlds reserves, but a lot less population pressure; only about twelve million people between them all. Now, let's say they can accumulate, in the next five years, a surplus of two hundred and fifty billion—which is quite possible. That's still only twenty-five percent of the total assets of all U.S. companies."

"Wait a minute," interrupted Vincent, "there's a hell of a difference between total assets and total shares outstanding; and many a company is controlled by an accumulation of only fifteen, twenty percent of shares. I could buy control of some pretty big companies with $250 billion."

"Sorry," Rand corrected him, "it's not that easy anymore. In the first place, the total of shares in all the companies listed on the New York Stock Exchange and the AMEX comes to a little over 900 billion. Second, you're forgetting about the premium the raider has to pay over market value and the percent needed to control in an adverse situation. Hell, in a *friendly* takeover the Germans just bought forty-three percent of the A&P's stock, and in the last ten contested takeovers in the over-100-million range the premium paid for the necessary stock was about eighty percent above market value. It really wipes out the distinction, for all practical purposes, between total assets and total share value; especially when you include in replacement cost such valuable intangibles as trademarks, goodwill, skilled labor force and so on. No sir, anyway you want to look at it, they don't have enough money to buy it up."

"You're talking," protested Phil, "about an adverse or hostile takeover; a situation where management yells 'the Arabs are coming' and forces a high premium and the acquisition of a big percentage of stock. Suppose they just use intermediaries and do it quietly."

Rand shook his head slowly from side to side. "The Williams Act," he said, "has made it mandatory since 1968 that companies making tender offers disclose who they are, the source of their funds and what they plan to do with the target. There's another problem, too. Remember, the Germans who took over the A&P were a three billion a year, two thousand store supermarket chain. They knew the business inside and out. Suppose your Arabs *were* able to buy, say, General Motors. What are they going to do with it? How are they going to run it? Those twelve million people are mostly uneducated, much less being able to handle sophisticated managerial tools and techniques. They just don't have the manpower to exert control."

"The Saudis have most of that two-thirds of the reserves," countered Vincent, "and they've been training their people for some time."

"To run oil fields," Rand replied, "but I'll grant you they're shrewd—too shrewd to put all their eggs in one basket like that. As a matter of fact, Saudi policy forbids the investment of more than five percent of their funds in any one country, let alone one industry. You couldn't *force* them to go against their own interests like that." Rand laughed: "The Jews have got to be getting a real kick out of this."

"The Jews?" McKenzie raised a patrician eyebrow as he spoke, "How so?"

Rand's smile broadened into a grin: "For fifty years the Jews have been accused of trying to buy up everything to control the country through business. Not just here; Europe, everywhere. Now that shoe's on another foot, and the fact that it's an Arab foot has got to seem to them poetic justice. Think about it."

Kazalakis, among whose talents finance was not numbered, and who knew it, studied the faces of the three men on the sofa.

Rand was giving them the business by staring at them with those pupilless eyes of his and they were appropriately ill at ease. Reading faces *was* a talent of Kazalakis, and he could read respect for Rand in them. In the case of McKenzie, it was grudging, but there nevertheless. Kazalakis had been wondering himself about the prospects of an Arab takeover of U.S. industry, having seen rumors to that effect reported in the summaries from press sources. Rand had effectively demolished his concern.

McKenzie broke the silence. "Gentlemen," he said, addressing the three men across from him, "would you excuse us for a few minutes, please?"

The three shot up as one man. Phil said something about getting some coffee in the kitchen and they filed out.

The dismissal of the agency's financial analysts after so short an interrogation of Rand surprised Kazalakis. He had thought McKenzie would have been far more demanding. Rand had handled the matter so easily it seemed almost perfunctory. Once the three men were out of the room, McKenzie dropped the use of fictional names and addressed Rand.

"Mr. Rand, I thank you for your courtesy in coming here to assist us. As must have been obvious to you, we are not concerned by the unlikely prospect of the Arabs, or the Jews, I might add," McKenzie said it with a twinkle Kazalakis had never before seen, "taking over U.S. industry. We *do,* however, have unverified information from a responsible source that the Soviet Union is planning a major economic move against this country. We have no idea what it might be, only that it would be damaging. At the same time, we have information from a different source, also unverified, that someone you may know, Gregory Ballinger, may be doing business with the Soviets, or on their behalf. We are, of course, investigating both reports."

"Do you have anything," asked Rand, "that indicates a link between the two reports?"

"No," said McKenzie, "and that's where you come in. Or, rather, where we would like you to come in."

McKenzie waited for Rand to speak, hoping he'd volunteer. Rand remained mute as the silence built up. McKenzie finally broke it.

"Do you suppose you could get close enough to Ballinger to find out whether there is a link between the two reports?"

"Assuming either of them is true," added Rand.

"Of course," said McKenzie.

Kazalakis had been watching the by-play between the two men as if at a tennis match. The contrast between McKenzie's initial reluctance and his quick acceptance of Rand made him uneasy and the conversation absorbed him. He had set this thing in motion and now felt vaguely threatened by it.

"I don't know Ballinger," said Rand, "I just know of him. Everyone in finance does, of course. I've enjoyed some modest success, but I'm just not in his league, not at all."

"From what I understand," replied McKenzie, "your success has not been that modest."

"Let me see if I can demonstrate the difference I'm talking about," Rand said. "Look. I'm a millionaire. When I do deals, that's where the numbers are—in the millions. That sounds like a lot, doesn't it? Well, it's not. Not when you consider Gregory Ballinger. He's a *bil*lionaire. When he does deals the numbers are in the *bil*lions. Let me ask you something. Suppose I gave you a million dollars in cash, currency, and told you to spend a thousand dollars a day, every day, seven days a week, and then come back to me for more when you ran out. How long would it be before you had to come back to me?"

Kazalakis replied, "About three years,"

"Close enough," said Rand. "Now, suppose I gave you a *bil*lion dollars in cash and told you the same thing—spend a thousand a day, every day, and come back to me when you run out. How soon do you come back?"

The two men frowned and there was a pause while they did the arithmetic in their heads. "I'll help you," said Rand. "Three *thousand* years! That's when. You see the difference? *That's* the difference between me and Gregory Ballinger."

"You make your point well," said McKenzie. "Are you telling us it's impossible for you to help us?"

"No," replied Rand, "I just want you to understand the problem. How many people are in his league? Ludwig is, Kashoggi may be. Hughes, Onnasis and Getty were. Men like that could go to Ballinger; a handful in the world. Probably only half a handful now. The point I'm making is that, if he perceives it to be in his interest, Ballinger might go to you. *You* certainly don't go to Ballinger. You'd never get near him."

"Somebody got near him," Kazalakis said grimly. Rand raised his eyebrows and regarded him quizzically.

61

"This would seem about as good a time as any," said McKenzie as he took from the floor beside his chair a manila folder and untied the maroon string which fastened it. "We have a few things we'd like you to examine—see if they are of any particular significance to you."

McKenzie withdrew from the folder a sheaf of 8 by 10 inch photographs and tossed them onto the glass-topped table in front of Rand. Rand picked them up and looked at McKenzie. "Ballinger's?"

"Ballinger's," came the reply.

"Where'd he keep it?"

"What difference does that make?"

"Where something is kept," said Rand, starting to examine the photographs, "can often shed light on what it's for."

"The safe in Ballinger's office," said McKenzie.

"Which one?" asked Rand.

"Which safe?" McKenzie's voice held a note of surprise.

"Which office," said Rand. "He's got them all over the world, including one in a personally owned yacht in Miami. The rest are all in Comco's name."

"This stuff," Kazalakis said, "came from the one in New York, in the Comco building."

Rand just nodded, continuing to examine the photographs. Aside from a birth certificate for Ballinger issued at Casper, Wyoming, the material seemed routine enough; original and issue stock of Comco, minutes of board meetings at which nothing remarkable was discussed. One item caught his eye and he held it up for the other two to see. "What," Rand asked, "did your people make of this?"

Rand was holding a photograph of a note written by hand on a sheet of lined paper. The handwriting was very small and precise. The note consisted of a list of company names with a percentage figure after each. It read:

| | |
|---|---|
| Metz Industrie, GmbH | 15% |
| Stresso, Sp. A. | 10% |
| Bombay Heavy Fabrications, Ltd. | 5% |
| Siderakis Eteria | 5% |
| Mekaniskafabrikenaktiebolaget Mälmo | 5% |
| Mazatlan, S.A. | 10% |

"They don't know," Kazalakis shrugged. "They say it could represent a position in each company listed held by Comco or by Ballinger personally, or a target for a position. On the other hand, it might be a market percentage enjoyed by each company, but who knows which market? In other words, they don't know."

"Do you?" McKenzie asked Rand.

"No, but whatever it is, it represents quite a geographical spread; West Germany, Italy, India, Greece, Sweden and Mexico. The percentages might also indicate the amount of voting stock necessary to exert practical control of the companies listed; but no, I don't know either. One thing that's curious, though. Metz and Mazatlan, within the last six months, contracted with Columbia Steel here in the states for pretty hefty orders."

"What's curious about it?" asked McKenzie. "I mean, aside from the coincidence that they're both on that list?"

"In the case of Mazatlan," answered Rand, "nothing. I remember wondering at the time, however, what Metz, sitting right up there next to the Ruhr, was doing buying steel from the United States. I mean, it's not as if Columbia Steel were Japanese, making steel with the latest technology and able to undersell everyone else.

It may be the biggest in this country, but Columbia Steel plants are among the most obsolete there are—open hearth stuff. When the Germans and Japanese rebuilt after the war, they went in for basic oxygen. Much more efficient."

"What do you make of it?" Kazalakis growled.

"Well, as I said," said Rand, "Mazatlan makes sense. They're on our border and the transportation cost differential might make Columbia competitive. For Metz, I don't know; maybe they're taking advantage of the devaluation of the dollar against the mark."

Something else about the list nibbled at the edge of Rand's mind, but he couldn't put his finger on it so he changed the subject:

"How badly do you want me to participate?"

Kazalakis was annoyed by the question. "The stuff you've just looked at cost a good man his life," he snapped. "You still haven't said whether or not you can do anything!"

"Please," said McKenzie to Kazalakis, waving his hand at him as if telling a dog to get down. "I'm sure Mr. Rand has something in mind. What is it Mr. Rand?"

"As I mentioned, it would be useless for me to approach Ballinger on anything. I've got to get him to come to me. You know the old saying about banging the mule over the head with a two-by-four? That's our situation here. I've got to get his attention."

"How do you propose to do that?" asked McKenzie. Kazalakis was sitting back, eying Rand suspiciously. He was even more uneasy. It was he who had brought Rand in to see a reluctant McKenzie, and McKenzie was doing all the work. Kazalakis didn't know what to make of it.

"The equivalent of hitting Ballinger over the head is a successful attack upon him economically. He hates to lose. If I can beat him in a business deal, make a dent in him that he'll feel, even if it's only in his ego, he might go for me. I'm small potatoes to him. He'd try to swat me like a fly, take me the way I took him, to even the score. While all that's going on, I'll be in a position to look and listen. No guarantees, but I might be able to help you. But I can't do it alone. I'm not big enough. Don't have the resources. I'll need your help."

Here it comes, thought Kazalakis. He started to speak, but McKenzie cut him off with "What would you need?"

"The ability to manipulate a couple of your proprietary companies for a while, including the right to liquidate them. If I win, you'll end up with a net gain. If I lose, you lose."

McKenzie leaned forward as if to speak, but Rand prevented it by continuing. He wanted to get his entire proposal on the table before McKenzie gave his answer.

"Also," Rand continued, "even though my assets are tied up and I can't, I won't play your game with my money. I'll need one million, cash, deposited in the Swiss bank of my choice, in my name, for purposes of credibility."

Kazalakis looked as if he were about to explode. Rand continued quickly, "That, you stand no risk of losing. The money will never leave the bank—we both know you can monitor that—and will be returned in full at the completion of the operation, win or lose."

It was too much for Kazalakis. "And who gets," he hissed from between clenched teeth, "the interest on the million dollars!"

"Why, I do, of course," Rand said pleasantly, looking right at McKenzie, "I'm sure Dr. McKenzie doesn't expect me to work for nothing."

"Of course not," McKenzie said, to Kazalakis' consternation. "What you propose sounds reasonable enough." McKenzie rose and extended his hand. "Mr. Kazalakis and I will be going now. If you'll be good enough to remain, Vincent I believe it is, will brief you on proprietary assets available for manipulation and you can make the necessary arrangements through him for your check. When you're through, I'm sure he'll be glad to drive you anywhere you want to go."

"Fine," was all Rand said and he shook McKenzie's hand, then took Kazalakis' with a grin. Kazalakis, glaring, squeezed Rand's hand hard, as if to convey a wordless warning, but said nothing. This turn of events was unexpected, but there was no point in letting Rand know that.

As Kazalakis and McKenzie moved out into the hall, the sound of their voices must have alerted the three men in the kitchen and they appeared, as if on cue. McKenzie took Vincent to one side and spoke with him quietly for a few moments, then rejoined the others. "Why don't you two men come with us?" he said to Phil and Edward. Dutifully, they fell in line behind them as McKenzie and Kazalakis left.

The presence of the other two men inhibited Kazalakis as they sat in the car while Phil drove them all back to CIA headquarters at Langley. They stayed together as they were processed through the new TRW security system to gain access. Then, as the others peeled off and Kazalakis and McKenzie headed for the elevators for the seventh floor, Kazalakis said, "Could I see you for a minute, sir?"

"I can see you have something on your mind," said McKenzie, "and I think it would be a good idea."

Kazalakis remained silent until they were seated in McKenzie's office and his secretary had finished running through his messages.

"I know that I sponsored Rand," Kazalakis began, "but I thought I made it clear that he's a rogue. Frankly, I'm concerned that we" (he employed the *we* to be politic) "appear to have given him a *carte blanche*. The million, okay, but we don't know what he plans to do with our proprietory assets."

"Any orders he gives can be countermanded," McKenzie said.

"Good," said Kazalakis. "I'll keep a close eye on him and if he—"

"No," McKenzie cut in. "Finance is not your field."

"But—"

"No buts." McKenzie's voice grew cold. "For the time being, you have no need to know any more than you do; and for purposes of possibly being required to testify under oath before an oversight committee, I don't *want* to know any more than I do. I give you credit for bringing Rand to us." McKenzie rose in dismissal. "One more thing," he said. "I want this entire matter handled through blind memoranda; no addressee, no signatures."

"Right, sir," said Kazalakis, rising and heading for the door, "soft file all the way."

Kazalakis steamed down the hall, burst into his own office and grabbed a bunch of message slips from his secretary without a word. He flipped through them like so many playing cards until he came to one from Farington. He dropped the rest back on his secretary's desk and swept into his office, closed the door and scooped up the telephone. He punched the intercom button, then Farington's three digit code.

"Three-one-eight," said Farington's voice.

"What is it?" asked Kazalakis.

"The cause of death came in from Seidman. It was the capsule; asphyxia. It was an old one from World War II. Christ knows where he got it. Cyanide-L."

"Rough way to go," remarked Kazalakis. He knew it wasn't all that quick and the death was agonizing.

"Yeah," said Farington, "but better than what he was going through, the poor son of a bitch!"

The vehemence in Farington's voice caught Kazalakis attention.

"What d'you mean?"

"They were using neurokinin on him. Seidman found that too."

Kazalakis whistled softly. The use of neurokinin introduced a note of sophistication he hadn't expected. It was a drug that causes severe pain, so severe that death by cyanide-L was preferable to Zlin.

Kazalakis' mind shifted back from Zlin's problem to his own. McKenzie's swallowing Rand hook, line and sinker was completely inconsistent with his attitude when Kazalakis first proposed that he be consulted, and his going for Rand's proposal, virtually sight unseen, was even more disturbing. The whole thing stank when one considered that McKenzie was a "reform" director.

"Paul," he said to Farington, casually, "off the record, from your friendliness with the female help around here, is there any scuttlebut on the director's meetings or appointments the last twenty-four hours? Anything out of the ordinary?"

"Not really," said Farington, "at least not that I've heard of. They had a meeting of the Forty committee last night."

"Okay, Paul, thanks." Kazalakis hung up. The Forty committee! Named originally for the number of the National Security memorandum which created it, the Forty committee was now called the Operations Advisory Group. But its function was still the same; to make the authorization decision on proposed clandestine operations. And he, Kazalakis, operating director of the clandestine service, had not even been aware of the meeting, much less its agenda.

Kazalakis mulled over in his mind this latest bit of disquieting news. There were all kinds of possibilities, not the least of which was that McKenzie, a lot shrewder than Kazalakis had heretofore believed, wasn't being inconsistent at all. His idea of reform might very well include getting rid of someone like Kazalakis; a non-WASP, non-Ivy League holdover from the go-for-broke days of covert activities.

It occurred to Kazalakis that McKenzie might be setting him up.

"Shit," he said to no one in particular.

# VI

Gear down and locked, full flaps, the Messerschmitt skimmed the top of the hill. Dead ahead, but considerably below, ran a river of headlights along Passaic Avenue, hemmed in by a Cyclone fence beyond which stretched out the runway of Caldwell-Wright airport. To avoid a long taxi back to his hangar, Rand, who was in a hurry, held the stick to the left and simultaneously shoved in full right rudder with his foot. The ship sank rapidly in a slip toward the threshold of the runway. Over the fence, Rand neutralized the controls, flared, and settled the hot fighter into a three-point landing just ahead of the large white numbers painted on the runway. Braking hard, he made the second turn-off and taxied back in a series of *S* turns, exhausts flickering bright blue warnings into the night.

On the apron, Rand closed the throttle, then set his mixture control to full lean. The idling Daimler-Benz coughed twice and the prop jerked back suddenly against compression as the engine died. As the fuel truck drove up, Rand lifted the canopy back with an effort. He was tired. The last twenty minutes of flight had been in full darkness, and night flight over a heavily populated area in a forty-year-old single engine aircraft is not prudent. It had been a long afternoon. His briefing on those CIA proprietary assets suitable for exploitation in accordance with the plan he had formed consumed more time than he had expected, but they had come up with just what he wanted. What he wanted most of all now was a hot bath, a good meal and a good night's sleep. He'd be lucky, he knew, to be able to manage the bath.

Rand impressed upon the line boy the honor that was his in being permitted to fuel the Messerschmitt without supervision.

With the boy's assurances ringing in his ears and a promise to return to help hangar the plane, he entered the pay phone booth outside the door to the operations shack. Charging the call to his home phone because he didn't have enough change, Rand dialed T'sa Li. She answered, after only two rings, with the noncommittal "hello" she employed when not expecting a call and the caller could be anybody.

"It is I," said Rand, whose crotchet it was to be grammatically correct when to do so would be jarring.

"Hi, I. You sound tired. You ought to cut down on all that running."

Rand smiled. "Or something, at any rate," he said. Then, too tired for more banter, "Baby, I need a favor."

"I've already given you my body. What more could any man possibly want?"

"That," sighed Rand, "is a totally sexist answer which, in about five more years, will probably be illegal under some federal regulation or other. At any rate, the answer is just as sexist. What I want is your body, dressed to the teeth, with me, tomorrow, in Switzerland."

"Do I get to eat?"

"The finest cuisine served in the first class section of the red-eye to Geneva."

"I'm sorry I asked. What's all the business about clothes?"

"Just pack the most ostentatiously expensive daytime stuff you've got—that Halston, maybe, or the green Dior. And bring some diamonds from the family stash; better bring something on them with you for customs, okay?" Rand paused. "Guess that's it," he said. "I'll swing by in a couple of hours."

"It is like hell," T'sa Li interjected.

"What's the matter?"

"How long am I going to be living in this one dress? A week? A month?"

"Oh, right," said Rand, sheepishly. "It's a round trip. We come back tomorrow night—you still game?"

T'sa Li's sigh was loud enough to be audible over the phone.

"I suppose so. I'm curious. What's in it for me? I mean besides jet lag, a headache, swollen ankles, diarrhea—"

"You mean apart from the intense pleasure of my company? Well, for example, you get to pick the airline."

"What?"

"Yeah, hon, I forgot to ask you. Be a love and make the reservations. Take your pick; TWA or Swissair. I'm stuck out here in Jersey and—"

"You round-eyed—" T'sa Li steamed.

"Wait a minute," Rand protested. "You're not being inscrutable—"

"White devil!" T'sa Li completed, then started in again. "You—"

"Now you're not only being sexist, you're being racist. . . ." But Rand was speaking into a dead phone. T'sa Li had hung up.

As Rand drove down Fifth Avenue, slipping the BMW expertly through traffic toward Central Park South, he positioned himself instinctively so as to be able to pull in to the front of the Plaza and hand the car over to the doorman. Abruptly, he changed his mind. He might need it immediately, and it took a while to retrieve it from the garage. He turned into Central Park South and parked in a no parking zone, trusting to luck.

Rand went straight to his room where, as he had requested in his second phone call, Alfredo Matarazza was waiting for him in the living room, watching television. Matarazza jumped up as Rand entered, snapped off the television set and said, "Hi, Boss. Where we goin'?"

"Downtown first," Rand replied. Then, noticing that the red "message waiting" light was blinking on the telephone, he picked it up and dialed the desk. He identified himself, listened, then grunted in satisfaction. T'sa Li had come through, as he had known she would. They had confirmed reservations on the Swissair night flight to Geneva with return the following evening. He was to pick up T'sa Li in—he looked at his watch—fifty-four minutes.

Entering the bedroom, Rand went directly to the *armoire* and selected a medium weight, woolen two-button suit in a gray pinstripe, a deep maroon tie and two white shirts. He lay them on the bed, then picked out two pair of black over-the-calf socks and placed them next to the other clothing. He returned for two sets of clean underwear, then went back to the door to the living room and said, "Fredo, I'm going to take a bath. Be a pal and make us some coffee. Or have a drink, if you'd prefer it."

"Sure you don't wanna drink too, Boss?" asked Matarazza, for whom there was no choice between the two.

"No, I want a stimulant, not a depressant," said Rand, heading for the bathroom.

Twenty-five minutes later, Rand, wearing the gray pinstripe and carrying only a small bag with a change of shirt, socks and underwear which would fit under the seat of the aircraft, was on the sidewalk, Matarazza at his side, headed for the BMW at the curb. His muscles were relaxed from the hot bath and his cardiovascular system stimulated by the coffee. As they neared the car, Matarazza moved ahead to open the door for Rand. Matarazza did not drive the BMW four-speed nearly as well as Rand did, but for Rand to have suggested otherwise, or to have expressed a preference to drive while in Matarazza's company, would have offended the burly man gravely. Matarazza had been the "wheel man" on many a criminal enterprise, and his driving ability, with big, heavy American automobiles at least, was a matter of great pride to him.

It was Matarazza who first spotted the parking ticket under the windshield wiper of the BMW. He picked it up, read it, and grunted in disgust. "What d'ya want me to do wit this?"

"Pay it," said Rand.

"Ah, Boss," Matarazza said, dejectedly, "didn't ya do what I told ya yet?"

"What was that, 'Fredo?" said Rand as he climbed into the front passenger's seat.

"Boss," protested Matarazza, "you don't pay no attention t'anything I say. What'cha do is, ya register the car under a scam name in Jersey. Then, when ya get a couple hunnert tickets, or whatever gets 'em really pissed so's they go to do something about it, ya sell it to yourself again under *another* name, reregister and the hell with it. You could give a fuck about tickets!"

"I don't get that many, 'Fredo," said Rand. "It's a lot less trouble just to pay them."

"But Boss," Matarazza protested, "ya don't unnerstand. It's the *principle* of the thing!"

Rand was still smiling over Matarazza's latest revelation of his philosophy of life as they turned into Mott street. It was heavily trafficked and it was apparent to Rand that there would be difficulty finding a place to park. He asked Matarazza to let him out in front of T'sa Li's building and do the best he could to be ready to pick them up when he came down with her.

Rand entered a Chinese restaurant, returned the bow of the

71

maitre d', who recognized him from previous visits, and crossed to the antique Otis used to convey patrons to the private dining rooms on the second floor. He pressed the button marked "3" and waited for the elevator to wheeze its way upward. When the elevator stopped, the door did not open. Instead, T'sa Li's voice came over a speaker, saying something in Chinese. "It's I, hon," he replied, and the door opened.

What one might take for a vestibule really wasn't. T'sa Li's apartment was guarded by a "spirit gate"; a baffle which forced one to enter via a series of ninety degree turns capable of being negotiated by humans but not by demons. The gate was of elaborately carved teak and very, very old. T'sa Li escorted Rand through the gate into her living room. It was western, but featured superb Chinese art and antiques.

Standing in the center of the room, in western dress, was a tiny whisp of an oriental woman. Her hair was completely white and she wore a broad smile as she nodded her head continuously in reply to Rand's "Good evening, Madam Li, how have you been?" Whether or not T'sa Li's mother understood any English at all, Rand didn't know. T'sa Li had told him, when they first met, that she did not speak the language. It was always a source of amazement to Rand how Madam Li could have been the mother of T'sa Li, who was five feet nine, much less that of her brother T'ang Li, who was six feet six and almost as wide through the chest and shoulders as he was tall.

"Mother," said T'sa Li, "insists that we have something to eat before we leave."

Rand knew from experience that it was useless to refuse and that he'd save time in the long run by agreeing and getting to it. "Thank you," he said to Madam Li, "that would be very nice. A bowl of soup would be perfect and leave us plenty of time."

T'sa Li translated and Madam Li, head still bobbing, led the way into the dining room. There three places were set at one end of a long dining table. In the center of the table was a beautifully arranged centerpiece made entirely of a variety of grasses. Rand assisted the ladies to be seated and waiters appeared silently at no apparant signal to serve a delicious soup wholly outside of Rand's experience.

The quickness of the service and the excellence of the soup did not surprise Rand, as he knew that they originated in the restaurant below. In fact, nothing about the building would surprise

Rand. As far as he could tell, an entire block of supposedly discrete four and five story buildings had all been connected, and housed God knew how many enterprises and people, all also somehow interconnected. The only ones he was certain of were T'sa Li's ample digs; those of her mother and bachelor brother, Tang Li; the restaurant and, although he had never seen it, a gymnasium of some sort maintained, T'sa Li said, at the basement level by her brother.

Madam Li finished quickly and, saying something to her daughter, rose. Rand rose with her.

"Mother," translated T'sa Li, "is very tired and asks us to excuse her."

"Of course," said Rand, and Madam Li exited, smiling and head bobbing again.

"Now," said T'sa Li, "would you like to give me a clue as to what's going on? I don't mean to pry into your business, but why drag me along? I mean, as I understand your schedule, the only opportunity we'll have will be for a cozy duet in the john of a 747, where I give you the stewardess special."

"Or I," smiled Rand, "could initiate you into the ancient and honorable rites of the Mile High Club."

"No, thank you," said T'sa Li, making a face.

"Well," said Rand, frowning slightly as he pondered how much to tell her, "I have a bit of a problem. You know and I know that, rumors to the contrary notwithstanding, there has never been any connection between your brother's alleged organization and me. That connection has been made in the minds of others by extrapolating from my relationship with you, and the belief that I have served for some time as a financial advisor to some of the relatives of my late wife."

T'sa Li knew enough not to interrupt Rand when he was in the midst of a rare moment of self-revelation. She was aware that he would not be saying what he was unless he thought it necessary in order to use her; but after all, she had used *him* initially to gain entry to the United States. She felt no resentment and was smart enough to know that usefulness is an asset in a woman; certainly in one who was not—could not be, by occidental standards—a raving beauty. If T'sa Li could help the object of her affections, she would do so gladly.

"Now I have, from time to time," Rand continued carefully, "helped some of my relatives by marriage make a prudent investment or two; some of them with the assistance of a particular bank in Switzerland. Geneva, to be exact. The problem arises in that I now want to use that same bank to conduct a rather substantial piece of business of my own."

Rand rose and started pacing the floor, hands in his pockets, eyes following the intricate pattern of the thick Chinese rug beneath his feet automatically, without really seeing it, the way a railway car's wheels follow the track.

"Absent circumstances to persuade them otherwise, my Swiss friends will assume automatically that I am acting in the same interests I always have with them." He paused and continued to pace.

T'sa Li decided to risk a question: "Is your bank cantonal, savings or private?"

Rand stopped pacing and looked at her sharply. By this time he should not have been surprised by further revelations of the extent of T'sa Li's knowledge—she had demonstrated many times over her exceptional intelligence—but that she should ask a question indicating familiarity with the principal kinds of Swiss banks, startled him. T'sa Li caught the look and, not wishing to scare him off, said, "Oh, c'mon now! The only thing Italians know to do with money is buy gold and bury it in the back yard, right? And all Chinese can think to do with it is buy diamonds for their women to wear or hide in the house!"

Rand laughed and started pacing again. "All right," he said, "you nailed me fair and square." Then, "It's a private bank. And if you know enough to ask that question, you know that it's a family business and they are careful to know with whom they are dealing and what's really going on. If I suddenly start making moves with money as if it were mine, not someone else's, the famed Swiss secrecy notwithstanding, I'm going to have to answer questions over in Brooklyn. Now, I could answer those questions alright, but I don't want to have to. You follow me?"

"Perfectly. I accompany you and just sit there, looking like a million Deutschmarks, and let them put your reputation together with my all-American good looks and *voilà;* you're off the hook and I end up answering questions from *my* relatives."

"Uh." Rand grunted as her logic hit him, "I hadn't thought of that."

"Well, don't let it bother you. I can handle it. But thanks," T'sa Li smiled, "for leveling with me. I appreciate it."

Rand grimaced. "I'd be afraid not to," he said, his voice holding a note of increased respect. He looked at his watch.

"Jesus."

"What's the matter?" asked T'sa Li, "We've plenty of time."

"It's 'Fredo. I left him outside with the car. He's going to drive us. He's already pissed at the Chinese for taking over so much of Little Italy. He probably thinks I've been abducted by Fu Manchu. I'm serious. We've gotta get out of here. 'Fredo'll be coming through the restaurant door any minute with a gun in his hand."

"He won't get far."

"That's not the point. Who needs it? C'mon, girl."

She said it in French, then German, finally in English:

"Ladies and Gentlemen, Captain Germain advises that we are about thirty minutes from our approach to Geneva and it will be necessary to fasten your seat belts soon. We suggest that those of you who will be wishing to use the rest rooms, do so now."

T'sa Li was way ahead of the Swissair flight attendant. Almost as she stopped speaking, T'sa Li emerged from the first class rest room module. In place of the slacks and sweater combination she had slept in through the night in her seat next to Rand, she was wearing a vintage Coco Chanel version of "the little black dress." In its stark simplicity it set off, as could nothing else, diamond earrings, a diamond necklace and matching diamond bracelet of such size, color and cut that she drew stares instantly from first class passengers who thought they'd seen everything.

"Jesus!" Rand exclaimed as she sat back down next to him, "take that stuff off and don't put it back on 'til we're in the cab. You're just begging to get hit on the head as soon as you set foot in the airport!"

"I want there to be no doubt in the minds of the customs people that I wore these *in* when I come *out* tomorrow night." ·

"You've got the provenance for that stuff, haven't you?"

T'sa Li looked at Rand archly. "I've got something that should do the trick," she said, "but I don't want to take any chances."

Rand shook his head as he said, "Not take any chances! I just—"

"Besides," T'sa Li continued, ignoring him, "I've got you to protect me, haven't I?"

"Oh, Christ!" Rand said. "Why do you do these things?"

"Because its fun!" T'sa Li's voice sounded almost like that of a little girl. "Men," she said, "don't understand anything!" T'sa Li's face was drawn up into a pout. Rand, seeing that further remonstrance would be pointless, gave up and started looking nervously at the other passengers, trying to spot any jewel thieves. T'sa Li, however, was not through. "Why," she asked, with her chin held up high, "do you travel about inconspicuously in a Nazi airplane?"

"Okay, okay, forget it!"

"With real guns sticking out all over it!"

"C'mon, lemme up!"

"I expect fully," said T'sa Li, with a sniff of final dismissal, "that someday you'll come by to pick me up in a tank!"

Rand did not reply. By this time he was slumped down in his seat, head turned away, looking out the window and trying unsuccessfully to pretend he didn't know her. Several minutes went by that way, then T'sa Li poked Rand in the side with a stiffened forefinger. On the third, vigorous poke, he turned around. She smiled broadly. "Friends?"

Rand smiled back. "Why do you do things like that to me?"

"Because its so much fun," she said. "You bite so hard!" Rand just smiled and shook his head. The flight attendant chose that moment to relay the Captain's command to extinguish all cigarettes and place all seatbacks in the upright position for final approach. Rand complied and turned his attention to the window. He pointed out Mount Blanc to T'sa Li, but a rainy fog obliterated almost everything below its summit. His ears distinguished between the gear going down, leading edge slats going out and the deployment of the flaps, taking a pilot's interest in it all until grunting a final appreciation as the Swissair Captain greased the monster aircraft onto the rain-swept runway.

As both Rand and T'sa Li had taken nothing but underseat carryon bags and a plastic dry cleaner's cover for T'sa Li's dress, they were not delayed by claiming luggage. They headed for the customs section, arriving ahead of the crowd, and T'sa Li straightened out the jewelry matter quickly. Minutes later they were in a cab and Rand instructed the driver:

*"Vingt-cinq rue du Rhône, s'il vous plaît."* Then, a few moments later, he added in English, "Cut across the rue de Chantepoullet, please, instead of going down Fazy, and stop for a moment at one, rue de Mont Blanc."

*"Ah, oui. Rhein? Tabac Rhein?"* the cabbie asked, inquiring

whether Rand wanted to go to a popular tobaccanist, and thereby confirming that he understood English.

"*Ah, merci,*" replied Rand.

That the cabbie could understand English was not lost on T'sa Li, either, and she determined to confine conversation to idle chatter.

"You don't smoke," she accused.

"A gift. For the man we're going to see."

"Then why not go to Davidoff's? It's the best. Even Lenin bought his cigars there."

"It's out of the way—Hey! How do you know about Davidoff's?"

"Never mind," said T'sa Li, who was as aware as any woman of the value of a little mystery.

The cab pulled in to the curb at the corner of rue de Mont Blanc and Rand entered the tobaccanist's, emerging a few minutes later with a small humidor filled with Havana cigars.

Twenty-five rue du Rhône was a thoroughly unprepossessing address and their destination was on the second floor. There, a small brass plaque announced, was quartered *Banque Thibaudault Frères.* Inside, a well-scrubbed young woman of perhaps twenty-three sat in a modest, wide-skirted dress, amber hair formed into a braided crown, behind a modern desk. The desk had no sides. It was a beautifully finished top supported by a burnished aluminum column set on a low pedestal. On the desk were an Olympia electric typewriter and a small Eriksson telephone switchboard.

When they entered, the young woman brought her legs together modestly, as they were quite visible. Then, eyeing first the very Nordic Rand and then the very oriental T'sa Li, she elected English as most likely to be the appropriate language.

"Good morning," she said softly, "may I help you?"

"My name is Rand. I have no appointment but I believe I am expected by M. Jacques Thibaudault. With me is Mlle. Li."

"Thank you. One moment," said the girl as she picked up the telephone, punched one button and then a second, twice.

"*Pardon,*" she said into the phone, "*un Monsieur Rand et une demoiselle Li pour toi.*"

Rand's eyebrow lifted involuntarily at her use of the familiar "*toi,*" but he said nothing.

"M. Thibaudault will be with you both directly, sir." She smiled and cradled the phone. No sooner had she finished speaking than a stout, balding man of about fifty-five, wearing a conservatively cut blue suit of typically heavy French material, emerged from the hallway leading to the rear. He was smiling as he held out his hand to Rand and said, with but a trace of French accent,

"Ah, M. Rand. After what arrived from next door yesterday, I have been expecting you at any moment!"

"M. Thibaudault," said Rand, turning to T'sa Li, "Mlle. T'sa Li, an old friend who enjoys my confidence."

"Mlle. Li," Thibaudault smiled and bowed, "Bienvenue, bienvenue!" Then to both of them he said, "You will have already met my niece, Mlle. Garance Genderon."

"We have, indeed," said Rand. They all smiled. The girl said nothing, but, as they turned to follow Thibaudault into the hallway leading to his office, Rand thought he caught Garance staring. His glance flicked down. She wasn't holding her legs together any more. Rand winked at her and she turned away, blushing. None of which was lost to T'sa Li, who managed to step on Rand's toe with one of her high heels. Hard.

It was not lost on Jacques Thibaudault, either, although he gave no sign of it as he thanked Rand for the cigars and seated his guests in his office. Thibaudault didn't know what to make of T'sa Li, but, as Rand had brought her here and it was Rand's business which would be discussed, *c'est la vie.*

"As I said," began Thibaudault, "when, yesterday, I received from next door—next door being British Bank of the Middle East at vingt-*trois* rue du Rhône—a cashier's check to your order for one million dollars U.S., I expected to see you momentarily, anticipating instructions. The check has, by the way, already cleared. What would you like us to do with the funds? Handle it in the same manner as in the past? An account with a number only?"

"No," said Rand, "I think this time we'll handle it a bit differently. Just open an account in my name with the full amount on deposit."

"That's all?" asked Thibaudault, incredulously, "No special instructions?"

"Well," said Rand, "there *is* something you could do for me; or, rather, allow to be done."

"Ah, *M'sieu,* if it is at all possible I should be delighted to assist so valued a friend and customer as yourself. How may I help you?"

"You may not be so eager," said Rand, "when you hear what I have in mind. I'd like to precipitate a government audit of your bank in the immediate future."

Thibaudault looked stunned. "Surely, *M'sieu,* you would not deposit one million dollars in a bank which you doubt is solvent!"

"Of course not."

"I can assure you, M. Rand, that the bank's affairs would be found completely in order by such an audit. I can also assure you that our liquidity is high, although I do not have the exact percentage at my fingertips. There would nevertheless be considerable inconvenience. There would be, for example, an automatic ten day interruption in all foreign transactions. There are ways, of course, of precipitating such an audit, but why should you do it? And why ask my permission? Why not just do it? *Je ne comprends pas!"*

"Were I to do such a thing," said Rand, in what he hoped would be a calming tone of voice, "a man as well connected as you would learn quickly enough who had been behind it. Then you *would* have good reason to believe I had doubts about the bank. But that is not the case at all—"

"May I," interrupted T'sa Li, "make a suggestion?"

Both men stared at her in surprise. Before they could recover, T'sa Li continued:

"I'm sure M. Thibaudault understands that you would not do such a thing without a good reason, Rick, and that he accepts your assurances, as demonstrated by your deposit, that you have complete faith in his bank. I'm also sure, M. Thibaudault, that M. Rand understands that, although you would come through a government audit splendidly, there would be substantial inconvenience involved, both for the bank and for you. It would seem to me that the fair thing to do would be for you to lend M. Rand some money—say, four million Swiss francs."

Thibaudault was flabbergasted. Rand was fascinated. Thibaudault's eyes kept jumping from T'sa Li's eyes to her diamonds and back again. He was very unhappy and the jewels gave him some degree of comfort. The woman might be quite impossible, but she was undeniably rich. The very rich are to be humored; it was part of Thibaudault's religion. He cleared his throat:

"I am afraid, *Mademoiselle,* that I do not follow you."

"M. Rand," T'sa Li replied, "has just deposited to his account in your bank the Swiss franc equivalent, at today's rate of exchange, of one million dollars U.S.; correct?"

"Correct."

"Suppose M. Rand were to apply to your bank for a loan of four million Swiss francs, stating on his application that he intends to use the loan, together with the million he has just deposited, to build a commercial building; an office building, say, here in Geneva."

"Wait a minute—" said Rand.

"Hear me out, please," said T'sa Li. Then, without waiting for a reply, "Credit the Swiss franc four million to M. Rand as a materials loan. Now you have, have you not, M. Thibaudault, in Switzerland a national equivalent of the Federal Reserve Bank we have in the United States?"

*"Oui, mais—"*

*"Bon,"* interjected T'sa Li. "Now, on the basis of M. Rand's deposit and loan application, what would you be in a position to do?"

Thibaudault's face was a study in perplexity. Then, as the full import of T'sa Li's words hit him, it dissolved into a beatific smile. "I could," he said slowly, savoring the cleverness of it with the appreciation of a connoisseur, "get a loan of a million Swiss francs for 361 days."

"Of course!" Rand exclaimed, grasping the idea completely, "You," he said to Thibaudault, "get the use of a million Swiss franc increase in operating capital for a year, and there's no cost to me because, as a materials loan—"

"It's payable on a receipts receivable only basis," cut in an enthusiastic Thibaudault, completing Rand's sentence for him, "so the money goes nowhere and we cannot, therefore, charge you any interest."

"Should M. Rand," T'sa Li said, to finish what she started, "decide in a little while that he doesn't want to build the building after all, he can so notify you, the loan can be cancelled, you are free to use the extra million as you wish and everyone lives happily ever after."

The three of them laughed, and Thibaudault lit one of Rand's gift cigars. Rand said, "Jacques, draw up the application right away, will you, so it'll be in the correct form. We've got to get back to New York tonight, but I'll be back here in a few days on other business. I'll drop by and sign it then."

They rose and, as they walked together out to the reception

room, Thibaudault asked, "But where are you to be putting up the building?"

"I dunno," said Rand. "This is your town. Pick someplace that's hot. It'll build up my reputation."

Garance Genderon rose as they crossed to the door and joined them for a final round of handshaking. Did Rand detect a subtle extra pressure on his fingertips as she drew away her hand? He wasn't sure. Not, at least, until in the crush at the doorway, he felt Garance's breast press hard against his arm. It had the firmness of youth. Rand felt a familiar stirring in his loins that did not diminish until he had gotten all the way down stairs.

Once out on the sidewalk, Rand, holding up his hand to hail a cab, said, "You've been holding out on me, girl!"

"Oh?" replied T'sa Li, sweetly.

"First," he said, "you know the difference between a cantonal, savings and private bank. Second, you know where Lenin used to buy his cigars in Geneva. Finally, we have that performance upstairs."

"The way things were going," T'sa Li said, "it looked as if you needed a little help."

"You were right. And you certainly *were* a help. In more ways than one. Old Thibaudault's absolutely certain by this time that I've taken on another organization as an account. Although why they would want to I'm sure he can't figure out, 'cause they have you."

"Hey! Hold it! don't you jump to *that* conclusion," protested T'sa Li. "I was working for an investment bank in Macao when we met, remember? I might have taken part in a few discussions, and I'm a member of a family, but not *that* kind of a family—okay?"

"Sure. It's none of *my* business, and it wouldn't make any difference to me either way. At any rate, thanks. I appreciate the help."

A cab drew over and they entered. The rain was now nothing more than a mist and the late afternoon sun was trying to break through. "Hotel des Bergues," Rand ordered the cab driver. "I figure," he said to T'sa Li, looking at his watch, "that we've got time for one decent meal. This place has the best site on Lake Geneva, and Soutter, the manager, is a friend of mine. If you tell me he's a friend of *yours*, too, I'm gonna kill you!"

At noon the next day, Rand groaned as he sank himself down in the hot tub in the bathroom of his Plaza suite. Two days and nights with nothing but the red-eye flights to and from Switzerland for rest had tired him greatly. He was concerned that by now the name of the flight might apply to him literally, because he intended to conduct more business that day and it wouldn't do to appear dissolute to a senior vice-president of Manufacturers Hanover Trust. He reached for a hand mirror and checked. Not too bad; some eye drops ought to do it.

Rand soaked for thirty minutes, but did not waste the time. After drying his hands on a towel, he proceeded to study Standard & Poors and similar publications, some European and written in French or German, seeking likely prey among Ballinger's holdings. From time to time he made a note on a pad he had placed on the toilet seat next to the tub, where his study materials were stacked.

Toweling off, Rand shaved, administered eyedrops and dressed in his most conservative suit: a navy, three-piece custom Brooks sack. He wore a white shirt, and a sterling collar bar held up the knot of a silver gray tie. He replaced the OM-1 Omega on his wrist with a platinum Bucherer auto-wind and shod his feet with black calf low-quarters of British hand-lasted construction. Satisfied with his appearance, Rand descended to the lobby and, having given Matarazza the remainder of the day off, had the doorman hail a cab.

Rand's appointment with Marshall Sinclair of Manufacturers Hanover was for luncheon in the bank's private dining room. Sinclair came out to greet him as soon as he was announced and, during cocktails, the two men occupied themselves with nothing more taxing than the pleasantries of the day and ordering luncheon. Then Rand said, "Am I correct that your bank, as any other, can always use a little extra operating capital?"

"Depends on the money supply and time of year," said Sinclair. "Things *are* a bit tight right now. Fed's clamping down. What've you got in mind?"

Rand, who was perfectly cognizent of the state of the money supply and current attitude of the Federal Reserve Board, said,

"Could you use a million for thirty days?"

"Sure could. How much do you want?"

"Three-quarters over the Fed."

"Done."

The two men finished their lunch and, while still at the table, Rand wrote out a check for one million dollars, drawn on Banque Thibaudault Frères, Geneva. Sinclair took Rand with him back to his office.

"With the five hour time differential," said Sinclair, "I'm not sure we can get confirmation today."

"Try."

Sinclair ordered that his message be put at the head of the line on the telex.

Good Ol' Jacques, Rand thought, as the return telex confirmed the check as good and that a hold had been placed on Rand's million at Thibaudault Frères, pending receipt of the check Rand had written to Manufacturers Hanover. Sinclair gave Rand a thirty day note and had his secretary call him a cab.

Forty-eight hours later, Constantine Kazalakis, striding up, down, back and forth in his office trying unsuccessfully to bleed off the increasing sense of pressure he felt building up within him, barked at Paul Farington:

"What's this outfit Rand's got our people all over the world buying stock in?"

"High-Tech, Inc., a micro-circuitry manufacturer. The plants are mostly in Texas. It's a spin-off from Summa Corporation after Hughes died. Ballinger picked it up through Comco. Comco holds fifteen percent of the voting stock. That's enough for effective control because the rest is pretty well spread out through the public. Everyone wanted to get a piece of a Hughes operation as a souvenier, I guess."

"Well," said Kazalakis, "I suppose we could always sell it and cut our losses if Rand fucks up."

"It'll be complicated," said Farington.

"Why? What d'you mean?"

"Rand's got all our people executing powers of attorney in his favor for every share they buy."

"My God. McKenzie's letting him get away with that?"

"Yes sir."

"My God."

# VII

At 6:45 A.M. the following day, Richard Rand was in his bedroom just stepping out of his jockstrap when the phone rang. Naked but for his sweat socks and running shoes, he crossed to the bed-table and picked up the telephone.

"Hello?"

"Ah," said the voice of T'sa Li, "You're *not* dead after all."

"Yes I am," said Rand, who had just returned from a five mile run in Central Park. After a layoff of four days, and notwithstanding a steam bath with Alfredo Matrazza, it had left him exhausted.

"In fact," he continued, "I have never been deader. I'm standing here in nothing but my shoes and socks and I'm not sure I have the strength to get them off. I've just run five—"

"Oh, for Heaven's sake," cut in T'sa Li, "why don't you just say you have a headache? Why do you have to be so *macho* about it?"

"Because," said Rand impatiently, "I don't happen to *have* a headache. But if this trend in the conversation continues much longer I can't make any promises. What's up?"

"Not, apparently, what I had hoped. Anyway," said T'sa Li, "I'm calling for mother. That bowl of soup you had the other day doesn't count. She'd like to have you over this evening for the rest of the meal. She says you're much too thin."

"There's an old occidental saying," said Rand, "that one can never be too rich or too thin. I really wish I could but I can't, hon. I'm taking today's Concorde to Paris and a shuttle back to Geneva. I've had it with jet lag for awhile. Gotta sign the papers for that loan you thought up, remember?"

"Sure. I also remember a blond receptionist, barely past puberty, who was wearing lemon-colored panties."

"What!"

"Am I wrong on the color?"

"Well, no. But—"

"Of course not," purred T'sa Li, "to show them to you she had to show them to everyone in the room. Well, darling, enjoy. When you're ready to play with the big girls again, let me know."

"Oh, c'mon, for Chrissake!" Rand exploded. Then,

"Look, you tell your mother I'd really like to some time very soon. Give her my regrets and explain, okay?"

"Sucker," drawled T'sa Li, and hung up.

Rand stood there a moment, grinning ruefully and thought of the tautly stretched little patch of lemon colored cloth. It gave him an erection. With a burst of newly found energy, he hung up the phone, sat down on the bed, stripped off his shoes and socks and headed quickly for a cold shower.

The flight to Paris aboard the supersonic Concorde was uneventful; a pleasant and restful amalgam of good wine, food and service. His only complaint was the snugness of his leather seat; yet it didn't stop him from dozing off from time to time as the digital speed annunciator at the front of the cabin called his lulled senses a liar by insisting that his comfortable aluminum cocoon was streaking east at Mach 1.9.

A terrorist false alarm caused a delay in Rand's connecting flight to Geneva. Arriving late, he took a cab straight to the Hotel des Bergues and, having overeaten aboard Concorde, omitted supper in favor of sixty pushups and a hot tub, then went right to bed.

Rand awoke the next morning feeling especially well. He was hungry, randy and eager to get on with the day that lay before him. It was a beautiful one; startlingly clear and with a crispness more appropriate to fall than early summer. Rand spent minutes just admiring the view of the mountains around Lake Geneva from his window. He called room service and, despite his hunger, ordered a continental breakfast. With perfect timing, the cart arrived as he stood in his bathrobe toweling dry his blond hair.

Rand tipped the waiter, took an appreciative sip of hot coffee and, carrying the cup with him to the desk, picked up the telephone and had the switchboard place a call for him to a number in Berne. He was halfway through a buttered hard roll when the telephone rang and the switchboard operator announced, "Ready with your call to Berne, M. Rand."

"*Merci,*" said Rand. There was some clicking, then:

"Embassy aux Etats-Unis."

"Good morning," said Rand. "Mr. Richard Rand for Third Secretary Halloway."

"One moment, please."

There was a hollow sound as Rand was put on hold, then:

"Halloway speaking."

"Yes. Richard Rand, Mr. Halloway. Just want to confirm our eleven o'clock appointment. I'll be signing the loan application we discussed in correspondence first thing this morning and I'm eager to get your take on the best way to handle the intangibles with the locals so that building will go up as soon as possible."

"Yes. Well, we'll certainly do our best, although as I told you in my letter, local counsel is a must. All right, I'll be expecting you at eleven and we'll have a car for you at the airport."

"Many thanks," said Rand, and he hung up. So much for the curious, he thought to himself. With the U.S. embassy at Berne certainly wiretapped, probably by a number of agencies, and a hotel telephone one of the leakiest devices since the invention of the two dollar fountain pen, anyone interested in why he was in Switzerland should be slowed down, at least. Rand was not going to Berne at all. He had just been informed that the two men he was to contact at eleven would meet him at the Geneva airport in an automobile.

Yielding to temptation, Rand smeared a thick marmalade on the remaining portion of his hard roll, devoured it, then poured himself another cup of coffee which he sipped as he dressed. He selected from his suit carrier a light gray cheviot, added a white shirt with french cuffs fastened with links made from two Krugerands and chose a deep maroon tie of watered silk.

Dressing completed, Rand rolled the breakfast cart out into the hallway as he left, took the lift down to the lobby, had the doorman hail him a waiting cab, then settled back in it for the short ride to the offices of Banque Thibaudault Frères.

As there was no one else on the stairway, Rand took the steps up to the second floor of twenty-five rue de Rhône, two at a time. Gaining the top, he paused, then opened the door and entered.

Garance Genderon was wearing her long blond hair down. She had on a dark green satin dress with a wide skirt. The dress buttoned up the front and the top two buttons of the scooped neck were undone, revealing a modest bit of cleavage. Under her pedestal desk, her stocking-clad legs were together, primly. She smiled warmly at the sight of Rand.

"Ah, *bonjour* M. Rand!" she said.

"*Bonjour* to you, Mlle. Genderon," replied Rand. He glanced downward. Garance Genderon was wearing patent leather pumps whose green matched the color of her dress. By the time his eyes rose, her legs had parted, raising the hem of her skirt like a curtain. It became inescapable to Rand that Garance' panties did not match her shoes and dress. They were a delicate egg shell that set off delightfully the paler flesh of her inner thighs; at least that portion of them visible over the tops of her hose, held up by frilly suspendors from an old fashioned garter belt.

Rand forced his attention back to business. "I told M. Jacques I'd be back in a few days to sign some papers. Is he in?"

"Oh," she said, "*Non*. But there is no problem, *Monsieur*. M. Thibaudault mentioned that you might be coming in in his absence. They are ready; he left them for you. If you will excuse me for a moment? They are in his desk."

"*Certainment,*" said Rand. Garance rose, dropping the curtain on her little show and walked with a lithe glide, skirt swaying, down the hall toward Thibaudault's office.

Rand seated himself on a leather sofa against the wall. He didn't have long to wait. Mlle. Genderon floated back into the room carrying a file folder. Two more buttons on her bodice were undone and her cleavage was now something less than modest. So obvious a play for him by someone half his age engaged both Rand's personal and profession curiosity. He had no objection to being seduced, if a bit blatantly, by someone so attractive. But he had to know the reason. Genderon was working for someone, but for whom?

It was a simple matter to sign the papers the young woman had spread upon her desk, despite the distraction as she leaned over from the opposite side, pointing with elaborate precision to where he should sign, breasts nearly falling out of her dress in the process. Rand felt as if someone was trying to get his attention by hitting him over the head.

The signing done with, Rand clipped his fat Mont Blanc fountain pen back into his inside suitcoat pocket, saying,

"Many thank's for your help. I'd like to repay your kindness. Would you be my guest for dinner tonight—"

"*Ah, oui Monsieur, Je—*"

"—in London?"

"London, *Monsieur?*"

"*Oui.* There's quite a night life to be enjoyed there, and some excellent shopping. You might enjoy it."

Mlle. Genderon hesitated, frowning. The offer, Rand surmised, exceeded what had been expected. She was probably unsure of her authority to accept.

"*Mon oncle,*" she said finally, "I shall have to ask my uncle. Oh, I do hope he says yes; I'd really like to go!"

"I'll phone you back at one," Rand said. "How's that?"

"Oh, yes. He should return very soon."

"One o'clock, then," said Rand, walking to the door. As he left she was still standing behind her desk, holding the file folder in both hands, looking worried.

Rand arrived at Cointrin airport at 10:43 A.M. After checking quietly to see whether he was being followed by anyone clumsy, he approached the car rental desk, identified himself and presented his European driver's license and a gold-colored American Express card. He signed the waiting rental contract and was directed by the attendant to the correct parking lot.

There were several identical black Mercedes-Benz 230 four-door sedans parked side by side in the rental lot. Rand had to check the license plates to find the one he had rented. He unlocked the door, got in, fired up the little four cylinder engine, backed up and drove out of the lot away from the airport.

Once on the open road, Rand looked into the rear view mirror and said, "Good morning, gentlemen."

Two heads rose up slowly behind him. They belonged to two men in business suits who took seats in the rear with sighs of relief.

"It must have been cramped back there," said Rand. "How long were you guys submerged?"

"Too long," replied the man immediately behind Rand. "I thought you were going to take us to Italy before you stopped."

"No such luck," said Rand as he turned into a scenic mountain overlook, parked, then twisted around in his seat to address them.

"Okay," said Rand, "who's who?"

The man directly behind him, thin, bespectacled and worried looking, spoke first.

"Robert Norris, Mr. Rand. I'm chief executive officer of Voltmaster."

"Your company's the one that manufactures transistorized electronic automotive ignition systems, correct?" asked Rand.

"Automotive, stationary power plant and marine applications," amplified Norris, a bit self-importantly.

Rand shifted his glance to the other man and Norris was glad not to have to look into those disconcerting pupilless eyes a moment longer.

"Arthur Simon," said the second man. He was lean but well put together. With gray eyes under thinning, sand-colored hair, he regarded Rand levelly as he said, "I'm CEO of Enerdyne. We manufacture electronic components."

"Including transistors?" asked Rand.

"Yes."

"Micro-circuitry chips?"

"No. That's beyond our capability at the moment. With the growing market, though, we'll be getting into it soon. We have approval from Langley. Transistors are obsolete for too many applications."

"Forget Langley and dump those plans," Rand commanded. "And both of you, please, take notes. If you have any questions on what I lay out for you, ask immediately. We can't afford any slip ups; this thing has to go right in every way, right from the start. Okay?"

Both men nodded. Norris took out a pad from a slender leather brief case at his feet and reached for a gold ballpoint pen. Simon took from his inside pocket a Mont Blanc pen similar to Rand's. They eyed him expectantly and, it seemed to Rand, a bit resentfully.

"The rationale," Rand began, "is as follows. Heat is the enemy of transistors. Your company, Mr. Norris—Voltmaster—will therefore modify its products so as to use chips. You will gain in reduction of size and, because of greater resistance to heat, increased durability. Where are you getting your present components—not just transistors, the entire component?"

"Bosch." replied Norris, "Robert Bosch, GmbH."

"All right," said Rand, "switch to Enerdyne. Specify components made with chips. No more transistors."

"But I've just told you," interrupted Simon, "that chips are beyond our capability to produce."

"Yes," said Rand, "and everyone in the industry knows that, too."

"Certainly."

"Good. Enter into a contract with Norris, here, to supply him with the components he specifies. A large contract. In the millions. As big as you can manage and still stay credible within the industry. Clear so far?"

"Yes," said Simon, "but quite *un*clear is where my company is to get the chips to go into the components we're obligating ourselves to sell."

"From High-Tech, Hughes' old company. Make the specs very detailed and precise and get the biggest contract with them you can swing. Multi-million, minimum. Got it?"

"I understand you," said Simon, "but do *you* understand that it may be too large a one? High-Tech, according to *Forbes*, is pretty heavily committed right now. With current production obligations, *they* may not be able to handle that big a deal without new hiring, overtime production—maybe even plant expansion. They may turn us down."

"Possible," said Rand, "but not probable. There's too much money to be made."

"They shouldn't have too much difficulty floating a loan to finance the added production," offered Norris.

"Right," confirmed Rand. "Now, Mr. Simon. Take delivery of as much of the High-Tech product as you can as soon as you can, *without paying for it*. That's critical. Under no circumstances are you to pay High-Tech anything on the contract without personal clearance from me. Not someone in Langley, *me*. Do we understand each other?" There was a pause and no one said anything.

"All right," said Rand. "Do either of you have any questions?"

"What's the time frame?" asked Simon.

"Everything by yesterday," answered Rand.

"I was afraid of that," responded Norris with a sigh and look of martyrdom as he sank back in his seat. Rand swung around and started the car. Pulling out into the road, he drove back in the direction from which they had come. Shifting into fourth gear, he glanced in the rear view mirror, caught Norris' eye and, taking his right hand off the wheel, made a downward gesture with his flattened palm. Norris sighed again pointedly as he and Simon sank down to the floor and out of sight once more.

Heathrow Airport, outside London, is divided into two sections for the reception of passengers; one for those from Europe, the other for trans-Atlantic flight arrivals. Rand and Garance Genderon, inbound from Geneva on BA, went through the European arrival section and the green light "nothing to declare to customs" area. Just outside were a number of men in top hats standing about holding signs in the air. Each bore a name. One of them read, "Mr. Rand."

Rand identified himself and with a courteous "This way, please, Mr. Rand," was ushered, together with Garance and the porter bearing their luggage, to a hired Phantom V Rolls waiting outside.

The trip to the Dorchester Hotel on Park Lane took only a half-hour. There, thanks to the polite professionalism of Paul Grunder, the reception manager, Rand and his young companion were whisked through a welter of Arabs and, in remarkably few minutes, ensconced snugly in a suite overlooking Hyde Park. It was 7:00 P.M.

"Now," said Rand to the girl as Grunder and the last of the bellmen retreated and the door closed, "tell me the truth."

"The truth, *Monsieur?*" Garance looked worried.

"The truth. Have you ever eaten English food?"

"Oh," said Garance, with obvious relief, "*non,* never."

"The cooking at home is French?"

"*Oui.*"

"Then," said Rand, "you deserve a change. I am not, however, a cruel man, so I won't inflict upon you what the English call food; at least not at first." He drew a wallet from inside his suitcoat pocket, removed from it an assortment of cards and, in a manner with which Garance Genderon would become familiar, sorted through them like a deck of playing cards. Abruptly he selected one card from the others, crossed to the telephone on an antique desk against the wall and made a brief call. Hanging up, he turned back to the girl.

"Dinner in one hour, and I suggest we dress. There are some places we might go later that require black tie."

Garance looked troubled.

Rand smiled. "Go ahead, girl, use the bedroom and bathroom. You'll have them to yourself for half an hour; I need only fifteen minutes. But I warn you," he grinned, "ready or not, in half an hour I'm going to be using both rooms!"

She smiled at him in relief. "Would it be possible—"

"Anything's possible," said Rand, "especially in a first class London hotel. Would you like a drink?"

"*Oui!* I'm terribly thirsty from the trip. May I have anything I like?"

"Anything legal."

"I'd give my soul for a large glass of cold, fresh milk!"

"Your honor, perhaps," Rand smiled, "but your soul will not be necessary. Lesson number one: in an English hotel, the hall porter is king. There is one, and a kitchen, on every floor. Scoot! I'll knock on the door when your milk arrives."

Garance Genderon scooted.

At 9:15 A.M., Rand and the Swiss girl were seated at table in the Elysée Restaurant on Percy Street, pleasantly sated by a splendid Greek dinner. Rand had declined *retsina* as requiring too much of an acquired taste for Garance to enjoy. He had not, however, spared the *ouzo*. Garance was clapping her hands and laughing as the last of a series of dishes was smashed with spirited Hellenic abandon when one of the Karageorgis brothers, who ran the place, approached a table set for two. The room quieted immediately in anticipation. Long blond hair fell onto Rand's shoulder as Garance leaned over to him and whispered,

"What's he going to do?"

"Watch!"

Karageorgis squatted down until his head was level with the table. He inched himself forward until he could, and did, clamp the table edge in his teeth. Then, to the amazement of Garance and the uproarious applause of the onlooking diners, Karageorgis lifted the entire table in the air using nothing but the strength of his jaw.

"There's a man," said Rand, "with a talented mouth."

Garance flushed. "You are a wicked man! But it's all right; I am feeling very wicked. I should like to go some place very wicked. Are there such places in London?"

Rand smiled at her appreciatively. She was wearing a classic full length white evening dress, strapless and sleeveless. It was ornamented solely by a gold Greek key design on the border of the cloth draped artfully over her exquisite form.

"They have indeed," he said and once more consulted the cards in his wallet. One by one he flipped through them; membership cards in London's private clubs: Ladbroke, Victoria

Sporting, Palm Beach Casino, Murray's Cabaret, until he came to the one he was looking for.

"Get yourself together, girl," Rand said, signaling the waiter for a phone to be brought to the table. He called Denise Rowe to reserve a table at Toppers on Poland street.

At 3:12 A.M., Rand and Garance were back in their suite at the Dorchester. Garance gave Rand her wrap to hang up, then sat down abruptly on the sofa. She clapped her hands together and giggled.

"Can you pick up a table in your teeth?" she asked Rand as he sat down in an ornate side chair across the room from her. She didn't wait for his answer, just started laughing at the thought of him trying to do it, shoulders rising and falling as she did, the nipples of her breasts keeping pace against the white cloth of her gown. She put her hand to her face. There was no sound now, just the rhythmic heaving of her shoulders.

"However badly I went about it," said Rand, "it couldn't be *that* funny!"

Garance dropped her hand back in her lap and shook her head from side to side, swiftly.

"No," she said, "it's not—not—funny at all."

Tears were streaming down the girl's cheeks. She was the picture of misery.

Rand wasn't sure whether it was the alcohol or something more. He was beginning to suspect it was something more.

"What's wrong, Garance?" he asked gently.

Still weeping, she rose slowly to her feet. Reaching behind her back, she undid a fastener, then held her dress up around her for a moment before letting it fall to the floor. She was naked except for a pair of white satin briefs. Slowly she turned her body sideways to him, controlling her sobbing with an obvious effort. She forced a smile. "My breasts," she asked him, lifting her head and holding back her shoulders, "they would be good enough for Topper, *n'est ce pas?*"

The reference was to the forty bare-breasted waitresses for which, among other erotic delights, Toppers Club is celebrated.

"They're fine," said Rand. "What's wrong, Garance?"

As if she hadn't heard him, Garance turned back, slowly, to face him directly. Then, bending gracefully toward him, as if in a bow, she hooked both thumbs inside the waistband of her panties, slid them down past her knees, then straightened up as they fell around her ankles. Catching her breath audibly, Garance lifted her right leg up and out of the tiny white garment and put it down to one side. Deliberately she did the same with her left leg until she was standing astride the little pile of cloth, legs parted. She put her hands, thumbs to the rear, on her hips, thrust her pelvis forward and lifted her chin.

"And my little girl," she asked, "is she not beautiful?"

Rand looked at the golden fluff that covered her pubis and said, truthfully, "She's beautiful."

The two of them remained motionless and silent for several moments. Then, slowly at first but at last uncontrollably, twin rivulets of tears flowed down Garance' cheeks. The sobs started again. Still, defiant of the emotion that rocked her, Garance Genderon held her pose.

"What's wrong, Garance?" Rand asked for the third time.

The dam broke. The lovely girl brought her legs tightly together and hugged herself, arms concealing her breasts.

"I don't know what to do!" she wailed.

Rand knew it wasn't the alcohol now. He rose, went over to the wretched girl and, taking off his dinner jacket, covered her with it. He reached down, picked up her panties and handed them to her. She turned her back to him and put them on; then, disconsolate, she sat down once more on the sofa. No longer crying, she drew her breath in irregular short gasps, struggling for control.

"I should have guessed," Rand said to her gently. "No one's tried to seduce me by taking my picture since I was seventeen."

"Taking your picture?" She looked up at Rand quizzically.

"An American figure of speech. That little trick of yours, flashing your panties at me; among adolescents in the United States twenty years ago, that was called 'taking a picture'. Don't ask me why."

"Young girls do that to boys they want to attract everywhere, I suppose," said Garance. Then, lowering her head, she said,

"It's the only thing I know."

"Why, Garance?"

"*Mon oncle.* He asked me to become friends with you; talk to you. He wants to know what you are thinking; what you are going to do."

"And for that he sent you to London with me?"

"*Non!* My uncle is a good man. He didn't come back in time so I decided myself to say yes. After all, I am already twenty-two.

I am an adult. My uncle has been very good to me. He raised and educated me after my parents died. They drowned in the lake when I was thirteen.

"Look," said Rand, "I'll make a deal with you."

"Deal?"

"A bargain. You go put on a nightgown and get into that bed and get some sleep. I'll sleep here on the sofa. Tomorrow, we'll go get a nice big breakfast at Grosnover House. That's another hotel just up the street and they serve the best breakfast in London. Then we'll pack up and I'll take you back home and we'll think up something to tell your uncle. If you'll do that, I promise to tell you exactly what I'm going to do. I'll even let you help me with something your uncle and I have already agreed on. How's that sound to you?"

Garance said nothing, just smiled through wet eyes and nodded her head in vigorous approval of the bargain. She rose and started toward the bathroom, then stopped and turned to him.

"It's a—what you say?—*deal*," she said, "but with one condition. I am the one who has been so foolish. I'll sleep on the sofa; you are at least entitled to your bed for your kindness."

"Okay," said Rand with a smile, "I'm too tired to argue the point with you."

At 5:21 A.M., Richard Rand was sleeping on his back in the massive bed with which the Dorchester furnishes its finest suites. The mattress rocked and, drowsily, he came partially awake. From a single, well-shaded table lamp a soft glow reached across the room. In the dim illumination Rand saw through sleepy eyes the figure of Garance Genderon towering above him, legs astride his shoulders. She was wearing nothing but a wisp of chiffon and lace bikini.

Noticing his eyes open, Garance steadied herself with one hand against the headboard of the bed. With her other hand she slid the little panties down, lifting first one leg and then the other to free herself of them completely; then tossed them aside. Looking down at him she said:

"I have come to take your picture."

"What?"

"I am twenty-two. I have decided. You are a good man. It is time."

Slowly and carefully Garance lowered her camera toward him. Rand reached up, cupped her buttocks in his palms and guided her lens down gently to a close-up of his mouth. She shivered as she felt the warmth of his breath between her thighs; then gasped in pleasure at the touch of his lips.

The next eight days were a pleasant jumble of sensory delights as Rand taught Garance what he knew of London and of love. He didn't have to teach her a thing about shopping. She was quite up to that, thank you, to the tune of some six hundred pounds sterling. Worth, Rand decided, every penny, after her masterful performance the day after they arrived in Berne. Before the Commission Bancaire of the Swiss National Bank, Garance was the personification of the troubled young lady concerned that those nice people who put their money in her uncle's bank might suffer because, she believed, Banque Thibaudault Frères was illiquid.

Thirteen days after Rand issued his million dollar check to Manufacturer's Hanover Trust in New York, and with one day left to complete processing and send the credit on its ten day journey from Geneva to New York, an audit of Banque Thibaudault Frères commenced by the Commission Bancaire put a hold on all international transactions of the bank. As there was nothing at all wrong with the bank's affairs, the audit took only seven days. On the sixth day, at the airport in Berne, Rand took his leave of a once more tearful Garance; he to leave for the United States, she for Geneva.

"You will come back, please," she said, hugging him tightly, "for more pictures!"

"I promise," smiled Rand. "How could I resist? You have become a superb photographer!"

Garance blushed deeply and, with a wave, Rand was gone through the security screen. She stood there in case he should have to return for some reason—a forgotten bag perhaps—until she had to leave to catch her own plane. An empty place inside her had been filled, but now it was empty again—and larger.

The next day, Monday, Richard Rand entered Manufacturers Hanover Trust's main office in New York City. It was the thirtieth day since he had given them his million dollar check and the bank had given him its note. At 9:07 A.M. he presented the note for payment and was promptly issued a cashier's check for one million dollars. At his request, the $6,250.00 it had earned in interest was given him in cash.

Eighteen minutes later, Rand deposited the million dollars with Bankers Trust, New York, endorsing the Manufacturers Hanover cashier's check to the credit of one of the banks for which Bankers Trust served as correspondent, Banque Thibaudalt Frères. Within half an hour, and nearly twenty-four hours before the delayed transaction in Switzerland would have actually transferred the million there to Manufacturers Hanover in payment of his original check, the telexed million dollar credit from Bankers Trust arrived at Banque Thibaudault Frères. The two transactions cancelled each other out, creating a "wash" and, true to Rand's promise to the CIA, their million dollars never actually moved.

On his way out of the Bankers Trust lobby, Rand stopped at one of the form-filled tables with chained ballpoint pens spaced throughout for the convenience of bank customers. Whistling a cheerful tune softly, he used the back of one of the forms and a captive pen to do a little arithmetic. After deducting for Garance Genderon's £600 shopping spree at the current dollar/sterling rate of exchange, Rand found he had netted $5,051.22 on the CIA's money, over and above what would be due him when it was finally withdrawn and returned.

Rand grinned at Alfredo Matarazza as he climbed into the waiting BMW double-parked brazenly in front of the bank.

"Boss," said Matarazza, "you look like ya scored. Whatcha do, heist the joint?"

"Sorry to disappoint you, 'Fredo. I made a little money, but it's all quite legal."

"Ah, Boss," said Matarazza, making a face. "Makin' dough legal's like fuckin' yer wife. Ya ain't makin' 'em pay when ya take what's comin' to ya anyway. It's the principle of the thing."

"You're wrong, 'Fredo."

"Huh?"

"It's the interest!"

# VIII

The first day of October in New York City was a duplicate of the thirtieth of September; at least according to the Channel 7 weather report Richard Rand listened to that morning. The day would be quite warm. Nevertheless, it *was* the first of October, and Rand made a mental note to have the flue in his sitting room fireplace checked so as to be ready for use as soon as the weather was cool enough to justify it. When the Plaza Hotel had been renovated completely after sale a few years before, Rand had paid well to have the flue unblocked. The lease specified that all expenses incidental to use of the fireplace, and the extra insurance premium, were to be paid by Rand. It was an extravagance, but one he could well afford and enjoyed greatly.

The weather report also prompted Rand's choice of a light blue summer-weight suit, a darker blue shirt and cream-colored necktie. On his feet he wore black and white wingtip shoes. On the "you never know in New York City" principle, he took with him a small Swiss folding umbrella as he left his suite and stepped into the gilded cage elevator to begin his descent to the ground where Alfredo Matarazza waited with the BMW.

The elevator dropped one floor and paused to pick up another passenger. A welcome addition for the brief trip, Rand thought as a comely brunette in her early thirties, strikingly well-turned-out in a maroon suit with matching sandals, bag and little melon-slice shaped hat, walked to the rear of the car, turned around to face front and, before the car could begin to descend again, sneezed with a healthy exuberance. She seemed a bit embarrassed by the force of her sneeze, and Rand found it hard to suppress a smile as she fought in a ladylike way to keep from sneezing again while gropping frantically with a white-gloved hand in her bag for a handkerchief.

Rand felt that a gentleman would not embarrass the woman further by taking notice of her difficulty; accordingly, he looked virtuously the other way. That was a mistake. He realized it as he heard her speak his name in a firm tone and, turning to look, found that what he had expected to be a lacy white handkerchief was, in fact, a Smith & Wesson "K" model revolver with rounded butt and shortened barrel. From the length of its cylinder and chamber size, he judged it to be of .22 rimfire magnum caliber and capable of very high velocity. He stared at the open ends of the exposed chambers; as he expected, the bullets were hollowpoints. The hole one of them would make upon entering him would be .22 calibre, but the hole it would make inside him after the hollowpoint had mushroomed would be closer to .44.

*"Gesundheit,"* said Rand.

The elevator stopped again. The doors opened and two young, determined-looking men of Rand's height but a good twenty-five pounds heavier, boarded. The woman put the gun and her hand back into her pocketbook, but held it in such a way that Rand did not doubt that he was still covered.

"We haven't very much time for conversation." said the woman. She was clearly older than the two men who had just joined them, and just as clearly in command. "Your Mr. Matarazza will not be joining us. He and your car are quite safe. Be cooperative and no harm whatever will come to him or to you. A different car is parked where your's was. Just get into the back quietly between these two gentlemen, sit back and relax. Is that clear?"

"I hope," said Rand, "you catch a hell of a cold."

The elevator reached the lobby and the four of them walked quietly out of the hotel and onto Central Park South. A black four-door Lincoln Continental sedan, emergency flashers on, was waiting for them. Rand couldn't get into position to see the license plates. He was herded immediately into the rear door on the street side. The woman and one of the men walked around to the other side of the car; she got in front, the man in the rear. The remaining man got in behind Rand and he was sandwiched between them in the rear seat. The uniformed driver got the big sedan under way immediately.

"I suppose I'd be wasting my time to ask where we're going?"

"And ours," replied the woman flatly.

The car turned north onto the Westside Highway.

"How," ventured Rand, "did you take out Mr. Matarazza? He's no amateur. There should be no harm in telling me. If what you say is true, he can tell me himself later."

Again it was the woman who spoke:

"Mr. Matarazza made the mistake of buying a cup of coffee from a street vendor. It made him ill. Some friends took him home. Your car is back in the garage. Would you like a cigarette?"

"I don't smoke. If I did, I don't think I'd try one of yours. I couldn't be sure I'd live long enough to die of cancer."

The Lincoln paused momentarily as the driver threw fifty cents into the exact change receiver and they crossed over the Henry Hudson Bridge into the Bronx.

"If this trip is going to be much longer," said Rand, "I'd like to stop at a men's room sometime soon."

"You'll be able to take care of that soon," said the woman. She spoke without turning around.

The car entered Van Cortlandt Park and drove through it slowly. There was a huge open area, more a plain than a field, covered with grass newly returned to green by fall rains after having spent most of the summer a burned out brown. Here and there a jogger, mind miles away, trotted along a path only he could see.

The road led toward the base of a hill covered with trees, leaves just going yellow, and a secondary growth of scrub brush. A turnoff climbed into the wooded area and they took it. Several yards inside, just far enough to conceal the car from the open plain because of a sharp bend in the road, the woman said, "Here." The car stopped.

The woman got out first, right hand deep in her handbag. The man to Rand's right exited next. Rand waited until the man to his left had gotten out, closed the door and walked around the car to join the other two. Then, at the gesture of the woman, Rand got out on the right. The driver stayed with the vehicle.

One of the young men beckoned Rand and he turned to follow him as the other took up the rear. Rand tensed, ready to fight or flee, whichever seemed appropriate, should either man produce a weapon. Neither did. After they had penetrated a few yards into the forest, out of sight but not earshot of the car, the first man stopped and gestured toward the ground. Rand unzipped his fly.

As he relieved himself, Rand could hear the woman's voice but couldn't understand what she was saying; especially as one of the helicopters that frequent New York City skies *whop-whop-whoped* over them and drowned out all other sound. He finished urinating and zipped his fly, then raised his eyebrows at the two guards. They nodded and fell into a flanking position, herding him back toward the car.

As the three of them reached the Lincoln, Rand saw the woman standing next to the open driver's window. In her left hand she held a microphone to her lips. It was attached to a curling length of wire that led back through the driver's window into the automobile. Her right hand was still in her pocketbook, pointing toward the ground. She raised it toward Rand as he approached.

The sound of the helicopter persisted and grew louder. Abruptly, the woman handed the microphone through the window to the driver, then motioned to Rand and his guards to walk down the road toward the plain. As they emerged from the woods, a Sikorsky six-passenger helicopter without markings settled on the plain just off the road. In the distance, one or two figures stopped to look; then, New Yorkers that they were, turned away and continued about their own business.

A door in the side of the helicopter slid open. The noise of the ship's turbine engine made speech useless, so the woman just entered, turned around and, with the gun now out of her handbag and leveled at Rand's midsection, motioned to him to board. Rand entered and took the seat she indicated. He was followed quickly by the two guards, one of whom slammed the door shut as the helicopter rose quickly and headed southwest toward the Hudson River.

"Kazalakis," Rand said to the woman.

"Let's just say that the pleasure of your company is requested at a meeting in Washington. A discreet meeting; one for which your usual colorful means of transportation are deemed inappropriate."

"Yeah," muttered Rand, "Kazalakis." He settled back down in his seat, lowered his head onto his shoulder and promptly went to sleep.

The Sikorsky was unpressurized so when, about an hour and forty minutes later, they descended to nine hundred feet at the Potomac River, the change in pressure registered in Rand's ears. He awoke and looked out the window.

As the ship followed the river south on the Virginia side, it struck Rand that they were taking the long way round to Langley. Within minutes they veered to the right over a tangle of freeways, then dropped rapidly. It dawned on him that they were not going to CIA headquarters. As a five-sided series of rings nested one inside the other came into view, their destination became clear: the Pentagon. Just why they were going there, however, was not clear to Rand at all.

The helicopter eased to a landing on the concrete slab used by military ferry craft based just across the river at Bolling. Military police were waiting. The door was opened by one of his guards, and the woman, again not trying to compete with the descending whine of the ship's turbine, gestured to Rand to get off first. He did so. Suddenly the door behind him closed and the turbine started to howl again. There was a blast of air from the rotor as it achieved flight speed, added it's *whop-whop-whop* to the general din and the ship lifted off.

A first lieutenant of military police said, "This way, please, Mr. Rand." He was holding in his hand a photograph of Rand which he did not bother to conceal. Rand followed him and three enlisted M.P.s fell in behind. They entered the building and, as they approached the desk where a visitor is required to sign in and obtain a pass either to hang on a chain round his neck or clip to his suitcoat pocket, the young officer leading him displayed written orders to the guard. The guard made a verifying phone call while the lieutenant made an entry in the log, signed it, picked up passes for himself and Rand, then led the way to an elevator.

Below ground level, the elevator doors opened and the officer led Rand down a corridor and through another check point. The M.P. on duty opened a door. It led into a small vestibule having another door on the left which required the officer to open it through the use of a combination lock set into it in the manner of a vault. Once that door was open Rand noticed that there was a turnstyle on the other side and then yet another door. The two men passed through the turnstyle, which Rand thought was probably used to record numerically those passing in and out for security accountability purposes, then they entered the door beyond.

The final door led into a small, room-sized theatre, about twenty by forty feet. There was a low stage and machine-operated curtains covered that portion of the room which would have been used for a screen were motion pictures to be shown. Similar curtains covered angled side walls where the stage wings would have been. An unused lectern stood to the left. As befitted a theatre, the floor sloped toward the stage and the seats were arranged in staggered, descending rows.

Five men sat in the front row. They turned round to watch Rand and the officer accompanying him approach them. Rand recognized all but one. McKenzie and Kazalakis sat beside each other. There was a separation of two seats and "Vincent," who had briefed him on CIA proprietary assets months ago, sat together with "Phil." The last man, whom Rand did not recognize, sat by himself in the last seat in the row, to Rand's right. He was in his early thirties and wore an expensive, two button wool suit in a light shade of gray, gleaming cordovan oxfords and a blue buttondown-collar shirt with a subdued, small-figured, black silk tie. Rand approved.

The officer who had brought Rand from the helicopter walked rapidly down the aisle ahead of him, saluted McKenzie, then walked over to the young man seated at the end of the row. He leaned over to him and spoke for a moment quietly. The man nodded and the officer brushed past Rand on his way out as Rand approached McKenzie and Kazalakis.

"Anyone," asked Rand, "care to tell me what's going on?"

"That," answered Kazalakis, "is what we were hoping you could tell us." His eyes looked upon Rand bleakly. "We had a deal," he continued. "You were entrusted with substantial assets and given a job to do. I was informed at 7:30 last evening that you have bankrupted one proprietary corporation and dissolved the other. The amounts involved are higher than I can count. I suggest it is you who owe *us* the explanation."

Rand regarded the two men levelly, then nodded his head to the right.

"I recognize everyone but the guy with the good tailor."

McKenzie answered him. "The young man represents the National Security Council. He is a staff member assigned to monitor this meeting."

Rand raised his eyebrows at this intelligence. It certainly explained why the meeting was held at the Pentagon rather than at Langley. White House staffers like to stay as close to home turf as possible.

"You're serious about this?" Rand asked Kazalakis. "I see two people I recognize from a prior meeting who are certainly capable of having followed what was done *as* it was done."

"Listen, Rick," said Kazalakis, throwing out a little smoke to cover the fact that he'd been cut out of the action in the interim, "since our last meeting I've had a hell of a lot of other things to do besides look over your shoulder. I'm not sure I would have understood it even if I had. But you're right. People have, naturally, been following what you were doing with our financial assets. But we trusted you. Damn it, Rick, *I* trusted you!"

"These guys," Kazalakis said it with a nod toward Vincent and Phil, "tell us there is no way they can calculate right now just where we are financially. Their job was to follow the pea from walnut shell to walnut shell. Now they tell us they can't even find the walnut shells! That, coupled with the news that you made a chunk of dough by manipulating that million that wasn't gonna be touched, has got some people, including me, a bit upset with you, Rick. So why don't you tell us what you've been up to? And try to keep it real simple, so's all us country boys can understand."

Rand looked from one to the other of them. Only McKenzie and Kazalakis did not flinch from the stare of his translucent eyes.

"Apparently," Rand said, with undisguised disgust, "I'll have to keep it simple because I'm dealing with simple people. Get me a blackboard."

The four CIA men just looked at each other but the NSC staffer, apparently familiar with the premises, rose, mounted the low stage and went behind the curtain on the right. From behind it he produced a green chalk board and wheeled it into position, stage center.

Rand watched as the NSC man, still saying nothing, returned to his seat; then, disdaining the steps, Rand mounted the stage himself with a single stride upward from the floor. He picked up a piece of yellow chalk from the tray beneath the chalk board and tossed it idly in his hand as he surveyed his small audience.

"The two companies you gave me to work with were Voltmaster and Enerdyne." Rand wrote the names on the board near the top.

"The target I selected was High-Tech. Gregory Ballinger controlled it. The object of the exercise was to take it away from him." Rand wrote the name *High-Tech* on the board.

"I had Voltmaster contract with Enerdyne for a product using a component, micro-circuitry chips, which was beyond Enerdyne's capacity to produce. That gave Enerdyne an excuse to contract for them with High-Tech." Rand drew arrows from one company name to another on the board as he spoke. "Clear so far?" he asked the assembly with a touch of sarcasm.

"While that was going on, you'll recall that I had your people throughout the world quietly buying up High-Tech shares and giving me power of attorney to vote them. The target was fifty-one percent of outstanding shares. We got fifty-six percent."

McKenzie interrupted him. "If we owned 56% of High-Tech, why all the rest of the hugger-mugger? Why not just throw the rascals out and be done with it?"

"Because," Rand answered him, "the mere fact of a takeover would not achieve our purpose. Only the way we did it, if sufficiently novel, would attract Ballinger's interest. Remember? Now, watch."

Rand returned to the chalk board and pointed to *High-Tech* with his yellow chalk.

"High-Tech needed to expand capacity to take on the Enerdyne contract. So, on the strength of the Enerdyne contract, they borrowed from Chase Manhattan. As security for the loan they put up the twenty percent of all High-Tech shares they retained as a corporate asset. Chase lent them fifty percent of the market value of the pledged stock."

"Now," Rand continued, annoying his listeners further by obviously enjoying what he considered to be his own cleverness, "after High-Tech had delivered a major portion of the components under the contract and demanded payment, I had Enerdyne *refuse* payment on the ground the components were not up to specifications and cancel the contract. While they were threatening suit, I surfaced my fifty-six percent interest in High-Tech and, on the ground that High-Tech was insolvent because it couldn't pay off Chase because Enerdyne refused to pay them, I fired the High-Tech board chairman, who had been installed by Ballinger and was his man, and replaced him with Vincent, here."

Rand stared at McKenzie and Kazalakis. "Okay," he said, in the manner of a graduate student teaching an undergraduate course, "can either of you tell me what had been accomplished up to that point?"

McKenzie and Kazalakis said nothing.

"All right," said Rand, "I'll give you a hint. At that point, using Agency funds, I paid off the High-Tech note at Chase. Now what d'you say?"

McKenzie and Kazalakis just frowned in concentration. Vincent, however, contributed to the classroom atmosphere by raising his hand. Rand pointed to him.

"When you paid off the note at Chase," Vincent said, "you got the twenty percent High-Tech shares Chase was holding as collateral. The loan was for fifty percent of market value. So you bought fifty-six percent at the market and got twenty percent more for half-price, for a total of seventy-six percent. In other words," Vincent continued, turning to address the others, "He got ten percent of High-Tech for nothing."

"Correction," said Rand. *You*, the CIA, the United States Government, got ten percent of High-Tech for nothing." His voice assumed once more it's professorial tone:

"All right, when the Enerdyne contract was cancelled, High-Tech stock went down on the market. Solution? Enerdyne reinstates the contract and the stock returns to it's former value. The Agency has lost nothing. *On the contrary,*" Rand smiled as he bore down on those words, rubbing it in, "as I controlled the money paid from Enerdyne to High-Tech, which is now Agency owned, the profits on that contract now go to CIA, as does the profit on the contract between Enerdyne and Voltmaster." Rand's smile broadened into a grin as he looked at the discomfited Kazalakis. "Simple," he said.

Kazalakis grimaced and rubbed his scalp vigorously with his right hand. Abruptly, he stopped rubbing but held on tightly to the top of his head, saying,

"So why the bankruptcy? Who's got the money now? Where did it all go?"

Rand glanced over at the NSC representative. He was writing rapidly in a notebook and scowling as he sought to catch up with Rand's exposition.

"Okay," said Rand, returning his gaze to Kazalakis, "remember where we are. Enerdyne has paid High-Tech. Now, Voltmaster, at my instruction, cancelled it's order with Enerdyne. Enerdyne, which could not sustain a loss that big, promptly went broke. They notified High-Tech that, although the product has been paid for, High-Tech should not ship it to Enerdyne because

Enerdyne is insolvent and it's customer, Voltmaster, has withdrawn. Of course I'm really just communicating with myself, here, for legal purposes. Again at my orders, High-Tech replies to Enerdyne that it doesn't want Enerdyne's property cluttering up High-Tech warehouses, so the property will be sold and whatever is realized sent as a credit to Enerdyne."

"Wait," said the NSC staffer, holding up his hand as if to signal a halt, "hold on for just a minute please." He was scribbling furiously as he spoke. This was worse than the math review class the first year he went for his MBA at Harvard. After a moment he caught up and, with a sigh, leaned back and said, "Okay."

"Was I going too fast for anyone else?" Rand asked, with exaggerated solicitude.

"No? Then bear with me for just a few minutes more and everything should be clear."

"At this point I had Enerdyne file a voluntary petition in bankruptcy and inform the court-appointed referee that there are millions in Enerdyne assets lying in the warehouses of High-Tech. The stockholders of Enerdyne, that is to say the CIA, get fifty cents on the dollar because of the share vs. share value of the merchandise in the warehouses. I then dissolved Voltmaster, at which point you all got excited and had me brought here."

Rand looked at the men before him. They looked numb.

"You *still* don't understand it, do you." It was a statement rather than a question.

"In other words," he said with a sigh of resignation, "I have now done the following for you, even though you are able neither to understand nor appreciate it: One." Rand held up his left hand and grasped his little finger. "I busted out one of your proprietaries, Enerdyne, and took all the money out of it for you."

"Two." Rand grasped the next finger. "The merchandise lying with High-Tech, millions of dollars worth, all belongs to you."

"Three." He grabbed another finger. "The money paid to creditor shareholders of Enerdyne all belongs to and goes to you."

"Four." Rand was down to his index finger now. "Voltmaster, another one of your little horseshit companies, is dissolved and you—not I—*you,* are left owning High-Tech Corporation, a first rate, listed company, once the pride of Howard Hughes, now stronger than ever, and a pisspot full of money."

Kazalakis looked over at Vincent. Vincent nodded his head.

"It works," Vincent said. "When the paper work is all done

we're going to end up owning a major enterprise and be way ahead financially."

"But this was not, was it Mr. Rand," McKenzie asked quietly, "what you were asked to do for us?"

"I beg your pardon?" said Rand. He was puzzled by the frostiness of McKenzie's tone of voice; he had expected praise, not an implied rebuke.

"My recollection of our conversation," said McKenzie, "is that you were asked to accomplish two things for us; neither one of which was the making of money. First, you were asked whether you could fathom the meaning of the notations recovered from Mr. Ballinger's safe. Have you?"

"No," said Rand, "I have not."

Secondly," continued McKenzie, "the point of all the financial maneuvers with which you have just dazzled us was, as I recall, to get you next to Mr. Ballinger so as to find out what, if anything, he is up to and on behalf of whom. Have you anything to report to us on that score?"

Rand brightened. "Yes. I've received an invitation to a party he's throwing next week."

"Where?" asked Kazalakis.

"Here in Washington. The address is somewhere on Massachusetts Avenue, Northwest. I haven't checked it out but it sounds like the embassy row area."

"We know about that one," Kazalakis said. "He gives these little *soirées* from time to time for his Washington 'friends'; people he controls. He makes Tongsun Park and his George Town Club look like the Red Cross. The FBI's been trying to get someone invited for years. We'll get you a rundown on probable other guests. Wait'll they hear we've got someone going in!"

"They better not hear that," snapped Rand. "I'm not working for the FBI. I've got my own job to do. Besides, the Bureau's a sieve. What some moralistic field agent doesn't leak to the press they'll hand over to the first militant who asks for it under the Freedom of Information Act. Get me the rundown, but let them find out about me from the surveillance and come to me. They'll get nothing."

"If you don't mind, Mr. Rand," said McKenzie with one eye on the NSC representative, "I'll continue to run the Central Intelligence Agency until relieved."

"Then run it," Rand replied testily. "In your capacity as director, give me a committment here and now that my role with you will not be disclosed to the FBI, or get yourself another man."

There was absolute silence. No one moved; even the NSC staffer stopped his pen in mid-scratch. Finally, McKenzie said:

"As you wish."

Kazalakis, seeking to relieve the almost palpable tension, said, "It should be quite a blast, Rick. Try to remember you're there on business."

Rand descended from the stage and rubbed the yellow chalk marks off his hands with his handkerchief as he said:

"Do I get to ride back with Shirley Temple, or have you made other plans?"

"We'll get a military driver to run you over to National," said Kazalakis. "You can grab the shuttle."

"Thanks," said Rand. "I'll bet you're the kind of a guy whose girl gets picked up in a limo and rides the subway home."

"Bullshit," said Kazalakis. "Just think about that extra six big ones you made on our dough in thirty days. We're still the ones who got fucked."

# IX

Esther Mary Blaylock had been named by her hard shell Baptist parents to reflect their devotion to the Bible. Like her brothers before her—two of whom survived childhood disease, poverty and deep Appalachian anthracite mines to have families of their own—she bore one name each from the Old and New Testaments.

Not that anyone ever called her by either of them; "Essie-Mae" had been her name for as long as she could remember, and that was eighteen years. She knew she was eighteen years old because she had had an eighteenth birthday just a little while ago when her Ma had give her her first store-boughten doll. Her old one, the one she had loved best, made for her by her Ma years ago, had been all tore up by the puppies. Even now Essie-Mae almost cried when she thought about it.

But she didn't cry. Essie-Mae knew that big girls didn't cry over dolls. They didn't really play with dolls anymore; they got the curse, married and had real live babies of their own. She knew that, but she wasn't sure how they got them. God sent them—she knew that because her Ma told her—but just how God went about it was somethin' her Ma had never gotten around to, replying to questions by saying Essie-Mae wouldn't understand and didn't need to "'till the time comes." It had something to do with sex, she knew, but until a few weeks ago she hadn't known what that was, either. Her Ma got mad when she brought the subject up because it "waren't fittin'."

It was all, thought Essie-Mae, probably because she was "slow." Years ago she had heard that word used to describe her in bits and snatches of conversation it was believed she couldn't overhear. It was why she didn't do well in school and had to stay home; why she could only read the small words in the Good Book and never really do like her Ma and Pa and read from it every day. It was why, until a month ago, she always had to stay home, never going anywhere except to church on Sunday, and why, she guessed, that at eighteen she still loved her dolly, whose name was Christina and who was a princess and very smart.

Not that Essie-Mae didn't know how to do some things; she could cook as good as Ma, and her brothers used to let her shoot their .22 squirrel rifle and Pa's .22 pistol they used to take on the sly. Got so's she could shoot good as them. Better even. And she could sew pretty things and had made clothes for Christina just like the ones other princesses wore in the picture book.

One thing more Essie-Mae knew about herself: she was very pretty; almost as pretty as Christina, who was beautiful. All princesses are beautiful and no one is as pretty as they are. Being pretty was nice, but sometimes it was a problem. It was one of the reasons she had to stay home all the time, because bad people sometimes did bad things to pretty girls, Pa said. She wasn't sure just what.

Essie-Mae Blaylock was happy. The only cloud on that happiness was some homesickness. She missed her Ma and Pa and the miner's cabin that clung to the side of the ravine. She even missed the white-painted wooden church in the holler where Reverend Baker told the scary stories every Sunday about what happened to sinners in Hell. But she only missed those things a little bit, so exciting had her life become in the last month.

Her Pa and Ma had explained it to her: A rich man who had been a sinner up in Washington, D.C., had been born again of the Lord Jesus and was doin' good things to make up for all the bad he done in the past. He sent a man to give Reverend Baker money to fix up the church and build a new parsonage and now he wanted to do something nice for Essie-Mae. The man who give Reverend Baker the money had seen her at the church, he'd said, on Sunday, and heard that she'd never been anywhere or seen anything. Reverend Baker told how she'd come along late and her Ma and Pa were poor now 'cause Pa had trouble breathin' and had to quit the mines.

Ma said the man up in Washington would let her dress up in all kinds of pretty clothes and they would take pictures of her to put in the catalogue and things. She would get to keep lots of the clothes herself to bring home and the clothes would all be decent and fittin' for a good Christian woman. He would see she got to church every Sunday and she could bring Christina with her. The people who took the pictures would send money home to Pa to help out.

Essie-Mae wanted to go. Maybe when she came back her folks would let Adam Morgan call on her. The way it was now, they had to see each other only in church or when she could let on she was going to the privy and see him a little out back. Adam Morgan wanted to marry up with her but her folks wouldn't hear of it. She liked Adam. He made her ache inside, and now that she knew what sex was all about, marriage didn't scare her at all; it would be fun.

Everything promised Essie-Mae came true. She sat in a window seat high up in a house bigger than the church back home. From the window, she could see the church she attended every Sunday since she arrived. It was made of stone and reached to the sky from the top of the hill. It looked like the one she saw in the picture book where princesses went to church.

Essie-Mae had all sorts of pretty clothes now, and they were hers to keep. Mr. Ballinger said so. He was the man who had found Jesus. Mr. Ward, who had driven her up from West Virginia in a car as big as a princess' coach, the one who had talked to her folks and Reverend Baker, told her all about Mr. Ballinger and what a nice man he was.

Her room was beautiful, with a big bed three times the size of her bed at home. There were pretty chintz curtains on the windows and funny openings in the wall where cold air came out so the room was cool, even when it was hot outside. Mr. Ward said that when the weather got cold, warm air would come out the same holes.

They all said she was pretty. At first, when the man who took the pictures came, she was shy. But it made sense for them to take pictures of her body. It was so they could know what kind of clothes to bring; just the way she had to look at her dolly so she would get it right when she made her princess clothes. Now she enjoyed showing off her body. After all, like Mr. Ward said, God give it to her. He made her body and anything He made was something good. It was a good thing to show off the work of God.

Mr. Ward was nice. He was the one who showed her how nice sex is. She had asked him, and he told her that it was something

112

men and women did together that feels good. She knew that much; she wanted to know what. All she had known was that the boy does it to the girl. Adam Morgan had told her that.

Mr. Ward had her take off her clothes and show him her body. It was all really easy and Essie-Mae didn't know why she hadn't figured it out for herself. It was just another way of kissing. Only instead of the boy kissing her lips up *here,* he kissed her lips down *there.* It felt wonderful. She got that ache and couldn't keep still. She loved it. It wasn't long before she got the photographer and Mr. Ballinger to do it to her too. Everybody, Mr. Ballinger explained, did it with people they liked. The men took off their clothes too, and held her and hugged her before and after they did it.

Essie-Mae liked and trusted Mr. Ballinger best of all; he was good to her. He didn't treat her as if she were "slow." He answered any questions she had so's she could understand the answer easily. Like her question about what bad men sometimes do to pretty girls. He told her she was a big girl now and had a right to know such things for her own protection. Essie-Mae was shocked by what he told her. It was awful. Bad men would try to put their pee-pee up inside her. Essie-Mae shivered at the thought of it. To change the subject, she told Mr. Ballinger of Adam Morgan. He said he sounded like a fine boy, but she should meet a number of men who were single so she could choose well.

As he took care of everything else, Mr. Ballinger said he would see to it that she met some goodlooking, unmarried men. The best way, he explained, was at parties. She could meet very important men, have sex with them and, if she decided that she liked one in particular, Mr. Ballinger would see to it that she saw more of him. Any she didn't like would not be asked to any more parties. If nothing else, she would get very good at sex. That, together with her ability to cook and sew, would make it easy to be a good wife to Adam Morgan.

Essie-Mae was excited. Tonight would be her first party. Lots of important people would be there, but Mr. Ballinger had invited one man just for her. He was tall and good looking; very fair, like the princes in the picture book. A lady would help her dress up to look older and more beautiful so she could please him better. Essie-Mae loved to play dress up. She couldn't wait for the party.

Richard Rand stood on the balcony of the fifteenth-floor corner suite he occupied for the night at Washington's L'Enfant Plaza Hotel. The sun was going down and the view, which ranged from the Washington Monument to the Capitol, was of a white city bathed in a pink glow. Nearby were new government office buildings, lights ablaze to reveal their post 5:00 P.M. emptiness, save for an occasional janitorial crew. The air was cool but, typical of early October in Washington, without chill.

From the light flooding through the glass doors into his living-room, Rand read once more the note he had received from Gregory Ballinger. Addressed to him at his home in the Plaza Hotel in New York, it was handwritten in a miniscule but very legible upright script. It said:

Dear Mr. Rand:

On Saturday evening, 11th October, at 8 P.M., I'm having a modest buffet for a few of my friends in Washington; persons you might find it useful to know, and whom I am sure would enjoy meeting you, as would I. I'd also like to take advantage of you to the extent of having you appraise an *object d'art* of a kind that I understand is within an area of your special competence.
Black tie.

Yours sincerely,
Gregory Ballinger

Albanside
Massachusetts Avenue, N.W.
Washington, D.C., 20016

The handwriting was the same as that on the list of foreign corporations from Ballinger's New York office safe that Rand found so maddeningly meaningless. The message was short but well calculated to attract his appearance, Rand acknowledged, with three lures packed into one paragraph: an opportunity to meet Ballinger; an opportunity to meet persons of influence in the Washington community and government, and a thinly veiled appeal to his libido. Curiosity, opportunity and lust; a potent and well-thought-out combination. Ballinger was living up to his reputation. He was confident, too; there was no RSVP.

Rand replaced the note in the pocket of his dressing gown and turned his attention to another document. He held it up to the

114

dying sun. No watermarks on the paper. It was a blind memorandum, but it's distinctive style betrayed it's FBI origin. The memorandum had arrived at his box in the Plaza in a plain manila envelope bearing no return address. The postage was in stamps, not a frank or meter, and the cancellation bore the name of an obscure town in northern Maryland.

The memorandum listed persons by name, occupation and alleged relationship to Ballinger. It included the Chairman of the Senate Subcommittee on Banking, who had acquired a small fortune by being prescient enough to invest in the stock of corporations which, shortly after his purchase, were merged into Comco after a tender offer well above the market.

Also on the list was a United States District Judge for the District of Columbia who was able to indulge his penchant for little boys discreetly and safely, courtesy of Ballinger, and who was believed to have reciprocated at least once with a masterfully-crafted but dubious anti-trust decision; the Assistant Secretary of the Treasury for Tariff and Trade Affairs, a former and future partner in the law firm representing Comco; a congresswoman and the wife of a senator whose lesbian love affair was accomodated by the ability to vacation on the same Ballinger-owned island in the Bahamas used to accomodate the Judge; a network news producer believed to favor Ballinger interests by selective reporting and editing in exchange for accurate leaks and otherwise difficult *entré*. Then there were the GS-18 career bureaucrats: A senior purchasing specialist, Department of the Navy and an associate deputy general counsel of the Internal Revenue Service. Both were believed able to count on positions at double their salary with Comco upon retirement. Both were valuable sources of information about the activities of their respective agencies. The employee of the Navy had a large appetite for women and his sexual preferences were considered unremarkably heterosexual; not so the IRS man, who required to be *en position voyeur* to achieve tumescence.

The memorandum concluded by noting that Ballinger had small affairs like that scheduled for this evening from time to time in Washington, New York, London, Paris, Hamburg and Rome. Some were elaborate costume parties; all reportedly catered to the one thing the guests had in common other than a relationship with Ballinger: prurience. The same persons might attend the large galas Ballinger also held, but the other guests would be typical "Green Book" types and the evening quite conventional. That he had been invited to the more intimate of Ballinger's affairs Rand considered a plus in his effort to get close enough to the man to acquire significant information.

Rand committed the names to memory, then left the balcony to bathe and dress for the evening. At seven-thirty he stepped into a big Checker cab obtained for him by the doorman and settled back for the half-hour ride through downtown Washington and up Massachusetts Avenue to Albanside, nestled in the lee of the highest point in the District of Columbia, Mount St. Alban, site of the National Cathedral.

Albanside was a massive, cut-stone mansion set well back from the Avenue. One approached and departed through separate wrought iron gates at either end of a circular drive leading through a *porte-cochère* illuminated by a great iron lamp hanging from the ceiling and secured against the wind by four iron chains. The front doors were of double height, and when Rand stepped into the vestibule at the request of a powerfully-built Oriental doorman, he could see why; even the vestibule ceiling was nearly twenty feet high.

At the interior door of the vestibule, Gregory Ballinger was waiting to greet him. Ballinger was taller than Rand, but thinner; almost ascetic. He had a thick shock of iron-gray hair and equally thick eyebrows to match. He reminded Rand of Oliver Wendell Holmes without the mustache. His complexion was tanned but still looked unhealthy as it was stretched tautly over the skull beneath so that facial tendons and major blood vessels were readily apparent. The hand that clasped Rand's was large and bony; it's grip strong. Ballinger's voice was low and well modulated as he said:

"Good evening, Mr. Rand. I'm Gregory Ballinger. You are very prompt. I'm so glad you could join us. Come in and let me introduce you to some friends of mine."

Ballinger didn't wait for Rand to reply, just turned and guided him from the vestibule into a huge room. The room extended the entire width of the house and was dominated by a staircase opposite the vestibule and across an expanse of forty feet. The staircase led upward to a wide landing from which, at either side, separate staircases climbed back and up in the opposite direction.

The right wall was devoted to a walk-in sized Tudor stone fireplace. Opposite it, in the left wall eighty-five feet away, four sets of french doors twelve feet high led out to a flagstone porch thirty by forty feet in size and bordered by a columned balustrade. The porch was half covered by a large awning; the rest was open to the sky. It overlooked an expanse of stone driveway extension and four-car garage, a large, graveled auxiliary parking area, lawn, flower beds and woods shared with the grounds of St. Albans School. The sharing was merely visual, however, thanks to a nine-foot-high stone peripheral wall.

On either side of the staircase, and cut through the rear wall of the room, were wide archways. Through the one on the left Rand could see an interior hall off which opened the doors to other rooms, one of them a library. The archway on the right led into a dining room whose table was set for a splendid buffet.

The floor under Rand's feet was covered by a vast Kirman-Lavehr rug of elaborately fluid design and soft colors that filled the room with a sense of warmth and opulence. Toward the walls, where the rug didn't reach, exposed parquet flooring of hand-fitted contrasting woods gleamed in reflected light through a coat of well-buffed wax. A chandelier containing a thousand antique cut crystal prisms flashed light throughout the room. When Rand glanced upward to admire it, he noticed that the interplay of refractions created miniature rainbows from prism to prism.

"It is a beauty, isn't it?" said Ballinger.

"Remarkable!"

"I had it made in Austria. Those prisms were salvaged from World War II bomb damage all over Europe. The designer was a genius to be able to make a coherent whole of it."

"He was indeed."

"I try to do the same thing in an entirely different genre."

"Comco."

"I thought you'd understand."

Ballinger escorted Rand from person to person, introducing him. The other guests, for the most part, betrayed no indication they had ever heard of Rand. He felt they accepted him as one bearing Ballinger's imprimatur. There was one man there to whom Rand was not introduced, nor had he been listed in the blind memorandum. A middle-aged Oriental, he seemed oddly out of place in occidental formal wear. He was standing near the staircase, almost like a sentinel. As he completed his tour of the room, Ballinger excused himself after asking Rand to make himself at home, then disappeared in the direction of the library. Rand busied himself with small talk, drifting from guest to guest, picking up an occasional glass of champagne from a tray held by a passing waiter.

Rand began to feel uneasy, as if something were out of place. He realized, finally, what was troubling him: he had arrived promptly at the appointed hour of eight—Ballinger had even commented on it. Yet, in the forty-five minutes which had elapsed since his arrival, not one other guest had appeared. Rand had been there on the dot, but every other guest had been there when he arrived. He didn't like it.

While musing upon the possible meanings of his realization, Rand was interrupted by Ballinger's voice, speaking from behind him.

"Ah, there you are, Rand."

Rand turned around. Ballinger stood there with a smile of anticipation on his face, studying Rand. At Ballinger's side and holding onto his arm was a woman Rand judged to be about twenty-two. She was five feet seven, and one hundred twenty-odd pounds. Jet black hair was worn in a shoulder length under-curl. It matched the black velvet of her floor length backless and strapless dress. The whiteness of her throat, shoulders and back looked as if it would be cool to the touch. Black velvet gloves that ran to her elbows and flared concealed her arms. If she wore any makeup, it had been applied so skillfully as to be nearly undetect-able. She smiled hesitantly, but enough to uncover flawless white teeth. She was, Rand thought, one of the most beautiful women he had ever seen.

"Mr. Rand," said Ballinger, "I'd like to present that *object d'art* I mentioned in my note, Miss Esther Blaylock. Essie, this is the gentleman I told you about, Mr. Rand. He will take you in to dinner."

Without waiting for a reply from either of them, Ballinger walked away and joined another group in conversation.

"Hi," said Essie-Mae.

"Hi yourself, Esther. I take it we'll be dining soon?"

"I reckon so. See? It's in there." Essie-Mae pointed through the archway at the heavily-laden dining room table.

"Don't it look good!"

"It certainly does, and so do you. What do you do?"

"I'm a model. An' you can call me Essie-Mae; ever' body does."

"Whatever you prefer," said Rand. The word "model" explained a lot to Rand about Essie-Mae. He'd once met one who in dress, bearing and surroundings was the quintessence of sophistication—until she opened her mouth. Her first sentence made Holliday's "Born Yesterday" portrayal sound like that of a Vassar graduate. It was all right with Rand. Recreational sex was recreational sex and Rand had bedded many an air-head in the past. None had matched the beauty of Essie-Mae. There was, at least, one area of kinship between them; Essie-Mae was hungry and Rand was famished. The announcement that supper was available in the diningroom came just in time. With unabashed quickness, he and Essie-Mae moved into position at the head of the line.

For the next thirty-five minutes, Rand and Essie-Mae occupied themselves with Ballinger's repast. Rand took pleasure in identifying for Essie-Mae the more exotic dishes. It was fun, for example, to watch her face register unrestrained revulsion at his description, highly colored and exaggerated for her benefit, of an octopus. She even turned away so as not to be able to see when he ate a piece. "Oh," she cried, "how can you *do* that!"

At the end of the diningroom table was an assortment of desserts. As Rand had had his hands full just trying to manage all there was for supper without trying to take on dessert, he had put it off until they were ready. He had already made up his mind in favor of the baked alaska when he asked Essie-Mae:

"Well, young lady, what would you like now? Baked alaska?"

Essie-Mae shook her head vigorously and grinned at him.

"Chocolate mousse?"

Another shake of the head. Her grin was now positively impish. Perhaps, Rand thought, she didn't know what those dishes were. He tried again:

"Baked Alaska is mostly iced cream. Do you like iced cream?"

Essie-Mae started to giggle.

"Well," said Rand, beginning to run out of patience, "why don't you just tell me what you'd like and we'll see if I can get it for you?"

Barely able to suppress her giggling, Essie-Mae leaned over to Rand and whispered in his ear,

"I'd like some sex!"

Though a bit taken aback, Rand recovered enough to reply,

"That's a very good idea and I'll keep it in mind for later on, but this hardly seems the time or the place."

Essie-Mae stood up and took Rand by the hand. Her voice had the urgency of childish enthusiasm.

"Come with me!"

She led him out the archway and toward a small door under the main staircase where it joined the rear wall of the livingroom. At the touch of her finger to a button, the door slid open noiselessly to reveal a small elevator. She pulled him in and pressed another button. The door slid closed and she pulled across the opening a brass folding gate. As the gate latched, the elevator rose slowly, stopping a few moments later. After the girl operated the gate again, Rand found himself on an upper floor in a large center hall. Essie-Mae led him through another door into her bedroom.

"Isn't it pretty?" she asked with obvious pride.

"It's very nice, but people will be wondering where we are. It's still quite early."

"Foo on them!" she said, peeling off her long gloves, "Let's take off our clothes."

Essie-Mae didn't wait for Rand to agree, she started to unzip her dress. When it fell to the floor she was completely naked, and the sight of her neutralized years of experience for Rand. He could have been seventeen again, so affected was he by her youthful physical perfection.

Essie-Mae decided to show off her body. She could tell the powerful effect it was having on Rand; she had noticed the same effect on Mr. Ward. She went into some of the poses they had taught her in the photography sessions. The effect upon Rand was immediate; he came out of his trance and started to undress. Quickly.

The couple's departure had not gone unnoticed. On the contrary, as soon as the elevator door had closed behind them the other guests, as if returning to theatre seats after an intermission, began to gather in front of the massive stairway with a murmer of anticipation; most were grinning, some had started laughing already.

As if on cue, for indeed it was on cue, Gregory Ballinger appeared from the library, waving his arms and shushing them.

"Quiet! Quiet, please. I must ask that you discipline yourselves. Remember, this must not seem at all funny; quite the contrary.

The man is no fool. The girl will take him in because she is genuine, but he'll tumble immediately at the first hint of a smile, let alone a laugh. So quiet, please. There's nothing to do now but wait."

Upstairs, Essie-Mae was shuddering in the throes of orgasm. Rand, a thoughtful lover experienced at foreplay, had raised Essie-Mae's appreciation of cunnilingus to a higher order, but was beginning to regret it. She was, he was sure, going to pull every hair out of his head.

It was some minutes later, while Gregory Ballinger was glancing impatiently at his watch and wondering what could have gone wrong, that Essie-Mae's first scream filled the mansion. Ballinger had made a point of instructing his guests not to run upstairs immediately, as too soon an arrival might tip off Rand. He needn't have bothered. Essie-Mae's cry, even though expected, was so expressive of horror and revulsion that it froze in mid-breath all who heard it. Her second scream was intelligible; a series of emphatic "NO!"s followed by a long, pitiful, *"Help* me! Oh, *some*body, *Please!"*

The effect was to galvanize Ballinger and his guests. As one they rushed up the stairs.

They found Essie-Mae in the hallway outside her room. She was sitting on the floor, naked, her knees pulled up to her chest, arms clasped around her legs, head down, rocking slowly back and forth, crying.

"Momma," she sobbed, "Momma; oh, dirty, dirty, dirty. Oh, Momma . . ."

Rand stood naked in the open doorway to Essie-Mae's room, leaning against the door frame and looking utterly bewildered.

The lesbian member of the House of Representatives hovered over Essie-Mae protectively. "Somebody," she commanded, "get a blanket!" Reaching down, she put her hands into Essie-Mae's underarms and guided her gently to her feet. Turning her around, she hugged the girl to her, saying:

"What is it, baby? What happened?"

Essie-Mae, still wracked by sobs, could get out only

"Bad things—dirty. I wa-want to go ho-*home!"*

The middle-aged Oriental appeared with a robe. The Congresswoman guided Essie-Mae to one side and helped her into it.

"Of course you may go home, my dear," Ballinger said to her. "I'll have Mr. Ward drive you there right away. Tonight. You can take your dolly, and we'll pack up all your pretty things and send them to you tomorrow." Turning to Rand, he barked,

"For God's sake, man, get some clothes on. And then I think you've got some explaining to do!"

Rand sensed that he was sinking deeper and deeper into a mire but could think of nothing more sensible to do than comply with Ballinger's order to dress. As he did so, he felt a growing sense of rage. Essie-Mae was completely ingenuous; no one could have faked her horror, loathing and rejection. What was more, as he had recoiled from his attempt at penetration when she screamed, she had pommeled him with surprising strength as she shouted "No" and "Dirty" at him. The blows hurt.

He had been had. It was all coming together; the fact that no one arrived after he did, even though he was precisely on time; the small number of guests, as few people could be relied upon to participate in so infantile and sick a joke. The entire evening had been a number on him by Ballinger; a deliberate, and successful, attempt to humiliate him publicly. It created the kind of story which would follow him, dog him, for years to come.

Rand finished dressing. He didn't bother with his tie, just stuffed it into his trousers pocket. He was aware that the hall was now empty as he tied his shoelaces and, filled with anger, left the room and trotted rapidly down the stairs.

Laughter greeted Rand as he was seen on the landing; mocking, derisive, humiliating laughter. The only one who wasn't laughing was Ballinger; he just stood apart with a faint smile on his face. As Rand got to the third step from the bottom, Ballinger spoke:

"There he is, ladies and gentlemen: Ricky Rand, playboy and entrepeneur. Renowned worldwide as a lover and financial genius. Yes, that's right, financial genius. Recently took over a company I controlled after going to a great deal of unnecessary trouble."

Rand stopped, seething, to hear Ballinger out.

"Such a waste of time, Mr. Rand. Why didn't you just ask me for it? I'd have given it to you to play with for as long as you were able. You'd have had to give it back rather soon, of course, as I'm quite sure your reputation for finance is as overblown as your reputation as a lover. After all, a man in his forties who can't even make love to a retarded teenage girl without traumatizing her!"

The entire assembly burst out in appreciative laughter. Rand, trembling with the effort to control himself, said:

"You're disgusting, Ballinger, you know that? Completely degenerate! Whatever your quarrel with me, nothing could justify the way you used that girl. I don't know what sick, filthy things you did to her to get her to react like that, but she didn't deserve them. And for nothing but a *joke!*"

"My dear Mr. Rand," said Ballinger, his voice rendered more smooth than ever by its heavy coating of patronizing disparagement, "you continue to disappoint me by your lack of wit. You see you still don't even *get* the joke. Do you?"

Rand could think of nothing to say.

"No," continued Ballinger, "you don't."

Ballinger was warming to his task, becoming expansive in his delight with his own cleverness.

"The joke," Ballinger continued, "isn't really on you at all; not, at least, the ultimate joke. You see I not only used her to play a little joke on you, but I used *you* to play one on *her*. Of the two of you, *you*, Mr. Rand, are the simpleton. The ultimate joke will come when our little heroine, finally over her shock at the depravity you attempted to inflict upon her this evening, marries some nice young man she loves and trusts completely, only to discover, on her wedding night, that he is every bit as depraved as you when he tries to perform the identical unnatural act. Isn't it perfect, Mr. Rand? Can't you appreciate the *symmetry* of it all?"

Rand could, and it was too much for him to bear. With an unintelligible roar of rage he launched himself at Ballinger from the height advantage of the third step. It was a clumsy and predictable move. Ballinger merely stepped aside like a matador and Rand hurtled past, landing running in the middle of the vast persian rug. He turned to face Ballinger and try again but Ballinger wasn't there. Before him instead was the silent Oriental, blocking his way.

"Get out of my way, old man!" Rand growled. The oriental remained motionless and impassive.

"I warned you!" Rand said, and shot out a left jab.

With a fluidity of motion that would have made Nureyev seem an oaf by comparison, the Oriental executed a little dance step, his arm swooped up in a smooth block that continued around to block the next jab and the next. Rand was moving as fast as he could, to no avail. The Oriental, on the other hand, seemed languorous in his motion.

Rand paused in his futile efforts to strike his opponent. At that moment the Oriental whipped his arms over his head, graceful hands held pointed down like *banderillas*. Before Rand could react, the hands struck downward and sharp fingernails cut him just above each eye. Ballinger made a gesture of dismissal and the lesbian lovers moved to the vestibule. The congresswoman opened the vestibule door and the senator's wife held open the great front door to the mansion.

Rand tried a feint with his left and a right to the body of his tormentor. The older man pirouetted, grasped the crossing right and accelerated it, spinning Rand around completely. As he faced the door, Rand felt a lifting of his left elbow and a simultaneous blow to his lower spine. The blow struck a nerve ganglion. The effect was to propel Rand, who felt at that moment as if he were weightless, into a running, stumbling, off-balanced rush out the front door, only to fall down the steps of the porte-cochere and land, face down, in the sharp gravel. Behind him he heard Gregory Ballinger's voice say:

"Good evening, Mr. Rand."

Rand struggled to rise. As he did so he heard another burst of laughter and the sound of the front door closing with a solid, final, thud. Blood was in his eyes. Then came the final humiliation as Rand realized that he was out in front of Ballinger's home, beaten, and on his knees.

# X

T'sa Li studied the sheet of plain white bond paper Richard Rand had handed to her. On the bottom it bore the inked impression of a rubber stamp that read:

*The Washington Star*
page *D-1*
Oct 13 7

The *D-1* was written in ink. The date stamp was slightly askew and the last digit smeared. Above the stamp, stapled to the center of the piece of paper, there was a newspaper clipping. It was captioned *The EAR*, and the first item in the column read:

UNEXPECTED TRIP . . . *Absolument Le Tout*, 'wigs, is wondering just what new wrinkle in *l'art d'amour* proved positively *too much* for the sweet young partner of Diviner Ricky Rand during Saturday night's *soirée intime* at Albanside, *Conglamarateur Extraordinaire* Greg Ballinger's Mass. Ave. manse tucked cozily next to the grounds of WASPier Than Thou St. Albans School. Ear hears that hot pilot Ricky flew out the front door on other than his own power and crash-landed on the driveway. Really, darlings, *where are standards?*

T'sa Li was smiling as she finished reading.
"It isn't funny," Rand said with some peevishness.
T'sa Li put the paper down on the small table beside her end of the sofa, stretched her legs out toward Rand who sat on the opposite end, and poked him with a stockinged toe.
"C'mon, boy, where's your sense of humor?"

"You think that's funny? What they did to that poor girl? How can you laugh at a thing like that!"

"God, you're touchy!" replied T'sa Li, "Of course I don't think what happened to the girl was funny. It was cruel. Very cruel. I was laughing at the article. There's an old Chinese saying, 'He who plays hardball must expect from time to time to get hit by foul tip.' "

T'sa Li turned off the table lamp by which she had been reading and the room illumination returned once more to the soft light from the flames flickering over seasoned hickory in the fireplace.

"You've been sulking up here for a week," T'sa Li observed. "Where'd you get the clipping?"

The fire brightened momentarily as a sharp, cool wind whipped over the chimney jutting out of the multi-gabled roof of the Plaza, creating a sudden increase in draft. Rand looked into the fire as he said:

"I haven't been sulking; I've been working. I've also been letting my face heal. The gravel scratches are gone but those cuts over my eyes have just had the stitches out. A quarter of an inch lower and I'd have been blind. A friend of mine in Washington sent me the clipping."

Rand made a face as he spoke the word "friend." The clipping had come by mail with a small note in Kazalakis' handwriting stapled to it saying, "What do we do now, Coach—punt?"

Rand dropped his hand onto T'sa Li's foot where it still rested against his hip, squeezed it and gave it a little wiggle from side to side. He looked over at her and said, apologetically,

"Hon, I need a couple of favors."

T'sa Li frowned. "You're not planning on doing something foolish, are you? There's a *real* Chinese saying that 'He who embarks on a voyage of revenge should first dig *two* graves.' "

"What I'm planning isn't foolish. I've got a job to do that I was given before that business with the girl came up, and I'm going to do it. My problem is lack of information. If I did anything now I'd be moving in the dark and that *would* be foolish. I've gone as far as I can with my own resources and I need help."

"My help?"

"And your brother's."

T'sa Li drew her foot back slowly, swung around and sat facing the fire. Watching the play of the flames, she said,

126

"You know I'll do anything for you I can. My brother is something else again." She turned to look at Rand. "Maybe you better tell me about it."

Rand reached a hand behind his neck and rubbed it vigorously.

"Yeah," he said after a pause, "maybe I should."

Picking up the two empty crystal snifters from the low table in front of the sofa, Rand went to the sideboard, picked up a bottle and held its label to the firelight. Satisfied that the bottle contained Fundador, he poured two ounces of the smooth Spanish brandy into each glass and returned.

"Remember," he said, "that day last Spring I got the call early in the morning? Well, that started it. . . ."

Rand took T'sa Li through the whole story, omitting only the events at Ballinger's party as he had related them to her before giving her the clipping to read. Now she had the context. He concluded by giving voice once more to his frustration at not being able to make anything of the note from Ballinger's safe. By the time he finished speaking, their glasses were again empty.

"Let me see it," said T'sa Li.

"See what?"

"The piece of paper from the safe. Do you have it here?"

"I've got a xerox. Wait a minute."

Rand went into his bedroom and extracted the paper from his briefcase. He turned to go back to the living room but found T'sa Li standing in the doorway, legs outlined through her negligée by the firelight behind her. She walked over to the bed table and switched on the lamp, then sat herself cross-legged on the bed and held out her hand. Rand handed her the copy of the note. "Those percentage figures," he said, "could be either—"

"Shhhhh!" T'sa Li held up her hand in the universal signal to halt. "Don't prejudice me with your thoughts. These things are like puzzles. It all depends on how you view them."

T'sa Li stared intently at the paper. Presently she said, "Okay. Now tell me what you were going to say."

"I was just going to say," said Rand, "that the percentage figures could be either a position in the stock of each company, or a target position, or a market percentage. Either way, it doesn't really tell us anything."

"Is there anything different now about any of these companies? I mean, since you got this? Anything you haven't told me about?"

"No. Wait a minute, I take it back. There was something in the newspaper today."

Rand went back into the living room and came back with a copy of *The Wall Street Journal.* He opened it to the third page and pointed to an article that announced the signing of a contract between Stresso, Sp. A., and Columbia Steel. Details were not released, but the deal was said to be in the high millions and of obvious help in reducing the U.S. balance of payments deficit. T'sa Li read it carefully, then commanded,

"Get me a pencil."

Rand looked down for a moment at the wine-colored dressing gown he was wearing until it registered upon him that he was unlikely to find a pencil there, then rummaged around once again in his briefcase until he produced a pencil and gave it to T'sa Li.

T'sa Li patted the bed beside her in invitation and Rand sat down next to her. "Look," she said, holding the paper out so he could see it too.

"Beautiful," said Rand, ignoring the proffered paper to stare into T'sa Li's negligée where it had fallen open to reveal her left breast fully. She looked up, caught him at it, and pulled the garment together.

"Don't be a wise guy. Watch."

T'sa Li took the pencil and drew a line under the last of the percentage figures on the list. They now resembled a problem in elementary school arithmetic. She glanced at the column and wrote the sum beneath the line she had drawn.

"Fifty," announced T'sa Li. "And, as all the figures in the column have a percentage sign after them, the rule is put the same sign after the sum. Fifty percent."

"Sure," said Rand, "but fifty percent of what?"

"Those three companies," T'sa Li asked, "Metz, Mazatlan and Stresso—how much of Columbia's capacity did their contracts amount to?"

"It wasn't released."

"Then find out. If those three match these percentages, you have your answer."

"Answer to what? What's the connection to Ballinger? What does it mean?"

"I don't know. But if my guess is right, and that's what it means —capacity—you know more now than you did five minutes ago."

"Yeah, I guess that's something. And I can find that out. But there's still something in the back of my mind about that list that's driving me nuts. Something that'll make it all add up!"

"Don't press," said T'sa Li, "if it's there, it'll come to you. Now, anything more *I* can do for you before we talk about my brother?"

"Yes. That girl. I can't just let it go like that. What happened is bad enough without letting what that sonofabitch said come true—that part about her marrying some poor *schmuck* and—"

"I understand," said T'sa Li. "What do you want me to do?"

"Her name is Blaylock; Esther Mary Blaylock. About all I learned from her before it happened is that she came from an area called Jeffersonville. It's in West Virginia. The nearest place of any size is Fairmont. Find her, see if you can talk her parents into letting you put her into a special school. Ballinger said she's retarded. Tell them it's an experimental government program or something. I'll underwrite it. What d'you say?"

"I'll give it a try, but even if I *can* find her, it'll be tough. They're going to be gun shy, and apart from that—I guess what I'm trying to say is that's pretty ingrown territory and they don't take to strangers. Now here I come, old slant-eyes herself, and—I mean, why me? Why not just hire a local private detective?"

"Because I'd have to explain what happened for it to make any sense, for him to know how to handle it. I'm not ready for that yet, it's too damn—"

"It's okay," T'sa Li interrupted, putting her hand over his and looking directly up into his eyes. "I understand. I'll do what I can. It may turn out to be nothing, but at least you'll know you tried."

"Thanks," said Rand, "but they don't pay off on trying. I'll give you a check."

"No. Wait. I'll tell you what I've spent when I've done what I can."

"Thanks, hon."

"Wait on that, too, 'till I've done something. Now, what do you want with my brother?"

"Look, please don't be offended, but you remember you told me you weren't a member of a 'family' except in the usual sense of the word? Well, that's not my understanding about your brother. From what my Italian in-laws tell me, the name T'ang Li is one to be reckoned with in the Tongs."

T'sa Li looked down at her hands, studying them. "And what if it is?"

"My relatives," Rand replied carefully, "belong to a confederation of members of their ethnic group exerting influence in Sicily, Italy, the United States, Canada and, to a much lesser degree, in a few places in the U.K. and Europe. For their numbers, they do well enough, but there are just not that many Italians."

Rand got up and looked through his bedroom window at the Manhattan night. "I've done some checking," he said. "Wholly apart from mainland China, there are twenty-two million Chinese in Asia; more than a million in North and South America; a quarter of a million in the cities of Europe; about a hundred thousand in Africa and seventy-five thousand scattered throughout the South Pacific. In every one of those overseas Chinese communities, the Tongs are active. All of those Tongs are allied in a confederation for the same purposes as the Italians: to moderate disputes and for mutual aid against outsiders."

Turning away from the window, Rand moved back to the bed, reached out and took T'sa Li's chin in his hand. He turned her head so he could look directly into her eyes.

"I am told," he said carefully and distinctly, "that your brother, T'ang Li, is high in the hierarchy of that umbrella confederation, the consolidated Tongs of the world." Rand spoke even more distinctly: "I am told that in matters of internal discipline, your brother is the most feared of men."

T'sa Li took Rand's hand away from her chin abruptly and gestured toward the window.

"You can hear anything you want to out there. I've heard the same thing, but never to my face, and never from my brother. It may or may not be true. I don't know. As I told you, I'm not a member of any such organization and I'd be the last one my brother would discuss something like that with. As to what I believe, that's something else. I won't lie to you. I think he *is* with the Tongs. That's one of the reasons I'm reluctant to have you meet him."

"Why?"

"You're an outsider. My brother has little to do with the occidental community himself, unless it's to meet a threat. He's very bright and learned to speak English well in Hong Kong, but he never had the educational advantages I did. He's much older. I'm the baby. His sister. And he's very old fashioned."

"In what way?"

"In the worst way possible, from my point of view. It's about you and me. We're not married. I'm not even bound to you in concubinage."

"He'd want *that?*"

"You don't understand. He doesn't look at things with western eyes. To be married is best, but concubinage at least brings with it a certain security. To his mind I have given up everything I have to offer a man and received nothing in return. He loves me but he doesn't understand me."

"What's he think of me?"

"He *thought* of you as an exploiter. The only reason you're still alive is my mother."

"Your mother? Not you?" Rand chuckled as he said it.

"It's nothing to laugh about. My brother is a red belt master. His art is the high T'ai Chi; his style, that of the tiger. He came by that rank in the traditional manner of our people. Do you know how one becomes a red belt master?"

"I suppose by passing a series of tests."

"You might call it that. It is arranged by the priests when they believe a challenger is worthy. A red belt master of any art may be challenged. There is a ceremony. The priests lock the two in a small room and they fight. To the death. There are only six red belt masters in the world. You owe your life to my mother."

Rand sat on the bed and stared at T'sa Li. She wasn't kidding. Seeing the effect upon Rand of what she had told him, T'sa Li smiled, shrugged her shoulders and let her gown slip down into a pile of chiffon around her hips. She tossed her head back, flipping her blue-black hair around her bare shoulders and raising her naked breasts toward him.

"After all my mother has done for you," she said, "don't you think you ought to take advantage of it?"

"Jesus!" said Rand, still under the spell of her narrative, "I'm not sure I can get it up with you any more. I mean, Christ, right in the middle of everything I'd be half expecting your brother to come smashing in here to do something exotic, like toss me over his shoulder and bite my nuts off in mid air."

T'sa Li lifted her buttocks a few inches off the bed, stripped off her negligée, wadded it up in a ball and threw it at him.

"Any more crap out of you," she said, "and that's just what I'll have him do!"

Rand grinned, grabbed the bedspread at one end, gave it a fast flip and rolled her up inside it in a ball.

T'sa Li wriggled around in her cloth prison struggling to free herself.

"Let me out of here, damn you," she yelped. "I've got claustrophobia!"

"I don't care if you've got gonorrhea," said Rand, freeing her, "I'm gonna fuck you anyway!"

T'sa Li was still asleep when Rand emerged from the shower, pulled a towel around his waist and entered the bedroom. His morning run had been as bracing as only sharp, clear fall air can make it and he felt at his peak. "Rise and shine!" he said.

T'sa Li groaned and rolled from her side over onto her back. Grasping the pillow beneath her head with both hands, she whipped it out from under her and put it over her face to block out the world of wakefulness. "Murrunf!" she mumbled from under it. Rand pulled the cover off her with a grin and started dressing. T'sa Li tried to tough it out, lying naked in the chill breeze from the open window, then gave up as the cold raised goose pimples up and down her body. Tossing the pillow away to her right she shot upright and hugged herself.

"Bastard," she said. Then, noticing that the pillow had knocked over a framed photograph on the back of the night table, she reached to pick it up.

"I hadn't noticed this before," she said. "My, you are vain, aren't you?"

Rand, who was tucking his shirttail into his trousers, paused: "Vain?"

"Not many men keep a picture of themselves in their bedroom."

T'sa Li examined the photograph. It was black and white. The blond, uniformed figure was younger, the hair much shorter. A medal of some kind hung at his throat. The uniform was unfamiliar, but then to T'sa Li one uniform was pretty much like another.

"You look well in uniform," T'sa Li said. She glanced at Rand. "Age hasn't hurt you any. Especially the eyes; they're just the same. What did you get the medal for?"

Something in Rand's posture alerted her. He was frozen in an awkward position, one hand holding up his still open trousers, the other down inside, pushing down his shirt.

"Is something the matter?" she asked.

"No," said Rand, starting slowly to move again. "That's not my medal. There were only about a dozen or so ever awarded."

"What is it? Why were you wearing it?"

"I wasn't. That's the Knight's Cross of the Iron Cross, with oak leaves, swords and diamonds. The uniform is 1943 *Luftwaffe.* That's a picture of my father. It's all I have of him."

"I'm sorry."

"No need to be. He's wearing that medal because he was one of the greatest fighter pilots the world has ever known."

"What was he like?"

Rand turned away to tie his tie in the mirror.

"I don't know. I never got a chance to find out. I've read everything there is to read about him, and there's quite a lot. I know what he was like as a pilot. As a father, I just don't know."

Rand turned to face her as he put on his jacket. "Maybe it's just as well," he said. "All my life I've been able to make him just what I wanted him to be."

"What do you want him to be now?"

"What *he* wanted to be; the best fighter pilot in the world."

"Then you both must be content."

"Yes. I just wish I'd had a chance to talk to him in other than my mind."

Rand, uncomfortable, changed the subject. "You have a gorgeous body, but the management isn't going to take kindly to you walking out of here stark naked."

"Oh!" said T'sa Li, startled out of her musings, "I'll just be a minute." She gathered herself together and fled into the bathroom.

Rand was not optimistic about T'sa Li's ability to dress in "a minute." He used the enforced delay to telephone a securities analyst for Brown Brothers, Harriman, who moonlighted discreetly, and asked him the details of the three Columbia Steel foreign contracts. His friend promised to call back.

As a result of his week-long study of the Ballinger empire, Rand was even more impressed by the strength of Comco and frustrated in his search for a way to strike a crippling economic blow against Ballinger. As these thoughts were going through Rand's head, T'sa Li, fresh and dressed in a light gray tailored suit, large-brimmed black hat, black kid pumps and handbag, entered the living room and joined him.

"Nifty," said Rand appreciatively, "very nifty indeed."

"Thank you, sir, she said," said T'sa Li. "Well, into the lion's, or, I should say, tiger's den!"

"If you think this is a bad time to interrupt your brother," said Rand, "we could make an appointment or something."

"There is no good time to interrupt my brother." said T'sa Li. "We might as well get it over with. Besides, I told you that my mother has smoothed things over considerably."

"The impression you gave me was that your mother was responsible for your brother not blowing me away. That doesn't mean he's very likely to give me the time of day."

"Oh, don't be such a 'fraidy cat. I was teasing you a little anyway. Mother explained it to him in terms of cultural differences and a matter of my own choice. He's as grateful as we are for what you did for us all, you know, and feels a debt of honor toward you, if the truth were told. He's gotten used to the idea. I think he chalks it up to another of the inevitably disastrous results of educating women. Come on."

T'ang Li's "den," a training room located in the basement of the same building complex as housed T'sa Li, her mother, brother and assorted enterprises, was reached by the same restaurant elevator used to gain their living quarters. As the cage moved downward, T'sa Li said:

"The elevator opens right into his training room. If he's doing anything, just step out and stand still. Don't move. Even if his back's to us, he'll know we're there. Don't interrupt whatever he's doing. He'll notice us when he's ready."

"Don't worry," said Rand, "I won't even breathe."

The cage stopped. When the door opened, they stepped outside and stood still. The room was small for a gym, perhaps thirty by thirty feet, Rand estimated. The walls and the ceiling, about fifteen feet high, were painted white. A hard rubber mat of pieces that interlocked like a jigsaw puzzle covered the floor. Rand had seen similar mats in health club weight-training rooms.

There were only three fixtures in the room, and they were identical: In the center of the room three poles ran from floor to ceiling. If looked upon from above, they would appear to be placed at the three angles of an equilateral triangle. Each was about the diameter of a telephone pole and covered with leather over hard rubber. The distance between each pole was a bit more than the width through the shoulders of a very broad-shouldered man. That the poles were hard surfaced and set very firmly into the floor and ceiling was apparent from the way they were being used by the sole occupant of the room.

Standing stock still, the figure of T'ang Li could properly be described as massive. He was six feet, six inches tall and had the shoulders of a football tackle whose hobby since birth had been bodybuilding. "Stock still," however, was a state in which it seemed T'ang Li would be found rarely. His body was animated by a restless energy which, because so well controlled by the discipline of his martial art, manifested itself in a dynamism producing a tension so great it was almost palpable. Watching him, Rand was fascinated.

T'ang Li was moving between the three poles with feline grace and extraordinary speed. It was T'ang Li's ability to start and stop moving, however, that was most remarkable. He moved in controlled bursts between frozen, split second pauses, as if illuminated by stroboscopic light. His body seemed to expand and contract repeatedly as he flashed through and among the three poles, his feet and fists striking them in passing so quickly that the sound of their impact seemed to lag behind his blows. And that sound was awesome; it and the appearance of T'ang Li was so suggestive of invincible strength that Rand forgot he was flesh and blood and from the smashing sound of his blows found it hard to believe the solid poles could stand much more of such an onslaught. The crunching blows were the only sound in the room. There were none of the usual shouts and grunts; Rand couldn't even hear T'ang Li breathe. There was nothing but the remorseless, rapid fire smashing of the helpless poles.

Rand couldn't be sure how long it was before T'ang Li flew backward through the air from the third pole, delivering a blow from each fist and foot to the other two poles as he passed between them, spun in mid-air and landed soundlessly on his feet directly before Rand and T'sa Li. He towered over the two of them, even as he bowed to Rand.

"My brother," said T'sa Li in English, "may I present to you my friend, Richard Rand."

"I am honored to meet one who was so helpful to my mother, my sister and to me. You have my thanks. I am in your debt."

Rand bowed. Not an oriental bow, but one just as correct: that of a Junker aristocrat. "And *I* am honored," he said, "to meet the respected master, T'ang Li. As to aid a friend is to reward one's self, there can be no debt between us."

"Then," said T'ang Li, "as a friend, permit me to earn a like reward and assist you in any way I can."

"Thank you," said Rand. "It is said that you have many brothers throughout the world—"

"Ah," said T'ang Li, "to speak of brothers is to speak of the things of men; matters which might distress the sensibilities of women."

"Meet you two for lunch in the restaurant, second floor," said T'sa Li, stepping into the elevator. "This is one girl who can take a hint." The elevator door closed and she was gone.

"There is a businessman," said Rand, "a very powerful businessman named Gregory Ballinger. His business is called Comco and it extends throughout the world, though headquartered here in New York. It has been suggested that his business operations may seek to accomplish more than the creation of wealth. Any information that you or your brothers could obtain about the origins of this man and his purposes, would be very helpful to me and much appreciated."

"I shall consult my brothers," said T'ang Li. Then he added, "We must not keep my sister waiting for lunch."

Rand took that to mean that the substantive conversation was over. Such was the power of T'ang Li's presence that Rand had found himself adopting the oriental's formal manner of speech. He decided not to press his luck. Whatever hostility T'ang Li felt toward him, he had concealed flawlessly. Discipline, thought Rand. He marvelled at the fact that after such strenuous exercise, and at an age in excess of fifty, T'ang Li not only was breathing as if at rest, there wasn't a hint of perspiration on those parts of his body which were exposed beyond the short, white, robelike garment he wore tied with a red sash.

Rand consulted his watch. T'sa Li had had no idea how long his conversation with her brother might take when she mentioned lunch. It was only a little after 9:00 A.M.

"It's just a little early for me," said Rand, "but a cup of tea would be just right."

"Ah," said T'ang Li, "down here I lose all track of time. One cannot wear a watch while striking the poles. It is also early for me, and many hours of training remain. Perhaps the two of you would excuse me until another time?"

"Of course. And I'm delighted to have met you at last." Rand started to put out his hand but checked himself and bowed instead. T'ang Li returned it and Rand stepped back to find that the elevator was down again, waiting for him. It gave him a creepy feeling and he was glad when the door shut between him and T'ang Li.

It was a good thing, Rand thought, that he had remembered to bow rather than shake hands. It wasn't the protocol of the thing, he just didn't relish placing his hand inside that of T'ang Li. Li's hands were huge, with a mass of calluses over permanently swollen knuckles. On the back of each hand, an inch above the wrist, was a callused, knobby protrusion, as if T'ang Li's hands contained an extra bone. Worst of all were the man's thumbs. They were deformed, probably intentionally, and curved backward upon their first joint like two hooks. T'ang Li had held his left wrist in his right hand as he spoke, but not before Rand had been able to see what he was attempting to conceal: what appeared to be a crude line drawing of a fish tattooed upon it in blue ink. Rand guessed it was a Tong symbol.

The elevator stopped at the main restaurant floor and the door opened automatically. Before he could exit, the maître d' came to the door and said:

"Miss Li is in the second private room, second floor."

"Fine. Would you send us up some tea, please?"

The man bowed his assent, released his hold upon the elevator door so it could close and the elevator resumed its journey upward.

"Well," T'sa Li greeted Rand as he approached her table, "you look none the worse for wear. How'd it go?"

"I would never, ever, want to fuck with your brother!"

"I should hope not! I mean, I'm pretty liberal, as you know, about what you do on your own time. But I'm not sure I could handle—"

"Oh, shut up. You know damn well what I meant!"

T'sa Li grinned. Her face shone with sisterly pride.

"He's a pretty impressive guy, isn't he?"

"Jesus! He is that."

A waiter arrived with tea and fortune cookies. Rand took the occasion to ask for a telephone and one was brought to the table promptly.

"I'll go powder my nose," said T'sa Li.

137

"Forget it. Just want to check in with the answering service."

Rand hit the buttons rapidly, listened a moment, said "This is Mr. Rand. Any messages?" then listened a moment more before hanging up with a brief, "Thanks." Then he took a wallet out of his breast pocket, ran through some business cards until he found the one he wanted and hit the buttons more deliberately while reading from the card and waited again.

"Mike? Rick. I got your message. Find anything?"

"Yep," came the answer over the phone. "Nothing startling. All three, Metz, Mazatlan and Stresso are solid outfits and the deals are straight out of a Wharton School textbook. Each one put up treasury stock as a guarantee of payment and Columbia did the same as a guarantee of performance."

"Gotcha," said Rand. It sounded good but there was still something about it that bothered him. That was getting to be the story of his life; negative instincts with nothing rational to back them up. He thought of a question:

"I don't suppose you've got the amount of the deals in terms of Columbia's production capacity by any chance?"

"Lemme see. Wait one."

Rand could visualize his friend leafing through his notes. He was wrong. On the other end of the line Mike was punching the keys of a remote computer terminal, then waiting for the requested information to be displayed on the viewing screen. In a few moments he said:

"Metz, fifteen; Mazatlan, ten; Stresso, ten. How's that for service?"

Rand let out a low whistle. The man on the other end of the line took it to be the compliment he felt he deserved:

"Good, huh?" The words in the earphone brought Rand back to the conversation.

"Terrific. I owe you one, Mike. Thanks."

"Any time. See ya." The phone went dead. Rand hung it up in slow motion as he looked at T'sa Li.

"You were right. I'm still not sure what it means, but you were absolutely right. It was production capacity all along. Look, hon —no offense, but I've got to make another phone call that I can't make from here. Mind?"

"Wouldn't make any difference if I did," said T'sa Li. "I've seen that look on you before. Go do what you have to do. I've got something to do, too, remember?"

"Right," he said, looking distracted again. "The girl." He looked at his watch and rose. "I've gotta get out of here." Rand bent across the table and kissed her.

"Keep in touch, huh?" Rand said. With a wave, he was gone.

Why is it, T'sa Li wondered to herself, that women always seem to be cleaning up after men?

# XI

Rand winced as the left front wheel of his BMW dropped into a pothole. He remembered not to brake and compound the problem by locking up the wheel, concluding darkly that only a *panzer* could negotiate New York's crumbling West Side safely. A block further north on Tenth Avenue, on the far side of a rundown Texaco station, he found what he was looking for and pulled over.

The interior of the telephone booth was filthy. Fruit peelings and an empty soda bottle on the floor had attracted a column of ants that wound its way around cigarette butts and other debris. An attempt to force the coin box had failed but left wounds. Among graffiti in several languages, the metal shelf beneath the phone bore the indictment: *Simpson smells girls bicycle seats.* Someone had scratched a line through the word *girls* and substituted the word *boys.* Rand wrinkled his nose in disgust. Nevertheless he was happy to find a booth that had not been converted into a pedestal-mounted phone nested inside an open weather shroud, the roadside madonna of the electronic age. At least inside the dirty relic one could conduct a conversation intelligibly despite competition from the hammering of passing diesel trucks.

Rand spilled a handful of quarters on the shelf. Ready to respond to the command of the operator for more money, he dropped a quarter into the coin box and dialed Constantine Kazalakis' direct line at CIA headquarters in Langley, Virginia. After pumping in the required number of quarters on demand, he could hear the phone ringing at the other end. Unless the police were tapping this phone as part of a drug or gambling investigation, unlikely at this location, it was the safest phone he could choose.

"Three-six-oh-seven." said a woman's voice.

"Richard Rand for Mr. Kazalakis, please."

"One moment, sir."

"Hello?"

"Greek? Rick. I'm in a phone booth so crummy it's gotta be alright. Listen, remember those percentage figures on that list we were talking about? Okay. They refer to production capacity of the outfit that's made deals with three of them on the list. In each case, the figures fit the capacity required exactly."

"Did you say three?"

"Right. The third was announced yesterday. It's in the papers. They're a great source of information. Try 'em sometime."

"Don't be a wise ass. Where does this put us?"

"Makes our man three for six so far. I don't buy his being clairvoyant so I don't like the trend. Might be a good idea to have somebody go to the outfit on the other end of all three deals and steer 'em away from the rest of the list."

"How can I do that, for Christ's sake? What do I tell them, 'don't make money'? Besides, it's a sure tip off we've got the list. You're gonna have to do better than that."

Rand sighed into the phone. "Okay, I'll keep digging."

"You do that. And stay in touch."

The line went dead. Rand hung up and stepped outside the booth. He paused to suck in some of the clear October air blowing in from the Hudson. The stench of the booth out of his nose, he slid back into the BMW, started it and headed gingerly out onto the disintegrating road. If he didn't get back soon, Rand knew, Alfredo Matarazza would have the street out looking for him.

Within a week Columbia Steel announced, with self-serving puffery about its "major contribution to the solution of the nation's balance of payments deficit," three separate contracts for the furnishing of steel to overseas buyers: Siderakis Eteria in Greece, Bombay Heavy Fabrications Ltd. in India and Mekaniskafabrikenaktiebolaget Mälmo in Sweden.

The financial press attributed Columbia's success in landing the contracts to the reduction of the Japanese steel industry's ability to compete against American companies resulting from the rise of the yen against the dollar. A check by Rand with his

141

friend at Brown Brothers, Harriman confirmed the capacity figures as five percent each, exactly as on the Ballinger list. Columbia Steel was hailed editorially in *Business Week* for demonstrating that the private sector, left unfettered by the federal government, could provide the leadership necessary to correct the country's basic economic imbalances, as witness the fact that fifty percent of Columbia Steel's production capacity was now under contract to foreign buyers for the next ten years. Network anchormen reported that the chairman of the board of Columbia Steel was now something of a hero in the business community.

Rand was still brooding over these developments four days later. Having no idea what to do next was contributing to his frustration when he picked up a message held for him at the Plaza's desk. It said only:

> Your reservation confirmed for dinner at the House of Li at 7:30 P.M. this evening.

Rand pocketed the note, went to a house phone and called the hotel garage. He asked that Alfredo Matarazza, on his way there with the car, be instructed to return and wait for him; then he went up to his rooms to freshen up. It was 6:33 P.M. and Rand felt better. If T'ang Li wanted to see him, there was a reason.

The maitre d' at the House of Li must never have a day off, Rand thought, as he had never once arrived when the man was not at his post. As he anticipated, Rand was directed to the rear private dining room on the second floor. There T'ang Li, who appeared to fill the small room by himself, rose to greet him with a bow which Rand returned before seating himself opposite the huge oriental. Menus were waiting and Rand selected something translated into English as "Mongolian barbeque." He had no idea what T'ang Li chose as he ordered in Chinese.

When the waiter had left, T'ang Li said:

"Mr. Rand, I am concerned for my sister. We have not seen her since your visit nearly two weeks ago. She mentioned to our mother that she intended to travel for an indefinite time but did not say where. Can you enlighten us?"

T'ang Li, Rand thought, was not one with whom to dissemble.

"Yes," he said, "she's on a mission for me to West Virginia. Jeffersonville, West Virginia. She's trying to find a young woman and persuade her parents to send her away to a school for the retarded. She doesn't have the girl's address and is trying to find her among rather reticent people. That's why I'm not sure just when she'll be back. The minute I hear from her, though, I'll let you know."

"Please do," said T'ang Li. His eyes bored into Rand's for emphasis, not the least discomfited by Rand's peculiar near absence of eye coloration.

Rand thought it time to try to change the subject.

"Have your brothers been able to learn anything of my businessman friend?"

"He is a friend of yours?"

"No. A poor choice of words. I know him, but he's not a friend. On the contrary, we are enemies."

"I see," said T'ang Li, but what he saw, Rand couldn't tell from his expression or inflection.

"Your enemy," continued T'ang Li, "seeks to enlarge those areas of the world in which he does business. Most recently he has been trying very hard to establish himself through his company, Comco, in the Republic of China. Taiwan."

"What are his chances of success?"

"None. In an information barter between the intelligence services of the Republic of China and Great Britain, the British advised that a recent defector from the Soviet Union, who professed to be a colonel in the Committee for State Security, identified your Mr. Ballinger as a general officer in that same organization named Mikhail Sarkov."

"What was the name of the defector?"

"Not revealed by the British, and I see no reason why the Taiwanese government would ask. The allegation alone was enough to block Ballinger."

"How do they rate the defector? Genuine? A plant?"

"That is still being evaluated."

"Anything more on Ballinger?"

"Supposedly he was sent to your country right after the war as a young lieutenant in the KGB to be a 'sleeper'. The defector claims not to know whether or not he has yet been 'awakened' and tasked."

"He must have been doing something to be made a general!"

"He is the builder and ruler of Comco. There is a difference between being able to awaken in your midst an industrial

143

giant rather than, say, the manager of a department store."

"You have a point," acknowledged Rand. "Does my government have this information?"

"Not known. But foreign governments are reluctant to share secrets with yours. A group of women washing clothes at the river bank are more able to control their tongues."

Rand felt embarrassed for his country but could think of no rejoinder; T'ang Li was right. Instead he asked:

"May I impose upon your brothers to continue their efforts? As I said, Ballinger—Sarkov, whoever he really is—is my enemy. Comco is an extension of him. Its operations are so complex that his chances of making a mistake and becoming vulnerable lie there, rather than with the man himself. I'm looking for a weakness I can exploit, any weakness at all."

T'ang Li nodded his assent. The waiter brought their meals and T'ang Li explained its many parts to Rand, relating it to his homeland, Mongolia. Like his sister, T'ang Li was proud of his Mongol heritage. The remainder of the meal was given over to his discourse on the history of his people; a small group of clans dwelling in the northeast corner of outer Mongolia and not to be mistaken for the far more numerous Tatars.

T'ang Li dwelt at length upon the life of Chinggis, one of the great conquerors of history, expressing resentment at the common belief his victories were the result of sweeping hoards of barbarians carrying every battle through sheer force of numbers and ferocity. He pointed out that there were no more than a million Mongols at the time against all the population of Asia, and attributed their success to Chinggis's skill in diplomacy, politics and psychological warfare as well as generalship.

The dinner was over in what seemed to Rand no time, and he left with his respect for T'ang Li enhanced by his newly acquired appreciation of the Mongol people.

The parking lot of the airport outside Casper, Wyoming, served as Richard Rand's introduction to the one characteristic of the area visitors were least likely to forget: the wind. Blowing constantly in the late afternoon of the last day of October, it carried as freight a cutting grit swept from the dry plains and a surprising cold that boded ill for anyone staying through the winter. Rand could feel the grit of the dust in his teeth and the cold start to numb his fingers as he struggled to fit the unfamiliar key into the door of a rental automobile. Successful at last, he slammed the door shut against the wind and took out a handker-chief to wipe the taste of the dust off his tongue. It made his mouth feel dry as he drove off toward Casper.

The airport disappeared behind him, and Rand felt loneliness seep into him as he passed through land he imagined resembled the back of the moon. To his right, blocking the setting sun and partially obscured by the dust haze, rose the Rocky Mountains. Although from time to time a dirt trail led off the asphalt into the distance, it was not until Rand came to the well-head pumps of the Big Muddy oil field that he felt in the presence of man. He greeted his first sight of Casper with an enthusiasm reserved to desert wanderers and others beginning to suspect they are alone on the face of the earth.

The motel Rand checked into had the inevitable western motif, but the bed was firm and the water hot. Rand thanked God for small favors and decided a bath was the only way to get the dust out of his pores before essaying the motel cooking. Steeping himself in the hot tub, he hoped fervently that his stay in Casper would not be long.

When the vital statistics window in the courthouse opened two minutes late at 9:02 A.M., Rand was first in line. Instead of the fossilized male clerk he had expected, the window was attended by a sunny brunette in her twenties. From his xerographic copy of the birth certificate Ballinger kept in his safe, Rand was able to give the girl all she needed to produce for his inspection the original record. It was kept in a large, leatherbound ledger in which all entries had been made with a steel-nibbed pen and india ink.

"Thanks," said Rand, "that's quick service."

"Oh, you're welcome, but I really can't take all that much credit. I had it out just yesterday for an FBI man. You're not with them too, are you?"

"Who's that?"

"The government."

"Oh, no," Rand smiled, "nothing like that. My name's De-Weed, Ernest DeWeed. *Time Magazine?* Your Mr. Ballinger's getting to be quite famous, you know. We're doing a cover story on him. Matter of fact, you might be able to help us."

"Sure!" The girl brightened visibly. "That what you need the birth record for?"

"Right. Just checking to be sure our information is correct. You know how people are always saying the press gets everything wrong? Well, we try to get it right at *Time.*"

The people behind him in line were beginning to get restive. Satisfied that the original entry was genuine and bore no indication of tampering, Rand handed the volume back to the girl. To the disgust of the others waiting, she asked:

"What else can I do to help?"

"Well, Mr. Ballinger must be pretty well known around here. 'Course, we've got a lot of information about his business success and everything, but that's all about his adult life. I'm supposed to interview someone who knew him when he was growing up. Going to school. That sort of thing. You know, find out what it was about him made him so successful."

"Well, gee," the girl answered, "I don't think you're gonna have much luck there—I mean school and everything. See, his Pa took off for the Mexican gold fields when the ones around here played out. His Ma died tryin' to have another baby, so maybe that's the real reason his Pa wanted to leave; memories an' all. Anyway, the two of them left here when Mr. Ballinger was like in the second grade. The *Call*—that's our paper—they did a story on Mr. Ballinger awhile back and the only one they found to talk to was an old lady used to keep house for them before they left town."

Rand frowned. "That does make it tough. I guess I better start with the same old lady then. You wouldn't happen to know her name or where she lives?"

"Sure. Everybody knows her. Miz Kaster. Lives two houses down from the public library." The girl pointed to her left rear. "You can't miss it."

She was right. Rand found the Kaster house easily from a sign over the metal mailbox fastened to the right of the front door. There was no bell so Rand used the knocker. Rand thought Miss Kaster must have seen him coming because the door opened right away. The woman who opened it was steady on her feet, wore a shapeless print dress with a knitted cardigan the color of rust thrown over her shoulders. Her hair was on the top of her head in tight, artificial curls and had a decided tint of blue. She appeared to be at least eighty years old.

"You the *Time Magazine* feller?"

"Yes ma'm."

"Sure you're not with the govamint?"

"No ma'm."

"All right. Annie called about you. C'mon in."

"Annie?"

"Annie Sedwick, up to the courthouse. Casper's a small town, mister, and a good thing, too. Annie said you're gonna write about Greg Ballinger. You for him or agin him?"

"Well, neither, really. I don't know him. I'm just one of a lot of reporters assigned to find out what we can about him for a cover story. He's been a very successful man and we think our readers would be interested in why. We have business reporters to explain all the financial things. I don't understand all that myself. What I'd like to find out is something about his youth. Miss Sedwick, was it? She said you could help me."

"Help who I want to," said Miss Kaster. "Sit down."

"You seem upset about the government," said Rand. "Miss Sedwick mentioned the FBI had been inquiring about Mr. Ballinger. Did they come here too?"

"They did. Told them nothing! Busybodies from Washington. Take the last penny a soul has and give it away to some good for nothing. Try to tell everybody how to live!"

"It's terrible," Rand agreed. He didn't want a lecture on the evils of the central government so he asked:

"Has Mr. Ballinger visited you lately, Miss Kaster?"

"No, no. Not for a long time. Sometime just after the war he came back for a visit. All grown up. Hardly recognized him. But I don't see too good anyway, don't you know. Can't expect him to come out here to visit an old lady he can hardly remember. Sends me a Christmas card every year, though. He's a good boy."

"I'm sure he is. Would you have any photographs of him as a boy?"

"No. Wish I did, now, but he's got the only one I ever had. When he came back he was so nice to me and wanted it so bad. They never took any down in Mexico and his Daddy died in a mineshaft. I didn't have the heart to say no. How could I? He'd just given me a thousand dollars cash money. You know, for all I'd done for him? So I didn't show him the rest. Now, don't you write that! What'll he think?"

"No. Of course not. You said something about the 'rest'?"

"The pictures. They're all I've got of him now. I figured if I told him I still had them, he'd want them, too. I didn't have the heart to part with them so I kept still."

"Pictures of Mr. Ballinger?" Rand tried to conceal his elation.

"Nope. Pictures *by* Mr. Ballinger. Little Greg, he was an artist. Used to draw houses and ponies and all sorts of things by the hour. Just give him some crayolas and paper and he'd be happy. I kept the three best. Framed 'em years ago, right after they left."

"Could I see them?" Rand asked.

"Don't see the harm. You wait right here."

Rand rose as Miss Kaster did and remained standing until she had left the room. What he had in mind was a long shot, but it was the only thing he could think of that held even the possibility of being able to verify Ballinger's identity.

Rand rose again as Miss Kaster reentered the room holding three ten-by-twelve-inch plain wooden frames against her breast. It was clear from the way she held on to them that they were dear to her.

"This first one," she said, handing it to Rand carefully, "is his best. Doesn't that look just like a pony?"

Under the glass of the frame was a childish line drawing of what looked to Rand like a deformed dog.

"That *is* good!" Rand gushed to a beaming Miss Kaster. She took it from him and pointed vaguely to the lower right hand corner.

"Don't see so good, like I told you; 'specially close up. Don't like to wear glasses with company. Make me look so old. But you see there? Look close and you'll see where he wrote on it *G-R-E-G.* I taught him to write his name!"

Rand was properly impressed. The second frame contained a rough box with a curlicue ascending vertically from one end, which Miss Kaster insisted was a house. The third and last consisted of a wavy horizontal line with the space below it filled in with brown crayon and that above it with blue. It was, assured Miss Kaster, a superb rendition of the front range of the Rocky Mountains. Rand agreed with her and was fulsome in his praise of Ballinger's artistic ability, saying:

"People should know about this, don't you think?"

"They certainly should!"

"Well, I'm going to tell people about it in *Time.* The only problem I have is that old saying, 'one picture is worth a thousand words.' I'm afraid I can't really do him justice. Tell you what; could I take these with me so we could print them in *Time?* I'd send them right back."

148

Miss Kaster snatched the Rocky Mountains back from Rand.

"Certainly not! What if the plane crashed? What if—"

"No, no, no!" protested Rand. "I can have them copied right here in Casper. I could have them back to you in half an hour." Before the woman could protest further, Rand took out his wallet and counted out ten one hundred dollar bills.

"Tell you what," he said. "You don't know me and I don't blame you one bit for being careful. Can't *be* too careful these days. Here." Rand handed her the cash.

Miss Kaster held the bills up close to her eyes. They widened when she recognized the figure *100* on the corners.

"You keep that," said Rand, "and if I'm not back in half an hour, *Time* will give you another thousand for your trouble. Is that fair enough?"

Miss Kaster sat down, holding both the money and the frames tightly. The money won.

"Well, I can't see why anyone would want to steal them. They mean more to me than anyone else. All right, young man. I'll trust you. But don't you let any harm come to them, you hear?"

"No ma'm!" Rand assured her as he took the frames. He looked at his watch. "Well, if I'm going to get these back to you in half an hour, I better run along."

Rand fought the wind back to his car, drove it to the next corner, went two more blocks and, satisfied that he was well out of sight of Miss Kaster or her neighbors, pulled in to the curb. With his pocket knife he opened the back of the frames carefully. It was difficult to extract the drawings as Rand used only the very tips of his fingers to hold but a millimeter of the edge of the paper. He put the three drawings between two of the frames to protect them, then cruised downtown Casper for six minutes before finding a commercial copying service.

A twenty dollar bill to the clerk on duty let Rand operate the Xerox copier himself. Gingerly, he made three copies each of the drawings, paid and left. Within three minutes more, Rand found a dime store, but it took another two minutes to find a parking space. He had fifteen minutes to go by the time he was able to use the crayons he bought in the dime store to color the Xerox copies. He picked the best three of his efforts, slipped them back into the frames and headed back to Mae Kaster's house. With two minutes to spare, he returned her precious works of art to Miss Kaster. She peered at them intently, but the combination of xerography, her poor eyesight and the glare off the frame glass led her to accept Rand's forgeries and bless him as he left.

"Upstairs on the second floor, Boss," said Alfredo Matarazza. "And don't worry. This lab's the one all them big defense lawyers use. Believe me when I tell ya. Ya pay top dollar but they get results."

"I hope so, 'Fredo. Wait for me, huh?"

Rand climbed out of the double-parked BMW as Matarazza put his left arm out the window on his side to give the finger to horn-blowing traffic backed up behind him.

The New York Technical Laboratory occupied the entire second floor of a building on West Twenty-first Street. It was operated by retired forensic chemists, physicists and technicians from several metropolitan area police departments, but N.Y.P.D. crime laboratory alumni predominated. Rand asked the girl at the desk for the fingerprint department and she led him back to a small office off a large, glass-walled room dominated by a butcher-block work table. The sides of the room were desks, counters, drawers, cabinets and comparison microscopes halfway up, and glass the rest of the way to the ceiling. A large hood like that over the stove area of commercial kitchens was positioned over the center work table. On one wall was a four-by-five-foot poster bearing a huge blowup of a fingerprint. Straight lines ran from bifurcations and anomalies in the ridges to the margin where they were numbered. From somewhere came the odors of acetone, formaldehyde and other chemicals Rand couldn't identify.

After a few moments Rand was joined by a corpulent, bald-headed man of about sixty who peered at him through thick lenses hung in steel wire frames. He held a slip of paper in his hand from which he read when he asked:

"You are Mr. Rand?"

"Richard Rand. Yes."

"How do you do. Morris Kaufman." The man held out his hand to Rand. As they shook hands he said:

"How can we help you?"

"I need some latent fingerprints developed from paper."

"How old are they? How long ago do you think they were made?"

"It makes a difference?"

"It can to your wallet."

"Tell me about it."

"Okay. If you've got a piece of paper you think somebody left his prints on yesterday, a week ago, last year, we can use that." Kaufman pointed through the glass toward the table with the hood over it. "Iodine fuming." he said. "Simplest way to go. And the cheapest."

"Now," Kaufman continued, warming to his subject, "there's another process, developed by the Swedes. It's called ninhydrin. The Swedes got a patent on it. You use it, you gotta pay a royalty. Couple years ago the FBI got caught usin' it without payin' off the Swedes and got their tit'n the wringer. Ninhydrin costs, but if the latents are old, there's no other way."

"How old?"

"Lemme put it to you this way—With ninhydrin, I could get Lincoln's prints off the Gettysburg address."

"These could be almost fifty years old."

"No sweat. Anything else you can tell me about them?"

"Yes. They'd be the prints of a small child. Six, seven years old. Those are the ones I'm interested in. The adult prints you can disregard."

"Don't know that I can guarantee to tell them apart. Not much difference in size between an adult little finger and a kid's thumb. The ridge detail is coarser, and if I find them one next to the other —it all depends. I'll do my best."

"I don't care about cost," said Rand. "If I can get it, I need ten fingers. If you can tell one from another, fine."

"You're looking for a set of knowns."

"Right."

"How much of a sample have you got?"

Rand handed Kaufman three manila envelopes. "Three separate drawings. You know how kids hold them down with their whole hand when they're working?"

"Yeah. Sounds like we got a shot."

"Fine," said Rand. "How soon can you have it?"

"I could drop everything else, but that costs extra."

"I told you I'm not concerned about cost."

"Give me a couple of days. Leave a number at the desk and I'll call you. The deposit is two bills. You can leave that with the girl too."

They shook hands and Rand headed back to the front desk.

Three days later Rand responded to a message from his answering service to call Mr. Kaufman at New York Technical Laboratories. Kaufman reported good news. From among the three specimens provided, he had isolated ten identifiable latents that were, in his opinion, those of a child. He had copied them, blown them up and prepared an exhibit which could be used for comparison purposes. Rand could pick up the package upon payment of the balance due of $1,200. Rand thanked him, promised to retrieve the materials that same day, and hung up.

Kaufman's was the last good news Rand received that day. T'sa Li had returned. Over lunch in the Plaza's Edwardian Room she reported the failure of her mission. Essie-Mae Blaylock was nowhere to be found.

"Could you find out anything about her?" Rand asked, "I mean, did she ever get back home?"

"I was afraid you'd ask me that."

"She didn't?" Rand was alarmed.

"She got back home all right. And ten days later she married that Morgan kid. The reason it took me so long to find that out is she proceeded to disgrace her family by running away from her husband on her wedding night. Nobody knows where she is and her husband won't talk to anyone about what happened."

Rand didn't feel hungry any more. He put down his fork and grew red in the face.

"You know what happened," he said quietly.

T'sa Li said nothing for a moment. Then,

"I really looked. I couldn't find her. She came home for an hour, grabbed some things and fled. I don't think anyone knows where she is."

"I know, hon. And I appreciate it. Let me know what I owe you."

"Forget it. I needed to get away anyhow."

"We'll argue about it later. That reminds me. Check in with your family, okay? They're worried about you."

"Already taken care of. Thought you might want company tonight after I'd given you my news."

The waiter interrupted to bring a telephone to the table. He gave Rand a look as he said,

"Call for you, sir. The police."

"Thanks," said Rand. He took the phone.

"Rand speaking."

"Lieutenant Portello. Twenty-eighth precinct." It was a middle ranking police officer who was rated as "all right" by Rand's Italian relatives.

"Yes, Lieutenant."

"So far as this department or Washington is concerned, and that includes the whole *geschmear,* even the military, your party ain't never been fingerprinted."

"You're sure?"

"Sorry."

"Okay. Thanks, Lieutenant. I appreciate your help."

"Any time."

Rand hung up the phone. His hand still on the handset, he leaned back in his chair and gazed distractedly out the window at Central Park South, seeing nothing. "Ballinger's never been printed," he sighed.

T'sa Li tried to think of something encouraging to say. She couldn't, and covered the silence between them instead by starting to pick at her food again. She was trying to spear an errant pea when Rand spoke her name, but it was his tone of voice that commanded her attention; it was strong and confident. "T'sa Li," he asked, fixing her with those terrible eyes, "how would you like to go to a party?"

# XII

"The hell you go to my brother! What am I all of a sudden? A child?"

T'sa Li was angry. She and Richard Rand were in his living room at the Plaza. They had finished lunch and she had said she thought going to a party was a great idea. She had remained agreeable when, a few minutes ago, he had explained that what he really had in mind was another mission. What had set her off was Rand's suggestion that it be cleared in advance with her brother, T'ang Li.

"Of course not," Rand replied in a placating tone. "It's just that your brother is being very helpful to me right now and when you were in West Virginia he was concerned. I see no reason to piss him off unnecessarily. You said yourself he's unhappy with the way things are between us and feels I'm exploiting you. I just want to take his feelings into consideration, that's all."

"What about *my* feelings!" she shot back. "Don't they count for anything? Do you know how *long*, do you have any *idea* how many *years* it's taken me to get the freedom I have today? I've come a long way, baby, to coin a phrase, and I'm not taking one step backward on that road just to make you feel comfortable!"

T'sa Li was working herself into a rage.

"You know what I think? I think you're afraid of my brother! Well, mister, I'm not! And I'm sorry, but I can't be the woman of someone who is!"

Rand's face drained of all color. "That stinks," he said, "that really stinks!" His voice was a throttled rasp escaping from a throat contracted rigidly by anger.

"I'll say this one time," he said, "and that's all: I am not afraid of your brother. That doesn't mean I've got some schoolboy bravado idea that I could beat him in a fist fight. Quite the contrary, there's no doubt in my mind he'd beat me to a pulp. The point is, if I had to, I'd fight him anyway. But if I could avoid it, I would. For a number of reasons, not the least of which is that I wouldn't be so stupid as to go up against him empty-handed."

T'sa Li could see that Rand's hands were trembling. He noticed her staring at the drink shaking in his hand. He put it down on the cocktail table and sat back down, trying to appear more composed.

"Look," said Rand, "I'm sorry I didn't see it from your point of view; but I think you could have stated your position without gratuitously attacking my courage."

T'sa Li was leaning back stiffly in the chair between the window and the fireplace. Her legs were squeezed together tightly and her arms folded across her chest. She lifted a hand to her nose and pinched it at the bridge for a long moment, then laced the fingers of both hands together and hugged her knees. Leaning far forward she said:

"I'm sorry. It was uncalled for. But let me ask you this: If you went to my brother, and he vetoed the idea, what would you do?"

"Come up with another plan, I guess."

"That's exactly my point. I've said I'd do it. You're willing to let my brother prevent me; let him exert control over my life. There are no circumstances under which I can accept that. None."

Rand remained silent, deciding to hear her out.

"If the situation were reversed," said T'sa Li, "would *you* accept it?"

"No," Rand replied slowly, "I wouldn't, but—"

"But I'm a woman." she finished for him.

Rand grinned sheepishly, like a little boy caught doing something he shouldn't. T'sa Li relaxed back in her chair and held up her hands, palms outward, fingers spread and pointed down, a small smile on her lips.

"You win," said Rand.

"*We* win," she corrected him. "Now. Care to fill me in on this super scheme of yours?"

Rand grinned and relaxed, exhaling audibly. "You go to a party at Ballinger's place in Washington."

"That much I knew. How do we manage that and what do I do when I get there?"

"This isn't one of Ballinger's kinky sex *soirées*," Rand said. "I wouldn't get you mixed up in anything like that. It's one of his regular blasts for half of official Washington. They were talking about it the night of my disaster. The screwballs will be there but everyone else will be straight. All the Congress has an invitation to every one of these and a lot of them go. My wife's family, family in quotes that is, owns a guy from upstate, Barry Carr. Barrington Carr the Third. A real blueblood and crooked as a ram's horn. He's divorced, in his forties, dumb, good looking and a real charmer. He'll be your date."

"Thank's a lot. When I'm not fighting off this lech you're fixing me up with, what do I do?"

"Don't worry about the lech. Your hero, that's me, will be outside in the bushes under the patio in case you get yourself in what they used to call 'distress'. But try not to. If I have to pop up it'll blow the whole operation. All you have to do is pick up a glass or two Ballinger's handled, so it has his fingerprints, go outside on the patio for air and slip it to me. I split and you go home and fight off Barry Carr."

"Wait a minute," T'sa Li objected. "It's November, remember? Nobody's going to be going out on the patio for air. They'd freeze. The doors will be locked."

"Not in Washington, hon. They have roses blooming into December. Wear a wrap and keep it with you. You'll be okay."

"Until I go home with Barry Carr," said T'sa Li. "I should have let you ask my brother."

Rand grinned at her. "Still time to change your mind."

"Not on your life! When is this fiasco?"

"The fifteenth. Plenty of time. I'll make a call and you'll be hearing from Carr in a couple of days."

"I can hardly wait," said T'sa Li. "I hope they have poison ivy in Washington into December, too. And you end up sitting in a patch of it. Jesus! How'll I keep a straight face all night knowing you're out there playing hide and seek in the bushes?"

Rand ignored her taunt. "Just don't take all night getting those glasses."

T'sa Li started to giggle uncontrollably. She pressed her hand over her mouth and looked away from Rand whom she could see was becoming annoyed.

"What's so goddamn funny?" he snapped.

"I just thought," T'sa Li gasped, "what if it rains? I can see you now, half drowned under a bush, cursing and swearing, all curled up in a wet little ball!" She made a face and mocked him: "Still time to change your mind!"

The grounds of the National Cathedral are open at all hours, and that was the way Rand came in. Driving slowly, he found a parking lot between the Cathedral and St. Albans School and left his rented Olds there. A brief walk down the hill and he was into the woods beside and behind Albanside. He paused to survey the walled-in area while he still had the height advantage of the hill and could see down and over the wall.

The sets of patio doors were closed, but their gauze curtains let light from the great living room blaze through. The patio itself was illuminated clearly. It was elevated to the same height as the peripheral wall and threw the area immediately below into deep shadow. The bushes were *arbor vitae* and forsythia, except under the patio where tall rhododendron provided plenty of room and good concealment.

Latecomers to the party were still being dropped off from gleaming limosines. The garage doors were all closed and two additional cars which appeared to belong to the house were parked on the large, crushed gravel driveway extension: a 450 SLC Mercedes backed up against some *arbor vitae* and a Volkswagen at the Belgian block curb separating the gravel from the lawn. Save for the activity at the entrance, the entire area enclosed by the wall appeared to be deserted.

Rand made his way through the woods and down the hill to the wall. He was wearing a chauffeur's uniform. It might give him a chance to talk his way out if detected and was also dark enough to blend into the night. Under his arm he carried a rolled up bath mat whose black color was selected for the same reason. Rand threw the mat up across the top of the wall against the possibility of there being glass imbedded there, then jumped up and grabbed the top of the wall through the mat with both hands. He pulled himself up far enough to shift his right hand to the other side of the wall and levered himself over the top, lying on his stomach on the mat. Swinging his legs around and still holding on to the mat, Rand slid with it down the other side of the wall and crouched low. He rolled up the mat and left it there.

For a full two minutes Richard Rand remained in the same position, absolutely still, as he tried to sense any movement which would indicate that his intrusion had been discovered. He could not. Staying within the wooded area, he worked his way completely around the back until woods gave way to shrubbery; then moved quickly through that lesser concealment to the rhododendron at the foot of the patio. Once there, he moved to the middle and sat down with his back to the patio foundation awaiting the burst of light and sound that would accompany the opening of the patio doors by T'sa Li or anyone else. He settled himself in for a long wait, fighting to stay alert against the temptation to nod.

T'sa Li had no difficulty at the party with Barrington Carr III. He seemed determined to flirt with every woman there under sixty, so she was left to herself enough to ease into a group where Ballinger was holding forth on the evils of inflation. He was drinking what appeared to be an Old Fashioned, and T'sa Li gave a silent cheer; the glass was a rental type, squat, smooth sided and easily concealable. All she had to do was beat a waiter to it when Ballinger set his glass down empty. She moved closer to be in a better position to make her move, then took back the silent cheer. Now as close to Ballinger's glass as he was, she could see that the combination of ice within, and the stuffy, humid air of the crowded room without, had covered the exterior of the glass with so much condensation the water was running down its sides. The glass would be useless for fingerprints.

T'sa Li was now on her own. She could hardly go out onto the patio and hold a conversation with Rand in the bushes about what to do next. She retreated to the ladies room to think it over. There was a small line at the powder room set aside for women, located off the same hallway as the library. Two sweet young things were ahead of her and sweet young thing number one gave her the idea. A hush-voiced, eyelid batting little nitwit whose eyebrows' darkness contrasted starkly with her salon-reddened hair, she was showing her wide-eyed companion her escort's invitation. On it was scrawled the autograph of a handsome senator with few brains but much money and a superb staff, who was considered presidential material by the innocent and the cynical. Two, thought T'sa Li, can play at *that* game.

Barry Carr, trying hard but unsuccessfully to charm a shrewd local anchorwoman, was only too glad to get rid of T'sa Li again at the cost of no more than his invitation and a ballpoint pen. T'sa Li threw her wrap farther back on her shoulders and pulled aside the bodice of her lemon satin gown to reveal as much of her breasts as she could without seeming obvious, then went looking for Gregory Ballinger.

Outside, Rand caught himself starting to nod when he heard what sounded like something or someone brushing against dry leaves. It brought his every sense alert immediately. Eyes now thoroughly accustomed to the dark, Rand searched the deep recesses of the woods but saw nothing. The same sound occured again and this time Rand was ready. He stared in the direction of the rustling and detected movement. By chance he glanced to the right and detected more movement; the place was becoming crowded. There were three people at least lurking about on Ballinger's grounds: himself and two others.

The first figure was moving toward Rand, whether intentionally or not Rand didn't know. He remained stock still. The first figure came on steadily in the direction of the patio. For the moment, Rand lost sight of the second figure. Probably holding still and listening too, Rand thought.

When the first figure got itself into the lee of the patio and the umbra of its shadow, Rand felt he could remain passive no longer; it was too big a gamble. He certainly couldn't afford to be ambushed, nor could he afford to be stumbled upon accidentally; either way, he'd be of no further use or protection to T'sa Li. He moved to intercept the first figure.

It wasn't hard for Rand to ease behind the moving shadow. It's destination appeared to be the patio. The shadow was attached to a small person, and one hand around the mouth from behind stifled any sound as Rand's other pinched shut the carotid arteries on either side of his victim's neck. Blood supply to the brain cut off, the figure slumped into unconsciousness in a moment.

Rand wasn't as successful in keeping his attack completely silent. To his dismay there was an audible thump as something the unconscious figure had been holding slipped from its grasp and fell into the accumulated dead leaves on the ground. Rand moved to retrieve it. The hair on the nape of his neck rose when he found a pistol and realized it might well have been used against his attack. He eased the figure to the ground and was startled as his hand slid over a soft breast. A woman!

Hand behind her head, Rand lifted her enough to permit some

of the glow from the patio doors to filter onto her face and was shocked to recognize Essie-Mae Blaylock, in spite of her boy's haircut. He held up the pistol. It was a .22 calibre Colt Woodsman semiautomatic; a fine piece no longer manufactured that Rand recognized immediately from its short slide and slender barrel.

T'sa Li stopped congratulating herself when Ballinger, having graciously autographed her invitation, handed it back to her. He did so with his left hand; the same one with which he held it as he wrote on it. The pen was useless for the retention of prints because of its rough surface. She had latents from Ballinger's left hand only. Her eye fell upon an ash tray on the sideboard next to Ballinger. It was saucer-shaped with rim depressions to hold cigarettes positioned like the four points of the compass. Its smooth, porcelain surface was ideal for her purpose, but T'sa Li didn't smoke, had no cigarettes with her and no reason to ask Ballinger for an ash tray. The problem stopped her for about ten seconds.

T'sa Li coughed violently. She threw her head forward and covered her mouth with her left hand. With her right she reached out past Ballinger and pointed wildly at the ashtray.

"Amftway!" she pleaded through her covered mouth, "Ampft-way!"

Ballinger, thinking himself in immediate danger of being vomited upon, swept up the ash tray with his right hand and held it out to T'sa Li even as he backed away from her quickly. She took it by the rim, noting with triumph that Ballinger was holding it with his right thumb pressed firmly into the top and all four fingers beneath it.

Spinning around as if to avoid further embarrassment, T'sa Li held the ash tray in front of her and fled toward the ladies room. Confronted by the ever-present line, she took the only avenue remaining to her. Ballinger watched with a tolerant shake of his head as she hurried out onto the patio to be sick.

Rand was having problems of his own. The delay necessitated by his discovery of Essie-Mae Blaylock prowling the grounds with a gun had allowed the second figure to get perilously close, and the closer it came the bigger it looked to Rand. Still holding the .22 Woodsman, he decided to try to draw the figure away from Essie-Mae. Rand bolted from his hiding place and ran for cover behind the Volkswagen. His tactic succeeded. The big figure stopped, then started back toward Rand's new hiding place. As it did so, it ducked to avoid a shaft of light from the *porte-cochère*. The figure didn't get down far enough and the momentary illumination was enough for Rand to recognize the figure as the powerful Oriental doorman.

Things were coming apart at the seams. Rand couldn't abandon Essie-Mae and if he tangled with the pursuing doorman, which seemed inevitable, the outcome was in doubt. Should he be caught, both Essie-Mae and T'sa Li would be completely vulnerable. He needed a weapon. The pistol was useless to him. The .22 long rifle cartridge was designed for just that; a rifle. Used in a pistol, the short barrel permitted the slow burning powder to create a surprisingly big blast of flame and loud report from the muzzle.

Rand shifted the pistol around in his hand so he could use the butt as a club. He needed better position; someplace where he could disappear for a moment and, with luck, ambush the big doorman and blackjack him with the pistol butt.

To help him ease slowly and quietly out of his crouch and sneak away, Rand put his left hand out to lean on the bumper of the Volkswagen. The dark caused him to underreach a few inches and his hand came to rest on one of the stubby muffler tailpipe extensions that are a VW trademark. It gave slightly under his weight, and Rand smiled coldly at the birth of a lethal idea.

With a hard twist, Rand started to unscrew the tailpipe extension. The car was new and the pipe came loose in his hand without difficulty. He moved quickly back to the Belgian block border of the driveway, reversed the pistol in his hand once more and rested the front sight carefully against the edge of one of the blocks. Laying aside the tailpipe momentarily, Rand leaned his full weight against the front sight and broke it from its holding groove in the gun barrel. He slid the slide back partially and saw that there was a round in the chamber.

The door to the patio opened and T'sa Li ran across the width of the patio to hang over the balustrade, head down toward the rhododendron, making choking sounds. Alarmed, Rand glanced toward the looming figure of the doorman. He, too, had been startled by T'sa Li's bursting unexpectedly on the scene and paused, motionless, evaluating the new situation.

It was all the time Rand needed. He stuck the sightless muzzle of the Colt into the Volkswagen tailpipe extension, placed the other end of the pipe against the Belgian block and pressed the barrel of the pistol into it firmly. As the big Oriental started to close on him, Rand brought to bear the .22 semiautomatic, now lengthened considerably by its gleaming, chromium-plated, improvised silencer. He aimed for the figure's head, now silhouetted against the light from the patio doors, and pressed the trigger.

There was a muffled *Pupf!* like that from a power lawnmower when the starter rope is pulled out but the engine doesn't quite catch. His pursuer hesitated for a moment, then slumped into the darkness. There was the sound of something hitting gravel, then all was still.

T'sa Li heard the noise and peered anxiously into the darkness. Having just come from the brightly lighted house, she could see nothing.

Still holding the pistol, Rand moved cautiously toward the fallen figure. Playing possum, he knew, was the oldest trick in the world and Rand was taking no chances. He listened for breath. There was none, but breathing slowly and silently from a wide-open mouth was another old trick. He had to chance it.

Pistol at the ready, Rand felt for the head, then slid his hand down so he could feel the carotid artery. There was no pulse. His hand felt warm and sticky. He lifted the head so that some of the window light could illuminate it. It was the doorman all right. Rand's bullet had taken him just to the right of the nose, under the eye. There was no exit wound. He dropped the oriental's head and made a crouched run across the open driveway extension to the shadow of the patio. T'sa Li saw the light reflect briefly from his blond hair.

"Rick?" she called in a shouted whisper.

"Yes," Rand answered in a hoarse whisper of his own. "You get it?"

"In my bag."

"Okay. Get down here. Hurry up!"

T'sa Li left the balustrade and strolled to the end of the patio and down the stairs to the driveway, obviously getting some air after being ill. She walked back to where Rand was crouched over an awakening Essie-Mae. He knocked the girl out again with pressure on her carotids, then lifted her on to his shoulder.

"Play along with me," he ordered T'sa Li.

Together the two of them walked nonchalantly out onto the driveway and toward the exit gate, Rand with some difficulty as he had the tailpipe-silenced pistol down the front of his trousers under his uniform jacket, and Essie-Mae Blaylock hanging over his shoulder like a drowning victim. They startled a chauffeur leaning, bored, against the side of a Silver Cloud Rolls. Rand shook his head in disgust as T'sa Li said aloud:

"I can't understand it, Charles; she didn't have that much to drink. Really!"

"Yes Ma'm," sighed Rand, and the chauffeur raised his eyes heavenward in silent commiseration as they left the premises and turned into the Cathedral grounds.

T'sa Li started to giggle.

"Not now, for Christ's sake," said Rand, "not now!"

"I can't help it," laughed T'sa Li, unable to obey him. "Look," she said, pointing up at the twin spires of the National Cathedral towering above them, "do you have any idea how much you look like the poor man's Quasimodo?"

Rand shifted Essie-Mae higher on his shoulder.

"Yeah," he observed sourly, "at least it didn't rain."

# XIII

Richard Rand folded the last of eight days' worth of copies of *The Washington Star* and *The Washington Post* with a grunt of satisfaction and placed it on a neat pile for disposal. Not a hint in any of them of a death at Albanside, natural or unnatural; nor was there any account of the finding of the body, anywhere in the Washington metropolitan area, of an Oriental dead of gunshot or other trauma.

Were his late opponent merely an illegal alien, Rand reasoned, Ballinger would not have gone to the considerable trouble necessary to cause a corpse to disappear. No; more likely the man was identifiable as his doorman and any linkage of him to Ballinger could range from the embarrassing to the dangerous. Rand wished now that he had had the presence of mind to have had T'sa Li at least take a look at the body. It was unlikely that she would have recognized the man, but all Rand knew now was that he was Oriental. T'sa Li could have told him what *kind* of Oriental; Chinese, Japanese, Korean or whatever.

So much, Rand thought, for Monday morning quarterbacking. He made a mental note to tell Alfredo Matarazza he no longer need stop each day at Grand Central for the Washington papers, rose from the sofa to place another hickory log on the smoldering fire and stepped back, eyeing it critically before replacing the fire screen. What he saw offered no encouragement that the log would catch fire. Rand retrieved his newspaper from the pile, wadded several pages into paper balls and stuffed them under the newly added log. After a moment they burst into flame. Replacing the fire screen, he crossed to the sideboard to pour himself a pony of Fundador before turning to his mail.

Rand chose the largest piece first. He checked the return address and, seeing that it came from the New York Technical Laboratory, ignored the other mail and tore it open. The package contained a chart, a report appropriate to a police department summary of evidence for a District Attorney, and a cover letter.

Rand started with the cover letter. After the usual bureaucratic references to file numbers, dates of previous correspondence and receipts of known and unknown specimens, there followed a predicative paragraph and a description of the tests and methods of comparison employed in the examination. Rand skipped to the information he wanted in the penultimate paragraph:

> CONCLUSION: It is concluded, therefore, that on the basis of dissimilar pattern order, i.e. the appearance of such configurations as loops, whorls, arches and tented arches in a different order of succession on fingers 1 through 10 in the known sample than that of the unknown; the absence of any tented arch pattern at all in the unknown sample and differing ridge counts, from delta to core, in those with the same patterns (in this case, all ulnar loops), that the known and unknown subjects are positively not identical.

Ballinger was not the person he purported to be. It did not follow necessarily that he was a Soviet "sleeper" but the *modus operandi* was so much in the classical KGB pattern that, coupled with what he had learned from T'ang Li, it made a very strong case; one that no intelligence agency could ignore. The further question remained: were Ballinger's accurate notes, secreted in his safe and indicating foreknowledge of all six Columbia Steel deals with foreign consumers, the result of intelligence-gathering operations? If so, was it in furtherance of the building of Ballinger's cover financial empire, consistent with his still being "asleep," or had he been "awakened" to carry out tasks laid on by his principals?

As usual, Rand thought, he had more questions than answers. He wondered whether T'ang Li had been able to come up with any more information. Stuffing the materials and the cover letter back into the envelope, he went over to the highboy at the rear of the room and reached up to the molding in the cornice. A light pull opened a secret drawer nearly six feet above the floor. He placed the laboratory report in the drawer underneath Essie-

Mae Blaylock's Colt Woodsman, closed the drawer and walked over to the telephone.

To the *cognoscenti,* be they of the intelligence community, the famous, notorious, celebrated or merely rich, the synonym for privacy during a visit to New York City is the Regency Hotel on Park Avenue. For its employees, discretion is the religion practiced most devoutly. It came as no surprise to Rand, therefore, when Kazalakis designated a room at the Regency as the appropriate place for the meeting Rand had requested. That, however, was the only thing about their conversation Rand had found unsurprising. That Kazalakis should agree with alacrity not only to an immediate meeting, but volunteer to travel to New York, Rand found as disconcerting as the information provided him by T'ang Li which prompted his request for a meeting in the first place.

Out of operational habit, Rand dismissed Matarazza and walked several blocks, checking for surveillance, before hailing a passing cab for the short ride from the Plaza to the Regency. He had no sooner entered the lobby than the assistant manager, whose vision rivalled that of a falcon, rose and greeted Rand quietly in fluent German. Assured Rand wished no special service on this occasion, he shook hands and retreated unobtrusively to his post as Rand made his way across the lobby and picked up a house phone to announce his arrival to Kazalakis. That accomplished, he crossed to the elevator alcove and gave the operator a floor number which was three above his actual destination. A quick trip down three flights of fire stairs and Rand was knocking at Kazalakis' door.

"It's open," Kazalakis' voice boomed through the door. Rand turned the knob, opened the door and entered. There was no one in the hallway, but the bathroom door was open. Across from the bathroom doorway hung a decorative wall mirror. Rand smiled. Kazalakis would be in the bathroom, probably with a gun, checking. The wall mirror would have a couple of paper match books between it and the wall on the far side to cock it unobtrusively at enough of an angle to reflect a full view of the passageway into the bathroom mirror.

When Kazalakis emerged from the bathroom a second later, he was drying his hands on a towel. He was in his shirtsleeves and no gun was in evidence.

"What would you have done if I were the maid?"

"Depends on how good looking you were," Kazalakis shot back with a smile. He pointed to a tray with an ice bucket and setups sitting on the cocktail table. "How about a drink? I've got bourbon, scotch and vodka."

"Thanks," said Rand, "I'll try a vodka and tonic."

"Help yourself."

Rand did, while Kazalakis poured some bourbon into a short glass filled with ice cubes, then raised the glass in a gesture of greeting. "Good to see ya," he said; then took a swallow. Rand stirred his drink by swirling it around with quick little motions of his wrist. It gave him a look of impatience that matched his mood. Without taking a sip he said:

"Ballinger's bad."

"Tell me about it." Kazalakis sat down in an easy chair by the window.

Rand sat on the edge of the sofa leaning far forward, his eagerness to speak betrayed by his body.

"Those six corporations, the foreign outfits that made the ten year deals with Columbia Steel? Well, Comco's got effective control of every one of them. *Every one.* Went for maybe all its reserves, a huge bundle, to pull it off. You won't find it on the books. Part of the reason it cost such a phenomenal amount is it was done through a maze of holding companies, some of them set up for just this move, so the foreign governments involved wouldn't pop to the fact that one of their homegrown pride and joy big employers and contributors to the economy had just been scooped up by a U.S. founded multi-national. They're touchy about that."

Kazalakis, legs stretched out and obviously at ease, reacted to this intelligence with a shrug.

"Maybe it's a good business move for Comco."

"To wipe out all its cash reserves for five companies? C'mon! They weren't getting Exxon or G.M. And it was done *before* the deals with Columbia. That makes the Columbia deals a Ballinger operation."

"It could *still* be a good business venture for Comco. Can you demonstrate to the contrary?"

"No," said Rand. He leaned back and, for the first time since their conversation started, took a sip of his drink. He looked at Kazalakis with a smile of anticipation and said:

167

"But I can tell you that Gregory Ballinger is not the chief executive officer of Comco."

Kazalakis looked down into his glass and frowned, as if he had spotted some disagreeable foreign matter in his drink.

"Oh?" Kazalakis' voice was controlled, guarded. He looked up at Rand and asked quietly, "Well, if Ballinger isn't, who is?"

"Probably a man named Mikhail Sarkov, a general officer of the KGB."

Again Kazalakis' voice was controlled, his words deliberate, as if each one had been selected with great care. "And your proof for that remarkable statement?"

"I can't prove he's Sarkov. I can prove he's not Ballinger. If you want, I'll give you the two sets of fingerprints." Rand took another swallow of his drink, then continued, "But I don't have to, do I? I'm getting the distinct impression that I'm not telling you anything you don't already know. Which explains your completely out of character trip up here to see me. You're here to find out just how much I know. Right, Greek?"

"You've been very busy," observed Kazalakis calmly.

"I guess you could say that," Rand answered. "So when do we blow the whistle?"

"*WE?*" came the barked response. The old Kazalakis was back. "*We* don't do anything. Let's get that straight right from the start. The United States Government will decide what to do in the national interest, and when. There's no *we* about it. *You*, I'll grant you, provided a valuable service in confirming from independent sources information that *we*, that is your government, received very recently. But if you don't know, you ought to know that this confirmation won't make an illegal alien case that'll stand up in court against the kind of lawyers Ballinger can hire, much less espionage or something like that. *Plus* nobody knows yet what the son of a bitch is up to. So he's bought the companies and made the deals. So what? *You* don't know or you'd have just told me."

Kazalakis was on his feet now, pacing the floor characteristically and punctuating his speech with vigorous gestures.

"Listen, Rick, the company's grateful for your efforts. I'm here to tell you that. But I'm *also* here to tell you that that's the end of it; we'll take it from here."

Kazalakis stopped pacing and faced Rand directly, fixing him with a bushy-browed stare. "Look—we know what happened to you down in Washington. Nobody blames you for being pissed at Ballinger. But stay out of it from here on, Mister, or *gha mauto stavrosu!*"

The epithet was familiar to Rand. He had heard it enough from Kazalakis during their air combat days. The English transliteration, "Fuck your cross," could not really convey the intensity of feeling expressed by the original Greek; the cultural frame of reference just wasn't there. But Rand got the message. He was to stay away from Ballinger from now on. Or else.

Rand said nothing. He put down his drink and stood up, faint irises giving his eyes an even colder look.

"I mean it, Rick," said Kazalakis, not unkindly, "don't get off the reservation on this one. Give it some thought."

"That much I can promise you," Rand said, then turned and left the room.

"Boss," complained Alfredo Matarazza, "why do you gotta always embarrass me?"

Rand, riding beside his chauffeur in his BMW coupe, lifted his eyebrows in surprise at the question.

"Well, I certainly don't mean to, 'Fredo. What's wrong?"

"It's this fuckin' car! Look, Boss," Matarazza twisted his bulk around to face his passenger as the BMW sped along the Westchester Parkway. "I know you're hipped on this Heinie heap, but believe me when I tell ya its the wrong car for goin' where we're goin'!"

"Jesus, 'Fredo!" Rand's voice carried fear. "Will you watch the goddamn road!" He sighed as Matarazza obeyed, then dropped the pitch of his voice in an effort to display an unconcern he didn't feel:

"This car is perfectly capable of a drive into Westchester to see my father-in-law. The only thing that could happen is that we both get killed when you take your eyes off the road. Which could happen in any car you could name."

"Sure, Boss. Sorry. But you don't understand. The point is we're goin' to see the Don. Now, how does it look you drivin' up in this little Heinie car? I park it between two Caddys or next to a Lincoln and nobody's even gonna see it! Like, you're a successful man, you oughtta *look* like a successful man. And if *you* don't look good, *I* don't look good. Ya see what I'm sayin'?"

"Alfredo, this car costs twenty-six thousand dollars off the

169

showroom floor in Germany. That's *before* I buy every ultra-high performance part the Alpina company makes for it, including a turbocharger, and *before* I pay to ship it to Brockton, Massachusetts, for Arno Witt to blueprint the engine and put it all together."

"Who's Arno Witt?"

"The best German engineer and mechanic this side of Stuttgart. And he doesn't work cheap. For what this machine costs I could buy both those Caddys *and* the Lincoln and get change."

"But Boss, it don't *look* like it. Who's gonna know?"

"Anyone who tries to catch it or follow it into a diminishing radius turn, that's who. She'll do a hundred and fifty-six and the handling'd make Ralph Nader come. You know your problem, 'Fredo? You're an ad agency's dream: a snob."

"Who's a slob!"

"Snob, 'Fredo," laughed Rand, "S-N-O-B, *snob.*"

"Oh, yeah," Matarazza smiled and turned to look at Rand, ready to give him the needle, "a high class guy with a college edjamacation, married a broad with no tits, snorts coke and his dick goes limp when the Russians fart. That's me all right!"

Rand laughed and held up both hands in a gesture of surrender:

"I give up, 'Fredo. Just *please* keep your eyes on the road!"

By now they were running past a long, high wall of fieldstone fitted together as only master masons from Italy two generations ago were able to do. The wall bowed in to a massive iron gate and Matarazza drove onto the apron in front of it, stopped and got out of the car. He walked over to a niche cut into the wall on the left about five feet high and opened what appeared to be a police telephone call box. Picking up the receiver, Matarazza stood for a moment with it to his ear, legs spread apart, coat open, swaying slightly from side to side as he engaged in a brief conversation in Italian.

Matarazza replaced the telephone and reentered the BMW. As he started up the engine with a throaty, high rpm *whoooup,* a concealed electric motor drove a worm gear and the great gate swung inward slowly and silently. Matarazza let in the clutch and eased the car through the opening in the wall.

The driveway of the estate of Don Luigi "Lou the Baker" Scarbacci looked like a well-maintained suburban street. Paved with asphalt and running between solid granite curbstones that antedated the preformed concrete era, it was impossible to see where it led as it disappeared quickly into a grove of blue spruce, emerging after a sharp curve, placed for strategic reasons rather than landscape esthetics, to split a wide, parklike lawn. The broad expanse of closely cropped grass also served a defensive role; it would be impossible to cross in daylight without being seen, and floodlights enabled it to serve the same function at night.

The lawn swept upward to the crest of a hill. At it's summit stood a multi-gabled and chimneyed, slate roofed mansion of eclectic architecture built of the same fieldstone as the perimeter wall. The appearance of the mansion was stark, the ground unsoftened by the usual shrubbery, and no trees stood near it. The low plantings at the building's base could not possibly conceal a man and were apparent only when very close to the house.

To the left of the mansion was a macadam parking lot that would have served a small supermarket nicely. It was complete with white lines painted to outline parking spaces. At the rear of the parking lot, detached from the house, was a four-car garage. All the garage doors were closed. Parked in the lot were a Lincoln Continental in deep blue which had been modified by the Murphy Company into a six-door limosine. Two spaces away was a standard black, four-door Fleetwood Cadillac sedan. Rand would have bet a million dollars that Alfredo Matarazza, to prove his point, would park the BMW exactly between the two behemoths, and that is exactly what he did.

"See, Boss? What'd I tell ya?"

"For your birthday, 'Fredo, I'm going to buy you a diesel locomotive. Its the only way you'll ever be completely happy." Rand jumped out of the car, much to the dismay of Matarazza who had run around the vehicle to open the door for him, then fell in behind Rand for the walk to the front door. The walkway skirted a large circle in the lawn filled with bark which protected the expensive bulbs that lay dormant underneath, waiting for the arrival of spring.

As the two men approached the front door it was swung inward by a large, muscular man of about forty. Behind him, standing on wall-to-wall carpeting in the center of a livingroom, amid furniture covered in heavy clear plastic, was a short, thickset man in his late sixties who walked forward to greet Rand, embracing him and kissing him on both cheeks. Rand returned the embrace warmly and the older man patted him vigorously on the back as they hugged.

"Ricky! Welcome! It's good to see you!"

"Don Luigi," Rand said as he stepped back from the embrace, "you've got to tell me what you're eating or drinking." Rand brought up his right arm and shook his fist. "Strong!" he said with a mock frown.

The Don smiled slyly. "Eatin' and drinkin' these days I gotta take it easy. No smokin', either. But the Doc didn't say nothin' about anythin' else. Probably figgured I'm too old. So I keep on goin' just like before. *That's* what keeps me young!" He gestured toward the man who had just closed the door behind Rand and Matarazza. "You know Augustino, my *consiglieri.*" It was a statement, not a question.

"Of course," said Rand, and the two men shook hands.

Finally Don Luigi Scarbacci noticed Alfredo Matarazza.

"He looks good," the Don said, nodding toward Rand approvingly, "you're takin' good care of him."

Alfredo Matarazza looked relieved. *"Si, Don Luigi. Grazi."*

"C'mon in the kitchen," commanded the Don. "This is no place for family to meet. Veronica has food and wine for us. Come."

The three men followed the Don down a hallway past a dining room on the left and a small chapel on the right. Through the chapel archway Rand could see the ever-present candles burning at both sides of a small, flower bedecked altar surmounted by a statue of the Virgin and flanked by ornately framed photographs of deceased relatives. The picture of his late wife was in its accustomed place.

At the end of the hall they reached their destination. The kitchen was designed for people who take food seriously. The refrigerator was a commercial model; double-doored and of stainless steel. The stove, gas fired, had six burners and a large hot-plate and would have done justice to any good restaurant. Over it was a large cooper hood vented to the outside through washable filters protecting a powerful electric fan. Against the interior wall was a long, pipe-legged table of butcher block, and in racks over it hung every imaginable kind of pot and pan; not suburban Revere Ware but heavy, restaurant grade aluminum. Interspersed were whisks, ladles and other paraphernalia of the professional chef. The ovens were separate and included a "proofer" for bread. It was not for nothing that Luigi Scarbacci had learned the baker's trade at Dannemora thirty-two years before. The skill that had earned him his nickname "The Baker" was one he took pride in maintaining.

A large bay window cut into the outside wall admitted the light that flowed over the big kitchen table set for four. Standing behind the table was Veronica Scarbacci, wife of the Don. The obedient victim of an arranged marriage at nineteen to a man of forty-four she hardly knew, Veronica Scarbacci was now herself forty-four. A simple print housedress with an apron over it covered her gaunt frame. Her hair was an artificial black and her eyebrows overplucked to thin, worried lines above dark, deepset eyes that mirrored years of pain; the pain of never hearing but *knowing* that her husband was repetitively unfaithful, the pain of funeral after funeral for male relatives who died violently, the pain of never having anyone she could talk to about the things that tore her soul—even the priest in the confessional cutting her off with a quick, fearful absolution when she tried through him to open her heart to God.

To Veronica Scarbacci, Richard Rand had always seemed a breath of fresh air from outside and she greeted him warmly:

"Rick! You look wonderful. Can you stay for awhile?"

"Well, I hope so. Your husband thinks I came all the way up here to see him, but it was really just an excuse to get some of your cooking."

Veronica Scarbacci smiled at the lie and her husband bellowed,

"Ha! She made the pasta, but *I* made the gravy! You tell me how you like it. The bread, I make that too."

The spaghetti, its sauce and the bread were superb and the three men said so often, although Rand admitted to himself that anyone in his right mind would have done the same regardless of the truth; an archangel would have hesitated before offending Lou the Baker Scarbacci.

Veronica Scarbacci's expression moved as close to happiness as it ever did. She sat with a glass of wine on the edge of her chair so that she could leap up to wait on the men quickly, her sustenance the stream of compliments won by her cooking. The Don told them again, as he did on every such occasion, the secret of the crispness of the crust of the bread he had baked: a shallow pan of water placed in the oven and a hot iron placed in it to generate steam during the final minutes of baking.

173

The meal over, Veronica Scarbacci followed custom by excusing herself so that the men, should they wish to, might talk business. In the moment, following, Alfredo Matarazza, sensitized by years of experience to know when it was appropriate for him to remain and when to leave, remembered suddenly that the BMW needed fuel and, "so's we don't hafta stop on the way back," left to attend to the matter.

"So," said the Don when the others had left the three of them together, "you have the look of a man with business on his mind, eh?"

"That I do," replied Rand. "Big business."

Rand looked levelly at his quasi father-in-law, who returned his gaze impassively, his face receptive. Augustino Della Croce, the shrewd *consiglieri* of the Scarbacci family, had the look of a watchdog whose ears had alerted him to a possible intruder. He watched Rand silently, missing nothing.

"How big a business?" asked the Don.

Rand took a deep breath. "I want to take over Comco."

Della Croce remained silent, out of deference to his Don, but sat back abruptly in his seat. Scarbacci reacted to the body language of his advisor by rebuking him with an upraised hand, saying, "We owe Riccardo a listen." His expression never changed.

Rand proceeded carefully. "What I have in mind is not a 'bust out' operation. Comco has put itself in a weakened position by massive spending to acquire control of certain foreign corporations. What I propose is to acquire effective control and then sell, right away. A quick turnover. The profit should be enormous; enough to make everybody rich. A hell of a score."

"How big a score," said the Don, "depends on how much we gotta put up, how long we gotta tie it up and what we get when we sell."

"Comco," said Rand, "is worth a billion. That's a thousand million dollars. To do the job will take thirty million dollars, maybe a year, maybe less, and the use during that time of the services of our friends."

"You come to us," said Della Croce, this time without interruption from the Don, "for thirty million dollars. What do *you* put up?"

"Almost every cent I have, five million, and my time and ability, which you know. That leaves twenty-five million I'll need from the people."

"You know how much twenty-five million can earn a year on the street?" asked Della Croce.

"Yes," Rand answered, "and it's nothing like a half to three-quarters of a billion dollars."

"How can you do this thing?" asked the Don. "Could you do it with General Motors?"

"No," said Rand, "G.M. is owned by too many people and institutions. Comco is vulnerable not only because its reserves are almost out but because its ownership is heavily in one man, Gregory Ballinger."

"This man Ballinger," asked the Don, "he mean something to you? You sure this is strictly business, nothing personal? It's a bad thing," the Don continued without waiting for Rand's answer, "to mix feelings with business." He tapped his temple with a forefinger. "Affects the judgement."

Rand didn't know whether the Don knew of his humiliation at the hands of Ballinger. He did know, however, that it would be the height of folly to assume that Don Luigi Scarbacci was uninformed about anything important that touched the life of any one connected to him.

"I have clashed with him before," Rand said carefully, "and took a company away from him in such a way that I got a percentage of it free. With his money, as a matter of fact. Naturally, as I scored off him, he was angry with me and retaliated. I would be lying not to admit that there is bad blood between us. But I promise you that my plan is sound. Complicated, but sound. It will be the biggest score ever made."

"Bullshit," said the Don, "the income tax is the biggest score ever made. And every year they break the record again." He looked out the bay window and rubbed his chin in reflection. The Don had the greatest confidence in his "son-in-law." The man had many times over demonstrated his genius for finance. It was also true that he was a mature man. Still, the prospect that Rand's plan may have been generated out of hate rather than the more reliable emotion, greed, gave him pause. Finally he turned back to address Rand:

"Twenty-five million is a lot of eggs to put in one basket. I don't ask you the details of your plan because I probably wouldn't

175

understand it anyway. I have confidence in you, Riccardo, but twenty-five million? I dunno. I have the whole family to think of, you know."

"Of course, sir. I realize that," Rand responded, "but what I propose would earn enough to take care of everybody."

"Maybe," said Della Croce, "we should do like the doctors do for an important operation."

"What's that?" asked the Don.

"Get a second opinion."

"From whom?" Rand snapped. "Who're you going to get can second guess me?"

"There's still the man in Florida," said the *consiglieri*.

"He's sick," said Rand.

"His mind ain't sick," Della Croce retorted.

"For five years now you didn't need a second opinion!"

"No, and you weren't askin' for no twenty-five million, either!"

"*Basta!*" said the Don. Both men fell silent immediately. It was clear a decision had been taken and it remained only for it to be announced; further debate was out of the question.

"Gus," said Don Scarbacci, "has a point when he says we're breakin' new ground here talkin' this kind of money on your say so. An you should understand he don't mean nothin' personal; it's his job to think that way. You, Rick, got a point when you bring up your record with us; a track record like that deserves respect and consideration. You got some reputation. Enough, I figure, that with such a prize you should be able to raise front money for this scam a number of places, not just with us. Tell you what: you need twenty-five? I'll give you fifteen of our people's money if you can come up with another ten from someplace else. You do that and I'll let you move fifteen of what we got in Switzerland anywhere you want. Fair?"

"Very fair," said Rand, holding out his hand to the Don. "I'll see what I can do and get back."

Luigi Scarbacci did not reach out to take Rand's hand; he merely raised his own, palm out. His eyes grew bleak and age fell away from him to reveal the icy strength that had made him the ruler of one of the biggest crime families in the United States; survivor of five attempts at assassination and the killer, directly or indirectly, of one hundred and seven men over a period of forty-three years.

"Riccardo," he said, "you know what you're doin'? I have to

know that, with Gus here as a witness. You know I love you like I would my own son, but you gotta understand you'll be puttin' up more than five million. You understand?"

"I understand," said Richard Rand, "that I'm putting up my life."

"I'm sorry to talk about such things with you, Riccardo, but if this thing don't go down the way you say it's supposed to, and somethin' happens to the fifteen—well, it's not just that I won't be able to help you. My people will be lookin' to me to take care of it. And I'll hafta do just that. Even then, could be I'd end up goin' down with you. So I'm puttin' up somethin' else, too. You understand? This is, like you said, big business."

Rand nodded soberly. "I understand completely."

The Don rose and smiled abruptly. "Okay, then," he said, "so much for business. You got a dog yet? You oughtta get a dog. Wait'll ya see the Doberman pups I got out back. Raise 'em myself. Some guys, ya know, they raise pigeons. But what the fuck can a pigeon do for ya? Ya feed 'em, love 'em, take care of 'em and they'll still fly away to some other guy on ya. A Doberman? He'll stay with ya 'till the end and anyone fucks with ya, he'll tear their balls off."

The Don opened the back door and gestured the two men to precede him. "Wait'll ya see 'em," he said, the pride unmistakable in his voice. "Bein' on the same side of the fence as one of these cocksuckers'd make the devil shit!"

# XIV

As she had promised him over the telephone, T'sa Li had her brother with her in her apartment when Rand arrived, wearing a soiled trench coat dripping from the cold November rain that washed and chilled Manhattan as only moist cold can. She shied from his wetness, saying with mock exasperation,

"The rug you're dripping dirty water all over is seven hundred years old. Let me have that ratty coat. If it wasn't so wet I'd offer to burn it for you."

"This coat," replied Rand in a tone of appropriate grievance, "is an old friend; maybe not as old as your rug, but it's kept me warm for many a year and I'd appreciate it if you'd follow the custom of your people and at least respect it's age." He shrugged his way out of the coat and handed it to T'sa Li.

"You could have fooled me," she said. "It looks a lot older than the rug. Well, c'mon in. Tea's ready."

T'ang Li was standing in front of the sofa politely, his expression reflecting nothing of what he thought of his sister's banter with Richard Rand. He and Rand bowed to each other and T'ang Li sat down, his broad shoulders taking up fully half of the back of the sofa. His sister sat next to him and started to pour tea as Rand seated himself in an ornate wing chair. Between them was a low table holding the tea service. The long spout of the silver teapot held by T'sa Li had been fashioned into the graceful neck and head of a dragon which glared at Rand from an inlayed jade eye.

The tea was steaming as Rand took a swallow and was rewarded by the pleasure of its warmth seeping into him, chasing away the wet chill. After a moment he said:

"That's good. I think I may live, after all." Rand paused uncertainly, not sure how to proceed. "I'm at a disadvantage, Mr. Li. I have a business proposition to make to you and your associates but I don't know the protocol. I'd like to have what I propose accepted or rejected on it's objective merits and I'd hate to have it shot down for an unintended breach of courtesy or custom. I guess what I'm trying to say is that I'd like your help in presenting what I have to say properly. Am I making any sense to you?"

T'ang Li nodded soberly and said:

"Yes. I understand. My first advice is to permit my sister to finish her tea before you go further; she has some matters to attend to and there is no need for us to bore her with such a dull subject."

T'sa Li's expression was one of resignation. Rand knew she was annoyed but she said nothing to challenge her brother's injunction. Instead, she took another sip of her tea, put it down and said:

"Against my better judgement, because its not worth it, I think I'll go put that coat of yours in the dryer. God knows it can't hurt it." The two men rose with her and remained standing until she had left the room.

"My sister," said T'ang Li when they had seated themselves again, "is not in any way associated with me in business."

"So I understand from her."

"It's better that way."

"Yes."

"How may I help you?"

"Well," Rand answered, "I'm not sure, because I'm not really sure of your jurisdiction, I guess you'd call it, in your organization. I'd hasten to add that I'm quite aware that that's none of my business, so let me just say that my proposal would involve your associates investing a great deal of capital, plus their active participation, under my direction, in a joint venture. With, of course, a commensurate participation in the profits. Am I speaking to the right person?"

"You say a large amount of capital is involved. How large?"

Rand gambled and upped the ante. "Fifteen million dollars, U.S."

"No," said T'ang Li, "you are not talking to the right person. For such a sum there is only one person for you to talk to. There is also the question of your wanting to have our people under your direction. No, only one person can decide something like that."

T'ang Li stared at Rand. It was obvious that he was trying to decide whether to shut the matter off then and there, or give Rand the opportunity of a hearing at the highest level of his organization. That would be a serious concern, for whether his associates decided to participate or not, Rand would perforce learn something of a secret guarded closely from the occidental world. Rand appreciated what must be going through T'ang Li's mind and waited patiently for him to decide.

Abruptly, the huge Oriental rose from his seat on the sofa. He did so without leaning forward or using his hands on the arms of the furniture like ordinary men; he just rose straight up, with complete smoothness, as if powered not by muscle but hydraulics. "You'll need your coat," he said to Rand, then left the room through the same door as had T'sa Li. Alone, Rand waited.

In a few minutes, both T'sa and T'ang Li returned. T'sa Li had Rand's coat with her and he detected a hint of sarcasm as she said:

"Well, that didn't take too long. You must come over for tea some time."

Rand grinned and put on his coat; it was still damp but at least warm from the heat of the dryer. Out of deference to her brother, he refrained from kissing T'sa Li, saying only, as he followed T'ang Li through the spirit gate, "I'll be back when I can stay. That's a promise."

"Sounds more like a threat to me," said T'sa Li and, as the angle of the spirit gate caused Rand to be temporarily out of the sight of T'ang Li, she reached down and goosed him. Rand snapped his head around but she was already back on the other side of the spirit gate; all that remained to receive his glare was a suggestion of perfume and an unladylike giggle.

Rand sat patiently in the rear of the big Checker cab. It seemed at least an hour ago that T'ang Li had hailed it outside the House of Li, but was probably only half that time. He couldn't see his watch because of the blindfold that T'ang Li had, without apology, fastened expertly around his eyes soon after they drew away from the curb. The driver, Rand reasoned, would be one of T'ang Li's Tong men. He had given up some time ago trying to follow in his mind the left and right turns. He had heard the sounds of bridge traffic, but then he had heard such sounds twice. He might well be back in Manhattan after a brief diversionary excursion into Brooklyn, the Bronx or Jersey. The cab slowed, turned and moved slowly over what felt like the heavy timbers usually laid over the large excavations in New York streets occasioned by subway or other major construction underground. Almost at a halt, the cab eased over a projecting timber and came to a stop. No move was made by the driver or T'ang Li to get out of the cab.

A moment later, the reason for remaining in the taxi became clear. There was a whirring sound and the entire cab jerked upward in the embrace of what seemed to Rand must be the world's oldest, most worn out, freight elevator. The long wearing of the blindfold was beginning to have it's effect upon him too, Rand thought; he was starting to experience vertigo—the elevator seemed to be swaying sideways, then actually going down again. With a heavy jolt, the sensation of movement stopped and, to Rand's relief, he heard the cab doors open. He was assisted out and then walked down a hall. They took a ninety degree turn and stopped. What sounded like a metal fire door was opened in front of him and T'ang Li finally spoke: "Step up," he said. Rand raised his left foot, reached it out and was surprised to find it land at the same level. "Now the other." said T'ang Li, and Rand repeated the move with his right foot.

Rand was now standing on a thick carpet or rug. The giant hand grasped his elbow more firmly and guided him into a sharp right turn followed by a ninety degree turn to the left. Spirit gate, Rand thought as he was led forward across the resilient floor-covering until he could feel the seat of a bench or a chair against the rear of his calves and, at the signal of a slight downward pressure on his arm, sat down. He eased backward and found that he was in a high-backed chair.

Rand expected the blindfold to be removed at this point but it was not. To his darkness was added silence; possibly for psychological effect, he speculated. There was a heavy aroma of incense in the air. From a sense he could not specify, Rand gained the impression that he was in a large room. Something almost imperceptible happened, a change he could not at first identify. Then it dawned on him; vibration. He could sense it even through the thick floor-covering. Rand put this new sensation together with the erratic freight elevator ride and concluded that the room he was sitting in was in the bowels of a large commercial building, near the power plant. His speculation was cut short by the voice of T'ang Li:

"What you see and learn here is to stay here. Is that understood?"

"Understood and agreed," Rand answered firmly.

Unseen fingers unfastened the knot of Rand's blindfold and he felt it slip away. He held his eyes closed for a moment in anticipation of their reaction to light after so long a period of total darkness. When he opened them, he was pleasantly surprised as the lighting was low; in fact it seemed to dim and brighten slightly in cycles, as if the electrical power supply was uncertain. Because his eyes were accustomed to darkness, he was nevertheless able to see clearly.

Rand found himself seated in a comfortable, teak framed, tapestry-upholstered upright chair of Chinese design. He had been right about the room; it was twenty by forty feet at least and the ceiling was very high, almost lost in shadow. About fifteen feet in front of him the floor was raised about two feet higher in a series of three shallow steps that extended the width of the room, much like the sanctuary of a traditional church.

The rear wall was given over to stylized representations of a dragon, a fish, oriental pictographs and other symbols meaningless to Rand. The floor was covered by a wine-colored carpeting that ran from wall to wall, over which lay a fortune in antique Chinese rugs. Directly before him, at the center of the raised portion of the room, was a spirit gate that appeared to have been fashioned from decorative screens of intricately carved teak, holding deep green silk in panels upon which were embroidered pastoral scenes of ancient China. To the far right and left of the screen spirit gate were braziers from which wafted the incense he smelled. On the floor, level with Rand and set at angles so as to form a pair of arms extended outward with the spirit gate as their center, were two carved teak benches capable of seating, Rand estimated, at least six persons each. The low light was shed by traditional paper lanterns which shielded not the traditional flames but modern electrical bulbs fed by the unsteady supply that caused them to vary in intensity in unison.

The low glow of the lanterns left the corners of the room in shadow. As Rand was taking in his surroundings, the spirit gate on the dais quivered slightly and eleven men, between forty-five and an advanced age Rand could not estimate, filed into the room from both sides. Rand rose. The men lined up in front of the two benches and bowed to Rand and T'ang Li. Rand followed T'ang Li's lead in bowing back, then sat at a subtle pressure on his arm. Immediately the men who had just entered sat on the benches behind them. One, whom Rand took to be the eldest, said in halting English, "Welcome." Rand nodded in return.

T'ang Li clapped his hands and, again from the spirit gate, several young women entered. Unlike the men, who wore western clothing, the young women were in Chinese dress. They served Rand tea, then the others apparently in order of age. Rand sipped his tea and waited. Another older man inquired as to Rand's health, which Rand acknowledged was good. More tea sipping. A third man asked Rand if his trip to the meeting had been comfortable and Rand assured them all that it had been.

The tea finally consumed and, at another signal from T'ang Li, the cups collected and removed, Rand waited patiently. He received no cue from T'ang Li. He was on his own, acutely aware of being under polite, but very close, scrutiny.

"Is it possible," the eldest said at length, "we may assist you?"

"Yes, sir," Rand answered, relieved that things were finally getting underway, "and I believe I may be of assistance to you."

"Please discuss."

"You are familiar with the multi-national conglomerate, Comco?"

The eleven heads nodded almost imperceptibly. "I propose, said Rand, "with financial help from you gentlemen, or those you represent, together with that of similar investors, to acquire control of Comco; then sell it at great profit."

"How great profit?" asked the eldest.

Rand, who had gotten fifteen million from the Don contingent upon his obtaining ten more, decided to ask for fifteen. He could always settle for ten and, if he got the extra five, would have that much more leeway. "I'm investing five million dollars, U.S.; I have the promise of another fifteen and I'd like fifteen from your people. For thirty-five million dollars, those participating can expect to divide the proceeds of the sale of a billion dollar corporation."

One of the younger men spoke. In his mid-forties, face smooth and hooded eyes hard, he asked: "With all respect to your reputation as one very clever in financial matters, I'd like to know how you believe you can buy a corporation worth a thousand million for only thirty-five?"

"Comco," replied Rand, "is controlled by Gregory Ballinger. He's a greedy man. I propose to bait a trap that will appeal to that greed. I am aware that I cannot cheat an honest man. Ballinger is not honest. That's how I'll beat him."

"Not only does that not answer my question," said Rand's interrogator, "you demonstrate that you do not know your proposed opponent. Comco is controlled by a Russian named Mikhail Sarkov, although I grant you that he uses the name Ballinger. But he is neither greedy nor dishonest. Not by the standards of his culture. He is a *cruel* man and an *ambitious* man, even ruthless and zealous; but not greedy or dishonest. Now, how does that information affect your ambitions?"

Rand addressed all eleven rather than just his most recent questioner:

"Ambition can be a form of greed far more powerful than lust for wealth; especially if it is ambition not for self but for something held more dear than self—one's nation, for example. I understand that Sarkov is a KGB general. He has exiled himself voluntarily from his homeland for a lifetime in the service of his country. A man who would do that must be very ambitious for his nation. My bait will be the same, and I suggest that under the circumstances, its lure will be even stronger."

For the first time, a man on the right bench spoke. He was about sixty, with white hair and a neatly cropped white mustache.

"There is perception in what you say, but you have still not answered the question put to you: how are you going to do it? What are you going to do with our people's money?"

As he would be using Tong personnel as well as money if he was successful in enlisting them, and he would of necessity have to take them into his confidence to some degree anyway, Rand saw no reason not to respond at least partially to this central question.

"I intend, with your assistance and money, to gain control of an issue of Comco stock."

This revelation caused a discussion in Chinese between the eleven men. It was, toward the last, quite spirited. Rand, of course, had no idea what they were talking about. Finally the man with the smooth face and hard eyes said:

"Mr. Rand, your proposal—or your explanation of it—is inadequate. Surely you are aware that even were you successful in obtaining control of a Comco issue, the issue funds would not be a part of the general corporate till. You would have achieved a voice—even a commanding voice if you had actual control of the majority of the stock—only as to the disposition of the proceeds of that particular issue. You would have no say at all in the running of the corporation, much less control of it. Besides, corporations usually suppress—retain for the corporate treasury—up to forty percent of every issue. What you have told us makes no sense."

"What you say," Rand replied, "is true up to a point. I am counting on Ballinger thinking as you do. But there is a way to start as I have told you and end up owning Comco."

"And how is that?"

Rand shook his head. "That is also my contribution. But if I told you that now, you wouldn't need me."

Another spirited general conversation in Chinese ensued; it seemed to Rand to flow back and forth between the two benches. The conversation slowed finally, and the eldest appeared to be polling the other ten, who replied in monosyllables. At last the room was silent and Rand waited to hear the fate of his proposal. The eldest spoke:

"I regret to say but we are divided. Some feel you have been as informative as can be expected and your reputation and personal investment of five million should be sufficient. Others, however, insist on knowing more than you will reveal."

"Then," said Rand, his voice heavy with disappointment, "I take it that my proposal is not accepted."

"Not necessarily. A moment, please."

Rand, puzzled, waited as the eldest Chinese spoke quickly in his native tongue to T'ang Li. The great Mongol beside him bowed and walked forward up the three steps and out the spirit gate, apparently having to bend down to pass through as Rand could see his head descend after he was behind the silken screen. Abruptly, T'ang Li's head appeared again and he returned to the room side of the gate, bowed to the old man, spoke to him in Chinese, then stood at the side of the screen. The old man turned to Rand:

"We had hoped that those of us who have spoken with you could be of one mind. We are not. Were this matter of less importance it would end here. But the prize you offer is very great. Unprecedented. What has been decided is likewise unprecedented. Just as you have chosen not to reveal some things to us, we have not revealed all to you—where you are, for example. There is still no reason for you to know that, but in the interest of maintaining these negotiations I can now inform you that we are an advisory group, and the person we advise has decided to be revealed to you, if you accept the conditions of such revelation."

"I am certainly honored by the offer," said Rand, "but if the condition is that I reveal how I expect to acquire control of Comco at this point I'm afraid—and I mean no disrespect—that my reasoning must remain the same."

The old man peered at Rand and said quietly, "That is a matter for negotiation. It has nothing whatever to do with revealing to you whom we advise. The condition is that you agree never to disclose what is revealed to you here."

"I agree," Rand said quickly.

"Do not be hasty, Mr. Rand. There is more. A penalty clause, you might call it. Weigh what I say carefully, then give us your answer." Rand said nothing, waiting for the old man to continue.

"In the event you choose for any reason to break your word and reveal the identity of the person you are to meet, it will cost you the physical removal of your eyes and your tongue."

It was the matter-of-factness of the way it was said more than the grisliness of the thought that took Rand aback. Thus it was several heartbeats later that he said, calmly,

"I understand."

"But do you agree?"

"Yes."

T'ang Li moved to the screen and, with his enormous reach, grasped it at both ends. With one motion he lifted it aside to reveal a dragon throne of carved, lacquered wood and sumptous tapestry upholstery dominated by green and gilt. There, seated in the throne rather than on it, was the one person in the world Rand least expected to see.

Madam Li, her tiny figure cloaked in a gown that could have come from the tomb of an empress, sat erectly. Her head no longer nodded but was held regally high. Glance strong and countenance firm, gone was the aura of age; in its place was that of power.

"You are surprised to see me," observed Madam Li.

"That," Rand replied, "is an understatement."

"Some knowledge of the culture and mores of old China might help you understand," said Madam Li. She smiled, softening a bit her now formidable appearance. Her English was accented but correct as she said:

"In our society—and it remains as it was everywhere but on the mainland—when a man marries, his bride is chosen for him by his family. It is a mutual arrangement, as the family of the bride is also choosing a husband for their daughter. We have found, over the centuries, that this way is best. It contributes to the stability of the family, which is the center of life and its principal institution. I know that may seem cold to Western ears, but the difference is that in the West, you marry whom you love; in the East, we love whom we marry."

Rand marvelled at Madam Li's voice. It was strong, vibrant and that of a mature woman, not an old one. He wondered just how old she was.

"We have been in this business of civilization for a long time," Madam Li continued, a tiny but commanding figure from her throne, "and we have learned to take realistic account of the qualities you call 'human nature'. A young man marries and works hard as, let us say, a merchant, so that he may better care for his family by adding to its wealth. He devotes his energies to his business and his passions to his young wife."

"Now it is a fact of life that, as a man grows older and more successful, his passions seek other outlets. Our society recognizes this fact and provides for it. The husband is permitted, even encouraged, to take a concubine. His wife will even help in the selection. After all, who should be more knowledgeable of what it takes to please a man than his wife? This cycle may be repeated several times until a man has a wife and three or four concubines."

The eleven men on the benches before Rand sat in respectful silence as Madam Li spoke. The only reaction Rand was able to observe was the shift of their gaze from directly up to the throne as she began to speak to a lowering of heads and looking at hands as the diminutive but powerful woman discussed male passions.

"It is also acknowledged in our culture," Madam Li continued, seeming to ignore all but Rand, "that when a man's passions require another woman, his mind becomes preoccupied with those passions to the detriment of his business. Therefore, as the family has the primary interest in the success of the business, it

187

is the custom of our people that when a man takes his first concu-bine, he turns over operating control of the family business to his wife, so that she may see to it that the family does not suffer from the natural consequences of the nature of men. So it was with my husband, who has now joined his ancestors after an honorable and joy-filled life. Before he left us, he had taken three concu-bines I selected for him, each pleasing him more than the last. I had long before taken control of the family business; hence my appearance before you now."

"I see," was all Rand could think of to say.

"I am sorry you had such a long trip. It was necessary that I be able to arrive here before you."

"It was not uncomfortable, thank you. I take it then that you have had the benefit of my conversation with your associates?"

"I have. They defer to me to resolve the impass you have come to, but I believe that impass more illusory than real. There should be no difficulty."

Rand frowned. "I'm afraid," he said, "I don't understand."

From the looks on the faces of the men on the benches, Rand could tell he was not alone in his puzzlement. The eldest thought he understood and said, bowing toward Madam Li:

"With your permission." Then he turned to Rand and said,

"By this revelation, you have been afforded a privilege rare even for one of our people. Perhaps you will be moved to respond by an increase in trust and reveal to us your plan so that those of us who wish to evaluate it may do so."

Rand felt decidedly uncomfortable, as if he were walking in a minefield. He regarded his next words as steps and took them very carefully:

"I am very much aware of the honor done me, and the trust placed in me, by Madam Li having revealed to me her role in your organization—indeed, her role in life. I prize that honor and shall guard it well. Nor would I now take the position, as I did earlier, that I ought not reveal to you my plan because you could then execute it without me. I am certain that Madam Li, as an honorable woman, would not do or permit that. But there is a further reason for my declining to disclose my plan. There are a dozen people here; a dozen possibilities, not for treachery, but for mistake. I mean no disrespect, just as you meant none toward me when you thought it necessary to establish a severe penalty for the possibility of disclosure by me of what I learned here. It is just not a prudent way to proceed. As with the identity and role of Madam Li, the stakes are too high."

Madam Li had an impatient look. "You have both misunderstood me," she said. "When I said the impass was illusory, I meant exactly that. It was mentioned that corporations often retain a substantial part of any issue as a treasury asset. The fact is that they almost always do. If the issue stock goes up, the company has a more valuable collateral to offer for capital. If it goes down, they can buy it back for less than the offering price. The company can afford to hang on to it, the average man cannot. Either way, it gives the stock flexibility, a high and a low, so the public can play with it, trying to buy low and sell high. Isn't that so, Mr. Rand?"

"Exactly. As was said, they usually retain up to forty percent of each issue."

"Which, of course, tells us what you are going to do with our money. Not how, but I'll give you credit for knowing that; it's your problem. But we do know now *what* you are going to do, don't we?"

Rand felt gooseflesh rising on his arms and the back of his neck. No one had any business being that goddamn smart! A bit ruefully he said, "Yes. I'm sure you do. Congratulations."

Madam Li ignored the compliment: "As I said, the impasse was illusory."

Rand wasn't sure how many, if any at all, of the eleven advisors had followed what Madam Li had said and shared her understanding. If they didn't, and Rand thought that was probably the case, they weren't going to announce it to their leader and peers. In any event, the matter had been decided; the Tongs would participate. Madam Li stood. Rand followed all eleven men in rising immediately. Even on the dais, with Rand below her, Madam Li was not quite up to Rand's height; yet he felt as if she towered over him as she said solemnly:

"There is one more facet of our culture with which I must be sure you are familiar before this matter can be considered settled. In an undertaking of this magnitude, where so much is entrusted to you, the highest form of collateral is required. Do you follow me? Or must I be more specific?"

Rand couldn't suppress a smile. Madam Li detected it and the expression on her face became lethal. "You find what I have said amusing?" Rand felt suddenly as if he were sitting in a giant refrigerator. His concern was no longer for his enterprise, it was for his life.

"No, no!" he heard himself saying quickly, his voice half an octave higher from the constriction of his throat. He got hold of himself and said: "It's just that I was experiencing a strong sense of *déjà vu*. The truth is that the collateral you require has already been pledged as security for the other fifteen million I mentioned. I'm certainly not looking forward to being held in escrow while rival claims to my hide are litigated in the streets."

To Rand's enormous relief, Madam Li smiled at his rejoinder. "Very well, then," she said, "my son will escort you to your home. Let him know your needs and he'll see to them. Please note that I said my *son,* not my daughter. She is a beneficiary, not a participant, in the family business."

"Forgive me," said Rand, "but is she aware of your role?"

"Yes. But when she assists me, it is strictly as a dutiful daughter to her mother."

"I understand. Thank you."

Madam Li turned and Rand joined all the others present in bowing low. When he rose again, Madam Li was gone. T'ang Li reaffixed the blindfold and led him out of the room, saying nothing. Back in what Rand assumed was the cab in which they arrived, Rand experienced the same sensations in the elevator until an incident of pronounced swaying brought sudden understanding. The vibration he had felt and the surging of the electrical current now made sense. He was not and had not been in an elevator at all. The vibration had been from an auxilliary motor generating power—thus the surge. It had been necessary to generate power because they had been aboard a ship. It could have been moored at a pier in Manhattan, Brooklyn or Jersey, but what he had believed a freight elevator had really been a hoist used usually for cargo. The sudden jolt as the cab on its pallet hit the dock confirmed Rand in his belief, and it was with relief that he realized how easily he could have been dropped into the river had things not gone satisfactorily. He kept his realization of where he had been to himself. As the cab engine started and they moved off, T'ang Li spoke:

"There's something else you should know about Ballinger. When I tied the blindfold I could see small scars above your eyes from the wounds you received in Washington. Would you mind telling me how you got them?"

"An old man," replied Rand, "my height but very slight. Moved like a ballet dancer. He did it with his fingernails."

"White Crane," said T'ang Li. "You're lucky you can still see. Had he wanted to, you'd be blind; both eyes stabbed out."

Rand grunted at the thought. "What do we know about this guy, White Crane?"

T'ang Li smiled. "White Crane is not a person, it's a style of martial art—soft but deadly. The man you discribe can only be Sung Bok, a red belt master of White Crane. He works for Ballinger—he and a corps of North Korean fanatics skilled in Tae Kwan Do. White Crane's a dying art; the young don't want to put in the many years needed to master it, nor subject themselves to the mental discipline. Be very careful of him. Sung Bok is one of the deadliest men in the world."

Wing Ha, sixty, Hong Kong Chinese, rich and respected internationally as an able entrepeneur, achieved his position in life through talent, a devotion to homework and to his Tong; the latter supplying capital at critical points in his career. Wa Sun Teng, forty-nine and Taiwanese, was known to be on the most intimate terms with the highest members of the government of the Republic of China. A descendant of the revered Dr. Sun Y'at Sen, he embodied that juncture where private enterprise and government meet in Taiwan. His Tong enjoyed a bilateral alliance with that of Wing, as well as membership in the umbrella organization chaired, if not ruled, by Madam Li.

Save for their Tong associations, the facts concerning both men were public knowledge in the international financial community and had secured for them an appointment with Gregory Ballinger. Thus they found themselves in the uncomfortable position of standing in Ballinger's office atop the Comco Building in Manhattan.

Although neither man was accustomed to such treatment, their preparation for this day had led them to expect and understand it. Gregory Ballinger was standing, too, as he returned their bows from behind his table desk. Messrs. Wing and Wa knew that they had but a short time in which to interest Ballinger. If they were successful, chairs would be brought in and the audience would turn into a conference; if not, their own discomfort would serve to hasten them on their way after having taken up a minimum of the time Ballinger budgeted so tightly.

The room was bright from the cold December sun. It caused the spectacular metallic golds of a collection of portraits of women by Gustav Klimt which occupied the south wall to flash brilliantly. Pointedly, even rudely, Ballinger looked at his watch as he said:

"Good morning, gentlemen. How may I help you? More to the point, how can you help me?"

"We are here," rejoined Wing, "because we feel we can help each other. But first, I hope you will excuse the formality of our request that you keep what we have to say in the strictest confidence, even should you reject our proposal. Secrecy is of the essence in this matter. Indeed, it is one of the reasons we come to you as the need for it precludes our forming a company of our own to accomplish our purposes."

"That is understood," said Ballinger. "You have my word. What are the other reasons you come to me?"

"Comco," replied Wing, "has the capacity to produce what we want produced; a capacity few other companies share. May I explain?"

"Please do."

"You are, no doubt, familiar through press reports at least with the work going on at the Princeton University Plasma Physics Laboratory in an attempt to produce energy through controlled thermonuclear fusion?"

"Project Matterhorn," Ballinger replied. "They recently achieved a plasma temperature of eighty million degrees. But they'll have to get to a hundred million degrees and sustain it for at least one second before they can get more energy out than they pump in. From the point of view of practical application, it's got years to go."

"Just so," Wing rejoined, "provided, of course, that one employs that method—heating—to achieve fusion."

"There is no other way," asserted Ballinger with a trace of impatience. "Whether one employs Princeton's magnetic coil method or the laser method, the principle is the same: superheat the gas until the electrons are stripped away so the positive and negative particles are moving at random."

"Forgive me for contradicting you," Wing responded, "but there *is* another way. Let me explain it like this—"

"No," interrupted Ballinger, his brusque manner in contrast with the politeness of his visitors, "wait." Ballinger depressed a

192

small button on the side of the medieval monk's writing desk and spoke as if to the room:

"Roger."

"Sir?" came the hollow reply from a hidden speaker.

"Get a hold of Scott McBee. I want the two of you in here right away."

"Yes, sir."

If the awkward silence that ensued as the three men waited bothered any of them, they gave no sign of it. Wa wondered whether the microphone that had picked up Ballinger's voice had really needed a button to be pressed to activate it. He decided that if Ballinger wanted to record anything said in his office there was nothing to be done about it and dismissed the thought. Within two minutes there was a knock on Ballinger's door. The knocker did not wait for a response, his knock having been more of an announcement of his arrival than a petition for *entré*. First through the door was a tall, raw-boned, rumpled redhead. He crossed the room with a vigorous, rangy walk and took up a position in front of Ballinger's desk, facing the two Chinese. He said nothing and it was obvious that he had either played this role a number of times before or held a high place in the confidence of Ballinger, so easy was his manner.

The second man was shorter, younger, and slender enough to appear still able to have bought his clothes at the prep school department of Brooks Brothers. He wore horn-rimmed glasses and hair cut in a manner not fashionable since the 1950's, when he must have been a little boy. He walked as if on hallowed ground and took up a position to Ballinger's left at a deferential distance.

Nodding toward the rangy redhead, Ballinger said to Wing:

"Dr. McBee is a physicist. Explain it to him."

Wing addressed McBee. "Just before Mr. Ballinger called you in," he said, "I told him that there is an alternative method to the production of energy through controlled thermonuclear fusion."

"I am not aware that there is any method for there to be an alternative *to,* " challenged McBee. "No one's done it yet. Princeton's still got a good way to go."

"On the contrary," said Wing, "it has been done. On Taiwan. I mentioned the need for secrecy—"

"Impossible!" cut in McBee. "No laser or magnetic accelerator of that size exists on Taiwan. Everyone in the field knows even what the Soviets have in the way of that kind of hardware. It's just too specialized. No one could have built such a thing in secret."

Wing was conciliatory: "You are quite right, Mr. McBee. No one had to on Taiwan because we used a method other than heating to achieve sustained fusion."

McBee looked incredulous. Before he could speak, Wing asked,

"Are you familiar with the work of Dr. Bogdan Maglich?"

McBee knitted his brows. "No," he answered, "can't say that I am."

"Dr. Maglich," Wing continued, "applied for a United States patent on a completely different method in 1972. His theory was quite sound but, to date, lack of funds has kept him from advancing to the point of producing more energy than that consumed —the *sine qua non* for success in this field, as you have just pointed out. My principals on Taiwan suffered no such capital starvation. Dr. Maglich's work has been followed to its logical conclusion. We are at the point of producing operational hardware. *Now* do you appreciate somewhat more the need for secrecy?"

"Wait a minute!" exclaimed McBee. "You say this Maglich method doesn't use heat? What *does* it use?"

"Colliding beams. A beam of deuterium is shot out and then bent back upon itself. The beam shapes itself into a figure eight orbit inside a cell. Actually it is a series of such orbits which superimpose into what Dr. Maglich called a *migma*, Greek for mixture. The deuterons in both the upper and lower loops of the figure eight move clockwise and collide nearly head-on, where they begin to interact and fuse."

"How can they fuse without superheating?" asked McBee.

Wing's reply was matter of fact: "As you know, Doctor, in fusion what counts is the relative velocity with which one nucleus strikes another. Heat is irrelevant. And the Maglich system is ordered, not random. The applications are obvious. The cells are relatively small and ideal for powering military lasers. Combined for increased output, they are ideal for powering deep ocean submarine detection devices. Large stacks of the cells would form a public utility power plant. And it is *not radioactive*. We can ignite clean fuel, such as Helium 3."

McBee snorted. "Helium 3! Where are you going to get that?"

For the first time, Ballinger interrupted McBee: "What's the problem?"

"Helium 3 is a rare isotope of helium," said McBee. "It is found naturally only in the atmosphere of the planet Jupiter."

Wing knew he had overreached and reacted quickly. "It is very rare. And for that reason, perhaps a poor choice for purposes of illustration; but it *is* available in very limited amounts through special production, albeit at high cost. Let's not lose the point: the method is nonradioactive and can ignite clean fuel."

McBee bored in: "You mean to say that you get direct electrical current production?"

"Correct," Wing affirmed, happy to get off the subject of Helium 3 and onto more easily defended ground. "No steam generators and so forth. The energy released by the process is carried off by charged bodies collectable by positively charged plates around the cell. An external circuit is connected to the plates to draw off the electrical current."

The room was silent as McBee held his hand over his mouth and looked at the collection of Klimts as if he had dismissed the subject at hand and was now evaluating the art currently on display in Ballinger's office. In fact, however, McBee didn't even see the pictures he was staring at; his mind was racing over what he had heard and recalling like a computer pieces of knowledge and arcane formulae from the world of physics. A brilliant man, Ballinger had hired him for his ability to digest information rapidly and pronounce accurate judgements as to the feasibility of projects which depended for their success on applied science. Although Ballinger had not said so in his introduction, McBee held a Ph.D. in chemistry as well as physics and was counted by Ballinger as one of the three most valuable men around him.

Abruptly, McBee turned away from the wall gallery and looked hard at Wing. "What is the collision rate in one of your *migma* cells?" he asked.

"It is proportional to the square of the beam intensity."

"The output of electricity from each cell?"

"One megawatt."

Once more the room lapsed into silence. Ballinger broke it: "Well," he asked McBee, "does it work?"

"It could. It violates no laws of physics and obeys the quadratic law, the basic law of colliding beams. But without testing the actual hardware, I couldn't say whether or not their application works."

"But it makes sense?"

"Yes. It makes sense."

"All right," said Ballinger. "Thank you. On your way out, have four chairs sent in."

Ballinger's mind had been attracted like a magnet to three possibilities: getting in on the ground floor on a usable energy advance more revolutionary in it's practical effects than the atomic bomb; immediate high-technology military and naval applications which would give any power acquiring them the possibility of armaments dominance and, finally, the possibility of getting a foothold on Taiwan; an ambition of Ballinger's long frustrated and growing more and more important as the USSR and the People's Republic of China became increasingly antagonistic. Wing's companion, Wa, had not said a word so far. He didn't have to, to have an effect upon Ballinger's thinking. Ballinger knew from his unsuccessful prior efforts to penetrate Taiwan economically that Wa could accomplish anything he wanted to in Taiwan. That was the key; finding something to motivate Wa, who was in a position to pick and choose his deals. And here Wa was, coming to him.

Two men arrived with four chairs and Ballinger and his youthful assistant joined the Chinese in being seated.

"What, gentlemen," asked Ballinger, "do you propose?"

"With the understanding, as part of the contract, that secrecy is of the essence," said Wing, "we propose to agree with Comco to produce, to our specifications, *migma* cell components. Again, for reasons of secrecy, we would do our own assembly."

"And possibly," interjected Ballinger, who would have taken just such a precaution himself, "manufacture of one key component yourself so that no one could pirate the technology?"

"Mr. Ballinger," replied Wing smoothly, "we wouldn't be here had your reputation not led us to believe you can be trusted."

"Well," said Ballinger, looking directly at Wa, "somebody on Taiwan must not have heard of my reputation for trustworthiness."

Wa fielded the thrust diplomatically: "Many times junior officials take decisions that are not the best. Things, as they say here in the United States, sometimes 'slip through the cracks'. Such problems are not at all unresolvable, given the ear of the right senior officials."

"That's reassuring," said Ballinger. "How big a contract, in terms of money, do you have in mind?"

"Thirty million dollars U.S."

"That's a lot of money for my company to risk in a new technology venture. If you aren't as successful as you hope to be in sales, I could be stuck with an awful lot of very expensive junk."

"There will be no risk for your company at all," assured Wing. "As part of the contract, we will deposit in *Banque Thibaudault Frères*, Geneva, thirty million dollars U.S. releasable to you on an accounts receivable basis."

"You are very confident," Ballinger observed.

"Mr. Ballinger," said Wa, "as we mentioned to you initially, we come to you not for capital but for manufacturing capability and confidentiality. The thirty million is already covered by an option for gallium arsenate laser application of a military nature. Our confidence is, I assure you, well placed."

While this colloquy was going on, Roger, the young administrative assistant Ballinger had not bothered to introduce, frowned, then leaned forward clasping his fingers together rigidly, displaying increasing concern. Finally he sat back, took a note-pad from his inside pocket and scribbled on it furiously. He looked at what he had written, underlined some words, then handed the pad to Ballinger who read:

*No reserves.* Will require issue to capitalize.
*Supervision,* and you are stretched thin right now.
Suggest *no decision now.* Let me do study.

Ballinger looked at the pad with a deliberately blank expression, as if it were a poker hand, but his mind raced. Roger Johansen was the possessor of one of the first of the exceptionally demanding combined J.D. and M.B.A. degrees pioneered by Yale. He was right about the lack of reserves—they had been used to finance the purchase of the companies he had enter into the deals with Columbia Steel. It followed that to finance the manufacturing called for by this proposal would require Comco to let out a new stock issue for that purpose. Certainly such an undertaking would require supervision and he *was* stretched thin at the moment. Johansen was right. Good business judgement called for a hard look and just the sort of study the young man was so well-equipped to undertake. Given the facts as his assistant knew them, Ballinger would have offered exactly the same advice.

But there were other essential and overriding facts and considerations that Johansen did not, could not ever know. The fact that Ballinger was a Soviet national whose country's vital interests must take precedence over any other considerations; that Ballinger couldn't afford to let the Chinese go elsewhere because he couldn't let slip this opportunity for a high-technology intelligence windfall, to say nothing of the strategic requirement for an economic foothold in Taiwan. The conventional wisdom of business would have to yield. He handed the pad back to his assistant, saying to Wing and Wa with a tolerant smile:

"My young friend wants to do a study of your proposal. And it would be a good one, I assure you. But I got where I am by taking decisions intuitively—something they frown upon in graduate school, I'm sure. I'll probably lose Roger one of these days to AT&T or IBM or some place like that where he'll feel more at home."

Ballinger rose and the others followed. "Very well, gentlemen," he said briskly, "if you'll send me a proposed contract, specifications and a *Depotauszug* from your Swiss bank—make it in Swiss francs, please; God knows what the dollar will be worth next week—if everything looks okay to the lawyers, we have a deal."

# XV

Gray dominated the streets and sky of New York City on the 25th of December as T'sa Li left a cab at the entrance to the Plaza Hotel. Even here the curb was not clear of the dirty amalgam of soot, salt and slush that a sudden freeze had welded to every piece of exposed asphalt in Manhattan. At minus 6 degrees Fahrenheit with a wind that gave it the effect of minus 17 degrees, all efforts at removal had been abandoned as useless. Besides, it was Christmas.

That thought was small consolation to T'sa Li. As she stretched out her leg in an attempt to reach the safety of the red rubber mat and the doorman's hand in one long step from the cab, a frigid gust ignored propriety and blew up under her skirt to take shameless advantage of her momentary vulnerability.

Chilled in her most intimate area, T'sa Li hugged her camel's hair coat and ran with short, choppy steps, large shoulder bag bouncing off her hip, directly into the lobby, not pausing until she had gained an open elevator. Still marking time briskly as the car arrived at Rand's floor, she gave his door three hard raps and was standing there, legs pressed tightly together and shivering, when Rand opened the door and stood for a moment regarding her.

"Cold out, huh?" he asked.

"Christ! Get out of the way and let me in. I'm freezing my *ass* off!"

T'sa Li didn't wait for Rand to move. She pushed him out of the way and went directly to the fire, holding out her hands to absorb it's warmth. Rand walked past her to the sideboard and poured a pony of brandy. "Here," he said, "drink this and give me your coat."

T'sa Li shrugged the strap of the calfskin bag off her shoulder and let it fall to the floor so Rand could slip off her coat. He tossed it over one arm and started out of the room.

"Where are you going with that?" T'sa Li asked.

"Hang it up. It's not a bad coat; treat it right and it'll last for years."

"It already has," she called after him, "too many."

Rand came back into the living room and made for the sideboard again.

"Which reminds me," said T'sa Li, "did you ever buy a new coat?"

"Yup. Brought one back from Geneva. Which reminds *me*. Did you bring it?"

"In my bag." T'sa Li took a last sip of her Fundador, put down the glass, extracted a manila envelope from her bag and handed it to Rand. The flap was open. He took out the enclosure and glanced at the last page. The signatures of Wing and Wa were there as was a notarial acknowledgement. With satisfaction he noted that the document was dated the day after the two men had met Ballinger in his office.

"It's none of my business, of course," said T'sa Li cheerily, "but what are you doing lending those guys thirty million dollars?"

"You read it?" Rand's voice rose as he spoke, reflecting surprise more than offense.

"Sure. I'm curious."

"That's what killed the cat."

T'sa Li stretched herself out on the sofa. "Care to check out this pussy for signs of life?"

"Cut it out," Rand admonished, "it's only eleven o'clock in the morning."

"Isn't this one of your Christian holidays?" pouted T'sa Li, "Where's your sense of tradition?"

Rand grinned, "Never mind!"

"Well then, what are you doing lending those guys thirty million. They don't need it and you don't have it."

"Goddamn, Sally," said Rand in exasperation, "I tell you about this and your brother'll have my ass!"

"Those are my family's people; you *don't* tell me and *I'll* have your ass."

Rand conceded: "All right, all right; won't hurt to run it by you anyway. But for Chrissake keep it to yourself that I ever said a word to you."

Rand didn't wait for her assent, just continued: "Those guys made a deal with Ballinger I put them up to. Ballinger, naturally, wouldn't let me get within ten miles of him. But I need a legal connection with the deal—one that will hold up in court. I've also got to be able to prove I didn't know what was going on between Wing and Wa and Ballinger. So I lend them the thirty mil sight unseen—I'm not told what the money's for. In exchange for my giving up the protection of knowing what they're doing with my money, they pay me eighteen percent interest if the deal I know nothing about goes through. If the deal flops, I get nine percent. That way I have a legitimate interest in the deal, don't know what it is, have a stake in the outcome nevertheless, and it all makes sense. *That's* why I'm so glad to get my hands on the loan agreement you delivered; especially with that early December date on it."

"That," T'sa Li asserted, "can't be why you look so relieved— I take it back—smug. You had that contract wired from the beginning. What was the source of tension? Aside from the fact that you're in your usual spot—way out on a limb?"

"Switzerland," Rand answered. He looked at her with a gleam in his eye. "I had to get Jacques Thibaudault in with the show. He was happy as a clam at high tide to have fifteen million more come in and issue a thirty million *Depotauszug* to Comco on an accounts receivable basis; but he damn near died when I told him he couldn't hold onto the money—that I was going to spend it all. Jesus, did he scream!"

"I'll bet he did; you blow it and he not only loses the money, he gets kicked out of banking and into jail. How'd you bring him around?"

"Told him it was time to pay his dues. Without my people's money, he's nothing. Then I sweetened it with the promise of a payoff that would have broken his icy Swiss heart to turn down. It went fine. Fun, as a matter of fact."

"What are you going to do with the money?"

Rand drained his brandy glass, sat down on the sofa beside T'sa Li and rested his right hand gently on the inside of her right knee. "You saw," he said, inching his hand higher up the inside of her stockinged leg, "a couple of weeks ago, that Comco let out an issue? That was to finance the Wing-Wa deal. My family's people and your family's people are buying it up all over the world. What the hell, the prospectus looks good. One, it's Comco. Two, it says the money raised will be used to produce a new kind of electrical power generator. What's the magic word these days? *Energy.* Can't miss. So far as Ballinger can tell, the issue is being bought up by thousands of unassociated individuals and entities worldwide. Everything normal. Everything cool."

"And what he doesn't know is—?"

"That all those people and investment groups are giving me control of those shares through powers of attorney."

T'sa Li had seldom seen Rand look more self-satisfied.

"So," she said, "you end up controlling the Comco issue for the Wing-Wa deal. Your own deal. So what?"

*"That,* lover, is going to *stay* secret for awhile. After all, I've got to keep you interested, haven't I? A little mystery is good for the love life; and I can't think of anything I haven't done with or to or for you in bed."

"In that case," T'sa Li retorted, "your imagination is even more pitifully limited than I feared." Rand's hand was halfway up the inside of her thigh now. She reached down and drew it up to her vulva, then clamped her thighs tightly around it.

Rand ignored her.

"Well," he said, "frankly, love, I was counting on you to come up with some of those ways known only to the emperor."

"All thirteen, I suppose," said T'sa Li, rising in annoyed frustration to warm herself at the fire again. "Make you a deal," she continued testily, "you come up with even half the thousand and one ways and I'll get mother to brief me on the emperor's best."

"I'll bet she could, too!" Rand agreed. "Speaking of something to eat, how about lunch?"

"Well," sighed T'sa Li, "as I always say: if a girl can't get fucked she can at least get fed." She spoke without turning around, continuing to stare at the fire.

Rand said, "I'll get your coat," and left for the bedroom. When he returned moments later, T'sa Li was lost in reverie at the fireplace. Rand stood quietly behind her.

"Here's your coat."

"Just put it over my shoulders." T'sa Li was still unable to tear her gaze from the fire. Rand did as she asked. For a moment she was still; then, reacting to the unexpected weight on her shoulders, T'sa Li looked down at herself and clutched the heavy fur that cloaked her body down to mid-calf. She turned toward Rand, her face mirroring surprise and questioning.

"What—?"

"Why so surprised?" Rand asked, innocently. "I told you I bought a coat in Switzerland. Surely you couldn't have thought I'd ever give up my old trenchcoat? It's a part of me."

"But—"

"It's an old Christian tradition," Rand teased, "to give one's girl a mink coat at Christmas. In this case, a cerulean."

T'sa Li whirled around, kissed Rand full on the mouth and said: "You bastard; you set me up!" Eyes gleaming and with a huge smile, she dashed away to the bedroom to look at herself in the full-length mirror on the bathroom door. She posed to the left and right, admiring herself in the silvery fur, then raced back into the living room to throw her arms around Rand.

"To hell with lunch," T'sa Li beamed. "I'll bet I know the traditional Christian way to say 'thank you'—I think they call it a 'Merry Christmas'!"

She pulled Rand toward the bedroom. He didn't resist.

After several hours during which Richard Rand and T'sa Li devoted themselves assiduously to increasing their carnal knowledge of each other, Rand reacted by dozing and his mistress took advantage of the opportunity to yield to a now rather insistent bodily urge of a different kind. As Rand seemed to be settling into a deeper sleep, she picked up a magazine from his "to be read" pile of periodicals on the bed-table, tore off the mailing wrapper and took it with her into the bathroom.

The flushing of the toilet awakened Rand. He reacted to long sexual bouts with two warring urges of his own: to drift off into sleep, and to eat. As he hadn't had a meal since breakfast, hunger won. Realizing that T'sa Li had preempted the bathroom, he decided to keep his mind off his growling stomach by some business reading. From the bedside pile, he picked up *The Wall Street Journal* for 24th December and was attracted immediately to an article headlined *Columbia Steel Sues in Mexico*. The article went on to say that the first of twelve monthly shipments of steel due under Columbia's contract with Mazatlan S.A. had been rejected as not up to specification. This assertion was contradicted strongly by Columbia, which had filed suit in Mexico for that country's legal equivalent of specific performance and goods had and received.

Alarm swept Rand. There was a slow fuse burning somewhere but he couldn't trace it to the charge. Frustrated and uneasy, as well as hungry, he threw down the *Journal,* went over to the bathroom door and knocked on it rudely.

"Yes?"

"What's going on in there?"

"What d'you think's going on? I'm reading."

"That's what I thought. You can do that anywhere. C'mon, I'm hungry."

T'sa Li's reply was drowned out by the sound of the toilet flushing. There followed the sound of the sink being used and, as Rand sat back down on the side of the bed to wait, the bathroom door opened and T'sa Li stood in the doorway naked, one hand still holding onto the knob of the open door, the other braced against her cocked hip and still holding a copy of the current Hong Kong weekly *Far Eastern Economic Review.* The light was still on in the bathroom and it backlighted her body so strongly that Rand could see clearly the tiny wisps of public hair between her parted legs.

"I'm sore," announced T'sa Li with a mock pout.

"C'mon," said Rand, "you were in there long enough to read the *Encyclopedia Britannica.*"

"I don't mean *that* kind of sore," said T'sa Li, "I mean *sore* sore. Right in my you know where."

Rand laughed and rose from the bed. "Well, if you don't stop posing in that doorway and put some clothes on, you're going to be a lot sorer in a minute."

"God! Is that all you can think of?"

"I dunno. Try me."

It was T'sa Li's turn to laugh as she bent down to retrieve her panties and bra from the floor beside the bed while waving the Hong Kong magazine at Rand. "Did you read this yet?"

"No. Why? Something good in it?"

"Interesting," T'sa Li said as she tossed the magazine back on the pile and stepped into her panties. "They've got an article about civil law around the world, and the U.S. doesn't come out all that well. It can take over *four years* for a civil suit to come to trial in courts in the big metropolitan areas here. People complain about India, Mexico, Germany and what have you taking forever; but four years! Even Italy doesn't take more than six usually and sometimes a payoff can work wonders in Mexico and —what's the matter with you?"

Rand looked striken. He sat down on the bed again, slowly, let the air out of his lungs, then took a deep breath.

"Jesus!" he said, "That's it." Rand paused as the enormity of what he had just comprehended sank in. "Shit!" he exclaimed, punching the mattress.

"What the hell are you talking about?" asked T'sa Li insistently, pausing with her panties at mid-thigh.

Rand jumped off the bed and began to pace back and forth at it's foot.

"Ballinger. That's what I'm talking about. The son of a bitch is a genius. It's so simple! How the hell could I have missed it?"

T'sa Li pulled her panties up tight against her crotch. With her fingers she smoothed the elastic around her waist, then eased it where it cut a little too tightly between her legs. "Are you going to tell me or not?"

"Later," said Rand, appearing to have made up his mind about something as he strode over to the telephone and lifted the receiver. He gave his room number to the operator and asked for an outside line, then dialed and waited impatiently. T'sa Li gave up and bent over to let her breasts fall into the cups of her bra, then reached back to fasten it's clasp. She had straightened up and was pulling on the cup tops to adjust them when Rand barked into the phone:

"This is Richard Rand. *R-A-N-D.* In New York. It is urgent that I talk to Deputy Director Kazalakis immediately."

There was a pause, then: "Of course I know it's Christmas! The world doesn't stop because it's Christmas; most of the world isn't Christian. No, the duty officer *won't* do. And if you don't patch me through to Kazalakis, I want your log entry to reflect that refusal—All right. For the next fifteen minutes I can be reached at area code 212, number 759-3000. Thank you. He hung up.

"Well?" asked T'sa Li.

Rand put on a robe and sat down to wait. "Litigation time," he said to her. "That was the key. Now it all fits together."

When the stewardess pushing the cart down the aisle of the 7:00 A.M. Eastern Airlines shuttle to Washington paused beside Richard Rand to collect his fare, she yawned unexpectedly. Rand, slumped down in the aisle seat in the "no smoking" section, got a clear view of the fillings in her upper teeth before the embarrassed woman was able to get a palm over her mouth. She held it there long enough to muffle the words, "Fare, please," then quickly took the boarding pass and forty-one dollars cash Rand handed her. "Thank you, Mr. Olay," she said. Thus was Earl Olay, Brooklyn, N.Y. added to the passenger manifest for Wednesday, 26th December.

Thirty-three minutes later Rand walked out the front door of Washington National Airport's south terminal, turned right and followed the curving sidewalk to the parking lot marked: "Reserved for Members of Congress, Justices of the Supreme Court and diplomats. All others will be towed away at owner's expense." Rand smiled to himself. Those suckers in Georgetown could scream about noise 'till doomsday; Congress was never going to close down Washington National. If the runways were long enough, they'd have the Concorde landing there. He spotted Kazalakis' bushy head resting, eyes closed, on the top of the driver's seatback in a nondescript two-year-old Ford LTD. Walking over to the car he jerked open the door on the passenger's side and barked at Kazalakis, "You can't park here, Mister!"

Kazalakis didn't move. He opened one eye slowly, peered at Rand and said:

"Fuck you."

"Merry Christmas."

"And if you have any friends, fuck them, too. Get in."

Rand did as he was told, then, as Kazalakis started the car and drove out of the parking lot, asked:

"Where're we going?"

"Nowhere until I find out whether you know what you're talking about. Calling me on Christmas, for Chrissake. It's guys like you cause so much divorce in this business. Okay. You said you figured out the scam. Tell me about it."

"Don't you want Matthew, Mark, Luke and John along to interpret for you?"

"Listen, hotshot," Kazalakis retorted, "I didn't get where I am by being a *complete* nitwit, despite what you might think. You just tell me what you've got. If it sounds like you haven't been smoking anything stronger than hash, I might risk bothering somebody important with it. Okay? Now, what've you got?"

"Okay," said Rand, "follow me through on this: We know from

the entry job that Ballinger had a list of companies in six different countries with percentage figures after each company. We know that the percentage figures matched the percentage of production capacity of Columbia Steel that each company contracted for. We know that Ballinger, through Comco, controls all six companies, and did before they entered into the contracts with Columbia Steel; that makes the contracts his operation. If we don't know for sure, we've got damn good reason to believe that Ballinger's a KGB general officer here as a sleeper. At his age and position, it's a good bet he's been put to work by now, so it's reasonable to assume that his operations involving Columbia Steel, which happens to be one of the nation's biggest basic industrial corporations, are on behalf of his principal, the USSR. Follow me so far?"

"I follow you," Kazalakis answered, heading the car up the George Washington Memorial Parkway toward McLean. "I don't necessarily agree with you, but I follow you."

"What don't you agree with?" asked Rand.

"Never mind at this point; just keep on going."

"Okay," Rand continued, "I couldn't figure out what he was up to, even when I saw yesterday that the Mexican company rejected the first monthly shipment of steel under it's contract and Columbia sued in Mexico. Then I got in a conversation about the delays in settling civil litigation and it hit me."

"What hit you?"

"The scam, the angle, the whole move."

"Well," said Kazalakis, pulling off the road onto an overlook site on the Potomac river palisade, "it doesn't hit me. Explain it."

Rand blew his breath out through his nose impatiently and said:

"Look—let's say two or three of the foreign contracting companies reject the first shipment by Columbia as allegedly not up to spec, right? What does Columbia have to do? What *can* it do? Nothing but sue, right? Now look where they are: Even if those foreign courts don't rule outright in favor of the hometown boys, it's a sure bet they drag the case out 'till Christ knows when. Years. Columbia's under contract to devote a total of fifty percent of it's capacity to the foreign contracts for ten years. That leaves it's remaining fifty percent capacity available for the domestic market. If three companies pull the rejection stunt, then Columbia's got to divert thirty percent of it's remaining capacity from the domestic market to honor it's contracts to supply the three companies and make up the rejected steel. With thirty percent of it's capacity not yet paid for and the need to take thirty percent of it's domestic-devoted capacity to replace the rejected steel, sixty percent of Columbia's capacity is tied up by just those three companies!"

"Wait a minute," said Kazalakis, "why doesn't Columbia plead fraud—a conspiracy between the three companies? I mean Columbia *knows* the steel is up to spec."

"No good," Rand replied. "Columbia doesn't know of any connection between those three companies. It doesn't know about Ballinger. And even if they did know, proving it'd be something else again. Damn hard to do. Even if they could, the cases are *still* tied up in litigation for years."

"Okay," said Kazalakis, "so Ballinger breaks Columbia Steel. What's the point of going to all that trouble to do that?"

"You're right," Rand confirmed, "it wouldn't be worth it. But that's not what he's trying to do."

Kazalakis looked puzzled. "Then what—"

Rand interrupted, "Ask yourself this: with Columbia's production capacity tied up to the tune of sixty percent by just three foreign companies, what's it reasonable to believe will happen?"

"Oh," Kazalakis speculated, "I suppose Columbia stock will go down on the market."

"Right again," said Rand. "Let's say the stock goes down by, say, ten points. Will the public panic?" Rand answered his own question. "No. Everybody knows Columbia's a huge outfit and the stock will probably go up again in a little while. Management will feel the same way: next month everything will be fine. Bullshit! Next month a couple *more* of those Ballinger-controlled foreign companies will reject shipments. Then the public *will* panic and Ballinger's agents can buy up Columbia stock at bargain basement rates. The following month, no rejections, just to make it look kosher. The month after that, the whole cycle is repeated, blaming America's out of date steel technology. Just wait and see, Greek; Watch the come-off. That's *just* the way it'll happen."

Kazalakis was silent. He took one hand from the wheel and brushed his forehead with the sleeve of his overcoat by pulling his forearm across his face. Abruptly he started the car, drove back on the parkway and proceeded at high speed in the direction of Langley, Virginia.

"What's up?" Rand asked.

Kazalakis ignored the question. "How many of those foreign companies did you say have actually rejected their shipments?"

"Only one for sure. It was in the paper. *Wall Street Journal.* It reported the filing of the suit by Columbia in Mexico."

"So the rejection probably took place a little while ago?"

"Right. Didn't become public knowledge until the suit was started. That had to take a little time to prepare."

"Yeah," acknowledged Kazalakis. He turned into the roadway leading to CIA headquarters, stopped at the gate and made a phone call from the guard shack. Kazalakis parked the car in the main lot and the two men walked into the lobby, were cleared through the TRW machines, clipped on badges and went straight upstairs into Kazalakis' office. The stocky Deputy Director for Operations sat down behind his desk, waved Rand into a chair and picked up his phone. Punching three numbers, he waited, then said:

"Paul, get me the NSA report on Columbia Steel's overseas communications. I want it all for last month. Right away. Thanks."

Kazalakis hung up and stared straight ahead, ignoring Rand, fingers of his right hand drumming impatiently on the top of his desk. Presently there was a knock on the door and Paul Farington entered, nodded to Rand, handed a thick file folder to Kazalakis and stood back awaiting further instructions. "Thanks, Paul." said Kazalakis, dismissing him, and Farington left the room as quietly as he had entered it.

Kazalakis started reading the file. After a few minutes of silence he slammed it down, saying:

"*Ahhhh,* shit!"

"What's the matter?"

"You were right. There's cable traffic here screaming about rejection of the first month's shipments to India and Italy, too."

"So," said Rand. "You want to know what's going to happen next?"

"Jesus! There's more?"

"Oh, sure."

"*God* damn! How do we stop it?"

"We don't. It's too far along."

"There's gotta be a way. There's *always* a way!"

"Oh, there's a way to handle it, all right." Rand had in mind his own attack against Ballinger and Comco, which had the virtue of also being underway.

"Hold it," said Kazalakis. He picked up his phone again, hit the buttons rapidly, then said: "Kazalakis. Is he in?" There was a pause, then: "I've got Rand in here. It looks like he's doped out the Ballinger operation. I think you should hear what he's got to say." There was another pause, then Kazalakis said, "Right there," and hung up. "No sense," he said to Rand, "having to repeat yourself. Let's toss it all to McKenzie."

Alexander McKenzie received the two men cordially and, over glasses of Harvey's Bristol Cream, Rand repeated to McKenzie what he had said to Kazalakis.

"You said there was more," Kazalakis prompted as Rand finished bringing the CIA director up to date.

"There is. Just detail, actually," said Rand. "The operation should go like this pretty much: If, as is likely, Ballinger has been able to acquire on the market over a period of time, say, twenty-five percent of the outstanding shares of Columbia Steel, it's of the B variety, or money stock. Some fifty percent of the A, or voting stock has been pledged by Columbia's management against fulfillment of the foreign contracts and either is, or soon will be, tied up in litigation in foreign courts. While that's tied up, Columbia's board chairman can't vote it. The twenty-five percent of the B stock owned by Ballinger carries with it automatically twenty-five percent voting of the A stock, and Ballinger, through the six foreign companies, still owes Columbia for the rejected steel.

"Let's say," Rand continued, "that Columbia stock goes down in the market on the average by half—not unreasonable to expect when these troubles come to light. When Ballinger pulls the string and the foreign companies accept the rejected steel in a compromise of the law suits, the stock returns to normal and the stockholders will be even. But Ballinger will have bought at half that amount, so he'll have bought it all at the expense of Columbia Steel. You see the beauty of it?"

The two men looked at Rand and nodded soberly. "Now," wound up Rand, "if Ballinger repeats the rejection cycle again, and he's certain to, Columbia's management will have to step down and hand over control of the corporation to Ballinger.

Management will have no choice. Ballinger can stand the litigation because he's tied up nothing. Columbia has it's capacity tied up. There'll be no way out. The Soviet Union takes operating control of one of America's industrial giants. Absolutely brilliant."

"You told me," said Kazalakis, "there was a way to handle it. How do we stop them?"

"You can't," said Rand. "It's gone too far. The only thing to be done is to counterattack the takeover vehicle: Comco."

"How do we go about that?" asked Kazalakis.

"Never mind," interrupted McKenzie, "that won't be necessary."

"Rand and Kazalakis, faces mirroring their curiosity, regarded McKenzie silently. Rand finally spoke:

"I beg your pardon?"

"Please listen to me carefully," said McKenzie, resting his elbows on his desk top and leaning forward toward Rand and Kazalakis in emphasis. "I want what I say to be understood very clearly by you both. There will be no, I repeat, no, counterattack mounted against Comco, Ballinger or his operation. You are quite correct, Mr. Rand, both in your identification of Ballinger as General Mikhail Sarkov of the KGB and your assumption that what he is doing is performing a task laid on him by his principals. You have also, quite remarkably I must say, deduced the details of the Soviet plan to take over Columbia Steel."

Rand looked stunned; Kazalakis embarrassed. Kazalakis attempted to speak but McKenzie cut him off:

"You were not informed, Mr. Kazalakis, as you had no need to know. You had no need to know as Deputy for Operations as there is nothing for you to do. Let me make myself clear: you are *ordered* to do nothing to interfere with Ballinger's plans. I can assure you both that this matter has been evaluated carefully by the National Security Council and the decision has been taken at the highest level, that is the *highest* level of your government, to permit the Soviet Ballinger operation to go forward to it's logical conclusion. Is that understood by both of you?"

Kazalakis and Rand sat in their seats in shocked silence.

"Well," insisted McKenzie, "is that understood?"

"Yes, sir," Kazalakis managed to croak. He sounded as if he were strangling. No wonder McKenzie had accepted Rand so quickly after first resisting his recruitment. That goddamn Forty

Committee meeting; they must have decided to task the whole fucking intelligence community to find out what was going on— Rand was just a wild card backup and the holdover deputy isolated. Beautiful! If the community comes up empty and Rand does the job, fine. If Ballinger gets the wind up, Rand moving around in the brush draws the bullet that makes Ballinger feel secure again. And if the thing blows up in their face, the perfect choice of scapegoats: need an outsider for plausible denial of government involvement? Meet Richard Rand. No good? Need a high-ranking agency head to serve up to an oversight committee? Here's Constantine Kazalakis with an apple in his mouth. Beautiful.

McKenzie spoke again, breaking Kazalakis' angry reverie: "And you, Mr. Rand?"

"I understand what you're saying, all right," said Rand in a voice so low as to be just above a whisper. "What I don't understand is, why?" Rand's pupilless pale eyes fixed McKenzie balefully. "And while we're on the subject of understanding one another," said Rand, "understand this: you can order *him* around," Rand nodded toward Kazalakis, "he works for you. Just remember, I don't."

"Very well," McKenzie replied smoothly, "perhaps I can persuade you. The rationale is quite simple: Détente, however well-intentioned, has proven a disaster to this country. The Soviets have cheated to such an extent on SALT that they are very close to clear ICBM superiority. The Soviet navy has already achieved parity and will shortly be superior to ours. There are now Soviet air and naval bases on both coasts of Africa. The Middle East, our primary source of oil, is being encircled by Soviet clients. They've made a mockery of the Helsinki agreements, taken us to the cleaners in bilateral trade, especially in agriculture and high-technology products, stolen the KH-11 satellite and used the revolution to get our best fighter plane and the Phoenix missile guidance system from Iran. The net result is that the Third World countries are on the verge of being 'third' no longer, but going into the Soviet camp. The balance of power is being altered rapidly against the United States."

"None of that is news," Rand rejoined. "Anyone who can read knows that."

"My point exactly," said McKenzie. "The American people know it and are uneasy. They suspect that something has gone very wrong but they don't know what, or what to do about it. Détente has been sold to them for so long as such a good that they must be prepared, emotionally and psychologically, for it's termination. Our people must be convinced beyond doubt that Soviet treachery has nullified American efforts to act morally and ethically to make détente work and advance the cause of peace. America must reestablish herself quickly as the dominant power in the world. The situation can be likened to that of 1941."

"I tell you these things," McKenzie continued, "because I know that you have the knowledge, and possibly the assets, to mount a counterattack on your own which might at least delay, if not thwart, Ballinger in his plans. That must not happen. I can assure you that to do so would be directly contrary to the national interest of the United States. 1941, Mr. Rand. Now do you understand?"

Anger coursed through Rand, causing his hands to tremble noticeably. "Yes," he said, nearly choking on the words, "Pearl Harbor." He fought his anger for control, won the battle, then continued in a tone of voice that betrayed the rage still seething in him just below the surface:

"The Soviet takeover of Columbia Steel is to be permitted to happen as an economic Pearl Harbor. The idea is to rouse the American people so strongly against the Soviet Union they'll accept the end of détente and whatever economic sacrifices are necessary for another last minute rush to rebuild American military power."

"Precisely," said Alexander McKenzie. He sat back with an air of satisfaction. Rand looked over at Kazalakis. His dark head was nodding and his expression indicated not only understanding but assent. That assent was enough to destroy Rand's fragile self-control. He leaped to his feet, saying:

"You people are crazy! You know that? Out of your minds! The whole thing is extremely dangerous and completely unnecessary. You want to end détente? Fine. All you have to do is expose the plot and grab Ballinger. You expose him as a KGB general and hold him to swap for one of our guys. But you don't want to do that. Oh, no. You want Pearl Harbor so you won't have to tell people the truth!"

The anger in Rand's voice gave place to scorn. "The Soviets cheated on détente. Bullshit! You know goddamn well there're no rules in an international fight for power. How can you cheat when there aren't any rules? So they got our plane from Iran. Who put it there and then didn't protect it? Where were you guys all that year, huh? And you gonna tell me we didn't get all we needed from their Mig-25 that landed in Japan? That's what it's all about, Mister! All detente did was give both sides an equal chance to advance at the expense of the other without paying the price of war. We had exactly the same opportunity as the Soviets to exploit detente but we didn't have the brains or balls or both to do it. You can't blame *that* on the Russians. We opted for prayer and peanut butter while they opted for *panzers,* so we lose. Why don't you tell *that* to the American people in a fucking fireside chat?"

As he spoke, Rand moved directly in front of McKenzie's desk and the seated man seemed to lean further back in his chair as if to escape the force of his words:

"No," Rand answered his own question glowering at McKenzie, "we won't do that. Admit we were wrong and we might not be reelected. So we'll just keep on denying the imperatives of reality and promoting the myth of morality in international affairs and the American people can keep on taking it up the ass."

Rand looked from one man to the other. "Once," he said, "just once I'd like to see a national leader tell the people there is no Easter Bunny; that what it's all about is big fish eat little fish and the only thing that counts in this world is power and the will to use it. Is it the Russian's fault they're not stupid? So at Pearl Harbor thousands died and now tens of thousands of citizen's life savings are to be wiped out; sacrificed for the same old bullshit!"

Rand ignored Kazalakis. He rested his hands on McKenzie's desk top and loomed over it as close as he could get to the CIA director. His voice took on a chilling calm:

"You know what? You're going to have some people hysterical. Calling for war. Suppose it gets out of hand? Then what do you do? How're you gonna fight a war, huh? With what? Rusted ships with crews more interested in fighting among themselves? Thirty year old subsonic bombers? An army that wants marijuana packed in it's C rations? You expect them to hold against the Red Army?"

His passion spent, Rand turned away and repeated, dully:

"You people are crazy."

McKenzie's smooth diction wore a patina of sarcasm as he asked: "And what is your suggestion, Mr. Rand? That we capitulate to the Soviet Union?"

214

"No," Rand said, almost sadly, "just tell people the truth for a change. Tell 'em the facts of life. They're a great people. They'll come through. But they need time. Because it's *not* 1941. You don't *have* a depression-hardened generation out there. I agree that they don't know. But they deserve to be led, not conned. Don't do this to them."

McKenzie rose and stood behind his desk. "Well, Mr. Rand," he said with a forced friendliness, "it was good of you to let us have your views. We appreciate them. On the other hand, I'm sure you appreciate the fact that this matter has received a great deal of informed and thoughtful attention from your government and a decision taken for a different course of action."

McKenzie held out his hand to Rand. "That being the case," he continued, "I'm sure we have your assurance that you'll do nothing to interfere with the policy of your government."

Rand straightened and stared at McKenzie for a moment. Instead of taking McKenzie's hand he unclipped his visitor's badge and tossed the plastic square on McKenzie's desk.

"You have nothing of the sort," said Rand. He turned on his heel and strode to the door. As he reached it, McKenzie rose and called after him severely:

"I don't know just who you think you are, young man. You're as entitled as anyone else to an opinion of what's best for the American people. But I remind you that you've never been elected to represent them in any way. It's one thing to hold an opinion; quite another to take it upon yourself to interfere with the actions of your government. Just how far are you prepared to let arrogance take you? I'd like to know your intentions before you leave. I believe we're entitled to that."

Rand, who had reached the door and had his hand on the knob, turned and regarded McKenzie coldly, his eyes completely empty.

"That's something we have in common," said Rand, opening the door.

"And what is that, sir?" asked McKenzie.

"When it comes right down to it, we'll both do exactly the same thing."

"Indeed. Which is?"

"Whatever it takes," said Rand, and was gone.

McKenzie sat back down in his desk chair slowly. For what seemed to Kazalakis one of the longest moments he had ever lived, his superior said nothing. Finally, McKenzie spoke:

"That man is very dangerous. Eliminate him. Quickly."

"He may be arrogant," said Kazalakis, "but he's right, you know."

"Of course he's right. Since when has that been controlling? How many people can be in charge? Just makes him all the more dangerous. As for arrogance, the problem is he's not arrogant enough."

"I beg your pardon?"

"A truly arrogant man," explained McKenzie, "values himself above all else. He won't risk his own destruction for a cause greater than he is because it's inconceivable to him that there could ever *be* such a cause. Unfortunately for him, that's not your Mr. Rand."

"Sir," protested Kazalakis, "elimination's the ultimate sanction. It's not as if he had said he was going to interfere, he just advocated it. If we were to go around liquidating everyone with a contrary view—"

"All right, all right. Your point is well taken. But I want him watched closely. At the first sign that he *is* interfering, or even planning to interfere, I want him gone. If he gets out of control, don't even take the time to come back to me with it. Just do it. Immediately."

"Yes, sir." Kazalakis rose, then paused as McKenzie said:

"You won't have any trouble with that? I mean his being a long time friend and so forth?"

"If that were the case, sir, I'd have had to resign a long time ago."

"Very well then," said McKenzie, "see to it."

# XVI

Through breaches cut by the East Sixties at regular intervals in the elegant wall of apartment houses lining east Fifth Avenue, light from the newly risen sun flashed across intersections to penetrate the wooded border of Central Park, it's flora still leafless this cool, moist, late April morning. Richard Rand, running due south, entered the last of five miles at high cruise, feeling euphoric. Behind him, Alfredo Matarazza, driving the open coach inexpertly and suffering from hangover, felt dreadful.

Rand kept track of his progress by the patches of intense light seeping through the brush at each intersection, signaling that another block lay behind him. He knew he still had a great deal of reserve strength; too much, he decided. Accordingly, with only half a mile to go, Rand elected to finish his run with an 880 yard dash. Catching Matarazza completely by surprise, he rolled up on the balls of his feet, lengthened his stride and sprinted. Within moments he was too far ahead of Matarazza to be protected effectively. With an oath the long-suffering bodyguard whipped his horse and, seconds thereafter, lost his four and a half mile battle with nausea. The horse, more startled by the retching of his driver than the crack of the whip, gained on Rand.

Seeking to achieve a training effect by extending his body to it's limit, Rand got what he wanted; the last hundred yards were pure mind-absorbing pain. So deeply had he forced himself into oxygen debt that he staggered as he passed the tall pin oak that was his finish line and had to bend over, legs astraddle, hands propped against his knees to prevent himself from falling. A rushing sound like the noise between short wave stations filled his ears and he closed his eyes against the red haze that blurred his vision and threatened his balance.

It was Rand's critical need for more air that forced him from his bent over position. Thrusting his body erect, eyes still closed and head tilted to the sky as he inhaled huge breaths, Rand stepped out blindly to start walking off his exhaustion. So it was completely his fault when he walked directly into someone. "Excuse me!" he gasped.

Extending both hands automatically to steady himself and his victim, it was several moments before Rand's eyes focused and he saw, to his surprise and chagrin, that the person he had barged into was T'sa Li.

"It's okay," she said. "C'mon; walk and catch your breath before you fall on top of someone you don't know and get sued."

Rand tried to smile but managed only a grimace as he walked slowly north, one arm draped across T'sa Li's back and shoulder. If she minded having Rand's hot, wet arm over her hound's tooth jacket, she gave no sign. The jacket matched a full, pleated skirt. Black figured, knitted wool socks and black penny loafers covered her legs and feet. Under her jacket she wore a finely knit eggshell turtleneck sweater. The outfit, topped off by a black beret, made her look like a fashionable member of an Oriental auxiliary of the IRA.

Alfredo Matarazza, having problems of his own, was only too glad to use the excuse of the appearance of T'sa Li to drop back a discreet distance where his wretched state would not be noticed.

"What," Rand asked haltingly between breaths, "are you doing up so early in the morning?"

"You mean," she answered, "what am I doing here at all?" T'sa Li didn't wait for a reply. "Well," she continued, "I said to myself, 'If Muhammad won't come to the mountain—'After all, it's been a long enough time without hearing from you for even me to get the hint."

"Sorry," Rand managed between two more deep draughts of air.

"Oh," said T'sa Li, airily, "no need to be. I was hurt at first, then angry, then indifferent and, finally, curious. When something came up I thought you should know, it was enough excuse to satisfy my curiosity. I figure you had a reason, no matter how dumb."

218

"Yeah," said Rand, now purposefully laboring his breath to cover his uncertainty as to what to say.

"At any rate," T'sa Li went on, "what I came to tell you is that the Morton School returned the check for next month. They sent a nice note saying that Miss Blaylock, or, rather, Mrs. Adam Morgan, has now been discharged and is back with her husband —just fine, thank you. Since you've been paying for it, I thought you'd like to know the happy denouement."

Rand checked his pulse and noted with satisfaction that it was recovering rapidly. "You're right," he said, "I'm glad." He was too embarrassed to say more and uncertain whether or how to explain his neglect of T'sa Li. Sensing his predicament, she made it easier for him:

"I don't suppose you'd care to satisfy my curiosity? I mean a woman really wants to know. Advertising has a cumulative effect, you know, and a girl doesn't know whether to run out and buy a dandruff shampoo, mouthwash, deodorant soap, antiperspirant, charcoal insoles for her shoes, a premoistened cloth to wipe her genitals, a douche to flush her vagina and a spray to make it smell like strawberries—or all of the above."

Rand laughed.

"I don't care much one way or the other about the rest of it, but don't start fooling around with those douches and sprays. Other than sheer conceit, I've never been able to understand why so many women haven't figured out that humans are no different from the other animals. Even insects. The only real aphrodisiac is the one nature gives every woman free. Why spend a fortune on *Cinque de Chanel* or *Vol de Nuit* when what really turns a man on is *une femme au jus?*"

It was T'sa Li's turn to smile: "Well, from past experience with you, anyway, I certainly *thought* so."

"The answer to your question," said Rand, "is 'none of the above.' It's just that I'm making some moves that'll attract lightning and I don't want you under the tree if it strikes."

"Balls!" snapped T'sa Li. "How many times do I have to go down this same road with you? We've been over all this before and I *thought* we'd decided I have the right to make up my own mind about what chances I'm willing to take. So what happens? You shut me out without even *consulting* me. Unilaterally, *ex parte*, just like that!"

"Before was different!" Rand protested. "Before I was just pre-

219

dicting, nothing had really happened yet. We're way beyond that now. Everything I said would happen, did. Christ! Columbia went down twelve and an eighth before Ballinger brought it back by compromising those suits; and there was a hell of a lot of volume in that stock. He's loaded with it now. We know because he had to borrow to the hilt to pay for it because the Comco reserves were spent acquiring those foreign corporations. He's so close to pulling this thing off he can't think of anything else. All he has to do is stay cool for a month or so, then repeat the rejection cycle and the whole *geschmeer* is his. But he's extended to the limit. Vulnerable, really vulnerable. And he knows it. The minute something goes wrong and he feels threatened, he'll look to blow away whoever he thinks is behind it. And he won't give a fat rat's ass for the life of any bystanders caught in the middle."

Rand pulled the white towel around his neck out from under the collar of his warm-up jacket and wiped his sweat-drenched face with it. T'sa Li said:

"What are you going to do?"

*"Going* to do? I've already done it. Wing and Wa have already told Comco it's product doesn't work because of faulty manufacture, so Comco's not entitled to the money in Switzerland and it won't be released. Then they wrote to me, saying the deal failed so they're only paying me nine percent interest on my loan to them instead of eighteen. I challenged that, all still on paper, and demanded that they reveal the deal to me so I could verify the claim of failure. They wrote back, outlining the deal and the failure, with copies of the appropriate correspondence with Comco, so now I have that knowledge officially and can document exactly how I learned of it and when."

"What good does all that do you?"

"Don't you see? It gives me the lever I want. I've got control of the issue Comco let out to finance the Wing-Wa deal and produce the product; about all that's not in my control is what Comco held back in the treasury—they always keep some of every issue, both as an asset and to make it harder for someone to get control of the issue."

"Right," agreed T'sa Li.

"But," Rand continued, "Comco failed to produce to spec; it's been rejected. They might as well not have produced it at all. That means that the owners of that special issue stock are entitled to their money back, and the SEC'll enforce that right because it was on that basis—produce the product—the stock was sold through the prospectus. Anyway, 'though Ballinger doesn't know it yet, that's me. But Comco doesn't have the money to pay me off; it was spent to produce the faulty product. And we know there are no reserves left after the foreign acquisitions. Not only that, in real terms it would cost Comco double to pay me back even if they could: the amount of the issue to me and the loss of an equal amount spent to produce the useless product—that's sixty million dollars. Ballinger's got to be worried now—and that means he's extremely dangerous."

"How do you know?"

"That he's dangerous?" Rand's voice rose, reflecting what in his view was the silliness of T'sa Li's question.

"No," T'sa Li said crossly, "that he's worried. He's cool, a real pro; and you said yourself he has no way of knowing you're involved yet. Besides, even if you get the entire issue, that isn't the same as general stock in the corporation. You get control of the issue money but not the money in the general till. How does that make you a threat?"

Rand stopped walking and looked at T'sa Li admiringly. She was her mother's daughter. After a moment he said:

"I knew you had brains after the first five minutes I talked to you in Macao; and you promptly confirmed my judgement by taking me to the cleaners on that gold deal. But now I'm beginning to think you're so fucking smart you're dangerous."

"Confucious say," T'sa Li said in her best imitation of a Hollywood Chinese accent, "is always dangerous to fuck smart woman."

Rand grinned. "Well, you put your finger right on it.

"But you haven't answered my question," T'sa Li protested.

"No. And I'm not going to, either. Ballinger's worried all right, but not for that reason. He's in trouble if *any*body with a substantial block of issue stock demands his money back because he can't pay and that would destroy his image of omnipotence. That'd be bad because he's got Columbia Steel spinning now and if he's shown to have problems of his own it could give them hope; maybe enough to hold on as long as possible instead of throwing in the sponge as soon as he puts them through the wringer again. That's one reason. We also know he's worried because he asked Wing and Wa to come see him to talk about it; and when they told him they couldn't get away from the Far East until after the deadline, he offered to fly out, with a quorum of his board of directors no less, to meet them in Hong Kong. Now that constitutes *worry*. People beg to see Ballinger all the time. He hasn't walked across the street to see someone since Christ was a cadet."

T'sa Li stopped, leaned against Rand's shoulder, lifted her leg and slipped off her left loafer. She shook it out, inspected the interior carefully, then replaced it and resumed walking.

"What do you think he wants from them?" she asked. "Try to get them to change their minds and accept that stuff?"

"No. As you say, Ballinger's a pro. He knows that isn't going to happen. He's got to smell a rat; I'm gambling he'll smell the wrong one until it's too late. Could be he'll pump them; try to find out what's going on, but I doubt it. He's too much of a realist to waste time. My guess is he'll ask them for an extension, then try to find another buyer for the product. At least I hope so. Keep your fingers crossed."

"Why?"

"Uh uh; that's classified too."

T'sa Li stopped abruptly and looked Rand directly in the eye. "You don't trust me?"

"What you don't know, you can't be forced to tell," said Rand. "Trust has nothing to do with it."

Something in his tone sent a little spasm down T'sa Li's spine but she refused to let him know it. "I'm beginning to think a flair for melodrama is genetic with you. So what are *you* going to be doing for the next five days?" As she spoke, T'sa Li crossed her hands behind her and walked with exaggerated, stiff-legged steps, schoolgirl fashion. The act didn't fool Rand; he sensed the tension in her.

"Getting the hell out of town," Rand said, "out of the country, actually."

"Where?"

"Far as I can get from Ballinger."

"Where?" T'sa Li persisted.

Rand shook his head negatively. "Same answer. Same reason."

T'sa Li walked forward with a sudden spurt, then stayed a good six feet in front of Rand, letting the distance express her anger. Rand jogged forward to join her. She wouldn't look at him.

"What's the matter now?" Rand asked, weariness and irritation unconcealed in his voice.

Resigned to the fact that she couldn't keep ahead of Rand, T'sa Li replied icily, "Just good and pissed, that's all."

"Why?"

"You don't know? Because," T'sa Li said scathingly, "our deal was mutual respect, remember? 'No strings, just respect.' Well, where the hell is the respect in just cutting me off without a word? All of a sudden we've got secrets—correction, *you've* got secrets—that affect the relationship. I don't mean those little airheads you screw to practice your stroke or clear your sinuses or whatever; I don't like it but I go along because that's what 'no strings' means. I've got the same right to play and a deal is a deal and it's none of my business. What *is* my business is anything that keeps us apart. That's something I've got a right to know about. A right to—"

"For Christ's sake, woman!" Rand roared, "For just one minute use your head instead of your ass! Look: the minute the agency even *thinks* I may be interfering with the administration's little fucking of the American people they're going to move to terminate me. Fast. It's just a matter of time 'till Ballinger gets the same idea. *Plus,* if I fuck it up and don't deliver on this scam, both your family and my family will be looking to whack me out. I've got just one chance of staying alive: my margin for error is zero. One mistake, one little unanticipated development where I react the wrong way, and I end up a duck in a shooting gallery full of world class riflemen. Now if it offends you that I don't want you to go down with me if I blow it, well then I'm sorry but that's the way it is. And while we're letting it all hang out, even if I *didn't* give a shit about whether you live or die, I damn well value my *own* ass enough not to want to have to worry when they start shooting and I start running about whether *you* can keep your speed up and your head down. Now I'm sorry, but I just don't think that's unreasonable. Not at all."

T'sa Li walked on for a few steps in silence, head down, staring at the ground. She could think of nothing to counter Rand's argument. He was right. But the fact that Rand had logic with him didn't make her feel any differently. In his acute danger lay a powerful lure; almost a challenge to her love for him. T'sa Li felt an overwhelming need to be a part of this critical time in Rand's life; she felt she *must* share it or what they had together would be forever diminished. Unable to conceive of any other approach, T'sa Li implored Rand:

"Let me be a part of it, Rick; let me at least do *something.*"

What it took for a woman so proud as T'sa Li to utter that

simple plea was not lost on Rand; nor was he unaware that there are some things between a man and a woman that transcend logic. Putting his arm around her waist and turning them around to head back toward the park exit, Rand said, at length:

"All right, tell you what: if things go as I anticipate, after about five days a letter addressed to me will be arriving at the hotel. I'm going to try to be back in time to pick it up myself the minute it arrives, but I might not make it. I can't afford to have that letter sitting in my box behind the desk for anybody with half an ounce of wit to come along and grab. What'll be in it is too important to my operation; hell, it'll be *all* important. I'm leaving today; in a couple of hours as a matter of fact. I want you to hole up at my place and keep checking the mail and grab anything that comes in right away. I'll clear it with the management. Can you do that? You didn't get so mad you threw away your key, did you?"

T'sa Li smiled. "No," she said, "but I was tempted. *God* how I was tempted! Anyway, how do I recognize the hot letter? You get a lot of mail, boy."

"It'll be from out of the country. I'm sending it to myself. The address will be in my handwriting."

"Better print. With your squiggle it won't get out of the first post office. Either that or they'll send it to Russia or something."

"Very funny. As I said, when you get it, hole up in the apartment; don't even send down for food. Take up a bag of fruit or something. If I don't get there before the letter, I'll be there right afterwards. Got it?"

"Got it. And Rick?"

"Yeah."

"Thanks."

"Better hold off on the thanks until this thing is over," Rand said grimly, "you may end up damning me to hell—or wherever your heathen idols damn people to. I still think it's a bad move I'll probably regret."

T'sa Li looked at Rand sharply. "You're really that worried? It's not like you."

"Worry's a waste of energy. I never worry about something I can't control. If it's something I *can* control, then I do something about it instead of worrying. Fact is, I *enjoy* living on the edge and gambling. If you can't lose, you can't win. That's a basic fact of life. But I broke a rule just now and it bothers me; takes the fun out of it."

"You mean me. Letting me in, right?"

"Right. Anybody else involved is there because he's needed, knows the risk and takes it to share in the payday. Strictly business; no personal involvement. If he goes down, he goes down and it's too bad but he knew what he was doing just as I did. You're different: your participation isn't necessary and I'm personally involved; I care what happens to you. That could cause me to take a decision based on something other than operational necessity. Worse, it could cause me to get angry."

"And?" asked T'sa Li.

"Any prize fighter will tell you that getting angry at your opponent is a mistake. Revenge is a dish to be tasted cold. Besides, when I get angry—I don't mean pissed off, I mean really angry —I get rash. I can't afford that. When you live on the edge you're always leaning over, farther and farther. The trick is never to lean over so far you can't straighten up before you go over the edge. I'm way out there now. The odds are poor; even if I pull it off. I'm gambling that past company policy will hold."

"What's that?"

"We—this country, it's intelligence community—have never terminated anyone for revenge or spite. We don't do it nearly as often as people think we do, and then only for impersonal reasons of state. The closest we ever got to there being any emotion involved was the Kennedy vendetta against Castro. Emotion is frowned upon as unprofessional; poor tradecraft. And they're right. If that policy holds and I get away with what I'm planning, they'll be super pissed but they won't order me dead. Don't get me wrong; they'd whack me in a hot minute to stop me; but once I've done it they'll just make the best of it. I hope."

"Then why so concerned?"

"Because I haven't gotten away with it yet—and to do it I've got to expose myself. From then on it's the old race against time routine. Only I don't get to know when the race starts. First indication I'll get is the first try—assuming I survive it. Even then I won't be sure; might be some of Ballinger's people. Now you, you come under the heading of something I can do something about. Only I didn't. So when I expose myself I expose you too. Sure you don't want to change your mind and stay out of this mess?"

"I'm sure," said T'sa Li. She gave him a sidelong glance: "How about you?"

"Yeah," said Rand. "Well it *has* occurred to me that I may have bitten off more than I can chew."

"Boy," T'sa Li said, "you really are strung out, aren't you?"

"What d'ya mean?"

"A few minutes ago you were leaning too far over the edge; now you're biting off more than you can chew. You're mixing your metaphors—old worn-out ones at that. It ain't like you not to do no good in English."

"Kiss my Heinie ass," Rand muttered.

"See?" said T'sa Li. "Now you're being redundant."

Rand shook his head, "I walked right into that one, didn't I?"

T'sa Li was happy. Rand was smiling again.

Despite having prepared for it when he packed his suitcase with appropriate clothing that morning, the change from Spring warmth to the cutting chill of a late Fall afternoon still caused Rand to pause at the top of the mobile stairs nestled against the Boeing 747 at the Pan American ramp in Bogota. Tightening his torso muscles involuntarily against the cold, dry air, he proceeded down the steps at a brisk clip and kept moving rapidly until he had gained the terminal building.

Rand's modest luggage, one suitcase and one briefcase, helped make his passage through customs swift. From there he walked directly to the Pan Am ticket counter, confirmed his return flight reservation for five days hence and inquired after any messages. There was one. The clerk handed Rand a plain envelope addressed to "Sr. Richard Rand, Nueva York, Estados Unidas de Norte America."

Rand grinned as he read the address, then walked away quickly so his amusement wouldn't become apparent to the clerk, who would never have understood it. There was no word "North" in the name of Rand's country, but one would never know that growing up in central or south America. From the Rio Grande South, the arrogation of the term "American" by citizens of the United States was resented deeply. The insertion of the word "Norte" was a subtle way of letting *gringoes* understand that the word "American" is not a synonym for "Yankee."

Rand was still smiling as he opened the envelope and extracted the sole contents, a key to a pay locker bearing the number twenty-seven. The irony in the address, Rand noted, lay in the fact that it was undoubtedly written by an ethnic Chinese. The

226

beauty of Madam Li's Tong organization arose from it's geographic universality; members could be found among every major community in the world, including some allegedly communist Chinese on the mainland.

The locker was easy to find and yielded a tan saddle leather briefcase with solid brass fittings and latches. Rand added it casually to his luggage and proceeded directly to the terminal entrance, took the first cab in line and settled back for the ride to the Bogota Hilton. He was at peace with himself again; the peace that accompanied committment. Rand was reconciled even to the involvement of T'sa Li. She had, after all, elected freely after full appraisal of the risk; that her reward, if any, would be psychic only, was her business. For the next five critical days the operation was being carried forward by his associates, Wing and Wa. There was nothing more Rand could do until the fifth day, when the critical move would be his to perform. Which was why he was in Columbia.

*"Herr von Randenburg; sehr angenehm!"* Front office manager of the Bogota Hilton, Ernst Walter Bogner-Martinez, crashed his heels together and bowed to Rand, who bowed in response and replied in clipped East Prussian that he assumed his accomodations were the best, as required. Bogner-Martinez was horrified at the thought of anything less for the *Reichsfreiherr*, an ancient title little used in recent years but rightfully Rand's father's and his own, were he a German national. It was not just for purposes of security that Rand posed as a German in Bogota; a West German, paying in hard Deutschmarks, is generally treated abroad much better than a Yankee with increasingly worthless dollars. The noble name and title, especially to a Columbian proud of his own ethnic German extraction, was just icing on the cake.

Accordingly, Bogner-Martinez himself led Rand and the bellman to Rand's top floor suite. With a flourish Bogner-Martinez opened the drapes in front of the glass doors leading onto a private balcony. The view of the mountains was spectacular as the dying sun etched sharply defined purple shadows into the darkening green. Rand tipped the bellman handsomely but merely thanked the manager; to have offered him money would have been to insult the class-conscious man.

Rand saw them out, then opened the sliding glass doors to the balcony and stepped out into the cold night. He frowned as he noted that adjacent balconies to the right and left could be reached easily by an able-bodied man and that even those below offered access to an athlete. Chilled, Rand retreated to his sitting room, closed the glass door and studied the latch. He didn't like what he saw. Turning his attention to the briefcase he picked up at the airport, he placed it on the sofa. It was unlocked. Inside were several packages wrapped in newspaper. Rand checked the paper; it was local and dated the previous day. He started taking out and opening the packages.

The first, a small one, proved to be a box of fifty rounds of calibre 7.65mm center-fire rimless ammunition. It was Gecco brand, of German manufacture. Rand selected the largest package next, thinking it might be a firearm. It wasn't; he found instead an item he had requested specifically of T'ang Li: an electric hand drill whose motor was compatable with the electrical current in use in Bogota. A chuck key was attached to the power cord, and taped to the handle was a flat tin containing sized metric high-speed metal cutting bits.

The next wad of paper yielded a hard leather speed-scabbard holster for a semiautomatic pistol. It was angled, flat and small. Worn on his right hip under an unbuttoned suitcoat, the fact that Rand was armed would not be noticed.

Rand hefted the next package but couldn't guess it's contents. Unwrapping it, he was surprised to find a sterling silver cigar case, slightly tarnished, it's shape fluted to hold individually four large perfecto-shaped cigars. The top was secured by a tight slide fit. Rand removed it and exposed the top quarter of four cigars that smelled to his inexpert nose like very good ones. The weight of the case puzzled him. He picked out the first cigar and found that all he had was a cut-off quarter of a cigar. Beneath it the container was filled with loose 7.65mm ammunition. The next cigar proved to be just that—a cigar, as did the third in line. The fourth was another cut-off and beneath it, nestled like a missile in it's silo, was a Maxim silencer. Rand extracted and studied it. Sterile.

The final roll of newspaper contained a Colt pocket semiautomatic pistol in .32 auto calibre. The piece had a concealed hammer, grip and slide safeties and a commercial blued finish. Nevertheless it was stamped on the slide *U.S. Property,* unusual as military pieces commonly were finished in a nonglare "Parkerized" surface. The barrel was threaded to accept the Maxim

228

silencer. The pistol, Rand knew, had last been manufactured in 1946, was a fine weapon, and the commercial finish indicated it had been in clandestine service at some time in the past. Rand smiled to himself at the thought of someone trying to trace his new weapon.

Dropping the slide safety, Rand jacked the piece out of battery. It was empty. He stuck his thumbnail into the breech opening and held it up to the light. In the reflected light from his nail he saw a clean bore with sharp lands and grooves. Satisfied, he engaged the slide catch and released the magazine. Opening the box of cartridges, he charged the magazine, inserted it into the butt of the Colt and released the slide catch. The slide went forward, stripped a round from the magazine and chambered it. Once more Rand slipped out the magazine. He added a cartridge and replaced it once again. The pistol was now fully loaded and cocked. He slipped on the slide safety and put it aside, thought better of it and tucked it into his waistband.

Wadding up all the newspaper into one large ball, Rand found it too large for the wastebasket. Still carrying the paper ball, he studied the glass door for a moment, then left the room and walked down the hall until he encountered a maid.

Rand gave her the newspaper, tipped her, then asked her, in poor Spanish, for a push-broom. After some difficulty in explaining that he did *not* want his room swept, but wanted instead a broom to do it himself, the maid, in exchange fo another generous tip, sold a push-broom to the crazy guest.

Back in his room, Rand unscrewed the handle from the broom and laid it carefully in the track behind the sliding door to the balcony, then tried to open the door. It moved perhaps three quarters of an inch before the broomstick stopped it. Rand grunted in satisfaction, then took the electric drill and moved toward the door to the hall. He chucked a 4mm bit into the drill, plugged in the power cord, then turned the deadbolt so that it went home into it's receiver on the door jamb. Rand snapped on the drill and proceeded to drill a hole through the receiver, then into and through the bolt itself. When he had finished, he blew out the metal dust and rubbed his finger over the hole, feeling for burrs. Finding none, he unchucked the bit, reversed it and reinserted it, shank first, into the hole he had just drilled. Thus assured that it would be impossible for anyone to enter his room by manipulating either the bolt on the hall door or the latch on the balcony door, Rand felt free to undress and shower.

The hot water playing steadily on the base of his neck and shoulders made Rand feel sleepy. Tired from his long trip and with nothing to do until morning, he ignored a slight hunger in favor of the prospect of a good night's sleep. Naked but for his radium-dialed OM-1 Omega, Rand slipped between the crisp sheets. He thought of leaving a call for the morning but dismissed it. He would rise when damn well ready.

Rand slipped his hand around under his pillow until he found the Colt, then moved it to a more comfortable position. He smiled as he closed his eyes. There are times, Rand thought, when it is more comforting to fall asleep holding the cold butt of a pistol than the warm breast of a woman.

# XVII

At 8:32 A.M., Thursday, 30th April, Richard Rand sat dressed fully before a small cart which bore the remains of his continental breakfast. He checked his watch, then rose to stare through the opened drapes at the panorama of Bogota in the sliding glass doors to the balcony. The bright, cold morning air intensified normal hues into the artificial vividness of Technicolor.

The telephone rang. Rand crossed to it so quickly the second ring had barely begun when he answered with a crisp, *"Ja."* The switchboard operator announced deferentially a long-distance call from Hamburg. The caller advised that Rand's purchases of coffee to date were sufficient; it would not be necessary to extend his stay. As he hung up the phone, Rand's relief that his boring pose as buyer for a bogus consortium of German coffee distributors was at an end was superceded by a sense of anticipation.

Looking about for his briefcase, Rand noticed the broom handle still in place in the track of the balcony door. He removed it to the closet, made a last-minute check to see that he had left nothing unpacked, placed his suitcase in the closet next to the briefcase from the airport locker and closed the door. He slipped the cigar case into his inside jacket pocket, holstered the Colt, donned a German made black capeskin military cut topcoat and matching calfskin gloves, then picked up the briefcase he had brought with him to Bogota.

Although Rand had removed the drill bit from the deadlock on the door to his suite when he admitted the bellman with his breakfast, he checked the small hole as he left, decided it was too noticeable and went to the bathroom for a piece of soap. He rubbed the soap into the hole, filling it, then tossed the soap into the wastebasket, opened the door and placed the multi-lingual "Do not disturb" sign over the doorknob. Once outside his suite, with the door latched behind him, Rand checked the hallway for the presence of others. Seeing no one, he slipped his door key into the keyway of the lock cylinder and eased the cylinder slightly off-axis to the left. He withdrew the key carefully, then bent down to inspect the keyway to be certain it had remained off-axis after the key was free. He hadn't lost his touch, Rand thought, and by the time this morning was over his life could well depend upon attention to such little details. He headed for the elevator en route the diplomatic section of Bogota.

When his taxi let him out in front of the German embassy, Rand made a point of straightening his tie and adjusting his cuffs until the cab was out of sight, then proceeded on foot to the United States embassy, not far away. The Marine guard took no notice of him as he entered the reception area; not so the young woman with deep auburn hair worn shoulder length who sat behind the reception desk. One did not come across many tall, lean, Nordic types in Bogota; especially one whose intimidating eyes and black leather coat made him look like the Gestapo man in every Warner Brothers B thriller from 1939 to '45. It had been *de rigueur* to watch them all on the late-late show her last two years at Barnard. She was tempted to say something like "You haf relatifs in Milvaukee, yes?" but thought better of it. Instead she asked politely,

"Yes, sir; may I help you?"

"I hope so," said Rand, handing her his U.S. passport. "I'd like to see someone who can execute a notarial acknowledgement."

"A notary public?"

"Something like that, yes."

"All right," the woman said, picking up the handset of her PBX. "If you'll have a seat I'll check with the third secretary. He's already in the office and should know about things like that."

Rand concealed his alarm. The third secretary was usually the resident CIA officer. "No need to trouble high officials," said Rand, knowing full well that a third secretary was anything but high level. "Well," the auburn-tressed woman frowned, "how about the legal attaché? He should know about things like that too."

Rand winced inwardly again. The legal attaché in every U.S. embassy is the resident FBI agent. To object again, though, might kindle the woman's suspicions.

232

"Whoever," he said without interest in his expression.

"I'll try Mr. Wormser for you. He's the third secretary. He'll know."

Rand waited, standing, as she pushed the intercom button on her PBX. "Mr. Wormser? There's a Mr.—uh," she looked at Rand's passport, "Rand here; a U.S. citizen. He needs something notarized. Are you tied up?"

As the woman listened to the reply she looked down at her desk. After a moment she looked up at Rand and, with her hand over the mouthpiece of her phone, said:

"He says that's something you can have done at any lawyer's office in the city. And if it involves local business it's better to handle it that way."

"Tell him," Rand said impatiently, "I'd prefer to do it here. If I do it locally I'll have to have it legalized—have the local judge attest to the authenticity of the notary, then the Interior Minister's office verify the judge, the Foreign Office swear that the guy from the Ministry of the Interior is kosher, and you people that the Foreign Office guy is okay. It goes on forever. All sorts of seals and ribbons and God knows how much time. Besides, I want it to file a claim in the States through the embassy; it's not a local matter."

The woman nodded her head rapidly, setting her glinting locks bouncing, and held up her hand to stop Rand's explanation as, once again, she spoke into the phone:

"He says it isn't local and he wants to avoid the local red tape and everything, okay?" She listened another moment, then hung up, saying: "You're in luck. He has no appointments until nine-fifteen. The early bird gets the Wormser. Follow me."

"I'm half afraid to, after that one," said Rand, following anyway. "No wonder they shipped you down to Bogota."

"Well, I can't go to Germany; I've got relatives in Milwaukee."

"I beg your pardon?"

"Never mind. Here we are." She knocked on a door, opened it and said, "Mr. Wormser, Mr. Rand." She stepped aside to let Rand enter and then closed the door behind him.

Wormser, about forty, had a budding paunch and looked like a basset hound in horn-rimmed glasses. Ivy League in dress and grooming, he was standing behind a standard middle-level bureaucrat's desk, manufactured for the Government Services Administration by Federal Prison Industries. A framed color photograph of a comely woman holding a well-scrubbed child was on the left corner, a government issue double-decker In-Out basket, the senior grade wooden one, over on the right. The rug was multi-hued indigenous Columbian and the chair to which Wormser waved Rand after they shook hands was a native-carved wooden antique of unusual sturdiness and artistic interest. On the wall was the standard issue color photograph of the president, signed with an auto-pen. The photograph of the Secretary of State was unsigned.

Rand opened his attaché case and extracted an original and two copies of a document prepared before he left New York. It was complete in every detail, down to the jurat of the U.S. embassy in Columbia for official acknowledgement of Rand's signature; only the date, time and his and the official's signatures remained to be filled in. He placed it, facing himself, on Wormser's blotter and rose, drawing his fountain pen from his suitcoat pocket as he did so. He handed Wormser his passport and said:

"I'm going to sign this document in your presence, then ask you, if you will, to acknowledge it. Okay?"

"Certainly."

Rand bent over the paper to sign it, saying:

"As I explained to the young lady, this is a claim against a U.S. corporation that I want to file immediately, through the embassy, as time is of the essence legally. If I used a local notary, by the time everybody got through attesting to the authenticity of everybody else, I'd lose a week and you guys would have to shuffle five times as much paper."

"I quite understand," said Wormser, who had reseated himself.

As Rand rose from signing the document, Wormser pressed a button concealed by the overhang of the top of his desk. In the ceiling, a wide-angle lens of fixed f: 3.5 aperture photographed Wormser, Rand and the document; then a tiny motor drive unit advanced the film and recocked the shutter. Wormser then turned the paper around, filled in the date and time and signed in the space provided. That done, he reached into his drawer for a handpress and affixed the seal of the United States; then took out a rubber stamp and pad and employed them to print his name and commission under his signature.

"If you want to file this through us," said Wormser, "we'll require a copy as well as the original."

"Sure," said Rand, "I've provided for that. If you'll just block stamp all three in and give me back one copy, I'll be out of your hair."

Wormser picked up his phone, still on intercom, and punched the number for the steno pool. Within moments an attractive black woman entered and was given the three documents for blockstamping. Rand had barely enough time to comment on the weather to forestall questions from Wormser when the woman was back. He checked the original and his copy. They were blockstamped into the embassy at 8:47 A.M., 30 April. He placed his copy back in his briefcase, shook Wormser's hand and followed the black secretary out to the reception area. As he passed the auburn-haired receptionist, he leaned over and said quietly, *"Ve haf vays uf making you talk,"* then waved and was gone.

Eleven minutes later, Rand's taxi delivered him to the Bogota office of IT&T. He asked for and received the attention of an English speaking customer representative.

"Do you," asked Rand, "have telephone facsimile transmission services available?"

"Yes, sir."

"All right, I'd like to transmit a document to New York."

"Yes, sir. This way, please." The man led Rand to what resembled a booth used by students of languages. In it, on a desk-high shelf, were a telephone and a device the size of a briefcase. It had a roller and, to one side, a cradle to receive a telephone handset.

"Just use this telephone to place your call, sir. If you'll give me the document, I'll get the machine ready. Is it more than one page?"

"No." Rand handed over the blockstamped copy of his claim.

"All right," said the attendant, slipping the document around the roller and checking to see that the spring-loaded clips held it securely, "when they're ready to receive on the other end, just put the receiver in this cradle here and push this button. When the light comes on, it means the transmission is finished. Pick the receiver back up and complete your call. When you're ready, just stand up and someone will bring you back to me. Don't forget to remove your document. You'd be surprised how many people leave them in the machine."

"Fine," said Rand and, as the attendant left to assure him privacy, he picked up the phone and called New York.

"Feld and Feld, good morning," said a voice that sounded as if it were at the other end of a long, hollow log.

"Good morning. Mr. Rand for Aaron Feld, please."

"One moment."

"Aaron Feld."

"Counselor!" Rand beamed as he spoke. "I take it from the firm name that the big day's arrived. First time I had to specify *Aaron* Feld. Once the word gets around, you'll be lucky to hang on to your clients. I'm thinking of switching myself."

"Yeah," drawled Aaron Feld, "Rhona made us a firm officially yesterday. And you're right—I think we're gonna have to change the name to Rhona Feld and Husband."

"That sounds about right," said Rand. "Say, got your facsimile machine warmed up?"

"Ready to go."

"Okay," said Rand, "the way we discussed. Put your extension on conference call and hook your machine to it, then call you-know-who's office and tell 'em you're going to transmit something for their president from a client. Okay?"

"Gotcha," said Feld, "wait one." Rand's phone gave off a signal that told him he was on hold. He remained there for three minutes, then Feld came back on the line to say "Shoot." Rand cradled his receiver on the machine and pushed the button the attendant had indicated, then sat back and waited. The roller spun rapidly as an electronic head scanned the document slowly from left to right in ultra thin lines, translating what it picked up into electrical impulses and sending them out over the wire. The receiving machines reproduced each scanned line exactly. When the scanner had covered the entire page, it stopped and signaled by a light. Rand picked the phone back up and waited. Presently, Feld's voice announced:

"Done. You're gonna explain this to me when you get back, aren't you?"

"You know all you need to know—and maybe all you *want* to know right now," said Rand. "Remember, when this claim gets to general counsel, and it will fast, he's going to call you as my lawyer and ask our intentions. Be sure to let him know you're recommending an injunction against their use of the issue money until the claim litigation is decided, then let him talk you out of it. I know that goes against all your lawyerly instincts, but do it

236

anyway. Just be sure you get their promise, immediately and in writing, not to do anything with the funds from that issue. Okay?"

"You're right about that going against all my lawyerly instincts," said Feld, "and not just my lawyerly ones, either. I've got a well-earned reputation in this town as a tough son of a bitch to deal with and this is gonna make me look like the biggest patsy in the bar association. You know that, don't you?"

"Relax," Rand laughed. "When this is finished I guarantee you a reputation as the biggest prick in practice."

A woman's voice interrupted. "Rick? This is Rhona. I was listening in and I *heard* that. Just make sure that reputation's that he *is*—not *has*—the biggest prick in practice. I couldn't handle the consequences!"

"Congratulations, Rhona," said Rand, "and don't worry about it. *Aaron* couldn't handle the consequences!"

"Very funny," said Aaron Feld. "When I get the written assurance, how do I get in touch with you?"

"You don't. I'll get in touch with *you.* Put it away someplace secure—and I don't mean the office safe—then you and Rhona stay in the middle of a bunch of friends day and night until you hear from me."

"Hey! Wait a minute!" Aaron Feld protested, "Just what kind of a jackpot've you got us in the middle of, anyway? What's—"

"It won't be for long and the pay is good. Thanks, counselor," said Rand, and hung up.

Rand removed from his briefcase an envelope addressed to himself at the Plaza and sealed his copy of the blockstamped claim into it. He slipped the envelope into his inside suitcoat pocket as he stood to signal that he was ready to pay his bill and leave.

Rand had his cab wait as he saw personally to the application of the correct amount of postage for airmail at the Bogota post office and assured himself that his crucial document was safely on it's way, then had the cab take him back to the Bogota Hilton. As he walked through the doors into the lobby he checked the time on the clock over the desk: ten minutes before the 11:00 A.M. checkout time. All he had to do was to pick up his packed bag and the airport locker briefcase and he'd be ready to leave.

Alighting from the elevator and approaching his suite, Rand noted that the breakfast cart had been removed from the hall in front of his door. The "Do not disturb" sign was still in place on the doorknob. He fumbled for his key until another couple six doors down the hall had entered their rooms, then squatted down to examine the keyway of his doorlock. It was aligned perfectly. The hair at the nape of Rand's neck rose and he came to his feet slowly. Looking both ways up and down the hall, he spotted a stairwell entrance all the way down on the right. Carefully, Rand backed away from his door for about six feet, then turned and walked quickly to the stairwell door. In keeping with fire regulations, it was unlocked.

Instead of going downstairs, Rand went up, to the entrance to the roof used by maintenance men. The door was locked but, again in keeping with regulations, it opened outward. The lock was simple and yielded easily to Rand's American Express card. He took off his coat and shoes, folded them into a neat bundle, then turned his suitcoat inside out and folded it as if to be packed in a suitcase. He placed the jacket and his necktie on top of his overcoat and shoes, then carried the bundle out onto the roof and squatted to place them carefully in the lee of the door shed. Still squatting, he fished out the cigar case and extracted the Maxim silencer. Rand replaced the case, pocketed the silencer and made his way to within four feet of the edge of the roof.

To avoid being observed from the ground below, Rand crawled to the edge on his hands and knees, then prostrated himself to look over it. The balconies were in plain view below him. He counted them, located that of his suite, eased back and repeated the procedure until he was lying flat directly above his balcony. Rand drew the Colt, affixed the silencer to it's muzzle, then rolled over on his back. He unbuttoned his shirt, placed the pistol inside it next to his body, buttoned the shirt halfway back up and tightened his belt as hard as he could against his stomach. Thus assured that his pistol would not be lost in the process, Rand eased himself over the edge of the roof and, hanging momentarily by both hands, dropped silently on stockinged feet onto his balcony.

Once more Rand got on his belly. The drapes were closed and he could see nothing of his suite's interior. As he had relied the previous night on the broom handle to secure the glass doors, they were unlocked. With the broom handle now in the closet, the door was free to slide. Rand twisted his body so he could retrieve the silenced Colt from inside his shirt with his right hand, then released the safety and held the pistol muzzle to the sky.

With his left hand flat against the glass of the balcony door, Rand slid it open with one smooth, quiet motion in an attempt not to alert anyone who might be waiting for him inside the room. It didn't work. As Rand held back the drape to take a look, the sudden draught warned a slender, dark complexioned man in his forties sitting in a chair so positioned that he could command both the front door of the suite and that of the balcony. Time stopped for Rand when he saw the assassin, his mind noting vividly not only the silenced 9mm Browning P-35 already aimed chest-level at the balcony door opening, but also the closely cropped mustache, pomaded hair and expensive, European-tailored suit.

The Browning fired as the drape went back, making a soft *thump!* that trailed off into a metallic ring as the slide returned to battery with metal to metal impact. As Rand was on his stomach, the 9mm jacketed hollow-point bullet went three feet over him with a hissing *snick!* At that moment Rand squeezed the trigger of the Colt. With the sound of a pop-top beer can being opened, the Colt recoiled once in Rand's hand. The 7.65mm bullet, coursing upward, took the seated intruder just under the right eye and exited a half inch above his crown with the plopping sound of a ripe tomato bursting on a kitchen floor. Rand could see clearly the small blue entry wound and then, as the man pitched toward him, the hole the size of a quarter torn out of the top of his skull. Brains, hair and blood dirtied the ceiling.

Rand gained his feet as the intruder's body hit the floor and started to convulse. A series of scrambled nerve signals from the traumatized brain started spasms at the body's toes that rippled upward repeatedly, bowing in series legs, spine and neck.

Rand stepped inside the room, closed the balcony door and stood aside, watching coldly, as the body on the floor, like a rooster preparing to crow, entered final spasm with a slow-motion stretching of the shoulders backward and head and neck forward. It's eyes bulged and from the now wide open mouth the tongue protruded slowly to maximum extension. The body became rigid in that posture, quivered momentarily, then relaxed slowly, tongue receding perhaps a quarter of an inch back into the open mouth, the open eyes, no longer under pressure, glazing over into total lifelessness. "Now," said Rand to the corpse in a tone of mild exasperation, "what the fuck do I do with you?"

Rand pondered briefly concealing the body elsewhere in the hotel; even waiting until dark and throwing it off the balcony with enough force and deflection to make the apparent suicide seem to have been launched from several balconies away. Even as he turned these thoughts over in his mind Rand discarded them. The mess on the ceiling could not be concealed short of washing and repainting and the exit wound was welling enough sticky syrup of rapidly oxidizing blood onto the carpeting to require professional cleaning. On top of all that was the distinctive odor of blood and brains; a heavy sweetness, cloying and unmistakable.

"The hell with it," Rand said aloud; then opened the closet door, retrieved his suitcase and the airport locker briefcase. Stepping carefully over the body on the floor, he crossed to the front door and left, closing the door firmly behind him and once more seeing to it that the "Do not disturb" sign was secure on the outside knob. He headed for the stairwell quickly, retrieved his clothes from the roof and dressed inside the door at the top of the stairs. He replaced the pistol and accessories in the saddle leather briefcase, smoothed back his hair and left the stairwell for the elevator down to check out. It was 11:27 A.M. and Rand wondered whether he would be charged for an extra day. To his relief he was, giving him the opportunity to argue the point and thus fix the time of his departure in the mind of the cashier. He was gambling on the fact that it is difficult to fix time of death exactly; impossible in most cases. When the body was found he would be gone; there was nothing to connect him with the dead man, whom he had never seen before, and he would protest, should it come to that, any gratuitous imputation of knowledge or responsibility for what ocurred in the suite after his departure.

At the airport, Rand replaced the saddle leather briefcase in a locker and, as instructed days before in New York, pushed the key under the sand in the big cylindrical ashtray to the right of the bank of lockers. From there he went to the center of the passenger area and studied the arrival and departure information displayed on the closed-circuit television screens overhead.

Pan Am had a flight to Manila via Los Angeles leaving in twenty-two minutes. Using his U.S. passport, Rand purchased a first-class ticket on the flight to Manila with dollars. He looked about for a U.S. Customs preclearance station, found none and headed for the men's room. Once in a stall with the door closed, he searched himself for anything reflecting his operational alias. He intended to reenter the United States from Los Angeles as Richard Rand and knew that anyone coming in from Columbia, prime staging area for cocaine smuggling into the United States, would be checked carefully by U.S. Customs. Into the toilet bowl went his torn up German passport, return ticket to Hamburg, remaining Deutschmarks and pocket litter. He had to flush several times to get it all down. Readjusting his clothing, he left the stall, washed up, combed his light blond hair and left to board his plane.

The trip in first-class was pleasant and Rand spent most of it napping. Because the prevailing winds aloft were westerly, it was some five hours later that the 747 swung wide over the Pacific and picked up the glide slope signal from Los Angeles International Airport. The sun was bright at a little after 2:00 P.M. and the reflection from the ocean dazzling. Rand looked toward the Los Angeles basin and shook his head. A thick layer of dirty yellow smog lay stagnant between the coast and distant mountains. He hated the thought that he would have to breath such muck; it looked like the pictures combat artists had painted of Ypres in World War I under history's first attack by poison gas. The illustrators whose pictures he had seen as a boy had used just that color to portray the deadly, flesh blistering, nitrogen-mustard gas. He turned away in disgust.

With the cabin still eighteen feet off the ground, the huge tires of the big Boeing raised puffs of blue smoke as they chirped onto the runway under the sure hand of the thirty year veteran Pan Am captain. The seat belt dug into Rand's lap as the jet thrust reversers took effect and braked the now awkwardly lumbering craft down to taxiing speed. The first officer took over to turn the ship onto a taxiway to make it's way carefully across intersecting taxi and runways under the direction of LAX Ground Control, whose job it is to keep the ponderous giants and lesser craft sorted out as they move along the ground like so many albatrosses waddling and sandpipers darting on a beach alive with feeding seabirds.

There was a short wait for a nesting spot at the terminal for the albatross carrying Rand. Then, as a first-class passenger, he was one of the first to disembark and was number three in line at Customs. He grunted in resignation when asked to step aside into a booth to be searched completely, damning the cocaine trade for the inconvenience and delay. He turned over all his posessions for scrutiny, then stripped behind the curtain.

Rand did feel that he was kept waiting longer than was necessary to search the little luggage he had with him, not knowing that his name was on the watch list fed by the main computer in Washington to remote terminals at every customs station. Nor was he aware that every scrap of paper in his possession, including his currency, had been photographed as he waited; he was disarmed by the courtesy shown him as his possessions were returned with the advice that all was in order.

As Rand stepped onto the motorized sidewalk that carried him down the long passageway to the ticket counters, it did not occur to him that his every move was being monitored in a control room by several well-dressed men peering into black and white closed circuit television screens fed by cameras tucked into virtually every available nook and cranny overhead. So ubiquitous were the electronic eyes they went unnoticed.

Leaving the motorized walk with a little hop, Rand went over to the American Airlines counter to buy a ticket for New York. American was sold out for all but that night's "red-eye" flight. That was longer than Rand wanted to wait so he went over to United. There his luck was better; the clerk sold him a first-class ticket on a New York flight leaving in thirty-six minutes and was about to ask Rand whether he had any luggage to be checked when another man in the same uniform approached from behind the counter saying:

"They've got problems in the back with a ticket you sold this morning, Larry. I'll cover while you help 'em get it straightened out."

The agent who had sold Rand his ticket nodded and left. The new man smiled at Rand:

"We do our best but sometimes we blow it, even with the computer reservations. The rule is, 'you sell it, you straighten it out.' Now, did he get your bags checked?"

"No," said Rand, "There's only one. I'll carry on the briefcase."

Rand slid his suitcase under the counter and waited as the agent snapped a destination tag around the grip. Then he asked:

"Where do I board?"

"Gate one twenty-four, sir. You go down there to where the moving sidewalk is, take it out to the end, then follow the signs.

It's the last one, all the way back." The agent looked up at the wall-mounted clock. "Prob'ly be a good idea to get started right away. It's a good distance and the flight's on time."

Rand agreed, thanked the man and headed for the motorized sidewalk. He rode it out to the end, at first enjoying, then tiring of the feel of the rollers massaging his feet through the rubber tread and the soles of his shoes. He was glad to get off and start walking. The signs were clear and, as he walked further out, fellow passengers became fewer and fewer; still, it wasn't until he actually came upon Gate 124 that anything seemed out of place to him. It dawned on Rand then that he was alone in approaching the gate less than twenty minutes before departure time and there was no one in the departure lounge.

"Where is everybody?" Rand asked the agent behind the desk.

"We're losing money on this flight," the man answered, "but you won't be alone by any means. We just let the rest board already so not to delay departure. Smoking or nonsmoking; aisle or window, what's your pleasure?"

"Aisle, nonsmoking," Rand answered. The agent pasted his seat number onto his boarding pass, conducted him through the metal-detector and waved him on up the covered ramp to the plane, a 707 Rand could see through the lounge windows. It was nestled against the ramp, which bent at a forty-five degree angle before it reached the plane. Rand started up the ramp, feeling uneasy.

Rand's disquiet increased as he walked up the slope but, for want of anything further to alarm him, continued on his way. As he rounded the forty-five degree angle of the ramp, however, all doubt was resolved; he was in big trouble. The ramp abutted a plane alright, not ten feet away; but the aircraft door was closed. It was then he heard footsteps—several of them—coming up the ramp beyond the turn behind him. He was trapped.

As the footsteps came close, Rand jammed his hand in his trouser pocket and brought out a red-handled Swiss Army pocket knife. He opened the largest blade quickly, then ran the short distance to the airplane. There, where it fit against the plane, the ramp had a short accordian-pleated bridge which could be adjusted tightly to the aircraft fuselage against inclement weather boarding. The folds were reinforced by metal strips, but between the strips was a heavy, water-proof fabric.

Rand dropped his briefcase and with both arms held above his

243

head, struck the knife through the fabric between two pleats. He raised his feet off the floor of the ramp and let his body-weight force the blade down through the fabric. The method worked for about three feet, then the cut was too low for it to be effective any longer. As the footsteps were almost to the bend in the ramp ten feet away, Rand sawed at the cloth desperately. The rent he had cut extended downward another foot and Rand snapped the knife closed, pocketed it, grabbed his briefcase, pushed it through the cut and let it fall to the ground below. Then he grasped two adjacent reinforcing strips and spread them as far as he could to struggle through the rent himself and drop, just as a man's voice behind him said, "Hey!"

The drop was twelve feet. Rand held his legs together, knees bent, body bent forward and arms crossed over his chest. As his feet hit the ground and his flexed leg muscles took up the shock, he rocked backwards and fell along his right side, paratrooper fashion. Scrambling to his feet, Rand didn't bother to brush himself off, just picked up his briefcase and ran, bent over, around the aircraft to concealment behind the landing gear. There he paused to take stock.

When coupled with the attempt to kill him in Bogota, this latest threat argued against Ballinger as prime-mover. First, the initial attack was too soon. Moreover, it had followed his visit to the embassy. He must have been on the watch list and the third secretary had gotten on the horn to Langley and read them his claim against Comco. Kazalakis was being as good as his word; the agency couldn't know what he was up to yet, but just the fact that he had made a move against Comco had been enough to trigger a preemptive response. His latest predicament fit right in: Ballinger couldn't mount such an attack on short notice. He would have to rely on money to the right people—something that took time to arrange. The funny business with the airline smacked of government; fear of regulatory power was a far more effective stimulant to prompt and complete cooperation. An angry government could cost the company big money a hundred different ways and no employee wanted to risk being accused by his superiors of prompting such a vendetta by his recalcitrance. All other airlines would be covered like a blanket; ditto surface transportation. He had to get away from LAX. Fast.

Peering around the mammoth tire, Rand could see a portion of the General Aviation terminal in the distance. He ran underneath the covered ramp to avoid being seen, then hugged the wall and made his way along it until a man in coveralls shouted something at him. Probably a warning, Rand thought, for just then, with a tremendous howling against his unprotected ears, a taxiing 727 turned in toward a ramp twenty feet away. Rand scuttled by ahead of it.

Still crouching low, Rand darted across the taxiway itself and paused in the shelter of a drainage ditch lined with concrete. He raised himself up just far enough to see that between him and the General Aviation terminal lay a runway serving jetliners. What appeared to be a taxiway intersected it to his right—it was difficult to see clearly because of the angle, Rand's covering ditch being deep in the V of two swaths of concrete—and as a 707 hurtled from his left at well over one hundred miles an hour he learned that he was directly opposite the point where the pilots rotated the aircraft and lifted off. He covered his ears with his palms and received a severe buffeting from the 707's wing-tip vortices. The roaring vibration numbed him.

Rand glanced up and down the runway as the 707 angled into the sky, exhaust crackling like frying bacon. Clear. At least momentarily. Clutching his briefcase, he ran out onto the runway, only to be overcome suddenly by awareness of terrible danger as a shadow moved over him in an instant. Rand dived to the ground and braced himself for the shock of being crushed to death. What a fool he had been! Imagine a pilot not realizing that an intersecting runway would be feeding in aircraft with shorter landing roll requirements; the other strip was no taxiway, it was another runway!

As the shadow passed beyond Rand, the landing gear of a DC-9 straddled him, hitting the concrete beside him not eight inches from his head with a tearing sound, raising the stench of burning rubber to mingle with the taste of terror in his mouth. A fraction of a second later, with a stunning blast from two General Electric jets, the huge ship was beyond him. Rand rolled over and over to the side of the runway and onto the grass. He couldn't rise; he was trembling too much from the effects of a massive release of adrenalin.

Within moments, Rand's sense of self-preservation asserted control of his mind and body. He couldn't stay where he was; not only was there danger from aircraft, his presence in the highly restricted area must by now have been reported to the tower by the pilot of the DC-9. Rand got up on his knees, then to his feet and scrambled, clutching his briefcase, across the runway toward a line of light multi-engined aircraft tied down outside the General Aviation ramp. Gaining the concealment of the planes, he paused to look after his appearance, brushing himself off and running a comb through his hair. That done, he proceeded without further incident to the ramp entrance of the terminal, entered, then walked directly to the men's room, relief from severe stress having prompted in him the urgent necessity to urinate. Rand looked down into the porcelain fixture as he relieved himself, surprised by the force and quantity of his urine:

"Scared the living piss out of me!" he acknowledged to himself with a smile.

# XVIII

Brushed off, washed with paper towels, combed and once more presentable, Rand left the men's room of the Los Angeles International Airport General Aviation terminal, walked briskly to the desk manned by the fixed-base operator, Butler Aviation, and inquired about aircraft rentals. The clerk was sorry, but Butler offered charters only. He referred Rand to California Aero, whose office was nearby and who offered for rent anything up to a DC-3.

At California Aero, he showed his FAA multi-engine, land, instrument pilot's license; an FCC third class radio operator's license; a current medical certificate and his pilot's log showing an accumulated 2,205 hours and 21 minutes of flying time, most of it as pilot-in-command. Together with his credit card, the display enabled him to rent a Cessna 172 equipped for IFR flight "for a trip down the coast to San Diego" without question, whereas application for a more high-performance, longer range aircraft with greater useful load capacity would have required a lot more time and checking; too many companies had been burned by having their larger, faster planes rented for what turned out to be a marijuana run south of the border, only to have them impounded by Mexican or U.S. authorities when something went wrong.

For the benefit of anyone interested, Rand filed an IFR flight plan for San Diego and took off. After release by L.A. Control, he cancelled his flight plan and switched to VFR. Picking up the Colorado River Aquaduct Valley, he followed it east flying just high enough to be legal.

Although he had checked the weather carefully before departing, Rand worried as he headed between the peaks of the San Gorgonio and San Jacinto mountains. The wind was reported to be from the west, but a shift to either north or south could cause him to fly right into a deadly "mountain wave," a surflike clear air turbulence that spilled over the crest of a mountain peak or ridge and flowed in a powerful downdraft along the lee side. As the twin peaks loomed high above both wings of the Cessna, Rand braced himself. His luck held. The wind had not shifted and all he experienced were a few bumps and some mild wing rocking.

Rand passed directly over Palm Springs enroute to his actual destination, Phoenix. It lay some 400 statute miles to the east of Los Angeles and well within the 750 nautical mile range of the Cessna 172. He made the left bend around the San Bernardino mountain ridge and slowed to maneuvering speed as a precaution against turbulence, then swept right with increased throttle and left the aquaduct valley to fly over the Joshua Tree National Monument and on through the Gila Bend Mountains. It was there that the wind shift caught him.

With the stomach floating upward sensation associated with express down elevators, a downdraft hit and the Cessna lost 800 feet of altitude so fast the needle of the rate of climb/descent gauge was pinned against the down stop. Rand yanked on carburetor heat to keep ice from choking off his fuel supply, then added power to struggle back up to altitude fighting the controls as the plane bucked and lurched like an automobile driven too fast over a bumpy dirt road. The turbulence persisted until Rand flew out into the valley of the Gila River where it forked north and south from the east. Following it east, Rand said to himself, "IFR—I Follow Rivers."

Camelback Mountain to his left, Phoenix came into view and instead of cutting power for his descent, Rand nosed the aircraft down with his trim control, using the added speed to make up for time lost fighting turbulence. He radioed Phoenix approach and followed instructions into the pattern, cutting his power back to 1,500 rpm to slip behind an Aero Commander on downwind. He dropped his flaps a quarter, trimmed level again and turned base behind the Commander.

Covering the end of the runway with his wing tip, Rand made his turns tight to make up for his lack of speed in the pattern. He gave the Cessna half flaps on base, full on final to drop the ship right on the runway numbers and turn off at the first intersection at the command of Phoenix Ground Control. Minutes later, the plane was tied down outside the General Aviation terminal. It was 6:10 P.M.; the flight from Los Angeles had taken him three hours and forty-one minutes. Rand entered that fact in his log book and took a shuttle van from the tie-down area to the terminal.

At the Phoenix FBO office it was a simple matter to hire a young flight instructor to return the Cessna to Los Angeles the following day. The extra rental would be charged to his credit card account automatically. That accomplished, Rand got a fistful of quarters in exchange for a five dollar bill and placed a long-distance call to New York from the nearest pay phone. A low, cautious voice answered:

"Yes?"

"This is Rick, long distance. I didn't want to call collect. I need to talk to the man."

"I'll see."

There was a short pause, then: "In ten minutes, call 914-229-3842."

"Got it," said Rand, jotting down the number of what he knew would be a pay phone at the other end. He pressed the stop watch button on his Omega. Exactly ten minutes later, armed with another load of quarters, Rand dialed the number he had been given.

"Hello," came the voice of Luigi Scarbacci.

"It's Rick," Rand said apologetically. "Sorry to get you out of the house but I need a little help."

"Wassa matter? Where are ya?"

"In Phoenix. Uncle's looking to whack me. I need help to get back to the city."

"Our business—there's a problem?"

"Not as long as I'm alive to handle it."

"Where y'at now?"

"The airport."

"It's been a long time since I been there. They got a restaurant there?"

"In the airport?"

"Yeah."

"I'm sure they do."

"Go have somethin' to eat. Stay there. Have a second cuppa

coffee if you hafta. Some people will come by. Your cousins, come to take ya to a family reunion, unnerstand? Go wit them. I'm gonna reach out."

"I understand," said Rand, "and thanks."

"What're relatives for? Forget about it." The phone went dead.

A check of the airport put Rand in a bit of a quandry; there was more than one place to obtain a meal. One, a glorified coffee shop, had the advantage of being crowded, thus offering some protection against attack. The disadvantage lay in the fact that it did a volume business and moved customers in and out as quickly as possible. Rand had no idea how long he'd have to wait and didn't want a confrontation with management over his occupying a table at the height of the evening rush hour while lingering over a cup of coffee. He was trying to keep a low profile.

His other option was clearly a restaurant. It was decorated pretentiously, served precooked, frozen entrés reheated in a micro-wave oven for which it charged prices that rivaled in outrageousness only those charged for drinks. The place was small and the prices kept it from being crowded. Rand chose it as he believed that so long as he was willing to buy postdinner drinks, he would be left to himself until those sent to meet him arrived. Besides, there was the added benefit of low lighting and a waitress who had unbuttoned most of her blouse and was in the habit, Rand observed, of bending over rather far as she served. If he had to wait, Rand thought, he might as well enjoy himself.

Seated at his request among the tables served by Miss Cleavage, Rand ordered from her a whisky sour on the rocks, veal in lemon and wine sauce with creamed spinach on the side. He enjoyed the view as he was served both times and the waitress appeared to enjoy the fact that Rand was enjoying himself; whether in anticipation of a generous tip or for the psychic reward of his frank admiration of her charms, Rand wasn't certain. He concluded that it was probably a combination of the two.

Halfway through the surprisingly good creamed spinach, two men approached Rand from behind and stood without speaking at either side of him. Rand looked at first one, then the other. They were dressed neatly and conservatively; one in a light blue Haspel cord suite, the other in a light tan Brooksweave, complete with buttondown collar and rep tie. In all the times he had been in the company of relatives of his late wife, Rand had never seen any of them dressed like that. He lost his appetite.

"You guys," he said, "look as though you could afford to buy your own dinner. Go away."

"Wouldn't think of it, Mr. Rand," said Brooksweave. "We just want to speak to you for a minute. May we sit down?"

As the two men seated themselves at his table without waiting for his answer, Rand said: "Thank's for asking," and motioned to Miss Cleavage. She dipped into the gathering with a smile that made her cheeks plump out like her breasts and asked, "Something to drink, gentlemen?"

"Just coffee, thanks, for both of us," said Brooksweave. As Cleavage moved away to comply, Rand said:

"Make it fast, will you fellows? I'm expecting relatives for an after-dinner drink. Some cousins from Phoenix."

"Of course you are, Mr. Rand," said Brooksweave, "and here we are, just in from Los Angeles. After all, we have the same Uncle. That would make us cousins, wouldn't you say?" Brooksweave was smiling at what he took to be his own cleverness. He didn't wait for Rand to agree, continuing with the observation: "Jets travel much faster than small Cessnas, Mr. Rand."

"Okay," said Rand, pointing a thumb toward Haspel, "so you and the deaf-mute here are a couple of tough guys from the company. That should make you smart enough to know *I* know you're not going to do anything fancy in the middle of a restaurant with people around. Get lost."

"You're quite right that we'd rather not disturb the taxpayers," said Brooksweave, "and, if the truth were told, we both rather admire you; you're resourceful and you move fast. It's too bad you went wrong. I'm assuming you went wrong, of course, or we wouldn't be meeting this way. We're supposed to be out of this sort of thing directly, these days. You must really have them worried to have them make an exception just for you. Now— You're a professional. You played the game and lost. You know what has to happen. Right here, if necessary. Why not go out like a professional? Is it really necessary to make a scene?"

"Sure," said Rand, "you're going to blow me away right here. Bullshit. You said yourself you just got here. You can't have the way out set up and covered. There's just the two of you. You think I'm going to go for that? You go boom boom in here and you'll be lucky to make it to the front door. They're jumpy around airports these days, you know. Terrorists and all that. You start shooting in here, there'll be rent-a-cops with magnums all over the place. Half of them will shoot the other half in the ass, of course, but you guys'll get blown away in the crossfire."

Brooksweave sighed. "You're quite right, Mr. Rand. But you give us credit for no sense at all. Who said anything about shooting? Albert, here, is holding under his napkin a cyanide gun. No sound. You, our good friend, as the waitress will attest, will suffer a heart attack after a good meal. Happens all the time. But why upset the other diners?"

Rand shrugged his shoulders and, as a gesture of surrender that was also a signal to four men who had entered and, bearing the unmistakable stamp of family members, were being ushered toward his table by Miss Cleavage as if to seat them nearby, he raised his hands shoulder high. As the four ranged themselves silently behind Rand's uninvited guests, the oldest, close enough to have heard the tail end of Brooksweave's sentence, answered him:

"But there ain't no other diners. Look around ya, bud."

Startled, Brooksweave and Haspel did so. Miss Cleavage, together with the last of the few other diners whom she had advised of a terrorist bomb threat, disappeared out the door.

"Gentlemen," said Rand to the two seated men, "my cousins from Phoenix." They remained silent, looking glum.

"Which means," said the apparent leader of the four rescuers, "either of you do anything stupid you get a blade up under the left arm and won't nobody notice. I own this joint, see? Look, I don't even hafta worry about the floor. That's why I picked a red carpet." With a chuckle, he motioned to his subordinates. Deftly they removed from Brooksweave and Haspel two 9mm Llama semiautomatic pistols of Brazilian manufacture and without serial numbers.

Rand pointed to Haspel and said, sharply, "Under the napkin. Cyanide gun. Look out."

"Right," said the leader and took it himself, wrapping the two tubed device carefully in the napkin. "These guys ain't cops," he observed. "Not with no cyanide gun."

"You're right," said Rand, "they have no jurisdiction here. They got that thing from the Russians. They won't cause any official trouble."

"You want 'em wasted?"

"No. No need for it. Just keep them here overnight and turn them loose in the morning with no money or I.D." Rand smiled at the two men as he rose to leave. "Just like back on the farm, remember?" He walked out with the leader and one lieutenant, the other two remaining with the seated CIA men.

"What was that 'farm' crack about?" asked Rand's still unidentified savior.

"Those guys are trained at a place they call 'the farm'." Rand answered. "Part of the training is to take them out in the country and drop them off with nothing—sometimes not even clothes— to see whether they're resourceful enough to get back. One time, one guy was dropped off in his underwear; sleeveless shirt and boxer shorts, that was it. Know what he did? He got a piece of paper from some trash and a burnt stick from a fire. Used the burnt stick to write a big number on the paper, stuck it somehow on his shirt and jogged all the way back. Everybody thought he was a marathon runner who got lost."

"Not bad," said Rand's "cousin" as they left the main lobby for an exit. "Hey," he said, changing the subject, "that really is my joint, you know. Give it to me straight. How'd ya like it. How was the food?"

"Good," said Rand as they went through the doors to a steel-gray Cadillac limosine drawing up to the curb. Waiting for the driver to open the door for them Rand added, with a smile:

"I like your taste in waitresses, too."

The two men settled back in the seats of the Cadillac.

"You like that chick?" asked Rand's host. "She gives great head. I'll make her come over tonight an' suck your prick." The speaker stuck out his hand. "Sorry, shoulda introduced myself sooner. I'm Rocco Martini."

"Martini," Rand repeated, shaking the proffered hand, "weren't you at a meeting one time a few years ago, they had me come in and spell out a deal to the group?"

"Yeah, sure," said Martini as the limosine pulled into traffic, "the sit-down in Newark about the casinos in Atlantic City. I seen ya there. That's how I recognized ya."

"Right," said Rand. Then, deferentially, he added:

"Look, I really appreciate your saving my ass in there and the offer of the girl and all, but with those two guys out of the way I could hop the next flight to the city and get in late tonight— early tomorrow. And I need to get back fast."

"Not a chance," said Martini. "I promised your, what is he— father-in-law? Uncle-in-law?—I'd get ya back to him safe and sound and that's what I'm gonna do. Them guys have friends, ya know. They'll have all the airports around the city covered. No way. This car is yours. You can leave tonight if ya want and they'll drive ya straight through. I'll have a car full of boys follow behind and they can switch off drivin'. An I'll put that broad ya like in the back seat here an she can suck your prick all the way across the country." Martini chuckled at the thought. It left Rand feeling weak. "Thanks," he said, "but I think I better pass on the girl. By the time I got to New York I wouldn't be able to walk!"

Martini roared with laughter. "Okay, okay, you got a point there. But you gotta try her out before ya go. I insist. She's a great mechanic."

"You twisted my arm," said Rand.

The executive offices of Ha Kah Enterprises, a financial holding company belonging principally to Rand's ally, Wing, occupied the top floor of the Ha Kah Building which rose eight storeys from a street cut into the side of the hill overlooking Hong Kong harbor. From the private diningroom, one wall of which was nothing but insulated glass, the harbor view at 10:30 P.M., Wednesday, 1st May, was fascinating to the Comco directors.

The multi-course meal that had been in progress since shortly after eight had been extraordinary in it's ability to surprise and please the palate anew. Chinese hospitality proved to be everything tradition promised. Of course, as they had been told, no business was discussed and they had been warned that to raise such a subject before their host did would be the height of discourtesy.

Gregory Ballinger chafed under the delay imposed by Oriental manners. As a supplicant, however, he held his peace until, the final toast sipped, Wing broached the subject of how he could "assist his honored guest." Ballinger thanked his host for a superb meal and mentioned that, as Wing was aware, a small difficulty had arisen between them in a business matter. He asked thirty days grace while he, Ballinger, whose attention had, alas, been diverted by other affairs, set the difficulty right.

Wing commiserated with Ballinger. As the chief executive officer of a business with many differing enterprises, though of course not approaching the size and success of that of his honored guest, Wing had, himself, experienced difficulties from time to time. He wanted to be of assistance and, while thirty days were,

254

unfortunately, out of the question as not his to give, perhaps so talented a manager as Ballinger could, as his reputation indicated, do what others could not and solve the problem within fifteen days.

They settled on twenty. It would be a tight squeeze for Ballinger to acquire an existing corporation which could serve believably as the purported intended buyer for the product Wing and Wa had rejected, but he could do it. If Wing thought he had him, so much the better.

"I am prepared," said Wing, "to be of as much help as possible. Naturally I shall require a resolution of your board authorizing Comco to seek and accept the extension, with a certified copy of that and an acceptance of the minutes for the protection of my company. As you brought with you a quorum of your board, it is clear that you anticipated my request and will have no objection. For my part, I have prevailed upon an official from the office of Her Majesty's Governor to witness the certification, thus saving the necessity of legalizing a notarial acknowledgment. That should save you a day, at the least."

"It will, indeed," said an agreeably surprised Ballinger. "Thank you, sir."

Wing bowed his acknowledgement. "I have a secretary waiting. He will prepare minutes at your dictation so we can conclude our business this evening."

Ballinger cleared his throat and announced:

"A quorum being present, the board of directors of Comco, meeting in extraordinary session in accordance with paragraph III, section c of the by-laws, at the British Crown Colony of Hong Kong on Wednesday, 1st May, 10:20 P.M., will come to order. The secretary will record those present and voting. The chair will entertain motions." It was moved, seconded and passed that the reading of the minutes of the last meeting be omitted. Then a stout director said:

"I move that Comco apply for, and accept if offered, a twenty day extension of the date of delivery on our contract with Ha Kah Enterprises, Limited."

"Second," said the man to his immediate right.

"All in favor?" asked Ballinger.

There was a chorus of *ayes*.

"Opposed?"

Silence.

"The motion is passed. Any further motions?"

"Move we adjourn."

"Second."

"All in favor?"

"Aye!"

"Opposed?—Very well. The meeting is adjourned to the call of the chair."

A young Chinese, obviously Wing's secretary, rose. "Roger," Ballinger ordered, "go with this young man please and transcribe the minutes. Bring back copies for all of us."

The two men were gone no longer than the time consumed by one round of drinks, then assisted each other in distributing xerographic copies of the minutes to each board member. That done, Ballinger reconvened the board and the minutes were approved by motion. At that point Wing summoned into the room a man whose dress and bearing marked him unmistakably as British Foreign Service. After observing the signatures and the passports of the signatories, the Foreign Service officer acknowledged them with his own, then took out a small handpress. As Ballinger wondered how much Wing was paying for such special service, the officer impressed upon all copies the seal of Elizabeth II.

"Go," said the priest, "the mass is ended."

"Thanks be to God," responded the congregation of Our Lady of Mercy Catholic Church. All but Don Luigi Scarbacci.

*"Deo Gratias,"* said the Don. Richard Rand, who was not Catholic, assumed he was speaking Italian until, as he followed the Don and his wife in genuflecting and leaving the pew, the older man muttered "Ya start changin' things, who knows where it'll stop. A thousand years Latin was good enough for the mass. Now we got a pollack for a pope."

"Luigi!" hissed Mrs. Scarbacci.

On the front steps of the church she asked Rand, "Can you come back for lunch?"

"I'd love to but I really can't. Besides, your breakfast was enough for the day."

"How you feel?" asked the Don, "You didn't look so good last night."

"Forty-seven hours straight I spent in that car. The only thing we stopped for was food, gas, and I can't say in front of a lady. You folks saved my life. The brandy and hot shower worked like magic. Slept like a baby."

"You come back when you can stay," said Mrs. Scarbacci, kissing Rand on the cheek.

"I promise." Rand embraced the Don, then once more seated himself in the now excruciatingly familiar rear seat of Rocco Martini's limosine for the drive to New York, the car full of Martini soldiers, all fresh from mass, following faithfully. They stopped at the first roadside pay phone where Rand called Aaron Feld at home.

"Hey Rick," Aaron Feld complained, "how much longer we have to keep worrying? You've got us scared shitless!"

"Not long. How'd you make out?"

"You mean those written assurances? Perfect. Counsel was so worried about having Comco assets equal to the issue tied up he gave us a beaut. It's where my mother couldn't find it—and she can find anything except my old man. How about taking it off my hands so life can go back to normal around here?"

"Sure," said Rand, who had no intention of doing so but didn't want to argue the point over the phone. "You at the apartment all day?"

"Right. With all my wife's relatives to form a crowd, the way you suggested. There's not enough money in the world for you to pay what you owe me for what I've been going through."

"I'm sure you'll think of a figure when the time comes. I'm in Westchester now. I'll swing by on my way home."

"Thanks, pal. There are limits to what a human being can endure."

Chuckling at the thought of Aaron Feld trapped in an apartment full of in-laws, cousins and God knows what other relatives, Rand considered calling T'sa Li at the Plaza, but decided against it in favor of leaving immediately. Again the two-car motorcade headed south.

Rand released Martini's men with his thanks before the Feld's apartment house on Central Park West. He felt sorry for the men; he had been uncomfortable on the short trip to the city from Westchester and they had to drive all the way back to Phoenix. The Feld's apartment house was just a few blocks north of the intersection of Central Park West and Central Park South. It would be but a short walk to the Plaza when his visit was over.

The Felds, Aaron harried and Rhona happy, greeted Rand warmly and both saw to it that he met every relative there— Rhona out of pride and joy, Aaron in a spirit of revenge. After persuading Aaron to keep the document for at least another day,

Rand escaped and walked to the Plaza, enjoying the beautiful Spring Sunday afternoon en route to an uncertain welcome from what must by now be a thoroughly annoyed and famished T'sa Li.

As Rand knocked on the door of his own suite, he decided on dinner at Christ Cella's as a peace offering. When his fourth knock echoed back to him with a foreboding hollowness, Rand used his key quickly to enter.

The suite was empty. All was in complete order, but there was no sign that T'sa Li had ever been there. Disturbed as he was by her absence, Rand consoled himself with the thought that the maid had undoubtedly cleaned the apartment and made up the bed. T'sa Li had probably just gotten too hungry and lonely to stay there. But if so, where was his mail? He left the suite immediately for the desk in the lobby.

"Welcome back, Mr. Rand," said the clerk. Rand's alarm increased as he looked at his box behind the desk. It was filled with accumulated mail and the clerk turned automatically to get it for him.

"Thank you," he said. "Have you seen anything of Miss Li in the past few days?"

"No, sir. But I've been off."

"Right. Many thanks."

Rand waited until he was back in the elevator to start going through his mail. The letter he had mailed to himself from Bogota containing his copy of the claim against Comco was not there. He got off the elevator realizing he was in trouble, but it was not until he reentered his suite to the sound of the telephone and he picked it up that he realized the depth and severity of his reverse in fortunes.

"Hello?"

"Good afternoon, Mr. Rand. Do you recognize my voice?"

"Yes," said Rand, who would never mistake Gregory Ballinger's urbane air of superiority for that of anyone else. He tried to make the best of it. "As a matter of fact I was about to call you in the morning."

"To demand a meeting of my board of directors, correct?"

"Correct," Rand answered, his alarm increasing as he realized that once again Ballinger was ahead of him.

"Yes," said Ballinger. "Well, a meeting between us is certainly in order but I don't think it will be necessary to trouble my board;

they're a dutiful lot, but not the brightest in the world. They think you're out to squeeze Comco on that issue to spite me for personal reasons. But we know better, you and I, don't we? Very clever, that business with the Chinese. My board still doesn't suspect any connection between you. Didn't put it together myself until I received the description of the young lady it is said you prefer over the rest. When I saw her and recognized her from one of my parties, and realized it was the one that cost me the services of a valued employee, it wasn't difficult to figure out. Would you like to see her again?"

"I don't know what you're talking about."

"Now, Mr. Rand," Ballinger said patronizingly, "let's not be disingenuous. Perhaps you'd like to hear her scream?"

"No," Rand said slowly, the full impact of his predicament sinking in, "that won't be necessary. What do you want?"

"Your presence. In my office this evening. Eight sharp. The building will be open to you. Oh, and Mr. Rand?"

"Yes."

"Please don't forget to bring with you your copy of that claim you filed in Bogota and the assurance your attorney euchred from my simpleton of a general counsel."

"I'll be there," said Rand. "Don't hurt her."

"That, sir, is up to you." The phone went dead.

Hanging up the phone, Richard Rand paused with his hand still on the receiver to collect himself. He was in a fury; not at Gregory Ballinger, who was acting predictably, but at himself for not following his own judgement and keeping the woman he loved out of danger. He felt a sticky clamminess at his neck, armpits and cuffs and realized that he had perspired profusely.

After a moment, it occurred to Rand that, even had he not permitted T'sa Li to become involved, the situation would probably be no different; Ballinger would have selected her as his extortion target on the basis of his relationship with her alone. And there was still hope! T'sa Li was still alive and would remain so as long as she was perceived to be useful by Ballinger. Further, no matter where the essential claim copy was, Ballinger didn't have it. Rand checked his watch: 3:54 P.M. He had four hours and six minutes. He stripped and headed for the shower.

Soaping his lean body, Rand reviewed his situation. That he needed help was the understatement of the decade. Don Scarbacci could lend him muscle and firepower, and the motivation was certainly there; should Ballinger prevail, the Don would lose a great deal of money, certainly power and, possibly, his life. On the other hand, T'ang Li had similar assets to throw into the battle and his motivation would be superior; the life of his sister hung in the balance. Rand hated to face T'ang Li—the man had made his wishes concerning his sister's participation clear—but it had to be done.

As Alfredo Matarazza was not due until morning, Rand took a cab from the Plaza entrance and asked to be let off at the 42nd street IND subway entrance. He ran down the stairs to the downtown platform, token ready. A local was about to leave and he jumped aboard. The doors started to close and Rand blocked his and left the train, searching to see whether anyone followed. No one did. The local left and an express came in behind it. Rand boarded the express and rode it downtown to City Hall. From there he took a cab to within three blocks of the House of Li restaurant complex, walked to the opposite block and entered a dry cleaning store. He asked the proprietor for T'ang Li and was conducted to the rear of the store, behind a curtain, and was seated in an old kitchen chair. The proprietor made a phone call in Chinese.

Presently a door Rand had taken to be that of a closet opened. From it an elderly Chinese man beckoned to Rand to follow. Rand did, and was led through a maze of hallways and stairs until he found himself at T'ang Li's gym.

Perspiring from exercise, a robed T'ang Li was waiting for him, standing in the middle of the room before his three poles. Pointedly, he did not ask Rand to be seated; he just glowered and said:

"On the phone you said my sister is in trouble. Explain."

"Ballinger's got her. He just called me on the phone. He's figured out what I've been doing and he's holding T'sa Li hostage for some papers. If he gets them, we're beaten."

"Why my sister as the hostage?"

"Because of our relationship."

"Where was she when he took her?"

"I'm not sure. Probably at my place at the Plaza or nearby. I had asked her to stay there."

"And where were you?"

"On the way back from Bogota. The trip you had your people help me with."

"She has a home here. Why was my sister to stay at your home with you away?"

Rand took a breath. "Because, contrary to your request and my agreement, I asked her to stay there to receive and care for a document important to our enterprise."

The folds over T'ang Li's eyes seemed to droop lower as his massive neck and chest expanded slowly to even more enormous proportions. After a moment he said, in a voice as harsh as his words:

"You are without honor and a fool. For that, when my sister is safe, I will kill you. But you did not lie to me. For that I will kill you quickly."

Rand, who did not like being threatened, even when he deserved it, replied coldly:

"At least we agree that the task at hand is to free your sister. We are agreed on that, aren't we?"

"You are still alive," observed T'ang Li in reply. Then he asked: "Where is T'sa Li being held?"

"I don't know. But I do expect her to be on hand at a meeting tonight in Ballinger's office in the Comco Building at eight o'-clock. The call was to summon me there; the threat to T'sa Li to guarantee my appearance with the papers concerning our enterprise—the most important of which I don't have because I don't know where it is."

"Attend without them. If you had them and brought them you would both be killed immediately. Use your ability with words to delay. If I go early, they may not bring her. If I try to go in with you they'll kill her. I must use surprise after you arrive."

"That won't be easy," Rand volunteered. "Ballinger's got a lot of what appear to be North Korean heavy hitters working for him. It's Sunday. Nobody else'll be in the building. He could have men on every floor, and there's ninety-seven of them. It could take a year to fight your way up to his office, good as you are. There's a helipad on the roof outside the office, and I could get you a chopper, but it's bound to be guarded and one hell of a long way down to the street if they get in a good shot. I doubt—"

T'ang Li interrupted Rand with a curt gesture of dismissal:

"I do not need advice on how to free my sister from a trap," he observed acidly, "from the fool who led her into it."

Rand's jaw muscles tightened and his bleak, near vacant eyes grew remote:

261

"That's twice you've called me that, Mister," he said. "When this is over, if we're both still around, you come ahead and take your best shot. Only don't expect any free passes. I don't give a shit what color belt you wear on your pajamas; the fucking thing better be bullet-proof."

There was no reply as he left.

# XIX

Hunched forward in the commodious passenger compartment of a Checker cab as it sped south on Fifth Avenue, Richard Rand looked suddenly at his index finger in disgust. So preoccupied had he been with the fact that he was en route to Ballinger's headquarters with no plan but to attempt to delay harm to T'sa Li that he had failed until that moment to notice that for the first time since he was seventeen he was biting his fingernails. The realization sobered him; the bitten fingernail became a symbol of how far he had fallen. Only a short time before a man in charge of his destiny and on the verge of huge success, he was now but a pawn in T'ang Li's effort to rescue his sister. His sense of frustration was excruciating. Rand hated to be dependent on anyone or anything, and to be in such a position when the life of T'sa Li and the fate of his greatest enterprise was at stake rubbed his ego raw.

It was 7:53 P.M. when Rand paid off the cabbie and walked the remaining block to the main entrance of the Comco Building. It was still a few minutes before eight when he walked up the broad steps toward the templelike facade, past the massive Corinthian columns that the architect had borrowed from the late Pennsylvania Station, and arrived at the heavy glass doors protected by bronze grillwork. Rand peered inside. A light was burning in the lobby and he could see a guard's desk illuminated further by a reading lamp, but no guard was in evidence. He concluded that he was being observed to discover whether or not he had come alone.

Rand put his hands in his pockets and stamped his feet. It was still chilly after sundown and he hadn't worn a topcoat. Inside, the door to one in a bank of elevators opened and a party of five men emerged. As he waited, Rand heard electronic sirens in the distance, the night bird sounds of the city.

The lead man of the party from the elevator, an Oriental dressed in a dark business suit, unlocked the door. Rand stepped aside as the door opened outward to receive him, then entered without being asked. As the man who let him in held up a hand wordlessly, Rand stopped. He felt other hands from behind him put upward pressure on his elbows and he raised his hands shoulder high. The hands slipped around in front of him and felt carefully down his trunk to his crotch, then across the plains of his back. The hands circled around and down each leg to the ankle, then repeated the procedure with both of his arms after pulling them straight to his sides. A palm then pushed him from behind in the direction of the elevator.

While being searched, Rand had observed his escorts. All were Oriental and wore the same dark suit and white shirt with conservative tie required of IBM salesmen during the lifetime of Thomas Watson, Senior. None spoke, and Rand had no idea whether or not any of them understood English.

Only two of the Orientals entered the elevator with Rand. At the same time, another elevator door opened and more men in dark suits entered the lobby. The door to Rand's car closed and they ascended with the high-speed *whoosh!* of a skyscraper express.

The ride was a quick one. The inside annunciator panel above the door made it clear that there were no stops for this car before the fifty-fifth floor. As the fifty-fifth floor was passed, the rapid flashing on and off of the numerals announcing the floor between fifty-five and ninety-six conveyed graphically the speed of their ascent. Deceleration started a full ten floors below the ninety-sixth and the final stop was smooth as a Rolls gliding to the curb at a fashionable address. The doors whisked back and Rand, between his two guards, stepped out into the brightly lighted hallway in front of the glass double-doors leading into the lobby of the Comco executive suite.

Both glass doors were open and three more Orientals in dark suit uniform guarded the entrance. Rand turned to the man on his right and said:

"What're you guys, Moonies? Or do you all play in the same band?"

There was no reaction at all to Rand's remark. Like a boy

whistling past a graveyard Rand asked, "Mary had a little lamb?" as they walked through the lobby and around the Mayan artifacts on display. "Polly want a cracker?" he tried as they moved through the dim hallway leading to the door to Ballinger's office. His guard knocked on the door, then said to Rand in accented English:

"You see how funny in here, wise ass."

The door was opened and Rand squinted because of the brightness of the room as contrasted with the gloom of the hallway.

"Good evening, Mr. Rand," said the voice of Gregory Ballinger, "it was good of you to be so punctual."

Still squinting, Rand looked around the room. Ballinger was standing across from him and to his right, back against a drapery framing one of a series of floor-to-ceiling windows in the north wall. Further to the right, parallel to the tapestry-covered east wall, was a long, ornate wooden table with something resembling a lectern on it. To Rand's left, the west wall was full of books and the wall behind him was hung with paintings. He couldn't see them well as the overhead track lighting used to illuminate them had all been focused on the center of the room. There, in the only chair to be found, sat T'sa Lim staring at him, frightened.

T'sa Li's chair was large, old and of solid wood. It bore no upholstery and appeared to be from a medieval refectory; perhaps once that of a Benedictine Abbot. Her legs were roped to the front legs of the chair so that her bare feet were several inches off the ground and her forearms were bound similarly to the chair's heavy arms. Good sized as she was, the chair dwarfed T'sa Li, adding to her appearance of helplessness.

Rand's escorts ranged themselves at either side of the door through which they had entered, one standing in front of the door to a coat closet. To Rand's front left, in the northwest corner, stood the middle-aged Oriental he recognized from the Washington party. Diagonally opposite, in the southeast corner, a soft-looking young man holding a handkerchief by one corner was using it to tease a large gray cat. With his back to the table-desk stood what appeared to Rand to be a fugitive from the 1960's; a man in his mid-thirties, bald save for a fringe of hair permitted to grow to shoulder length. He wore a mustache beyond the corners of his mouth, slacks, a maroon turtleneck shirt and a rumpled sport coat. The man looked bored as he fiddled with a Bolex sound motion-picture camera. The combination of the cameraman and the fact that the track lights in the room had all been aimed at T'sa Li's chair gave Rand a hollow feeling in the pit of his stomach.

"As you can see, Mr. Rand," said Ballinger, nodding toward T'sa Li, "I have kept my word. Not a scratch on her."

Rand wasn't taking Ballinger's word for it:

"You all right?" he asked T'sa Li.

"Yes," she answered, her voice near a whisper. "I'm sorry, Rick."

Ballinger spoke before Rand could say more:

"And you, Mr. Rand," he said, "were to bring some papers with you as your part of the bargain. May I have them, please?"

"I'm not a fool," Rand replied. "If I had those papers with me, Miss Li and I wouldn't get out of here alive—and that's got to be the deal. The logistics shouldn't be too hard to work out."

"No, Mr. Rand," said Ballinger, anger breaking through his urbanity, "it's you who appear to be taking *me* for a fool. You are in no position to bargain. You're playing for time, Mr. Rand, but wasting mine. You want a bargain? I'll make you a bargain. *Lester!*"

The soft young man with the handkerchief looked up from his game with the cat. "Yes, sir?"

Ballinger merely gestured toward T'sa Li. Lester smiled, pocketed the handkerchief, walked behind the table-desk and picked up a black leather attaché case and put it down heavily on the desk top.

"Careful, you idiot, you'll mar it!" Ballinger snapped.

"Sorry!" Lester winced. He opened the case and from it produced an old fashioned hand-cranked meat grinder of the kind once common in every household kitchen. Lester walked over to T'sa Li's chair and, with it's bottom-mounted clamp, fastened the grinder securely to the left arm of the chair, then stood back, waiting for further orders.

"What d'you think you're doing?" Rand asked, stepping forward protectively toward T'sa Li. He was seized immediately from behind by the two guards by the door. Each twisted one of Rand's arms behind his back, elbow bent so that both hands were high between his shoulder blades in a hammer lock. With one leg behind for stability, the two used their forward legs to wrap around each of Rand's, pulling his legs apart and to the side. One of them, Rand couldn't tell which, grabbed the top of his head

266

by the hair and pulled it backward so that he had to look downward to see T'sa Li. Struggle as he might, Rand was helpless.

"Get on with it," Ballinger said to Lester. Then, turning to the bald man with the camera, asked "Ready?"

The man shouldered his camera and looked through his viewfinder. He twisted the lens one way, then another, pointing it at the arms of T'sa Li's chair. Satisfied with his focus, he said "Ready."

Ballinger nodded to Lester.

"Which one?" Lester asked, taking a rubber band from his pocket.

The red Ford sedan pulled in behind the fire engine parked at the curb in front of the Comco Building and the uniformed officer in the visored white cap riding in the passenger seat took in the scene with growing anger. Finally he left the car and strode up to a tall fireman standing on the steps in boots, rubber coat and helmet arguing with a crowd of Orientals and fumed:

"What the fuck's goin' on here, Hennesy, a Chinese fire drill?"

"I dunno, Lieutenant," said the hapless Hennesy as the Orientals surrounding him ignored the presence of his superior officer and continued to jabber "Fie-ah! Fie-ah!" and point toward the immense building. "These Chinks, or somebody, hit the alarm box on the corner there and these guys keep yellin' there's a fire. But them Chinks inside there," Hennesy pointed up the steps toward the entrance to the building, "they say there *ain't* no fire and they don't wanna let us in to check it out."

"Fie-ah! Fie-ah!" T'ang Li's men shouted at the lieutenant, some of them hopping up and down to lend emphasis to their alarm, "Fie-ah! Fie-ah!"

T'ang Li observed the scene for a moment more from his position behind a massive pillar to the right of the doors at the top of the steps. He decided he had run out of time. With a barely perceptible gesture he beckoned to one of the men concealed near him. The man he had chosen moved quietly over to T'ang Li. The huge Mongolian spoke to his subordinate in a low grunt and the man bowed, then stood rigidly still as T'ang Li struck a match and set fire to his clothing. The obedient Tong warrior didn't move a muscle as the flames from his burning clothes rose and seared him. Finally, when his underling was enveloped in flames, T'ang Li grunted again and the man ran out from behind the pillar and down the steps toward the firemen, screaming.

"Jesus!" the lieutenant exclaimed, "That oughta be enough for ya—one of them got out! Look!"

T'ang Li's sacrificial victim threw himself like a Kamikazi at the lieutenant. The tall fireman, Hennesy, knocked him down and covered him with foam from a portable cannister as the lieutenant waved the other firemen standing by the truck toward the Comco Building. Axes at the ready they marched three abreast up the steps shouting at the crowd of Orientals to "Get back! Get back, there! Jesus, Louie, I don't think none of these fuckers speak English!"

The doors to the Comco Building were of tempered safety glass and shattered into thousands of tiny pieces at the first blows of the fire axes. The steel blades cut through the softer bronze of the decorative grilles easily and T'ang Li, now in the vanguard of the crowd around the firemen, was one of the first inside as his men shunted aside Ballinger's North Koreans.

As the firemen shouted that elevators were not safe to use in a fire, T'ang Li entered the same car that had served Rand and was on his way up moments later to the continued shouts of "Fie-ah! Fie-ah" and the lieutenant's pleading bellow that "Somebody get these crazy fuckers outta here!"

With the rubber band so tight around T'sa Li's little finger where it joined her hand that the flesh on both sides of it was dead white from the absence of blood, Lester reached into his pocket again and withdrew a Swiss Army pocket knife like Rand's own. With growing horror Rand watched Lester open not the knife blade but a shining cross-cut saw blade Rand knew to rival in sharpness the teeth of a Barracuda.

"Don't do this!" Rand shouted as Lester lay the saw-toothed edge against T'sa Li's knuckle at the second joint and held the rest of her finger straight out against the chair arm, "I swear to Christ I don't know where it is but I'll find it and bring it to you! I promise!"

Ignoring him, Lester leaned hard on the sawblade and drew it back across the joint full length. T'sa Li gasped, trying desperately not to cry out as the blade, moving in the same direction as the angle of its teeth, sliced quickly to the bone. Quickly the soft little sadist shoved the blade hard forward with all his strength. This time going against the grain the teeth cut forward digging into the bone and T'sa Li could stand the pain no more. She screamed as nerve tissue was torn by the jagged teeth and the bone of her finger separated. It was a long scream that came from deep within her; born of agony and horror of mutilation.

The realization of the finality of her maiming numbed T'sa Li and she just moaned as Lester drew the blade backward quickly, severing the remaining flesh and tendons. Despite the tightness of the rubber band, blood welled from T'sa Li's stump as Lester, bloody knife still in his right hand, used his left to hold her severed finger up to the camera. That theatrical display completed, Lester placed the finger carefully in the top of the meat grinder and cranked the handle. A squishing sound came from the grinder, following which a trickle of blood presaged the emergence from the round, slotted spout what appeared to be a small quantity of a poor quality hamburger. Lester caught it in his handkerchief to keep it from soiling the rug.

"So much, Mr. Rand," said Gregory Ballinger, "for your bargaining position." He signalled the cameraman to stop filming and continued addressing Rand:

"You will tell me, right now, where that document is. If you do not, Lester will grind up another of Miss Li's fingers—this time without first cutting it off. Do I make myself clear?"

When the light blinked on and the chime rang to announce the arrival of an elevator car at the ninety-sixth floor, it alerted the three North Koreans guarding the doors to the executive suite lobby. They were, however, completely unprepared for the sight of the massive Mongol who sprang at them from out of the car the instant the doors opened. The middle guard, nevertheless, had the presence to get off a powerful forward kick. The ball of his foot would have landed directly under T'ang Li's sternum had he been there to receive it. But T'ang Li was not; he was five and a half feet off the ground in a leap directly toward the central defender.

As he reached the top of his leap, T'ang Li's right leg shot out to the side and his foot struck the guard on the right just under the jaw and ear. The lifting, twisting blow broke the man's neck with a snap like that of a dry twig. With his left leg, T'ang Li attempted a similar blow to the guard on the left. The defender managed to block it with his arm but the impact of the blocked kick drove him hard backward into the left door frame.

The central guard never got another chance to strike at T'ang Li. Descending from his leap, T'ang Li shot his right arm straight out, fingers spread wide and stiffened like steel rods, directly into the face of his opponent. The thrust came from the shoulder carrying with it the full force of T'ang Li's body weight. The stiffened fingers struck the guard's face athwart the nose and his facial bones, in a natural camming action, guided the outstretched fingers into his eye sockets. Such was the power of T'ang Li's thrust that his fingers kept right on going through the wet pulp of the man's eyeballs and the shell-thin bone at the rear of the sockets to penetrate into the warm, moist, unresistant softness of the brain itself. The Korean dropped like a hanged man when the rope is cut.

As T'ang Li landed on the balls of his feet the left guard lurched back into the battle. But before he could get his guard high enough to block it, T'ang Li turned his left fist outward and, rigid hook of his double-broken thumb leading in a sweeping backhand slash, tore out the guard's jugular.

Without waiting for the throatless man to fall, T'ang Li passed through the now unguarded doors, slipped around the art in the lobby and made his way quickly to the door to Ballinger's office. Hand tightly around the doorknob, he twisted it slowly. It was unlocked. He heard nothing behind the door. The knob reached it's stop, latch retracted fully. T'ang Li concentrated, placing his entire body under such tension that his surface veins bulged from knotted calf to throbbing temple.

Rand didn't know how to answer Ballinger. He was in a dilemma. He didn't know what T'sa Li had done with the claim he had mailed, or whether she had ever received it; but to ask her, or to indicate to Ballinger that T'sa Li, not he, might be closer to the document, would only focus Ballinger's barbarity on her more intensely. T'sa Li herself, whether because she was incredibly brave or had no idea where the claim was, said nothing; she just sat there, head down, biting her lip. She didn't sob, but tears trickled from the corners of her eyes to run down her cheeks and fall in droplets from her chin.

"Well?" demanded Ballinger.

Before Rand could speak the door burst open and T'ang Li hurtled deep inside the room to land, legs apart and bent, left elbow head high, forearm horizontal and protecting his face, right arm vertically before the left, both hands balled into great hammerlike fists. From his throat came a roar that seemed to rumble and reverberate with the deep chest tones of a tiger. It began deliberately, decided upon beforehand as a tactic to startle and intimidate those within the room; but as he saw his sister the sound took on a spontaneous note of terrible anger.

At T'ang Li's entrance the guards holding Rand released him to fulfill their primary mission and defend against the intruder. In a raging blur of motion T'ang Li's bloody left hook of a thumb dripped the gore of a second throatless victim. The outside bone of his descending right forearm broke the attacking right arm of the other guard who died as the Mongol giant whipped the same arm back up to crush his temple with the knoblike end of the bone of his forearm projecting from T'ang Li's cocked wrist.

Rand, taking advantage of his unexpected freedom, rushed toward T'sa Li only to pull up short as Lester, with exceptional speed, dropped T'sa Li's now unbound and bleeding right hand en route the grinder to draw a .38 calibre Smith & Wesson snub-nosed revolver which he stuck in her ear so hard it bent her head almost all the way over to her shoulder.

"Freeze!" Lester shouted at the entire assembly, "or I'll blow her brains right out her other ear!"

The room obeyed.

"Well done, Lester," Ballinger observed quietly. "You too, Mr. Li," he added. "I congratulate you for having gotten this far; I quite underestimated you. You, on the other hand, have underestimated me. As you can see, any further heroics by you or Mr. Rand and your sister dies immediately. You hear that Lester? Don't wait for any further word from me. The minute either of these two makes a wrong move, pull that trigger."

"Yes, sir," said Lester. It was clear from his tone and expression that he hoped to be given the opportunity to comply.

Ballinger turned to his camerman:

"Did you get all that?"

"You mean the fight? No, sir. It was too quick. I was still on Lester."

"Never mind," Ballinger replied, "we have an unexpected opportunity for some film that will be a classic. Lester: keep that pistol in her ear, but drag that chair over against the window. I want the floor cleared."

Lester experienced some difficulty trying to move T'sa Li and her chair one-handed. "Help him with that," Ballinger ordered the cameraman.

"Now then, Mr. Li," said Ballinger, "you came here looking for a fight? Good; you shall have one. Mr. Li, meet Mr. Bok. Sung Bok."

The middle-aged Oriental in the corner took a step forward and bowed to T'ang Li. Li faced Sung Bok, brought his hands together before him and bowed in return; then reached down to remove his shoes. Sung Bok did the same; then both men stripped to the waist and assumed fighting stances according to the styles of their respective martial arts. Each angled away from the other rather than facing his opponent squarely, both using versions of the "horse" stance; legs apart, knees flexed, weight on the rear leg.

T'ang Li went into a high version of the T'ai Chi number one position, elbows head high, left forearm horizontal, right vertical, hands balled into fists. It was the same posture he had assumed upon first landing inside the room; the style of the tiger.

Sung Bok raised both arms high before him fifteen degrees from the vertical, elbows straight, razor-sharp fingernail tipped hands open, fingers hard together and pointing down. His arms and hands looked like twin long-necked, sharp-beaked birds.

Rand, fascinated by these preliminaries, forced himself to glance at Lester and T'sa Li out of the corner of his eye. He focused on Lester's revolver and noted with relief that the hammer was down; Lester hadn't cocked it. That didn't mean that it had to be cocked before firing—the piece was double-action—but it meant that the force on the trigger would have to be several pounds to fire it, not the fraction of a pound that it would take were the gun cocked. There was much less chance of the gun being fired accidentally in the course of the coming battle. As the two men started to circle in the center of the room, Rand waited until Sung Bok approached and then eased toward Lester and T'sa Li without looking at them, as if trying to stay out of Sung Bok's way. He got closer but dared not try to go further for fear of being noticed and ordered back. T'sa Li looked bad. Her face was drained and Rand feared she was going into shock.

T'ang Li was a graceful man in spite of his great size but he could not compare in grace to Sung Bok. Lean and lithe, the North Korean whirled backward, feinted with his foot, and in a backhand move that seemed almost slow, his nail made a shallow

272

six-inch slice across T'ang Li's torso, just below his pectorals. T'ang Li's block, a descending right forearm, missed completely and he spun away with a high rearward kick that didn't. Sung Bok was hurled backward several feet but landed in balance and with no apparent damage. By contrast, T'ang Li was bleeding from his chest.

It was Sung Bok who whirled next, using a sweep kick that T'ang Li blocked with a hard arm blow but, because Sung Bok had no weight on the leg and let it go limp, the blow did no structural damage. Sung Bok came over and across T'ang Li's blocking arm with extraordinary speed and a thin red line appeared across T'ang Li's forehead. It was a very damaging stroke and T'ang Li knew it. Sung Bok wasn't showing off; that thin red line would soon start to drip blood which could make it's way past T'ang Li's eyebrows and into his eyes. There was no way T'ang Li or anyone else could survive against Sung Bok without perfect vision; the man was just too fast and deceptive.

"Good move!" Ballinger shouted to Sung Bok. Then, to the cameraman:

"Did you get that?"

"Got it," said the photographer, his eye glued to the viewfinder as T'ang Li, running out of time and realizing it, started to press.

T'ang Li moved with a speed astonishing for a man of any size, trying to crowd Sung Bok into a corner where he could employ his greater size and strength. But Sung Bok was a will o' the wisp and not to be pinned down. The North Korean's high held hands darted down daggerlike as he slipped away, aiming at T'ang Li's eyes. Only the larger man's skill and experience enabled him to save his vision; but deep cuts appeared just below his eye sockets and the blood ran down to fly off his chin as he moved his head rapidly in the furious course of battle.

Rand stole another look at Lester and T'sa Li. Shivering with approaching shock, she was the only one in the room not watching the two combatants. Rand eased a little closer. The revolver was still uncocked. It was then a desperate T'ang Li, now beginning to experience impaired vision, elected to gamble everything on one move.

Sung Bok was close, but not close enough. T'ang Li shook his head as if trying to clear his vision without having to lower his guard by using his hand to wipe his eyes. Sung Bok sensed the weakness immediately and moved instantly to exploit it. Down like twin striking falcons came the dagger-hands. At the same time, T'ang Li slipped forward, stealing some of the distance between them, and thrust both arms, fists together, straight upward before him.

T'ang Li's upward sweeping forearms knocked aside Sung Bok's swooping arms. The North Korean countered immediately by driving both stiffened hands directly inward to stab T'ang Li in the axillae, the unprotected hollows under his arms. As Sung Bok's nails cut in, the outside bones of T'ang Li's heavy forearms sliced downward to land with crushing force on his opponent's shoulders at either side of his neck. Both of Sung Bok's collar bones shattered at once.

Disabled, Sung Bok slipped backward in retreat but T'ang Li, anticipating the move, spun around and moved backward himself to stay in close contact. He brought first one and then the other of his elbows smashing backward into Sung Bok's sternum. As each elbow impacted, T'ang Li snapped the corresponding forearm up to pulverize Sung Bok's facial bones with the knuckles of his heavy fists. The Korean reeled and the giant Mongol spun around to finish him.

With his left hand T'ang Li measured his stunned opponent, then cocked his right fist like a boxer. Like a boxer, too, he threw a tremendous overhand right at Sung Bok's head. Unlike a boxer, however, as T'ang Li's fist neared it's target he snapped it around in reverse so that it was his wrist, three heavy, cartilage covered bones protruding, that smashed backwards into Sung Bok's forehead just above the bridge of his nose. As the Korean's skull fractured and caved inward his eyes bulged outward and slivers of shattered bone pierced the frontal lobes of his brain.

His own blood now blurring his vision badly, T'ang Li turned from the falling corpse of Sung Bok toward his sister. The sight of the great, bloody monster that was now T'ang Li caused Lester to forget his instructions to shoot T'sa Li first; terrified, he shifted his aim to T'ang Li and squeezed the trigger. Blind now, T'ang Li didn't see Rand leap forward and grasp the revolver in an attempt to catch it over the hammer and cylinder to prevent Lester from firing.

Rand missed. As he twisted the gun down by the barrel he felt it against his leg. There was a partially muffled shot and what felt to Rand like a searing burn from a hot poker laid along his thigh. Rand wrestled the revolver away from Lester and turned to

274

cover Ballinger only to note, unbelievingly, that Ballinger was gone.

In anger, Rand heard the rapid *whop-whop-whop* of a departing helicopter; then turned in fury upon the frightened Lester and the cameraman:

"Face down on the floor!" Rand shouted, covering the two men with the revolver. They obeyed quickly. Rand took out his handkerchief and wrapped it around T'sa Li's stump. "You all right, baby?" he asked her solicitously. "You all right?"

T'sa Li, in shock, did not respond. Rand turned to T'ang Li, who was wiping his eyes.

"We've got to get her to a hospital. You could use one yourself. What d'you say? That chopper was Ballinger. We can get him later."

T'ang Li shook his huge head. "Take her," he said. "I stay."

"Suit yourself," said Rand. "This girl doesn't have time for us to argue." He gave T'ang Li Lester's revolver, freed T'sa Li of her bonds and picked her up gently. T'ang Li shoved the Smith & Wesson into his waistband as Rand, carrying the still silent T'sa Li, left the room.

Wiping his eyes again, T'ang Li looked from the chair and meat grinder to Lester, still prone on the floor beside the cameraman. At that moment Lester's cat, cringing on top of the lectern, mewed. T'ang Li smiled.

Walking over to Lester, T'ang Li kicked him lightly in the ribs to gain his attention, then gestured the erstwhile torturer to his feet.

"Strip," T'ang Li commanded.

"Huh?"

"Strip!"

The fearful Lester undressed hurriedly, then stood, trembling, before T'ang Li. His look of anxiety faded as T'ang Li crossed to the tiny closet, opened the door and motioned the pink-skinned sadist into the empty cubicle. Lester stood against the rear wall and watched curiously as T'ang Li reached up and removed the single overhead light bulb, then closed the door to leave his prisoner in darkness.

Stepping over the prostrate cameraman, T'ang Li retrieved the cat from the lectern. He held it out by the scruff of the neck and shook it violently. By the time he arrived back at the closet the screaming, clawing animal was frantic. T'ang Li snatched open the closet door, hurled the raging little beast at the startled Lester, then drew the revolver and fired a shot into the closet floor before slamming the door.

Inside the pitch dark closet the trapped, fear-maddened cat, driven berserk by the blast and flame from the Smith & Wesson, screamed and raced around it's tiny prison trying vainly to escape. Encountering the soft flesh of Lester, who promptly compounded the animal's terror by screeching himself and trying wildly to fend it off, the cat tore up and down his naked body, claws and needle-sharp teeth slashing and digging repeatedly. As the talons and teeth cut into him, Lester screamed louder and the cat became even more distraught.

At that point, T'ang Li opened the closet door just far enough to reach in and fire another shot before slamming it closed again. The cat, now completely hysterical, repeated it's frantic attempt to escape and, once more encountering the bleeding, crying Lester, tore into him anew.

Thirty minutes and three more shots later, out of ammunition and Lester now silent with nothing from the cat but short, low half-growls, T'ang Li opened the closet door. The cat shot out and raced round and round the room, finally scrambling up a drapery to hang at the top from bloody claws, wild-eyed and shaking.

Inside the closet, T'ang Li noted with satisfaction, lay the naked Lester, seventy percent of his flesh shredded and both eyes torn out. He was still alive but the pool of blood under his mutilated body was widening rapidly. Sensing a human presence, Lester opened his mouth in an attempt to speak, but all he could manage was a barely audible whimper. T'ang Li shut the door to let him die in darkness, alone.

The cameraman, still face down on the floor, was sobbing in uncontrollable fear, each scream from Lester having added to his terror. T'ang Li moved to stand over him, looking down. Presently the prone man noticed T'ang Li's feet and, shaking, turned his head up to ask:

"What—are you—going to do—with me?" He could hardly get the words out. T'ang Li let him struggle through the question again before reaching down with a smile to give him a hand up. The cameraman wept in relief; then T'ang Li, still smiling, strangled him.

# XX

"You're Mr. Rand, the man who brought her in here?"

"Yes."

"Are you sometimes called 'Rick'?"    ·

"Yes."

"All right, you can go in now. She's been asking for you."

"How is she?"

"Physically, she's fine. We gave her a pint of blood and a mild sedative for pain. We had to take a small graft from her thigh to cover the open end of the stump. We don't expect any difficulty."

"Why did you qualify her condition with 'physically'?"

"Because she's depressed. That's not uncommon when there's been a mutilation; takes awhile to get used to the idea. Then there's often a feeling of chagrin, embarrassment, when one does something like that with such serious consequences. I mean, she's been saying things like, 'How stupid; I've used that thing in the kitchen for years.' That sort of thing. See if you can cheer her up."

"Right."

"Ah, one more thing."

"Yes?"

"I'm not sure just how to put this: These Chinese 'friends' of hers. They act like guards. It isn't really necessary, you know, and I wonder if you could—"

"I couldn't. But there's no need to be concerned. She's from a very prominent and well-to-do Chinese family. They have an obsessive fear of kidnaping. Just humor them; they won't cause any trouble."

Rand knocked on the door and entered before T'sa Li could respond. It was a private room in a modern wing of the hospital, well lighted by large windows. The scent of flowers hung in the air. T'sa Li was sitting nearly upright, supported by the raised mattress of her adjustable bed. She had managed somehow to make up her face and comb her hair. Hesitantly, expectantly, she looked at Rand. He smiled at her and said:

"I've gotta hand it to ya, kid; for a girl, you've got a lotta balls."

T'sa Li started to laugh and cry at the same time. She wept the tears all women weep at some point in their lives when a man they love says the wrong thing, or doesn't say the right thing at a critical time. She had longed for him to tell her how lovely she looked, even if it was a lie; but he was a man, and men are so *stupid* about such things! She laughed because the compliment he paid her, the product of a completely masculine value system, was so absurdly incongruous and inapt. In fact, the more she thought about it the harder she laughed; and the harder she laughed, the more puzzled the look on Rand's face, which just made it worse. She finally had to come to a gasping stop so she could breathe.

"I blew it, huh?" said Rand.

"Jesus!" T'sa Li smiled, the tear paths still wet down her face, "Did you ever!"

"Yeah. Well, I meant well."

"You always do," T'sa Li said with an exaggerated sigh. "I guess that's why I love you." She patted the side of her bed and wiggled her hips over to one side to make room for him. Rand eased himself onto the bed, slipped his hand under the covers, found the inside of her thigh and ran his hand up the soft flesh slowly, saying:

"You look great. What say I lock the door?"

T'sa Li snapped her legs together, stopping the progress of Rand's hand. "You're too late," she pouted.

"Huh?"

"*That's* what you were supposed to say when you walked in here!"

"Women in general," sighed Rand, "and you in particular, are nuts. You'll never achieve equality because you are completely without logic." He leaned over and kissed her, at first gently, then passionately. She reached around him with her arms, giving not a thought to the bulky bandage that enveloped her hand, and pressed him to her. When he released her she reeled momentarily from the heady combination of intense emotion and lack of breath, then made a point of opening her legs to release his hand. T'sa Li looked down the mirrored corridors of Rand's far-away eyes and said softly: "There are some things about being a woman that are beyond logic."

Rand's hand found it's destination, only to be snatched back quickly at a discreet knock on the door. A moment later the door opened just enough for a nurse to announce "Miss Li's brother is here."

"Ask him to wait, please," said T'sa Li; then, turning serious suddenly, she said:

"My God, I completely forgot. How's your leg?"

"It's nothing. Really. How'd you know about it, anyway?"

"I was *there,* remember? I saw you take the bullet meant for my brother."

"I thought you were out of it from shock."

"It was as if I wasn't a participant anymore, just an observer. I could see and hear but didn't have the strength to say or do anything. It was weird. But I knew what was going on. You saved my brother's life."

"Well, let's not make more of it than there was. I was *not* shot, just burned. The gun was twisted sideways. The bullet must have gone into the floor through the rug. All I got was the muzzle blast. Ruined my pants and scorched my leg. The entire treatment consisted of washing it and smearing on Vaseline. The bandage is to keep the Vaseline from ruining *another* pair of pants when I get a chance to change. The only thing permanent about it will be a tattoo from unburned powder under the skin."

"I'll be curious to see it."

"Yeah. Listen; let me get out of here so you can see your brother and I can go change my pants." Rand rose, then said:

"Oh—ah, I hate to bring this up now, but did you ever get a chance to pick up that letter?"

"Yes. It was already there in your box when I got there the first day. I put it in my pocketbook to take upstairs with me, then went out the Central Park South side to buy some fruit around the corner. A car looked like it might be following me so I stopped to pet the horse Alfredo uses in the morning to check it out; you know, so I could see what they'd do. When the car stopped right there in the middle of the street, I slipped the letter under the seat lid. I was on the other side of the horse so they couldn't see me do it. Then I ran back toward the hotel to try to get away. They just backed up the car, got out, threw me inside and drove off. Nobody said or did anything, even when I screamed."

"Good old New York. Okay. I'm going to get out of here while the gettings good. Your brother's pretty pissed at me for getting you involved, and after what's happened, who can blame him. First time he gets me alone I'm going to end up in here next to you, only I doubt I'll be in condition to take advantage of the situation. I want to stay away from him 'till he cools off a little."

T'sa Li laughed, "You don't need to worry about that."

"Well, I appreciate the vote of confidence but I've seen him fight. So, if it's all the same to you, I'll—"

"You don't understand," T'sa Li interrupted. "You saved his *life*. It's not just that honor won't let him raise his hand to you now; he *owes* you his life. That debt will never be repaid unless and until he does the same for you someday. That doesn't mean he has to *like* you; in fact he'll probably like you even less—my brother hates to owe anybody anything—but he won't harm you. Not now. Quite the contrary."

"Good. Don't tell him about the Vaseline. Tell him the bullet tore the hell out of my leg muscles and it's a miracle I can still walk."

T'sa Li laughed. "I'll tell him you'll never play the piano again." Abruptly, T'sa Li's smile vanished. She bit her lip as she realized what she'd said. Rand, looking stricken, took a step toward her. T'sa Li shook her head furiously and he stopped.

"It's all right," she said. "I'm okay. You go ahead. Send in my brother. I'll see you later."

At 5:55 A.M., Monday 4th May, Richard Rand stood impatiently just inside the lobby doors of the Central Park South entrance to the Plaza Hotel waiting for Alfredo Matarazza to appear driving the horse-drawn coach. Two minutes later Matarazza pulled to the curb on the north side of the street. As Rand approached him, Matarazza observed with surprise his employer's tan camel's hair sport coat, off-white shirt and tie that matched his chocolate colored slacks.

"Boss," Matarazza said, "ain't you gonna run today?"

"Not today, 'Fredo. If our luck's holding, your ass is sitting on a billion dollars."

"Huh?" said Matarazza, starting to rise as Rand swung himself into the rear of the carriage.

"Sit still," Rand commanded, "and drive this thing into the park. Find someplace quiet and pull over. This guy you pay to use this thing; he know about the shotgun under the seat?"

"Yeah. I leveled with him. He ain't done no time or nothin' but he's a knock-around guy and all right. That's why it costs so much. The risk. I told him to keep away from it on account of finger-prints and like that there, and we'd take care of him if anything happened. He stays outta there."

"Good," said Rand as the coach rolled behind the trotting horse up through the park. They continued in silence but for the clopping of the horse's steel-shod feet against the asphalt, then Rand said:

"Anywhere around here you see an opening'll do."

No sooner had Rand spoken than there was the sound of a large displacement engine behind them. Rand didn't like the unre-stricted note of the carburetor intake; a deep breathing, rushing sound that denied the presence of power-choking emmissions control equipment. These days, the only legal motors coming out of the factory like that were in interceptor-engined automobiles built for the government. Rand turned around for a look. A black Ford four-door sedan with blackwall tires was behind them. Men were in both the front and rear seats and both windows were down on the right hand side.

"Down 'Fredo!" Rand shouted. "Hit the deck!"

Alfredo Matarazza had never served in the Navy but he had "gone to the mattresses" several times during family wars over the years and he reacted immediately to Rand's tone of voice, dropping the reins and diving into the rear of the coach as the first shots rang out. One zipped overhead with the sound of an outraged hornet. The second, lower and at an angle, just missed the coach but creased the rump of the horse. The animal leaped forward into a headlong gallop, no reins to guide it and fright-ened as much by the sudden absence of control as by the stinging wound.

"Grab the reins, 'Fredo!" Rand shouted, snaking his arm up and under the seat lid to grope for the sawn-off shotgun. Mata-razza got hold of the reins at about the same time Rand's fingers closed around the heavy weapon. The Ford's tires chirped under hard acceleration as the car, with handguns protruding from both right-side windows, caught up with the careering coach as both vehicles entered a deep cut. Walls of fieldstone masonry rose twenty feet on both side of the road to shut out from the world yet another life and death struggle in New York's Central Park.

Rand swung the twin muzzles of the double barreled 12-gauge over the side of the coach. He squeezed the first trigger and the piece roared and bucked in recoil as seven .32 calibre lead balls of buckshot from the top barrel tore the arm from the shoulder of the passenger in the rear seat of the Ford. A second later the other trigger sent a blast from the lower barrel toward the front seat gunman but the driver, reacting to the first shot, had let up on the throttle slightly and the rifled slug missed the front side window. Instead of taking out the gunman, Rand's second shot disintegrated the auto's windshield, the massive lead slug exploding the head of the driver. The big interceptor started to weave from side to side as the right front gunman abandoned the struggle for control of the automobile against the dead weight of the driver's body.

The swerving of the Ford widened progressively until it side-swiped the left wall of the cut, bounced right, barely missing the rear of the carriage, then careened and started a tumbling, side-over-side roll down the road behind the fleeing Rand and Matarazza. As spilled gasoline from the carburetor bowl hit the hot exhaust manifold it burst into flame and a moment later the fire reached the fuel spilling from the gas tank where the filler pipe had been torn loose. With a roar the Ford exploded into a spectacular rolling fireball that showered burning gasoline and pieces of flaming tires in all directions; including forward where it set afire the back of Alfredo Matarazza's coat. "Holy shit!" the big man shouted as Rand beat out the flames, then turned from him to check the rest of the coach, "Holy shit!"

Matarazza wasn't able to get the foam-flecked, panic-stricken horse under control and stopped until the carriage neared Fifth Avenue.

"You okay?" Rand asked Matarazza.

"Sure. Soon as I change my shorts I'll be good as new. Better gimme that piece."

Rand handed Matarazza the shotgun and the older man lifted the seat lid to store it out of sight.

"Hold it," said Rand. "Let me take a look in there."

Rand broke into a grin as he saw the envelope bearing his own handwriting in the bottom of the seat box where T'sa Li had dropped it. He reached in and took it out.

"What's that?" asked Matarazza.

"This," said Rand, brandishing the envelope before putting it into the inside pocket of his sport jacket, "is one billion dollars."

Matarazza looked at Rand skeptically. "No offense, Boss," he said, "but I think you musta hit your head back there before I got the fuckin' horse stopped."

There was no small talk, no meaningless, good-humored banter so characteristic of the last moments before board meetings of major corporations are called to order, as Richard Rand and Aaron Feld awaited the signal from the stenographer that his Stenotype machine was ready. The presence of the stenographer was unusual and indicated to Rand that his opponents were wary of him and prepared to take advantage of the smallest slip. If any trace of Sunday night's activities in Ballinger's office had been left by his North Korean goon squad, it was not reflected in the faces present.

The Comco boardroom was on the ninety-sixth floor of the Comco Building and was reached through the same lobby as Ballinger's office. It occupied the southeast corner of the floor and was separated from Ballinger's office by the private dining room that took up the balance of the east wall between them. A strong wind had cleared the pollution, and at 10:30 A.M., Wednesday, 6th May, the boardroom windows offered a sweeping view of lower Manhattan, the East River and South Brooklyn.

Aaron Feld flicked through his file, expending nervous energy. He was, as usual, throughly prepared in the event Rand called upon him, but one of his most deeply held beliefs was that one could never do too much homework. Rand, on the other hand, just sat next to Feld in the side chair provided until they were invited to address the board. The stenographer gave a discreet cough and raised his hand as a signal of readiness, and a fiftyish man with iron gray hair and a seamed face sitting at the far end of the conference table rapped his knuckles on the tabletop and said:

"Gentlemen, if you will come to order, please."

The room could not be said to quiet down as it was already still; at most there was a slight decrease in the rustling of clothing, a stilling of nervous fingers playing with the pencils lying at the sides of legal-length ruled yellow pads set neatly at each place around the table. One chair, the seat opposite that of the man who had spoken, was vacant.

"Let the record note," the speaker continued, "that a quorum of the board is present and the stenographer will record the names of the directors present as he is given them."

In his turn each man around the table spelled his name to the stenographer. Then the man at the far end of the table spoke again, consulting notes, carefully weighing each word:

"This meeting has been convened by the president in the absence of the chairman of the board of directors and chief executive officer, Mr. Gregory Ballinger, in accordance with section 12(c)(2) of the by-laws, which treats of the unavailability of the chairman by virtue of illness or otherwise. The record will show that diligent efforts to locate Mr. Ballinger over a forty-eight hour period were unsuccessful and his whereabouts at present are unknown.

"The purpose of this meeting is to consider a claim by Mr. Richard Rand, here present with his counsel, Aaron Feld, Esquire, that the funds of a recent issue to which he subscribed were not expended in accordance with the offering registered with the Securities and Exchange Commission, an allegation which the president, for and on behalf of the management of Comco, denies. Mr. Rand, there is a vacant seat at the table opposite me. If you'd care to take it you may now present your case to the board."

Rand rose, moved to the head of the table and pulled the chair out of the way, preferring to stand. He laid a file folder on the table before him and opened it, eyes searching the faces of the seated directors and the company president. He was convinced that Ballinger had not been located. Ballinger would never have let this meeting take place. He would have defied Rand, forced him into court, then stalled, hoping to take over Columbia Steel in the interim and, with time, raise enough money to pay Rand off. The difference was that Ballinger knew what was coming. These men, leaderless, had agreed to the meeting because they didn't know what else to do; they wanted a look at his hand. Litigation would still be an option; Rand had to prevent that.

"I shall be brief and to the point," Rand said, and those around the table noticed that he remained standing and omitted such prefatory niceties as the word "Gentlemen." Rand meant to intimidate them; to fill the psychological vacuum created by Ballinger's absence.

"I do not merely own stock of your issue of 17th January a year ago," Rand continued, "I control the issue—most of that not retained by your company as treasury stock—thirty million dollar's worth. That fat folder you see at the feet of Mr. Feld, there," Rand pointed to it, "is filled with powers of attorney to me from shareholders of record of that issue. You are free to examine it if you wish. At this point I want to say that if at any time this board wishes to go off the record for reasons of it's own, I have no objection. And frankly, when you hear some of what I have to say, I doubt you'll want the rest on the record."

"Be that as it may," Rand went on, "I have a story to tell you. Two Chinese businessmen came to see me last year; a Mr. Wing and a Mr. Wa. They wanted to borrow money to finance a particular deal that, for their purposes, had to remain secret. That ruled out banks and other conventional sources of borrowing. I lent them the money under a contract specifying the interest rate would be eighteen percent if the deal went through; otherwise, half that amount. Here is a copy of that agreement."

Rand handed a xerographic copy of his agreement with Wing and Wa to the director on his right. "Messrs. Wing and Wa informed me subsequently that the deal they had entered had failed and that they would, therefore, be paying me only nine percent interest. I had no reason to doubt their word but business is business; I challenged the statement and demanded that they reveal the deal to me for verification purposes. Here are copies of that correspondence."

Again, Rand handed the papers down to the right. Aaron Feld watched intently from the sidelines, taking in every word. It was the first he had heard the entire story himself and he was fascinated.

"Please note the dates on these documents carefully," said Rand. "In the meantime, not knowing until I learned through the correspondence you have before you of the connection between my debtors and Comco, I noted that you people let out an issue. The prospectus was attractive and I and many others, relying on that prospectus, bought the shares offered. Many purchasers, for reasons of their own, have given me voting control of their shares. You can imagine my surprise when I learned that the deal my debtors told me had fallen through was the basis for your issue, and the reason for the failure was that Comco, at least allegedly, had not performed to specification."

Rand paused to pour a glass of water from the carafe on the

table and drink it, letting his words sink in. Then he continued his address:

"At that point, I did what any prudent businessman would do —and certainly anyone owing the fiduciary obligation I do to all those issue shareholders who gave me powers of attorney—and filed a claim immediately. At the time I happened to be in Bogota on business and, as you know, filed my claim through the U.S. embassy there at 8:47 A.M. on 30th April. Remember that well, please."

The roomful of men was watching Rand intently, with great interest, but without apparent alarm. He had their attention, but so far, that was all.

"And what do you suppose your general counsel did when he received my claim?" Rand asked rhetorically, his voice sweet reasonableness itself. "Why, he called my counsel up and they discussed my intentions, which were, of course, to litigate. Mr. Feld here mentioned the routine procedure of obtaining a preliminary injunction against the expenditure of assets of your company equal to the value of the issue so shareholders could get their money back if the court decided in our favor. But, to my unhappiness when I found out about it later, your counsel talked Mr. Feld out of it and, in my name, he agreed not to seek such an injunction in return for written assurances that Comco would do nothing with the issue money, or take any action which would change the facts, until the case was decided by the courts. That was—when, Mr. Feld?"

"9:21 A.M., the same day, April 30th. He sent it over the phone transmission machine. Here's a copy."

"Thanks," said Rand, taking the copy from Feld and handing it to the director on his right in the now familiar pattern. He leaned forward, knuckles on the tabletop to support him, voice dropping very low:

"And then," Rand purred, "what do you suppose I learned happened in Hong Kong on the first of May?"

The president looked stricken: "May we go off the record for a moment?"

"Be my guest," said Rand.

"I just want to hear what you have to say from this point informally."

"Certainly. We can go back on the record any time you wish. All right. What I found out was that after issuing written assurances to counsel for a claimant alleging misuse of issue funds that nothing would be done to alter the facts until litigation had been decided, on May 1st, at 10:47 P.M., this board entered into an agreement with Ha Kah Enterprises, the company of my debtors Wing and Wa, to extend the terms of your contract; the contract that is at the heart of the issue. *That,* gentlemen, was not just a violation of your word, not just a breach of contract, but fraud."

Rand handed out copies of the extension agreement and stood, waiting. The board members glanced at the document perfunctorily, some just passed it on without even looking at it and stared instead at the middle of the table. The president broke the silence:

"What do you want, Mr. Rand? Your money back? I suspect you know we don't have it to give you and that's not what you're here for." His voice was weary.

"You're wrong," said Rand firmly. "My money back is exactly what I want, what I demand for me and those I represent by power of attorney. If you don't have it, then I want it's equivalent."

"In what?"

"Treasury stock. Thirty million's worth, split between the general stock of the corporation and every issue Comco ever let out."

The directors sat looking at Rand, stunned at the implication of his demand. Finally one started to say "You're out of your—" but he was cut off by the president:

"You don't really expect us to give you that, do you? All you have a legal right to now is to control how the proceeds from one issue are disbursed; you have no say over the funds in the general till. We give you stock from every issue and you'll have operating control of this company. Why should we do that?"

Rand's tone grew icy. "You're not thinking, gentlemen. When I said fraud, I didn't mean civil fraud. You're not facing a lawsuit, you're facing a trial. That little stunt Ballinger talked you into going along with violated the Securities and Exchange Act and constituted *criminal* fraud. This claim here," Rand picked it up and waved it in the air, "is your ticket to jail. All I have to do is turn the originals of this stuff over to the S.E.C. and the Justice Department. Ask your counsel: you give me what I want and you become ex-directors. You don't—you become ex-cons."

All eyes turned to a thin man in an Oxxford pin striped suit seated halfway down the table. The lawyer didn't return the

287

looks, just stared down at the empty yellow pad before him, his silence acknowledging the truth of Rand's assertions. The directors turned from their counsel to look at each other, hesitating. Rand guessed what was on their minds and pressed, brutally:

"There's no use looking around for Ballinger to save your asses; he's too busy saving his own. It's not your money, it's his. Face it, he fucked you. And, all right, I'm fucking you too—" The roomful of men frowned and some reddened, startled and offended by Rand's candid admission; they weren't used to being spoken to like that.

Rand leaned forward again, voice soft with menace: "But while we're on the subject of being fucked, gentlemen, just remember that here in this room it's only a figure of speech. It stays that way if you pay me off the way I want. You don't, and that figure of speech could become literal fact for some of you in a broom closet at Lewisburg."

Rand brought his body erect and smiled at the ashen, horrified group. "Then, of course," he said, his smile breaking into a grin, "there's the bright side; some of you might grow to like it."

The silence was so complete everyone in the room but Rand seemed to have stopped breathing. It was the president, face drained, who said finally:

"Back on the record. The chair will entertain a motion that Mr. Rand's claim has been found valid and that he be reimbursed, on his own behalf and that of those shareholders whose powers of attorney he holds, by treasury stock of thirty million dollars value, as of close of the market yesterday, in equal portions from every issue of the corporation."

"So moved." The voice was lifeless.

"All in favor?"

The "ayes" were listless, defeated.

"Thank you, gentlemen," said Rand. "I'll wait for certified transcripts of the approved minutes and until the transactions can be completed. Who's your transfer agent?"

"Morgan Guaranty."

"All right," Rand said, cheerily, "I want to give you all time for lunch. Shall we say Morgan Guaranty at two this afternoon?"

"Suit yourself," said the president. "I don't think any of us has much of an appetite, anyway."

# XXI

Richard Rand and Aaron Feld paused on the steps of the Comco
Building shortly before noon and shook hands; the handshake
was more than a perfunctory parting, it had the heartiness of
teammates sharing a victory.

"Don't worry about lunch, for Chrissake," said Feld, "I understand. Say hello to T'sa Li for me."

"Will do. See you at two at Morgan Guaranty."

Feld smiled, "I'll be there," and walked off to the north, looking for a cab. Rand went directly down the steps seeking Alfredo
Matarazza and his BMW. But where he had expected to find the
swift German automobile was a sleek Cadillac limousine, one
man in the front passenger seat, two in the rear and Matarazza
standing, an apologetic look on his face, beside the driver's door.

"What's going on, 'Fredo? Where's the car?"

"Boss, I'm sorry, but I had to tell the old man about this morning. I mean it was just luck it was them got whacked out, not us.
He says from now on, 'till this thing is finished, he's gonna take
care of you."

"Jesus! You mean every where I go I gotta have a car full of
muscle with me?"

Matarazza looked at the ground and scuffed his shoe in embarrassment. "Not just one, Boss," he said, inclining his head across
the street to where a Lincoln sedan, all seats occupied, was standing in a "no parking" zone.

"Oh, come on, 'Fredo! This is ridiculous!"

"Boss," Matarazza chided him gently, "you're tellin' the wrong
guy."

Rand sighed. "Yeah, I know. All right, take me to the hospital.

And when we get there, goddamn it, keep the guys out of sight. The staff's already complaining about all the Tong guys. I come in there with a private army, they're gonna go bananas."

"Sure, Boss. We'll keep low."

Rand looked through the window at the occupants of the limousine. "Keep low? These guys? They hardly fit in the car. What do I do, sit on their laps?" Matarazza continued to look embarrassed as he opened the rear door and Rand climbed in to squeeze between two men who could pass for all-pro defensive linemen.

Five minutes later Rand fretted while men from the Lincoln checked out the hospital entrance. At their signal that all was secure, the Cadillac rolled to the curb and Rand emerged, walking rapidly enough to keep ahead of his guards as he entered the building. To the dismay of the head floor nurse, his hulking entourage spread out along the walls of the corridor outside T'sa Li's room and glared at the impassive Tong men deployed along the opposite wall.

"I know, I know," Rand said to the nurse before she could speak, "I'm sorry. Believe me when I tell you it's not my idea. Please be patient; I'll only be a little while."

"Well, she goes home in the morning," the nurse said. "She's a lovely girl, but if this is the way she lives, I feel sorry for the poor thing."

One of the men from the Lincoln moved to enter T'sa Li's room to check it out but Rand fixed him with an angry look and Matarazza intervened with an "It's okay" to avoid a confrontation. Rand knocked on the door.

"Come in." T'sa Li's voice was cheerful. Rand entered and said:

"What d'ya mean, 'Come in'? How about 'Who's there?' I could be Jack the Ripper for all you know. Don't be so trusting."

"Ha!" T'sa Li snorted. "With my brother's people out there, even the doctor has a tough time getting in."

"He better *not* be getting in!"

"Well," T'sa Li replied airily, tossing her head, "any port in a storm. I hardly ever *see* you."

Rand smiled. T'sa Li had, obviously, recovered. The more she needled him, he knew, the better her spirits.

"Guess what?" Rand asked.

"I give up."

"At two o'clock this afternoon I pick up thirty million dollars worth of stock in Comco. General stock and shares from every issue they've ever let out."

"You did it!"

"You bet your sweet little ass I did it—thanks to you, I might add. Without that stamped claim I'd have come up empty."

"But the embassy had the original!"

"Sure. But the government's in with the show on this Ballinger move, remember? That paper'd disappear like a fart in a whirlwind."

"But you can stop them now; make them leave Columbia Steel alone."

"Any time after two o'clock this afternoon."

There was a knock on the door and the floor nurse stuck her head in. "Your brother's here. And Mr. Rand, those men of yours keep staring at my nurses. I won't have it. If they can't be polite, they can just leave!"

"I'm leaving myself. I'll speak to them."

"No, stay," said T'sa Li. "You and my brother are going to have to learn to be civil to each other."

T'ang Li entered, frowned at the sight of Rand and spoke to T'sa Li in rapid Chinese. T'sa Li caught her breath, said something briefly in Chinese herself, then T'ang Li turned and left the room.

"You see?" Rand said, "I told you. He's really pissed. Want's no part of me. You'll play hell getting the two of us in the same room."

"No, no," T'sa Li protested, "It's not that at all, it's—"she stopped in mid-sentence.

"It's what?" Rand demanded.

"Nothing. He was just explaining why he couldn't stay."

"*Why* couldn't he stay?"

"What difference does it make?"

"The two of you may have been speaking Chinese but you both flunk inscrutability. I could tell something's up from your tone of voice. It's Ballinger, isn't it? Something about Ballinger."

"Yes."

Rand's voice was excited. "He's found him?"

"No."

"Well?"

"Oh, Rick; let it go. T'ang will catch him. It's what he does best."

291

Rand stood. "What did he say!"

T'sa Li started to cry. "They got one of those North Koreans to talk finally. They'd been watching all the Comco corporate planes; LaGuardia, Teteboro, all over. Nothing. The North Korean said they were going to take delivery of a new one today."

"Where?"

"He didn't know. My brother's men will be covering every airport in the area. Ballinger's a pilot himself. They'll get him if he shows up."

"What kind of plane?"

T'sa Li frowned. "A Citation? Does that sound right?"

Rand didn't answer. He bent to kiss her, stiffly, preoccupied, saying only "I've got to go."

"No, no, no!" T'sa Li wept and banged her injured hand against the mattress to emphasize each word. "How can you *be* so stupid? This sort of thing is my *brother's* business, not yours! What if something happens to you? What happens to me? What happens to this afternoon? By two o'clock you'll have *won*, don't you see? You go get yourself killed now and Ballinger wins! Why risk it? For stupid masculine pride? Don't little boys ever grow up? You're always talking about logic; where's the logic in that? It's stupid, stupid, *stupid!*"

T'sa Li had banged her bandaged hand again to emphasize her last three words. Blood appeared seeeping through the gauze. Rand stared at the growing stain and said coldly:

"Your brother's expertise is on the ground. He may well get him, and if he does, good for him. But once Ballinger gets airborne, even your brother can't jump high enough. Up there, that's *my* business."

"Crap!" T'sa Li shouted, banging her hand again. "So Ballinger gets away. So what? You did what you set out to do. *You're* the one who told me how important it is to keep the Russians from getting Columbia Steel. You're the one," T'sa Li said, raising her blood-soaked bandage and shaking it at Rand, "who persuaded me it was worth it to go through this; not for you, not for me, for the *country. That's* why I saved your precious letter. Now you're going to risk all that for the chance to be a goddamn hero? Well go on then! Get yourself killed! Lose everything! *Fuck* the country!" Sobs wracked T'sa Li, "Leave me—with—nobody. No—body." Her sobs prevented her from saying more, but she had no more to say anyway.

Rand spoke quietly. "You told me yesterday that there are some things about being a woman that go beyond logic. Well, there are some things about being a man that transcend logic too. This is something I have to do for the same reason your brother does; we're both men."

Rand paused for T'sa Li to answer but she said nothing. "Well," he said, "you could wish me luck, anyway."

T'sa Li shook her head and stared down at the covers of her bed. "Oh, you're so full of shit," she said. "Go on, get out of here."

In his anger, Constantine Kazalakis squeezed the handset of his telephone as if to punish the offending instrument for the bad news it had just brought him from Paul Farington at the New York CIA station in Rockefeller Center.

"You mean to tell me," Kazalakis shouted into the mouthpiece, "that with Ballinger out of pocket for two days, you've lost Rand too! I don't believe it! Don't tell *me* he got away from four guys in an interceptor! With a goddamn *horsecart!*"

Paul Farington's voice rang hollowly over the KYX scrambler phone, his voice piped into a safe-sized, combination locked encoder in his own office and out through an identical machine near Kazalakis' desk. As was his wont when his superior raved, Farington became even more unemotional in reply. He thought it served to calm Kazalakis, but the opposite was true; the Deputy Director for Operations resented the fact that his feelings were not transferable.

"I'm afraid the damage goes a bit farther than that, sir," Farrington said blandly. "All four of the people assigned to the removal mission were killed; two by gunshot and two burned to death in the car. We've just finished the clean-up and there'll be no repercussions, but those four were all the ones on Rand at the time because of the nature of the assignment. I've got regular people covering known haunts and so forth, and we'll pick him up again, but to mount another removal mission we'll need more specialists; he took out all we had in town."

"He took 'em out, my Greek ass!" Kazalakis barked. "It's gotta be those goddamn mob relatives of his protecting him. Those people I sent you were first rate. Now, for Chrissake, I gotta pull in more people from the pool and the best are outta the country."

"Yes, sir."

"Now listen to me. The FAA guys say Cessna was braggin' a

while ago that Ballinger's buying one of their new jets. He's a pilot and gonna take delivery himself; took a two-week type rating from Cessna out West somewhere a while back. He's gonna pick it up in New York somewhere, so you handle it. Call Cessna. Find out where. I'm sending a sterile plane to fly cover. I want that man protected until he finishes what he started. That clear?"

"Perfectly, sir. But air cover? What's the danger—"

"That lunatic Rand has a fully operational fighter up there, that's the danger. He's gunning for Ballinger for personal reasons and liable to do anything. He finds out about the Cessna and he'll go for it, believe me. If I knew how to get a hold of him I'd tell him about it myself. If you can't take him out on the ground, what I'm sending up there'll do the job in the air!"

Farington, who had mouth-drying visions of trying to explain to a Congressional oversight committee an air battle over New York City during his watch, said:

"Ah, sir; are you sure we want to go that route? I'm just thinking in terms of—"

"Goddamn it, just do it!" bellowed Kazalakis and slammed down the phone.

At that moment, several miles away across the Potomac river in a remote, barbed-wire enclosed corner of Andrews Air Force Base, three men in civilian clothing approached a small hangar labled only *T-314*. The lead man inserted a key in a lock, twisted it, and an electric motor activated a worm gear which raised the overhead hangar door. As the light advanced inside, it revealed in the shadowed interior the squat shape of a black-painted, French manufactured jet fighter bearing no markings at all.

"Flip ya," said the taller of the three men.

"Lemme see the coin first," said the man who had used the key. Then, by way of explanation to the third, added: "When we were flyin' for Air America, the sumbitch usta have a quarter with two heads."

"Hell yes," the tall man acknowledged cheerfully, "never take a chance I don't hafta; it's against my religion." He displayed both sides of an unaltered nickle, flipped it into the air and called "Tails." The three men watched it drop to the hangar floor and come to rest, obverse showing.

The man with the key said "Well, you won't go violatin' your religion today. Not flying that oil-burner against a prop job."

The tall man's smile was cold: "Yeah," he said, "like runnin' down a kid on a bike with a truck."

In the back of a cab speeding west on New Jersey's Route 46, Richard Rand felt a twinge of guilt for what he had done to Alfredo Matarazza. The trusting man had believed him when he said he was going down the hall to see T'sa Li's doctor and would be right back to resume his visit. Don Scarbacci's other men, relying on Matarazza's assurances, had made no move to follow Rand and he had made it out of the building unobserved. For a hundred dollar bill and the promise of another should he get a speeding ticket, the cabbie had been happy to employ all his aggressive driving skills to get Rand as quickly as possible to West Caldwell, New Jersey.

Rand was less concerned about T'sa Li's feelings. There just hadn't been time to argue with her; to explain that a man doesn't let another do his fighting for him. Maybe, he admitted to himself, he was rationalizing his obsession with Gregory Ballinger. On the other hand, it was always easier to rationalize *not* fighting. All he knew was that in quiet, unexpected moments, he kept hearing T'sa Li's scream as the saw blade tore through her finger. T'ang Li had an equal right to Ballinger's life and, if he got there first, so be it; Rand could live with that. What he couldn't live with would be letting T'ang Li have him by default or, infinitely worse, for Ballinger to escape.

In the race with T'ang Li, Rand could not, he knew, equal T'ang Li's assets on the ground; he had to gamble on Ballinger making it into the air. Rand had one, slim, advantage: he knew that the eastern distribution facility for Cessna jet aircraft was at the Dutchess County Airport in Wappingers Falls, New York. It had been built ninety miles north of New York City where its operations would not be hindered by FAA Terminal Control Area restrictions. His advantage was a slim one because T'ang Li would be checking all the metropolitan area airports as a matter of course and a simple question to fixed-base personnel at any of them would give him the location of the Cessna distribution center.

"Turn off here," Rand ordered the driver as they approached Passaic Avenue. Three minutes later he got out of the cab at the gate of Caldwell-Wright Airport and walked rapidly to his hangar. He left the hangar door locked and used his key to admit himself through the normal sized door at the far right of the building, relocking it behind him. Rand snapped on the overhead lights. Tail low, fuselage elevated on high, narrow landing gear, the wicked *E* model Messerschmitt seemed gathered for another leap into the sky to which it had been born so many years ago in Augsburg.

Rand crossed to the lithe fighter, mounted the wing and swung over the canopy. He reached around behind the stark, metal seat and, from atop the fuel tank, retrieved a black suitcase which he put down on the wing, then went to the rear of the hangar for a step ladder. With the ladder, Rand opened the engine cowling, exposing the big, engine-mounted, Oerlikon 20mm MG FF/M cannon and two 7.9mm Rheinmetall-Borsig MG 17 machine guns. Working quickly but carefully, Rand took the bolt for the 20mm out of the black suitcase and installed it in the machine cannon, then followed suit with the two machine guns. The wing-mounted weapons were next. They were reached more easily and Rand was soon finished. Despite his sense of urgency, he stood for a moment, wiping his oily hands slowly on a rag, admiring reverently the deadly beauty of the fighter; the most feared *Jagdflugzeug* of them all. Abruptly, he looked at his watch: 12:49 P.M. Urgency overcame reverie and Rand ran to the operations shack, looking for the line boy to help him roll the ship out onto the tarmac.

At 12:56 the line boy stopped cranking the starter flywheel, removed the crank from it's slot in the right side of the fuselage ahead of the canopy and handed it up to Rand. Rand waited for the boy to move away, shouted "Clear!" and let in the starter clutch to engage the great Daimler-Benz engine to the spinning flywheel.

Slowly the triple-bladed propellor swung over: once, twice, three times. Rand switched on the ignition and black puffs of smoke from oil that had seeped into the combustion chambers of the inverted engine belched from the twelve exhaust stacks. The powerful V-12 caught with a roar and the tightly strapped-in Rand trembled with the airframe until, brakes released, the ship was free to taxi in *S* turns to the end of the runway.

The operations shack emptied out to watch as Rand performed his magneto and control checks, scanned the surrounding sky and lined the ship up on the runway centerline. He set his gyro compass and altimeter, took a deep breath, set twenty degree flaps, held his control column hard forward and firewalled the throttle.

Slowly the Messerschmitt began to roll forward. It gathered speed quickly as the engine reached a deafening 2,480 rpm and the tail lifted. Moments later, behind 1,175 straining, eager horsepower, the steed that bore the last of the Teutonic knights into battle hurled itself once more into the sky. Gear retracting, white-outlined black crosses flashing back at the sun, it disappeared in a climbing turn, trailing a sound like distant thunder and leaving behind an inexpressible longing in the knot of pilots privileged to be present as the past lived one more time.

At 300 m.p.h. maximum cruise, the Bf 109E-3 was able to cover the eighty air miles between West Caldwell, New Jersey and Wappingers Falls, New York in sixteen minutes. Climbing time added, Rand was at 20,000 feet over Dutchess County Airport listening on the communications frequency by 1:20 P.M. The radio was crucial. The aircraft delivered to Ballinger would bear the Comco logo on it's vertical stabilizer, but Rand could hardly loiter at low altitude over the airfield in a Messerschmitt bearing full wartime *Luftwaffe* markings without causing a sensation and most certainly alerting Ballinger. He would have to rely on radio traffic. Few jet aircraft flew out of Dutchess and in communicating with the airport each would use designations such as "Gulfstream" or "Citation" in addition to FAA issued *N* numbers. If nothing else was said, such as "IBM" or "Comco," Rand would wait until the aircraft was climbing out to approach it for visual confirmation.

From a page of Cessna advertising in *Flying* magazine that Rand had torn out and brought with him, he checked the performance figures of the latest model Cessna jet available, the Citation II. It was capable of 443 m.p.h., but not until it had climbed to an altitude where jet engines are most efficient. It's ceiling was 43,000 feet. He'd have to catch him before he got that high because the Messerschmitt had a service ceiling of 34,450. At best he'd get one pass, maybe two, if surprise was complete.

Rand checked the area before him carefully, then threw the switch that armed his guns. He was in slow flight now to conserve fuel, a good time to clear his weaponry. Rand pressed the spring-loaded firing button and felt the entire airframe shake to the hammering of the 20mm machine cannon. Damn! He hadn't thought of the tracers. Every third shell glowed on it's trajectory and left a trail of white smoke. He was grateful for the altitude that, he hoped, would keep his burst of fire from being observed.

The traffic from Dutchess was modest. A Colgan Beech-99 turbo-prop commuter took off and a Cessna 182 landed. Someone in a Mooney asked for and received a practice radio direction steer. Rand leaned out his mixture even further to save more fuel. The day was beautiful, the Daimler-Benz muted. He thought in German and tried to recall what he had read of his father's *Luftwaffe* tactics. The martial music of his youth flooded into his brain. *Gute Augen haben*—have good eyes—his father was reported to have said when asked the most important asset of a *Jagdflieger.* Rand had read everything ever written about his father and a few battle and evaluative reports the man had written himself that survived in the *Luftwaffe* archives; several times he had mentioned the importance of constant scanning.

Only half Rand's mind was tuned to the Dutchess radio traffic; the other half was listening mentally to a song called *Erika.* Beneath his oxygen mask he mouthed the words along with the marching men singing in his brain: *Auf der Heide blüht ein kleines Blumelein* . . . He reached out to adjust a valve marked *Sauerstoff* and more oxygen flowed into his mask.

As Rand's head turned back from the valve, something tripped a trigger in his mind and he looked down again, intently. The sun was shining brightly off the broad ribbon of the Hudson River. That brilliant back-lighting was probably the only reason Rand was able to see the black shape that slipped along it, 5,000 feet below him; a duplicate of the little black-painted silhouette models used in his Marine air days to train pilots to be able to identify friendly and enemy aircraft. In those days, the *Mystère* was a friendly. But what was it doing here, without markings? Rand answered his own question: Kazalakis! The goddman Greek could read him like a book! This would be no turkey shoot of an unarmed transport; the son of a bitch would be combat ready, probably assigned to the dual role of protecting Ballinger and blowing Rand away. That the *Mystère* had not already climbed to challenge him could be due to only one thing; from the viewpoint of the jet fighter, Rand was in the sun, invisible. T'sa Li was right: he hadn't won yet. It was now or never.

Rand rolled the Messerschmitt inverted, pulled it through into a split S and dived on the *Mystère* at 370 miles per hour. *"Nähe!"* his father had written, *proximity!* Get *close* before you open fire!

The music in his mind was suppressed by Rand's concentration. The *Mystère* held straight and level so that Rand's dive brought him in behind and slightly to the left for a deflection shot. Still Rand held off, waiting to climb right up on his opponent before unleashing the lethal machine-cannon. He waited a moment too long.

With a flick of his control column the *Mystère* pilot broke hard left, counting on Rand's velocity to carry him beyond the jet's turning circle, unable to stay inside him. From then on the superior speed and climb rate of the *Mystère* would make swift work of the piston-engined fighter. Every instinct in Rand screamed for him to follow in a tight left turn. The Messerschmitt was equipped with automatically operating leading edge slats that would enable it to bite into the air at near stall speed and turn hard, possibly staying inside the *Mystère*.

*"Gegenüber!"* commanded the voice Rand's mind had created for his father years ago, *"Rollen Sie rechts ein!"* Rand obeyed instantly. Without thinking or even being conscious of moving the controls he rolled in the direction opposite the rotation of the *Mystère*. The right-hand roll, faithful to the laws of mathematics and physics though contrary to every human instinct, swept the blunt, sharklike snout of the Messerschmitt up inside the turn of the unmarked jet.

As the black fuselage crept into his reflector sight, Rand squeezed the trigger. The Messerschmitt shuddered as a glowing stream of cannon shells and tracer bullets reached out to the *Mystère*. At 540 rounds per minute, the black jet lasted only seconds under the impact of the tank-busting Oerlikon cannon before blossoming into dirty orange flame and dark, oily smoke through which Rand flew, zooming the Messerschmitt back up to altitude in a slow roll, his exultation accompanied in his mind by a symphonic orchestra playing triumphal strains of Wagner. He closed his eyes. "Papa," he said softly into his oxygen mask, "Papa."

"Cessna November three-nine-four-nine Bravo, say aircraft type." The voice from Dutchess radio sounded far away.

"Citation II," came the reply, "Say active runway, please."

The words snapped Rand back to attention like the siren of a traffic cop right behind him; the speaker was Gregory Ballinger!

"Active is six," Dutchess responded, "Winds from five-one degrees at four knots."

As Ballinger went through the routine of readying for takeoff, Rand's mind raced. The Citation II was certified for single pilot flight and could fly nonstop for 2,100 miles with a forty-five minute reserve. It was like Ballinger to think of that. No one would suspect him of planning intercontinental flight with that range, but it could be done by flying to Newfoundland, then on to Greenland, Iceland and Scandinavia. From there it would be a short hop to Soviet territory. He'd probably file local, zip over Connecticut to the sound and disappear. Rand headed the Messerschmitt southeast, taking one last look at the smoketrail of the *Mystère*. It went down to an oil slick in the Hudson, between two bridges. Rand was relieved; he wouldn't have wanted a school-yard catastrophe on his conscience.

Eighteen minutes later, Rand was over Long Island Sound, listening to Gregory Ballinger acknowledge a traffic advisory from Bridgeport approach. When questioned, Ballinger gave his altitude as "Going through twenty-three thousand to flight level four-one." Bridgeport answered with a snappy "Good day, sir." It was all the information Rand was likely to receive before Ballinger was by him.

From his slow cruise perch at 34,000 feet, Rand tried to pick out the white Citation rising toward him. He had almost despaired of doing it when he saw a flash of white against the purple of the distant horizon. The plane was right where it should be, but Rand had to be certain. He paralleled the coastline, keeping the rising jet in sight below him and, attempting to conceal his voice by adopting the affected bass and drawl of a second officer trying to impress his captain, said:

"Ah, Citation four-niner Bravo, do you read American three-twelve?"

"I read you, American," came the voice of Gregory Ballinger, sounding startled at being addressed in flight by a commercial airliner.

"Ah, four-niner Bravo, American three-twelve has a Citation in sight streaming excessive smoke from one engine. Don't know if it's you or not but you were the only call sign in recent traffic in the area. Suggest you rock your wings a bit; see if you're the guy."

The wings of the plane Rand had in sight below and to his left rocked as Ballinger's voice said, "Roger, American—if I'm the aircraft you have in sight, can you tell me which engine? All my instruments are in the green."

Like a diver rising from the board for a full layout back half-gainer, the Messerschmitt lazed up into a chandelle turn. Then, throttle to the firewall, supercharger at maximum blow, plunged into a howling full-power dive from above and behind the gleaming Citation. The jet was creeping out from under him! Rand reached for the nitrous-oxide valve.

The Daimler-Benz screamed under the super-fuel and the diving Messerschmitt fell like a peregrine falcon onto the helpless Cessna jet, pressing Rand back into his seat as it exceeded 400 m.p.h. still accelerating.

"American," Ballinger asked, "is it four-niner Bravo?"

The wing root of the Citation slid into Rand's gunsight. He hit his microphone button and spoke in his own voice, slowly and distinctly:

"Yeah, it's you. And me. *Motherfucker!*"

All else was lost in the shattering roar of the Oerlikon cannon and Rhinemetall-Borsig machine guns.

# Epilogue

As Alfredo Matarazza drove the Cadillac west toward one of the last of New York's once proud array of ocean liner piers on the Hudson riverfront, Richard Rand and T'sa Li sat quietly in the rear sharing between them portions of *The New York Times* and Washington's *Post* and *Star* newspapers. At their feet lay sections already read, headlines announcing the discovery and thwarting of a Soviet plot to take over American heavy industry, with Columbia Steel as the first intended victim; the escape, presumably to Russia, of Comco board chairman Gregory Ballinger, now exposed as KGB agent Mikhail Sarkov; and the text of a speech by the President of the United States announcing the breakoff of the latest SALT negotiations.

Rand, relieved that the most hard-line of public figures had not even raised the subject of the use of force against the Soviet Union, read instead with satisfaction a quotation from the President's speech:

> The sad fact is that the world does not share our historic commitment to morality in international affairs; it respects only power, and it is clearly dangerous to substitute the former for the latter as an operating principle. Henceforth, this administration will do the necessary to regain for the United States the position of mightiest nation on earth, confident that will serve the cause of peace as can no piece of paper backed by the hoped for good faith so recently disclosed to be an illusion.

Columnist William F. Buckley, Jr., called for a rebuilding of U.S. intelligence and covert activities ability, pointing out the danger of having nothing between the extremes of overt diplomacy or war with which to "effectuate the more eristic of our policies in advancing the national interest abroad."

Evans and Novak called for universal military training, citing growing realization that the all-volunteer armed forces could not "deliver either the quality or quantity of personnel required for a militarily strong United States."

Mary McGrory derided the overreaction to "what goes on in the business world every day and is only criticized when attempted by unlicensed Marxists rather than Anti-trust Division approved members of the *laissez-faire* capitalist protective association."

George F. Will said he hoped the affair and its consequences marked the end of the peculiarly American inability to distinguish between the world as it is and as one would like it to be, but he doubted it; the "addiction to analgesic illusion to relieve the pain of reality having become too much a part of the national character over the past seventy years."

Art Buchwald reported on an interview in which the decline of morality in international affairs was lamented by Idi Amin.

T'sa Li was reading an article in the business section of the *Times* reporting on the acumen of New York financier Richard Rand. He had led a group which took quick advantage of the confusion, generated by the discovery that the board chairman of Comco was a Soviet agent, to take over the giant conglomerate in a stockholder's coup, then turn it over just as quickly for a heavy profit. An article in the next column reported that all disputes over the quality of steel delivered to foreign purchasers by Columbia Steel had been settled with the predictable upward effect upon Columbia stock.

T'sa Li finished her reading and interrupted Rand's:

"You took quite a chance, didn't you?"

"Took *a* chance?" The wounded look Rand put on his face was so exaggerated T'sa Li started to giggle.

"I'm serious!" Rand insisted in mock protest. "Which one of the four hundred thirty-two I took in the last week alone did you have in mind?"

"Oh, stop it!" T'sa Li laughed. "I mean that bluff you ran on the date. Suppose someone on the Comco board of directors had realized that the 30th April on your claim and the 1st May on their agreement with Wing and Wa to extend their time was really the same day because of the international date line? What then?"

"It wasn't really that much of a chance. I did that because of the psychological effect. In real time terms I still had them by forty-five minutes or so. The time gimmick just made it easier."

"How about that plane that went down in the Hudson? I mean, it's not like Ballinger disappearing over the Sound without a trace; people *had* to see that crash in the river. How'd they handle it?"

"Any crash," Rand answered, "is under the jurisdiction of the National Transportation Safety Board. They have to determine the reason. Besides, the Hudson at that point is a navigable waterway. That puts it under Federal jurisdiction. They kept everybody away from the wreck site, announced it was a corporate jet belonging to Jacobus Construction, which just happens to be a CIA proprietary company, and that it went down when the turbine flew apart from metal fatigue. *Voilà.*"

"And all the rest of this?" T'sa Li gestured to the papers at their feet as the limousine glided to a halt across from the pier.

Rand shrugged. "They wanted to buy Comco in the worst way and the worst way was my way. It was that or see an American industrial giant legitimately owned and operated by 'organized crime'."

T'sa Li smiled. "Blackmail."

"Uh, uh." Rand grinned, "Extortion."

"No wonder they covered for you!"

"Oh, they did a lot more than that."

Rand helped T'sa Li out of the car as Alfredo Matarazza went round to the trunk for their luggage.

"What?" T'sa Li asked, smoothing the skirt of the beige traveling suit she had chosen for the first day of their cruise. Rand took her hand and they started walking toward the pier.

"Remember those six foreign companies Comco took over? The ones Ballinger used to make the steel deals with Columbia? I kept them for myself. All of them. That's on top of my end from the deal with our families."

"You're incorrigible!"

Rand didn't answer. They walked on a few feet more and T'sa Li felt Rand's hand tighten. Taking it as a sign of affection, she squeezed back, looking down at the ground to watch her footing among the uneven cobblestones of the wharf area. Rand's whole arm seemed to tighten and she glanced at him. He was looking straight up, into the sky.

"Whatcha thinking?" she asked, quietly.

Rand continued to look upward, as if searching. "You know," he said, "that business I told you about in the dogfight with that jet? The way I tried to remember all the things my father had said or written?"

"Yes."

"I was trying this morning to find the part about rolling opposite the rotation of the target in a turn. It isn't there."

"What do you mean?"

"I mean it isn't there. I went through everything I've got. There's *nothing* about rolling the opposite way!"

T'sa Li was silent for a moment, then asked:

"What do you make of it?" She felt his whole body tremble and looked at him sharply. Rand was still looking upward. His eyes were blinking rapidly.

"I think," Rand said, taking a deep breath to regain control of his emotions, "I think my father finally spoke to me."